Soul Savior

By: I. R. Miller

To everyone reading, who decided to pick up a piece of a fifteen-year-old's heart.

Please be careful with it.

Table of Contents

Chapter One: What's the Catch?......5
Chapter Two: The Deadliest Game of Hide and Seek......16
Chapter Three: Music for the Soul......24
Chapter Four: Minerva's Perspective......30
Chapter Five: Blue-Eyed Ghost?......34
Chapter Six: Minerva's Weird Behavior......41
Chapter Seven: Preparing to Fight a Kid......46
Chapter Eight: Minerva is Using Cheat Codes......51
Chapter Nine: The Last One but New and Improved......56
Chapter Ten: Oh Look, I'm Seeing Things......61
Chapter Eleven: What a *Ray* of Sunshine......67
Chapter Twelve: Teenagers Are Confusing......74
Chapter Thirteen: Ouch!......81
Chapter Fourteen: Ray's Perspective......88
Chapter Fifteen: Elias Sucks at Apologizing......94
Chapter Sixteen: Homeless Man Threatens Me......102
Chapter Seventeen: Ouch! Part Two......109
Chapter Eighteen: Under A-Rest......116
Chapter Nineteen: A Free Man (Or Something)......122
Chapter Twenty: A Glowing Staircase and a Gambler......129
Chapter Twenty-One: I Guess I Don't Like Poker......135
Chapter Twenty-Two: Fake It 'Til You Make It......142
Chapter Twenty-Three: Candles Are Annoying......148
Chapter Twenty-Four: Can You Not Do That?......155
Chapter Twenty-Five: A Bar Fight in the Basement......164
Chapter Twenty-Six: Poison and Other Party Drinks......170
Chapter Twenty-Seven: Lyle's Perspective......175
Chapter Twenty-Eight: Hangover Cure and Caramels......183
Chapter Twenty-Nine: You've Missed a Lot, Dude......194
Chapter Thirty: I Need a Break (Feat. Gary)......201
Chapter Thirty-One: Don't Ruin Our Dance Party......207
Chapter Thirty-Two: Try Not To Die......218
Chapter Thirty-Three: *Another* Evil Shadow Thing?......224

Chapter Thirty-Four: A Library Tries to Kill Us..232
Chapter Thirty-Five: The Deadliest Game of Hide and Seek (Reprise).......................238
Chapter Thirty-Six: The English Language Sucks..251
Chapter Thirty-Seven: I'm an Insomniac (But So Are You)..259
Chapter Thirty-Eight: A Giggle in the Garden..269
Chapter Thirty-Nine: Elias is Finally Helping...275
Chapter Forty: Coffee Confessions...282
Chapter Forty-One: People Like to Fight Me...290
Chapter Forty-Two: He Brought a Bear?..300
Chapter Forty-Three: Secret Tunnels Are Cool..309
Chapter Forty-Four: Tangled Up...316
Chapter Forty-Five: Okay, Who Gave Her a Rock?...324
Chapter Forty-Six: Ouch! Part Three..329
Chapter Forty-Seven: Mary's Story...335
Chapter Forty-Eight: I Challenge Thee to a Duel...341
Chapter Forty-Nine: Epic Battle Sequence: Activated...346
Chapter Fifty: This is Clearly Not Fair..352
Chapter Fifty-One: Elias Seriously Lacks Communication Skills.................................357
Chapter Fifty-Two: Meaningful Conversations Behind a Table.....................................361
Chapter Fifty-Three: The Power of Friendship and Apologies......................................365
Chapter Fifty-Four: Mary's Perspective..370
Chapter Fifty-Five: Uh Oh, Do You Have Insurance?...375
Chapter Fifty-Six: What Happens Now?..386
Epilogue...395

Chapter One
What's the Catch?

My life changed the day I answered that ad. If I'd known I would be running for my life only a few days later, I would have never called.

But how bad could a haunted mansion be? I mean, ghosts couldn't be real...

Right?

"As we go later in the day, we will see the temperature and humidity rise..."

The news reporter gestured toward the side, where the weather for the next week displayed on the screen.

Mom turned to face the TV. "He always sounds too upbeat for waking up at three in the morning. You're telling me that he can get little to no sleep and still sound like he got the full eight hours?"

"One of the many mysteries of the world, I suppose," I responded.

I mindlessly ate my breakfast as my eyes stayed glued to the TV. The local events were never too interesting, but occasionally we grabbed bigger news stories and clung to them. My eyes flitted towards the bottom of the screen, where small text shuffled across. I skimmed over most of it, but something caught my eyes:

UPCOMING NEWS: STRANGE REQUEST FOR AIDING WITH HAUNTED HOUSE.

With the school year starting, I could picture the haunted house workers preparing for Halloween in a couple of months. But the phrasing implied something different.

I hadn't even noticed that I spilled hot sauce on my shirt.

"Seriously?" I muttered as I went to the kitchen to grab napkins.

Mom looked me up and down. "Quincey, uhm, you have some sauce on your..." She gestured towards my chest.

"Oh, wow, I never would have noticed."

Mom rolled her eyes with a smile on her face. "Always with the sarcasm."

I dabbed the napkin on the spot, thankful I wore a black shirt. As long as it didn't get on the design, we're good.

"Up next, we will be covering an intriguing story involving a man and what he believes to be a haunted house after a quick commercial break."

"A haunted house?"

I grabbed a sweatshirt I found draped over the couch and tugged it on. "I guess so. It looks…fascinating."

"Sounds fake. Could it be for Halloween?"

"Maybe, but they usually wait until mid-September to start asking."

Mom shrugged and continued cleaning the counters.

I sat down in front of the couch, setting my plate with *tortilla espanola* on the coffee table. I gently nudged one of Ollie's beds out of the way so that I could lay my feet out in front of me.

He must have known what I had done, because he immediately perked up from inside a different bed.

"Ollie-bear, wanna come here?"

I patted the area beside me, and he ambled his way over.

"Oh, you're so tired, aren't you?"

I stroked our old dog's fur and felt the curls underneath my palm. His fur was getting unruly—we seriously needed to get it trimmed.

"How are your friends doing? I haven't seen them in a while," Mom called from the kitchen.

I sighed. "How many times have I told you? Rachel's off in New York, and Kayden is about to leave for—"

"College, right?"

I could practically feel the anticipation in her voice like a hand trailing down my back. Or maybe 'around my throat' would be a better comparison.

"I still haven't picked one out yet. Or what I want to do."

I didn't look at her as she started telling me about the importances of going to college. A commercial about hair products for straight hair suddenly becomes the most interesting thing in this house.

I glanced back at Mom, and she gave me a sympathetic smile as she set up her breakfast.

"Don't worry, sweetie, I won't make you do anything yet."

While she said that, she sat down beside me as the commercials finished.

"A man by the name of Elias Everard claims that there is a mansion that is haunted, and that he needs to find someone here who can help him. He didn't give many details, but whoever takes him up on his offer can get ample compensation."

"The only time I hear the word 'compensation' is when it's in those weird commercials with the car accidents."

But Mom seemed to be focusing on something else.

"You know…now that you aren't working at Driver's anymore, you could probably use some cash."

I didn't need her to lay it all out for me.

The news reporter left us a number for anyone interested to contact.

I wrote it out on the napkin, thankful that I had been carrying a pen with me, and decided I would call at some point that day.

"Why not call him now?"

"Because," I started, "maybe he doesn't want someone who just got out of high school to do this job. I don't know if you need any credentials for it. Also, shouldn't I be looking at colleges?"

I hoped that playing the 'college' card would work, but she shook her head.

"You could have been doing that all summer. Now do what you need to do before I call him for you."

It didn't surprise me that she approved of it. She had told me about her paranormal phase when she was younger, and she still watched those kinds of shows. Plus, the money would be nice. More than nice. If I could have my first year of college paid for, maybe I'd want to get started sooner.

Even then, I knew that this was a hoax—there was *no way* this could be real. But some part of me still got excited. The same part that swooned over the people written on paper, that longed to save the world after fighting in a magical war, that still believed in the unbelievable.

That part of me wondered if this could be real.

I pushed the thought from my mind. I had long stopped believing in fairytales, or that I would face no struggles in life if I kept going with a positive attitude. The world just didn't work that way.

I stared at the number written on the napkin. A feeling came over me that I couldn't describe. A yearning, or maybe a calling. It urged me to go for...something. What, I couldn't tell.

From the corner of my eye, I saw Mom giving me a thumbs up and an excited grin.

I sighed and pulled out my phone.

It only rang twice before someone picked up.

"Hello?" The voice that answered had a vague accent I couldn't place, and he sounded hopeful.

"Uhm, is this—" I looked at the napkin— "Elias Everard?"

I could hear his excitement easily, even through the phone. "Yes, yes, this is Elias! Did my ad make it into the news? Did you see it?"

"Yes, that is correct. Could I learn more about it?"

"Of course! Can you meet me at, let's say, eleven?"

I gave Mom a glance. She nodded.

"That'll work for me. Where would we meet?"

"Do you have the mansion's address?"

One more napkin check. "Nope."

"Here."

He waited while I got ready and began to slowly recite the address. I didn't remember there being a mansion at that end of town, but I didn't visit that area often, so for all I knew it'd been there my whole life.

"Alright," I said as I finished writing down the address. "Anything else?"

The other end went silent for a few moments.

"I don't think there is…oh, make sure you bring a suitcase—if you take me up on my offer, you'll likely be staying for a while. This is a bit of a…longer job. But I promise, it will be worth it."

I turned to look at Mom again, making sure that she heard the same thing I had.

"You get to live in a mansion?" She whispered.

"I guess."

I directed my voice to Elias again. "I'll meet you there."

With nothing else to say, I hung up the phone.

"Do we really trust this Elias guy? This sounds kinda sketchy."

There's no way this could be legit. He hadn't even mentioned the supposed 'compensation' the news reporter brought up. Could that have been used as a lure to get people to call? This was seriously starting to sound like a poorly planned scam.

"Okay, think of it this way. Is it a bit weird? Sure. But it can be a fun adventure! Even if it *is* a scam, you're still getting some cash for college. The only way to be sure is if you pack your bags and *go*."

Good thing I already had some things packed from my visit to my *abuela*'s a couple days ago that I probably should have unpacked sooner. But it's good I didn't; I just needed to throw in a couple of extra outfits and some other essentials. It'd only take me a few minutes before it's good to go.

Now, the question: am I really doing this?

I pulled back my sleeve and stared at the face of my watch: *9:48*.

Shrugging my shoulders, I pushed my way up to my room. Looks like I might be going ghosthunting.

I shoved down my suitcase as I tried to zip it. I didn't think I packed *that* much, but I must have more than I thought. When I couldn't think of anything I could take out, I just pushed harder, eventually zipping it up.

Mom knocked on the door. "You ready?"

I pulled the suitcase up. "Yeah, I'll be there in a bit."

Lugging the suitcase behind me, I met Mom by the door.

"Remember, keep your phone on, and text me often. If something feels off, pretend I texted you about some sort of family emergency. It would probably be something about your *abuela* getting angry at…I'm not sure, I'll think of something. You don't have to stay if you don't want to."

I bent down so that she could kiss my forehead.

"Stay safe, and remember that I love you."

I smiled. "Love you too, Mom."

I dragged the suitcase to my car and popped the trunk. The suitcase got shoved in, nestled between everything else in the back.

I peered into the car, seeing all the clutter where my feet would rest. I made sure to put it all in the back before sliding into the driver's seat.

I punched the address into the GPS and started the journey.

I didn't want to be alone with my thoughts, so I drowned them out with the radio. The radio knob clicked as I flipped through, eventually landing on a classic rock station.

Song lyrics flooded through my mind, and I hummed along to myself. Saguaros passed by, resting on the side of the road.

My thoughts scattered as I pulled up to the mansion.

It was *humongous*.

It didn't look like it had more than a story or two, but what it lacked in height, it made up for in sheer size. When parked in front of it, I couldn't see the edge of either side. It looked nice, the bricks painted white. It looked almost *too* nice to be haunted.

The man who must have been Elias Everard stood in front of the door.

He looked much younger than he sounded on the phone. I thought he may have been in his fifties, but he couldn't have been older than thirty. Despite his youthful appearance, there were still strands of gray in his hair. His fists clenched and unclenched at his side. He must've been nervous. But why?

As soon as I opened my car door, he turned towards me. He avoided making eye contact for longer than a few seconds, but he seemed excited, and even a bit relieved, that I came. Even with the weirdness of it all, I guess I was glad that no one else had gotten there before me.

"Elias?" I called out as I started walking.

"Yes, that's me! Come on over, I promise I won't bite."

This felt...weird, to say the least. But I already made the drive here, so I forced a smile as I finally made it over to him.

"Hi, my name is Quincey. I'm here for your ad?"

Elias grabbed my hand and shook it, a smile on his face. His palms were coarse, but his clothes looked nice. They reminded me of what a college professor might wear. What kind of crazy job would this be?

"It's a pleasure to make acquaintances with you, Quincey." He turned around to look at the mansion. "Isn't it beautiful?"

It still blew me away. "Very."

Elias faced me again. "Well then, I'm guessing that you want to know about what I have in store for you?"

"Tell me about it."

"Actually, it's kind of a long story, heh…"

"I've got time." My curiosity started to get a hold of me.

Elias took a deep breath. "I've been dealing with this mansion for quite a bit of time now. It seems that there are souls inside, and I've tried calming them down myself, but for some reason they seem resistant to my attempts. So, around five years ago, I started getting some help…"

Wait, something seemed off.

"Five years ago? How am I just learning about this now?"

Elias' eyes shifted away from me. "Uhm, usually I could find the people on my own. But, I started to get desperate, so…"

He really had a hard time finishing his sentences.

I gave him an expectant look.

"I really need you to bel- what?"

"Well? Are you going to explain what I'm supposed to do, or am I just gonna have to guess?"

His face lit up. "I- I guess I should tell you about the souls, shouldn't I?"

Based on the ghost movies I'd seen, they usually didn't know much about the ghosts, so I wondered how much Elias knew. I nodded.

"Alright then. According to what I've seen, there are at least three souls, but there are likely more. I'd guess that there are only a couple more. The first person you'll meet is Minerva. She was an 18-year-old killed by some kind of injury to the head, likely from the force of a blunt object. Her eyes are sensitive to bright lights, so they will help drive her away. Unlike most 18-year-olds I know, she is very mature—you mustn't rely on her being reckless. I have reason to believe she died sometime during the 1950s."

I raised my eyebrows. I didn't think he'd know this much about any of the ghosts if he couldn't seem to calm them down, assuming he told the truth. Nothing about this made sense—I kept waiting for some cameraman to come out and yell, "Surprise! You've been pranked!"

"Constance is the second. She won't harm you; instead, she'll give you peace. As of now, she is the only one you won't need to worry about. She will be primarily found in the ballroom, wearing a red gown from the Renaissance. With the style of the dress, it is likely she died somewhere in the mid-1500s."

Ballroom? Renaissance? This is insane.

"Lastly, the third will be Ray. He was killed after being shot in the stomach while running away from something—or someone. He is very unhinged, and will do everything in his power to hurt you. Though he seems small, he has some force behind his throws. You will need to learn to defend yourself, as his first instinct will be to fight you. It appears that he may have died in the 1930s, but with him it's harder to tell."

I nodded along, acting like I understood exactly what he talked about. Elias sounded invested in this story, so much to even create stories for each of these…ghosts? Illusions? I wasn't even sure anymore.

I would have easily called him crazy, but the fear in his eyes looked too real.

Any doubt about the craziness of it all got pushed aside. He probably just had a few screws loose in the head. Maybe he was one of those insane conspiracy theorists who believed in alien abductions or that they faked the moon landing.

"I feel it is also important to mention that while in their angered states, the ghosts' memories do not serve them well. I am unsure of how to explain it, but it seems as though they can't form new memories in their angered state. At least not lasting ones.

They won't remember much of what happens in between…encounters. Constance's memory should be normal, however, so she will be helpful once you find her. Along with their altered memories, they also seem to have different senses altogether. I've noticed that they'll usually see you as a different person—the person who betrayed them the most, I would guess. I'm not entirely sure *why* they do, but I assume it has something to do with their connection to the mansion and how they died."

Well, I guess that made a *bit* of sense, but I didn't want to try having him explain it again. It'd be fine; he was just some lunatic, anyway. *I'd* be fine.

"I feel weird asking this, but the news reporter brought up a kind of reward for this?"

Elias chuckled. "Oh, right. Well, uhm, I think that if you manage to help with this, I'll give you…twenty grand? Does that sound alright?"

Woah. Is this guy made of money?

My surprise must have been obvious, because Elias beamed. "So, you'll do it?"

If for nothing else, I needed that money. "Yes, of course. Do you have any idea how long it'll take?"

"I haven't really got an idea, I apologize." He paused, thinking. "Possibly a month or two? Be prepared for longer. Any other questions?"

"Nope," I said quickly. Now that I knew how much money was involved, I wanted to get started as soon as possible

Elias handed me a key. "There is some food there for you already, and I'll come by every so often with groceries. Wouldn't want you to run out of food now." He laughed nervously to himself. "Do you need anything else from me?"

"Maybe a tour?"

For how long it must have taken him to find someone, he didn't seem very prepared for that. His eyes widened. "Oh- erm, well, I actually have somewhere to be. Please pardon my lack of preparation."

I raised my eyebrow, but instead of giving any further explanation, he scurried off to his car.

Why couldn't he just give me a tour?

His quick escape set me on edge. What else in here could have freaked him out so much, other than the supposed ghosts? I had no idea how I would even *help* with the ghosts, but he already left. But I didn't want to bother him, so there was only one logical thing to do: go inside.

I turned to look over my shoulder just in case I could catch him, but he had already gone who knows where. With a sudden sense of dread I couldn't quite place, I made my way into the mansion, suitcase in tow.

Chapter Two

The Deadliest Game of Hide-and-Seek

When I got there, I tried to give myself a tour.

It didn't take long for me to realize that would be next to impossible.

The mansion could have been a maze. It took me at least ten minutes just to find a bedroom, which I decided would do as my own. Even after I found it, I still took another twenty minutes to find my way back to the kitchen area near the entrance. Most of the mansion seemed to be made up of hallways and corridors covered in paintings of snobby rich people. If I hadn't seen the outside and driven here myself, I would have thought it was a castle in Europe, not a mansion in the middle of Arizona.

So, with that in mind, I decided to just stay in the few rooms I needed—the bathroom, my bedroom, and the kitchen.

It didn't take long to put my things where they belonged. My small stack of books and journals sat perched on the bedside table, my clothes quickly found their way to the closet and dresser, and my bed soon became prime for sleeping in.

My suspicions from before were still there. *Is this really a haunted mansion?*

I called Mom and filled her in on the details. She ignored my skepticism.

"Hey, this will be an adventure! Just give it a try, and if he starts to ask you to do things you don't want to do, you can come right back home. I don't care about the money as long as you're safe," she said after I brought up the cash.

I agreed and hung up the phone. Elias hadn't explained anything, but I knew I would be fine. It certainly didn't *look* haunted, and I hadn't seen any ghosts yet, so what was there to worry about?

It only took a couple of days for the madness of it all to sink in. I had known that this sounded insane, but it hadn't hit me that I essentially trapped myself in a mansion for a crazy man until later. I brought up my worries with Elias during his grocery stop, but the look of terror I got when I asked him about the ghosts shut down the question before I got an answer.

He suddenly became antsy, hurriedly handing me the bags. When I asked if I needed to pay him back, he only said "it's my courtesy." I guess that's nice.

Now armed with more noodles than I could eat in only a week and a ton of iced tea, I felt ready to fight some fake ghosts.

Even though I was hesitant about the whole 'haunted' part of this, there were a couple creepy things going on. The floorboards would whine. The lights would flicker. There would be random chills. Sometimes I would think I was hearing talking underneath my music. But those didn't mean anything.

Definitely not.

I sat curled up in my bed, a bowl of noodles in my lap. Music played in the background as I ate, helping to clear my mind. I couldn't think about how weird this experience was if I screamed the song lyrics in my head loud enough.

I turned my volume down as I got hit by a sudden wave of discomfort. The sensation of eyes watching me crept into my mind. I paused the music so I could listen, my eyes scanning the room. For the past week or so, I was the only one who stood in the mansion. No ghosts had bothered me before, so why would they be coming up now?

My gaze flitted towards the door as I heard the sound of creaking floorboards.

I kept my eyes fixated where I had thought I heard the noise.

Another creak as an invisible weight shifted.

My heart started to beat faster in my chest, and I felt eyes peer at me from every crevice. I grabbed my pillow and clung it tight.

I'm okay, it's just my anxiety, I'm okay. Take deep breaths.

My stomach started to knot as I heard someone.

"Aren't you going to greet me?"

I swore loudly. The bowl of noodles, which had thankfully been placed on the bedside table, had been spared—my pillow didn't get the same treatment. I tossed it instinctively over to the voice when I noticed the figure of someone standing in the doorway.

A lot of things jumped out at me; her eyes were a milky white, a harsh contrast from her dark skin, and blood trickled from her forehead and down to her neck, staining the white shirt she wore underneath her suit jacket. Dark box braids hung loosely around, floating by her waist. The woman couldn't have been much older than me. Was there something on her belt...?

As I made eye contact with her—or tried to—she stood rigidly, as if a statue. This had to be the first ghost...ugh, why couldn't I remember her name?

"Well?" Her hand twirled lazily in the air.

"Uhm, hey?"

Her bitter laugh rang through the room, and that's when I remembered her name: Minerva.

"'Hey'? That's all you have to say, after all this time?"

What did Elias say? Something about them not seeing me as I am.

"Do I know you?"

I assumed that she was staring at me but couldn't tell with her pupil-less eyes.

"Don't play dumb, Anna."

Fear shot through my veins with every step towards me.

"After you went off and had that affair, you had to rub it in my face that *you won*, didn't you? Well, you didn't. I am *thriving*, and I am *never* letting you take this away from me."

In only a matter of seconds, her right hand went from being empty to having a pistol aimed at my forehead. I waited for the shot that seemed inevitable, squeezing my eyes shut. I couldn't bring myself to look at her. It became hard to breathe.

When I peeked my eyes open, I noticed that Minerva's eyes, which were a milky white before, had turned a dark red. If this was in a cartoon, I would think that she's just angry about...something.

Usually that 'something' didn't lead to *murder*, though.

Minerva quickly put on a silencer. She cocked the gun, and fired the first shot. I barely missed it as I ducked. Despite the silencer, the sound still reverberated, if only a bit muffled. I wanted to curl up and wait for the headache to die down, but Minerva didn't give me that luxury.

"You want to play, Anna? Well, I've got a game we can play." She cocked the gun again. "You hide, I'll seek."

I still had no idea who this Anna girl was, but it didn't really matter, because she royally pissed off Minerva. If I wanted to have any chance of escape, I would need to pretend to be her—it didn't look like she'd believe me otherwise. I pushed down my fear as far as I could before I spoke. "Yes, let's play!"

Minerva's voice, which had been a regular volume earlier, had become deathly quiet. "How's this—I'll give you thirty seconds to run away like the coward you are before I blast a bullet-shaped hole in your head. Are you ready?"

I had already scrambled out the door before she finished saying *ready*. The decision to not explore the mansion earlier started to blow up in my face. I ignored the burning in my legs that grew more and more painful and obvious the more I ran. All I knew was that I had to run, and I had to run *fast*.

"Twenty-eight...twenty-nine...thirty! Ready or not, here I come!" Her voice dripped with insanity and her footsteps echoed through the hallways. I passed dozens of doors, all closed. I didn't have time to stop and check if they would make a good place to hide, because Minerva already started to come closer and closer.

Her laughter was broken and wicked. It grew louder and louder, closer and closer. If I wanted to keep my head, I'd need to hide.

I finally found an open door leading to a bright sunroom with furniture covered in drapes. I bolted inside and noticed a closet, also hidden by a drape, from the corner of my eye. I threw the tarp down to the ground and flew the closet door open, carefully squeezing myself in. I managed to squeeze my way in, ignoring the discomfort. I tried to breathe as quietly as I could when I heard Minerva slowing down.

"I know you're here, Anna! Why won't you come out and play with me?" She somehow managed to sound angrier than earlier. I held my breath as she came closer to the room I hid in. Everything in me went rigid. My heart was like a fast drum beat in my chest. One thought swirled in my head: I could die right here, right now, and I had the audacity to think that this would be a normal, completely safe little job.

From the side of the wardrobe, I could see a sliver of the outside. I kept an eye out for Minerva—I couldn't hear her footsteps anymore, so she must have known where I hid. The door to the room remained ajar, and from across the hall, I could barely make out the two doors of neighboring rooms. Minerva came up to the one on the right and slammed open the door.

Minerva stumbled back, covering her face. When she removed her hand, the room in front of her had gone dark. I saw the right of the hallway, where she had come from, and I noticed the diminished lights.

As she went to the room right next to it and repeated the pattern while grunting, the memory of what Elias had told me slowly came back to me.

She's eighteen, mature, and...what else?

Her focus shifted to the room I trapped myself in as she snapped around. I jumped, hitting my head.

Now is NOT the time to give away my spot, I thought to myself.

My heart pounded in my chest as she covered her eyes with one hand, searching the wall with the other. I trembled as I tried to wrack my brain for that missing detail.

When she found the lightswitch, it finally came.

Bright lights! She can't stand bright lights!

I tried to keep my hands from shaking too badly as I pulled out my phone. After the flashlight app opened, I would just press the button and hope for the best.

Minerva began to exit when she turned to look over her shoulder.

I angled my phone so that the light would get her—hopefully—right in the eyes. It would be my only chance to not get blasted.

She flung the wardrobe doors open, and I'd never slammed down my thumb harder than I did at that moment.

Minerva clawed at her eyes, stumbling back. I booked it as soon as I got out of her way, pushing past her.

"I'm blind, you bastard!" Her voice was a peril screech. My only goal was to put as much distance between the scary woman and myself as possible.

I didn't know how much time I'd have until she recovered, so I kept pushing myself. The corridors were a maze full of twists and turns. Every sound amplified. My heart raced, and my chest felt like an inflated water balloon. I felt the wicked cramp in my side, and I clutched it as I desperately continued onward. My head throbbed, but I had to go and not look back.

I managed to get some distance before I heard the faint echo of Minerva's yelling. It could have been moments or minutes. My legs threatened to give out; I hadn't run this hard and long in a very long time. I scolded myself. *I don't have time for this!*

I turned one of the many corners and got caught at a dead end. I barely slowed myself down fast enough to not hit the wall. My stomach sank. When I looked behind, I didn't see Minerva, thankfully. With the coast clear, I swirled back around and tried to find my way through the puzzle. The ache in my side got worse, and my heart felt close to bursting. Sweat caused my shirt to cling to my back and arms. I really wished that I had done more sports.

In the quiet, with the only sounds being my footsteps and breathing, I heard the smooth but accented voice of a woman.

Find the record.

"What the hell?" I muttered to myself. I looked around, but I stood alone.

Whether the voice belonged to the next ghost or just a hallucination, I didn't care; it was the best bet I had. There were many important things the voice didn't care to explain, though—for example, which record? How about where the records were?

The mystery woman didn't want to give any other information, so I sucked it up and tried thinking of somewhere that could have records.

There might have been some in a bedroom, assuming there were more after the one that I claimed, but that didn't feel right...damn it, why didn't I think to look around the mansion more?

An idea popped into my head.

The ballroom.

Elias had mentioned that the mansion had one, and that the only calm ghost would be found there. What was her name...maybe Constantine? I couldn't remember, but hopefully she'd still be able to help. She might even know where I could find some records.

A lot could go wrong, but I didn't have time to think about that. So I kept running.

I ran and ran and ran.

Eventually, I found myself in front of a giant pair of double doors. I skidded to a halt, noticing a plaque beside the right door.

Ballroom Chamber.

"Thank God." Relief flooded through me.

I froze, remembering Minerva was still very clearly chasing me. When I heard nothing, I willed myself to relax.

Reality hadn't hit me until that moment, standing in front of the ballroom doors, running for my life.

"Ghosts actually exist."

Saying it out loud gave it a sense of finality and certainty. *This is real.*

This was all like a very vivid, scary dream.

It just so happened that the dream was about to kill me.

Footsteps that had to have been Minerva's began to echo louder and louder—I'd wasted enough time already.

I didn't have anything left to lose, so I pushed open the ballroom doors.

Chapter Three

Music for the Soul

My footsteps echoed through the ballroom chamber as I ran in. I slammed the doors shut behind me, chest still heaving.

I turned around, examining the room. It could fit a decent sized apartment inside. Cloth-covered tables were scattered around the room, framed with wooden chairs. Rich people from centuries past were solidified in paintings, watching my every move. When I lifted my gaze towards the ceiling, I saw paintings of children dancing around, framed in gold leaf.

Minerva isn't here yet, I reminded myself. *But I don't have much time. No time for breaks—I gotta get moving.*

I briskly made my way across the room, looking for anything that could help. While the room had a lot of space, it didn't take long to see that it would be useless to keep looking. The only things to be found were the lonely tables.

Where people dine, only sit three. You will find the player, and you will be free.

"What the hell does *that* mean?" I muttered. As weirdly ominous as the voice was, it gave me something to look out for; a table with three chairs, by my guess. But I still didn't know what she meant by 'player.'

I explored my surroundings again. Maybe three chairs? Circling around, I tried finding that very thing. The problem was *none of these damn tables had three chairs.* Everywhere I looked were tables with at least four, but that wasn't what the weird poem-prophecy-thing said, now was it? No, of course it had to be *three*.

Okay. If I was in an action movie, what would I do?

Well, if I *was* in an action movie, I probably wouldn't be in this situation in the first place. Since I couldn't quite get out of here without risking Minerva finding me, I needed to find the next solution.

I ducked down low, hoping for a floorboard that might've stood out from the rest. No luck.

I could practically feel my time slipping away, like an imaginary hourglass that hovered next to me as I examined the room.

Panic rose in my chest as I heard the faint sound of Minerva's indistinct yelling. I swore under my breath.

Where was that Renaissance ghost, anyway? Unless another ballroom kept itself hidden in this mansion, I should've found her by now.

I stumbled against the wall, feeling my limbs start to collapse under me. My arm rammed into the brick, and then I felt it; a sort of design on the wall. Until I got up close, I couldn't even see it. I paused for a moment, feeling around it. I couldn't quite tell what exactly it would do, but I had to take a shot. I slammed my fist into it, and that's when I heard the sound of mechanics whirring from inside the wall.

Is this mansion even real?

I didn't know if they had secret headquarters whenever the mansion had been built, but one moment I stood in front of a brick wall, and the next I stared into a secluded room.

And, lo and behold, there sat a table with three chairs.

I cheered quietly, but not for long; Minerva couldn't be far behind.

I scrambled in and began to sift through the records. Resting on a side table sat a record player, rusted from time. Spider webs covered the corners of the lid and thin layers of dust lay on the rotator. Around the floor were dozens of records.

"Who in their right mind would throw all these records on the floor?" I murmured as I tried not to step on any of them. By some miracle I recognized a couple and brought them over the record player. Well, I tried to until I got interrupted.

No, dear, not those. It will be from the 1950s; that is when Minerva died.

I checked the copyright dates.

"Damn it, too recent." I gently placed them down and continued my search through the records. I heard the room seal closed behind me; a sort of automatic system probably triggered it.

Desperation became imminent as I put more and more records in the 'not-from-the-50s' pile. Why couldn't there be an arrow, or some sort of neon sign that said *MAGIC RECORD HERE*? I felt trapped in an escape room, except this one was way more dangerous.

I heard something outside: footsteps.

I cursed as my searching became frantic. I barely read the dates anymore; I just looked out for the five.

Just as I began creating a will that no one would hear, I finally found a record from the right decade.

If this wasn't the record, I was screwed. I could hear Minerva getting closer to the secluded room. I took a chance and slipped it into the record player.

The door opened as the music started to play.

I clenched my fist, knowing I would be dead in seconds. On my tombstone it would read 'the idiot who went to a mansion and somehow died.'

Except no bullet shot.

As I slowly turned around, I saw Minerva, her gun pointed right at me. She stood frozen like a statue. Both of our breaths slowed as rock and roll filled the room.

She blinked a few times before her eyes returned to the pale white. Her eyebrows furrowed as she looked at me.

"You aren't Anna."

To my surprise, I laughed. A genuine, hearty laugh.

I was alive.

Really, truly alive.

It felt *great*.

"Yeah, no. I'm not."

Minerva sighed, relieved. I didn't feel quite as safe yet—she still had a pistol aimed at my face. I swiped the pistol away, which seemed to snap Minerva back into reality.

"Oh God, I tried killing you, didn't I?"

"You almost succeeded, too. I'm still processing that I'm, you know, breathing."

"I- I'm sorry, I don't know what came over me. I could have sworn you were Anna…"

We seemed equally surprised, just by two different things. I waited until I could be certain I wasn't dead.

Well, I reasoned, *if I'm going to be living with her for however long, I should be friendly.*

I held out my trembling hand. "Uh, hi. My name is Quincey, and I'm here to calm all you ghosts down, whatever that means."

Now that the shock wore off, Minerva didn't seem very pleased. She stared down at my hand for a few moments before hesitantly taking it. "Minerva Mitchell. Businesswoman. Tell me, what does tha—"

Before she had the opportunity to finish her question, someone else walked in. I jumped, not wanting to go through another near-death experience so soon. Matter of fact, I didn't want to go through another one *ever*. But considering this all happened after one day, I had a feeling I wouldn't be so lucky.

When the woman in the red gown walked in, I recognized her immediately: Constance, the only ghost that wouldn't try to kill me. Thankfully.

"Greetings. My name is Constance."

I recognized the voice as the same one from earlier. I felt even more relieved. *I can get a break from running, finally.*

She must have seen it in my face, because she gave me a knowing smile. I tried to say something, but Minerva cut me off.

"Why hello there, Constance. It is a pleasure to make your acquaintance." She took a bow.

Where was that when I *met her?*

"I know *you*, Minerva," Constance teased, "I was introducing myself to the lovely lady who calmed you down. Dear, what did you say your name was again?"

"Uh, Quincey."

Minerva grumbled something inaudible.

I held out my hand for another handshake, and Constance took it gladly. Her hands were gentle and soft, just like everything else about her.

Actually, it dawned on me right then that I could feel them. Weren't they supposed to be see-through or something? They certainly didn't *look* transparent. Were there different kinds of ghosts, like ones that could interact with the world? Minerva was definitely about to kill me with the very-much-solid gun.

They were staring at me. I was still holding on to Constance's hand, so I quickly let go.

"Sorry," I mumbled.

"It is perfectly alright. Everyone gets lost in their head sometimes."

Minerva rolled her eyes, but Constance narrowed her eyes at Minerva. "Stop behaving like a child. You *are* a businesswoman, are you not?"

Instead of giving a sarcastic remark, she seemed startled by the sudden sternness of her voice.

She adjusted her suit jacket. "Yes, I am."

"If that is the case, then show it."

Minerva stood up straighter, and relaxed her expression. Relaxed it as best as she could, at least.

Satisfied, Constance turned back to me with a smile. "Shall we go for a brisk walk? There is much to discuss."

Chapter Four

Minerva's Perspective

I was so surprised when I saw Anna.

More prominently, I was angry.

How dare *she come back to me? She already ruined my life once.*

What would she do this time? Would she beg for forgiveness, down on her knees for so long that bruises began to flower on her pale skin? Oh, maybe she would plead, her hands clasped together and tears streaking her perfect cheeks.

Perhaps she would just taunt me again for my fate inside this mansion.

How did she find me?

All of these thoughts brewed in my mind as I stared down at the lady in question, minding her own business in one of the bedrooms. She sat on her bed, eating a bowl of noodles, and didn't even notice me until I spoke. She had the *audacity* to act clueless about who I was.

I was just so filled with fury that I whipped out my precious pistol and was ready to start blasting without thinking of the repercussions. If I had taken a moment of thought, I would have remembered that Anna would likely be dead. I had no clue what decade it was anymore, but a lot of time had passed since my first day here in the mansion.

I chased her through the mansion like a lioness on the hunt. She moved slower than I remembered. She had a tendency to outrun me when we went on our morning jogs together. The memory turned sour in my mind. She always strove to be ahead of the competition; it was one of the things I loved at first but quickly became annoyed with.

The longer the pursuit went on, the more insane I felt.

I checked the rooms ahead of me. They would be the ones she passed.

With nearly every door I opened, my eyes were greeted by seething light. I hissed as I frantically searched the wall for a lightswitch. These damn lights were going to get the best of me.

I walked inside one of the brighter rooms: a sunroom with furniture covered in drapes. I didn't think much of it until I heard the creak of wood from the closet.

She must have remembered my weakness, damn her, because when I opened the door I instantly became blinded by a bright light. I shrieked, covering my eyes as I did so. I felt her bump into me as she ran away.

I let out a yell of frustration.

My vision eventually came back to me, and I followed the most logical path. I had no way of telling which direction she actually went, so I prayed that she went the same direction.

I found myself in front of the ballroom. I could hear her shuffling, giving away her location easily. It wasn't a good place to hide, anyways, with its wide open space and little area out of sight.

I opened the doors and couldn't see Anna at first glance, much to my surprise. Her red hair usually stuck out, especially in areas with little color like this.

I ducked down, looking under the tables. The knees of my trousers became dirty. When I saw nothing, I stood up and dusted myself off. One can never let their appearance be anything but their best.

She had to be here somewhere.

I backed against a wall, trying to scan the room, when I felt something against my back. Some sort of design imprinted on the wall. I narrowed my eyes before jumping back when I heard the sound of something mechanical behind it.

A door? I thought to myself.

I saw a glimpse of red hair from the crack. I aimed at the back of Anna's head as music filled the air.

I froze.

Everything registered all at once:

The lyrics to my favorite song.

The records littered all over the floor, missing their sleeves.

Anna, her hands covering her ears. Except—it wasn't Anna.

Before my eyes, Anna's auburn hair changed to a curly, bushy brown. Her patterned dress turned into a simple frock and pants. She turned around, and her eyes weren't brown; they were gray.

"You aren't Anna."

The mysterious girl did the last thing I would have thought her to do: she started *laughing*. I stood before her with a gun to her face, and she *laughed*.

"Yeah, no. I'm not."

Such a silly girl; she couldn't even protect herself in the face of danger. Had she really thought that she could have survived my rage?

She never stood a chance.

The lyrics to the song still played. I forgot the name, but I remembered the tune. It was my brother's favorite song. I could have chuckled as I thought about how he would belt the lyrics in his room and how Mother would holler at him to quiet down. I remembered the days of sneaking out at night to see some girl or having a sip of booze. They were simpler.

What was I doing before this moment? I couldn't remember.

She tapped my pistol away, and then I began connecting what happened. "Oh God, I tried killing you, didn't I?"

"You almost succeeded, too. I'm still processing that I'm, you know, breathing."

"I- I'm sorry, I don't know what came over me. I could have sworn you were Anna..."

She held out her hand for an official introduction. I didn't trust it, but I eventually shook it, surprised by her firm grip.

A shadow formed behind me as someone else walked in. The girl, whom I'd learned was named Quincey, jumped beside me as this new woman walked in.

Before me stood easily the most stunning woman I had ever seen.

Her hair, raven's black, cascaded down her to her waist in gentle waves. Her lips were painted a ruby red and turned in a gentle and warm smile that reminded me of my mother's. Her red gown shimmered with brilliant embroidery, flowing down to her ankles. Her amber eyes were warm and intelligent. She was *beautiful*.

Her voice entranced me, melodious and soft with a gentle accent.

I straightened. When she spoke, I saw a sense of recognition flow over Quincey. What type of recognition, however, alluded me.

I introduced myself with a bow, but the woman who had introduced herself as Constance focused her attention on the girl beside me. I grumbled toward the ground as Constance gave the smile to Quincey I so desperately wanted. They shook hands, and I longed to know the feeling of her skin brushing against mine.

Constance asked Quincey a question, but no response came from her.

She finally came back to reality, but Constance continued to be gentle. I rolled my eyes and immediately earned a quick scolding from Constance. Her quick change caught me off guard, and all I could do was try to look more relaxed, however unnatural and vulnerable it made me feel.

Constance invited us for a walk. I would have followed her anywhere.

Without anywhere else to go, Quincey and I continued close behind Constance.

Chapter Five

Blue-Eyed Ghost?

Constance remained silent the rest of the way to the kitchen. There was no way to tell what she thought about as she scanned the pictures in every hall we went through. It was as though she tried to pick her favorite among the thousands. Whoever lived in this mansion before now must have really liked these people encased in the paintings.

My heart finally slowed from my brief fling with death. Minerva fell into stride beside me, although she didn't speak. When I tried looking at her in hopes that she'd start a conversation, she avoided my gaze. She had the face of a woman who knew she could convince anyone of anything. The confidence she showed felt almost unreal—although she refused to do so much as look at me. I kept going, tapping my fingers against the sides of my legs with anticipation.

The silence became unbearable. I had so many questions about everything, but I couldn't say any of them. I couldn't pick which ones were more important.

My suffering got cut short when we reached the kitchen. Was it really that close to the ballroom? It felt much farther from all the running, but Constance seemed to know a shortcut. She probably knew the mansion well.

How long had she been calmed? Elias said that she's the only one I wouldn't have to worry about calming but never explained how. It was good that she's calm, though, right?

"Quinton?"

Minerva stared right at me, one arched eyebrow raised.

I met her with a glance. "It's Quincey."

"I don't care." Constance met the comment with a glare. Minerva cleared her throat, trying to sound kinder. "Did you hear what Constance said?"

I had to give her credit for at least *trying* to sound nicer, even if she wasn't good at it. "No, sorry."

"She wondered how you found out about the mansion. I believe it's been a few months since our last visitor."

"Well, uhm, I heard about it on the news. It sounded fake. Elias definitely sounded like a madman. But I needed a place to stay and some extra cash, so I called Elias, met him here, and he gave me the rundown. His information was vague and instructions were virtually nonexistent. I thought this whole thing was some sort of delusion until...about an hour ago."

Minerva watched me intently. "Okay, lady, let me guess. You seem pretty young, so I'd say you're 23? 24?"

"Uhm, I just turned 19 a couple of months ago."

"Oh my," Constance said softly as she began making food.

Minerva barked out a laugh. "He thinks a 19-year-old is competent enough to handle murderous ghosts? He must be desperate."

Now I'm being ridiculed by ghosts? I glared at Minerva. "You're not one to talk. You're only 18."

Minerva opened her mouth to counter, but Constance cut her off before she could even start.

"You two need to get along." It wasn't that hard to tell that Constance was already getting stressed with us. "If Quincey is going to be living with us for however long, everyone needs to learn how to handle each other. That means no harsh retorts, and no arguing as best as you can. Minerva, I trust you can do that. Do you both understand?"

Despite the gentleness of her voice, her knuckles were white as she gripped the table. I sighed and agreed, as did Minerva.

"Thank you."

We fell back into that uncomfortable silence. Minerva clearly didn't trust me, but I couldn't say that I trusted her, either. The only thing we managed to agree on was pleasing Constance, but I had a feeling that Minerva's intentions were a bit different from mine from the way she looked at her.

As Constance prepared the food, I noticed her giving Minerva some longing looks. I had no idea what could be behind them; Minerva didn't know Constance until 15 minutes ago, but Constance seemed to have a connection to Minerva already. Elias had mentioned that the angry ghosts would have memory problems—maybe they had met before, but Minerva forgot.

"Do either of you know how many more ghosts there are? I know that there's definitely one more, but I don't know how many are after him."

"So you know about Ray?" Constance asked.

"Yeah, I think."

"What information do you have on him?"

"Not a lot. I'm pretty sure he got killed sometime in the 1930s. Maybe he got shot? He's very angry, I know that. There isn't much else Elias told me. He doesn't seem to be much of the *explaining* type."

"Well, you know nearly as much as we do. He is very strong for such a small teenager—"

"A *teenager*?"

Constance sighed. "Yes, unfortunately. It is very sad to think about."

Something inside me flared. "No, *that* is where I draw the line. Elias said I would probably need to fight him, and I am not going against a *kid*. I don't care if I 'have' to in Elias' eyes, that is *not* happening."

"I am sorry Quincey, I do not think you have any other choice."

I stood up. "That's it, I'm *done*. I already did one, that's good enough for me! I'm calling Elias and telling him that I'm going home."

I knew Constance was saying something as I walked away, but I didn't hear her. My anger fueled me all the way to the front door. I flung open the door. I took a step and...

...immediately got sent back.

"What?" I whispered.

I tried stepping out again, but after reaching the bottom step, I stood in front of the door once again.

I walked out again and again, but every time I would just end up in the same place. Always standing a few feet from the door.

I swore loudly and pulled out my phone to yell at Elias, but then I felt a compassionate hand rest on my shoulder. I exhaled as I turned to Constance.

"I am truly sorry, dear. I tried to tell you before you had walked away. The only way you will leave is if you calm us down, or..."

"Or?"

Constance sighed. "I will simply say that the people who came before were not quite as clever as you were. Minerva and her weapon met them before I did."

A shiver ran down my spine.

People *died*?

Part of me was ready to give Elias a nice slap across the face. It's one thing to not explain what I needed to do; it's something completely different to leave out the part that I might not be leaving this 'project' alive.

I wanted to try the door one more time, but I knew it wouldn't work. Whatever magic was over this place had me trapped here.

"Would you like to come back to the kitchen? The soup is ready, and some food might help calm you down."

I nodded. "Thank you."

"You are very welcome."

She led me back to the kitchen. I tried to calm myself and not have a big reaction in front of them, but Minerva's disappointed look didn't help. I tapped my fingers to my thumb, a trick I had learned to keep myself distracted.

I sat down a few seats away from the others and took a sip of the soup. All that running must have made me hungry, because I quickly downed it.

"What kind of soup is this?" I asked as I wiped some remnants from my mouth.

"I am not certain of a name, but it is a recipe my grandmother created."

Minerva also seemed to enjoy the soup, although it was hard to tell with her. Unless she was annoyed or mad, she didn't seem to reveal much.

Constance cleared her throat. "If my memory is correct, Ray is from the…1930s? What major events happened in that time?"

"The Great Depression is pretty much the only thing I can think of."

"Then we will try forming a plan using that as its base…can you tell me what exactly that is?"

Minerva shuddered. "It was awful. I was born towards the end, but my family still struggled from the effects of it for years. My brother and mother told me what it was like; no one had enough, and black families like mine were hit the hardest."

I hadn't thought much about what different families faced in those big events like the Great Depression. I obviously knew that racism existed, but it really didn't make sense to me. The fact that people would judge other people just for their skin color was stupid. Though maybe it's a bit easier for me—I certainly *looked* white, even though I was half Latina. My *abuela* thought I needed to get more sun so I actually looked like her grandchild.

"Imagine our friend here," she gestured towards me. "She said herself that she's in need of cash. Take her case and spread it across the globe due to something called the stock market crashing. Loads of people needed work because failing companies laid off their workers. Everyone was living in poverty. To put it simply, it was a bad time."

Part of me was offended that she just used me as an example for a downscaled version of the Great Depression by calling me broke. The other part of me knew that she was definitely right.

Constance didn't seem to understand, but she nodded anyway. She spoke slowly. "So you are saying that the people struggled with money, so there were little to no financially stable people?"

Minerva nodded.

"That *is* horrible. I can not even begin to fathom it."

Minerva shrugged. "It was easier for me than it was for the rest of my family. Growing up, it was all I ever knew. They had to adapt."

I questioned how much Elias actually knew about the ghosts, because I definitely didn't get told this. Maybe it didn't matter enough to him, but it felt important to me. For the first time, I sympathized with Minerva.

"Well," she said as she brought her bowl to the sink. "Time to catch some Z's."

Minerva wished us goodnight as Constance took my dish to the sink with hers. I wasn't sure if ghosts even needed sleep, but it couldn't hurt. After Minerva left, Constance walked up to me.

"I know you are young, and we are putting a lot on you, but I truly hope you can do it. We all hope so, even if some of us," she rolled her eyes in the direction Minerva had gone, "prefer not to vocalize it."

With that, she glided into the darkness, her soft footsteps quickly fading into the distance.

With that, I was alone again.

I took a deep breath, soaking in everything that had happened these past few hours.

I sat at the table, drumming my fingers along the side. I wanted a way to get on Minerva's good side. Maybe I could make breakfast tomorrow? What do ghosts even eat, anyway? It looked like they enjoyed food still, like the soup that Constance made.

Nevermind, I thought to myself. *I burn every other meal I make.*

I leaned my head against the back of the chair and closed my eyes. Now that I had some time to myself, I felt exhausted. I definitely should have done more gym classes, because my body felt like it would collapse any minute.

I felt a cold breeze. As I opened my eyes, I saw an angry man in front of me.

Or, there *was* an angry man in front of me. He vanished into thin air quickly after, like a wild animal being found. I did remember two things, however; his eyes, an unnaturally vivid blue, and that he was utterly *pissed*. Shivers ran up my spine as I stood, pushing my chair in behind me. My eyes flicked around the room, trying to see any other signs of the mystery man. Other than the brief visual, however, nothing hinted towards him ever being here.

I felt the pounding of my heart in my head.

I think I just need some rest. Bad sleep gives you hallucinations, right? I think I read that somewhere...

Maybe I could just accept it as a hallucination. I would have said that Minerva and Constance were as well, but the damage that they created and everything else was too real to be a figment of my imagination. That's different—they actually stuck around. He disappeared after a second.

Besides, as long as he didn't attack me, that was good enough for me.

Minerva's right. We all need some sleep. I have to start looking ahead to the next ghost: Ray.

With that final thought, I shuffled to my room and slipped into my bed. Even though I tried uselessly to convince myself it had been in my head, I still hoped that the man with the blue eyes wasn't watching over me again.

Chapter Six
Minerva's Weird Behavior

The sound of ceramics shattering broke the calm of the morning.

I shot up, startled. At first I thought someone broke in, but I didn't think anyone was dumb enough to come here. I yanked my sweatshirt down and threw my hair up in a ponytail before running out to see the cause. Minerva's yells were muffled. I thought I heard "get away from me," but I couldn't tell. I ran toward the noise—it had to be the kitchen—and flew open the door in time to hear the sound of another dish crashing to the floor.

Minerva stood alone in the kitchen, staring at the wall. Shards of broken plates surrounded her. Her whole body shook as she breathed.

I froze. Tension hung in the air like a heavy fog.

Eventually, the tension broke, and Minerva relaxed. She slumped forward, clearly exhausted. Whatever had been here before had taken all the energy out of her.

"Are you—"

She startled before turning around. "How long have you been there?"

"I just got here," I lied. It didn't feel appropriate to tell her that I knew she just had some sort of freakout, so I just sat down. Minerva nodded curtly before turning toward the cabinets to start making breakfast.

I did *not* want to deal with the whiplash of a Minerva breakdown, so I sat in silence. I searched the area around me; maybe she saw something that caught her off guard. Could it have been the blue-eyed ghost?

It didn't matter anymore. Minerva and I were alone now.

I fidgeted around in my seat, needing to move. I felt close to bursting as Constance came in, pulling up a chair beside my own. I hoped to talk to her, but she started a conversation with Minerva, so I waited.

At least Minerva seemed better now. She flipped pancakes like a showman, making jokes I didn't understand. They made Constance laugh, though, so they must have been good. Unless Constance was just laughing out of courtesy.

It didn't matter to me, though. I'd take this experience over Minerva trying to kill me anyday.

Constance set down her drink as Minerva served up the pancakes. Her amber eyes devoured us, as though searching for something. "Now then, I believe we should discuss the events of the previous night."

"Do you really think that is necessary?" Minerva huffed. "It should still be brilliantly clear in our heads."

"Quincey is the first to calm you down, and we have learned that she is here for the long run. You may not like it, but she simply cannot leave, which means she is in an *extremely* dangerous position. You nearly killed her, and that was just in the first few days!" She abruptly stood up. I sunk into my chair, shriveling from the raised voice. Minerva might have been scared, but she didn't make it quite as obvious.

Constance must have seen the fear in my eyes, because she took a deep breath and sat back down.

"I apologize; that was inappropriate. Now, shall we discuss this civilly?"

I *could* discuss it civilly, but even though the conversation was about me, I couldn't think of one useful thing to add. When I looked to my side, I saw Minerva watching Constance with some intensity. I couldn't tell what went on inside her mind, though.

Constance exhaled before smiling. "I believe that we are all in agreement that Quincey will most definitely need our help if she wishes to survive this. She is like a child—she can not handle this on her own, at least not yet."

I wanted to cut her off, but she just lifted a finger, and my argument died in my mouth.

It'd be nice if they could at least act like I'm in the room, too.

"So, as Quincey is the one with her life at risk—what with her being the only living person in the mansion—I believe it would only be appropriate to ask her what she thinks we should do." She smiled at me, waving a hand in my direction. "What would *you* like us to do?"

I hadn't actually thought of that. I hoped that they would know what to do, but it became clear that they were expecting me to take at least a bit of charge. But what did they want me to do? I have no idea what's happening anymore.

Constance shook her head solemnly when I didn't answer.

"She can't even come up with a plan!" Minerva exclaimed. "This bundle of nerves is supposed to be the one to help all of us? I don't think so! You two can keep going with this insane plan, I'm done!"

She put her stack of pancakes, which she barely touched, on the counter next to the sink and fled to her room. Constance sighed when we heard the door slam shut behind her.

"Truly, I want to make sure you know how grateful we are for you. Who knows how much longer Minerva would have been on that rampage."

"Probably a few extra decades," I said. I decided it was time to ask a question that came up the day before. "How does Elias know about all of you, but can't save you himself?"

Constance frowned. "I am unsure of why he is unable to, although it seems that he has tried. On occasion, it seems like he has been with us since I arrived, but that is impossible—I died many centuries ago. Even though he is not able to help us escape, it feels nice to have his presence here with us now and then."

I remembered what happened earlier. "Also, there's something I'm wondering about..."

"Hm?"

"Earlier, when I was on my way to the kitchen, Minerva kinda looked like she was having a crisis. Like, throwing-plates-at-the-wall level breakdown. I don't think it came from nothing, though. I think she may have seen someone, or something. Any ideas?"

I knew *I* hadn't seen anything, but who knows; they were ghosts, I wasn't. Maybe they could see things I couldn't.

Constance shook her head in dismay. "Sadly, no. Ray has yet to appear since April. It is nearly…September now, so that would have been," she counted her fingers, "six months ago? It has been quite a while, so I do not think he is appearing again. If he does want something—which I doubt, as he has gone this long on his own—what could it have been to make Minerva so angry?"

I shrugged. "I don't know anymore."

She sounded so unnatural, and I just realized why: she didn't use any contractions. It was like she's still learning English. Since she's French, that wouldn't be too far of a stretch. I didn't want to ask her about it right then, though, because I didn't know if that would be offensive. Maybe I'd ask her at some other time.

"If it wasn't Ray," I wondered aloud as I stood up and started to walk around, "and it wasn't you, who could it have been? I'm the only living person here, if you don't count Elias' visits. Are you sure there's no one else?"

Constance walked around to join me with a serious look. "I lost certainty in most things a long time ago, but I will protect you as best as I can. I refuse to lose another child."

I paused. "Another?"

She hesitated before continuing. "Around the time I passed, I was pregnant. I was 23, and it would have been my third child. Sadly, we found out a week or so before my death that the baby would not make it. My husband and I wanted to name him Solomon, after his father. He died when my husband was at a young age."

I could hear the sadness in her voice as she spoke, as if she were barely holding back tears. "I- I'm sorry, that's horrible."

Constance smiled with melancholy. "Oh, it has been an awfully long time now. It must have been centuries since then. I like to think that little Solomon is up in heaven somewhere, dancing with all the other little angels."

"How do you still believe in heaven?" I whispered. "Even after everything that's happened?"

"Well, when you truly believe in something, you do not need to rely on the good things to know—you know because you are still here, even after terrible times."

We stood in silence, as though mourning the lives lost; the one of Solomon, and the one Constance would have lived if none of this had happened. Tension was so thick in the air, it could have been cut with a knife.

Or pierced with a bullet.

Because, of course, that's when Minerva decided to blast one from the doorway. Her eyes were wide as the bullet shot inches away from my face.

Chapter Seven
Preparing to Fight a Kid

I curled into myself as the bullet shot. The ringing stayed in my ears like the bullet hit my brain instead of the area next to me. My heart beat frantically, like a terrified bird inside a cage. Through my blurred vision I saw Constance trying to calm down Minerva, but I wasn't processing it, like scanning the words to a book but not actually reading them. Tears spilled over as I squeezed my eyes shut. I could feel my heart rate rising until it pounded between my ears. The bullet lay beside me as I hit the ground with a quiet thud. I tried some breathing techniques I learned—long, deep breaths—but my throat constricted. My hands trembled as they clenched my hair, squeezing and releasing.

Constance and Minerva were next to me now.

"…—alright, you are alright, you are safe…"

"…—what happened, I swear I don't know what happened…"

The two women talked over each other, like a slurring drink or two different songs playing at once. I tried a breathing pattern my therapist, Adrianne, taught me during one of our sessions; breathe in for four seconds, hold for seven, breathe out for eight. Four, seven, eight.

In.

Hold.

Out.

A few minutes went by. Minerva and Constance stood on either side of me. They were silent now. My heart slowed to a reasonable pace. I must have stopped crying, because I felt thin streams on my cheeks drying. I took the sleeve of my jacket and wiped off my face; I was a mess.

I remembered the bullet that lay by my side, and I felt another jump of my heart, not quite as bad as before.

I rubbed my forearms up and down, reassuring myself that I was still there and safe, all in one piece. Constance's hand traced my back, and Minerva's rest on my leg. Having other people there comforted me, even if they were technically dead.

"How are you feeling? Are you alright?"

Constance's voice broke through the pristine silence.

I turned to her and nodded, slowly standing back up. My legs shook, but I balanced myself quickly. I politely asked Constance for a handkerchief or tissue, and she left and came back with a whole box.

"Thank you," I said with a croaky voice.

Constance smiled and squeezed my hand.

The comfort I received from Minerva, however, seemed to disappear now that she knew I wasn't going to be totally ruined. Why had she shot at me, anyway?

As I watched her back away, I didn't think I would get an answer.

She put some distance between us, and although she didn't look at me with much more than annoyance, I hoped that there was a shred of human decency behind her tough exterior.

Something about the way Minerva looked at me reminded me of someone. It was on the tip of my tongue, but I couldn't quite place it until she looked me right in the eyes.

The man with the blue eyes.

I bit the inside of my lip as I debated whether or not to bring it up. We had enough troubles already, what with Minerva acting up and the Ray dilemma. By chance could Minerva have been yelling *at* the man with the blue eyes?

I was overthinking this. Angry Man's likely just another ghost in the mansion; Constance said there were more. Could the blue eyes belong to the final ghost?

If so, I am *definitely* not leaving this alive.

"May I ask, does Ray have blue eyes?"

Constance raised an eyebrow. "No, he has green eyes. Why do you ask?"

"Nothing," I lied. I wanted to wait before telling them.

Minerva narrowed her eyes. "That's a rather bizarre question. You sure there's nothing else behind it?"

I hadn't expected to be challenged on it, so I didn't have a backup plan set up. I sighed and explained it anyway. "There's this ghost I saw earlier. At least, I think he's a ghost. I didn't get a good look at him, but there were two things I do remember; his eyes were blue, like, *really* blue. Practically glowing. He was also *really* angry. Do either of you know who he is?"

Constance and Minerva locked eyes, similar to the silent communication between parents when a kid asks about something they shouldn't. I felt dumb for not knowing what they were thinking and for being treated like I was a fifth grader. It's so dumb—Minerva's younger than me. The way they looked at each other made it feel like they had been like this for years, not a day.

They finally remembered that I was there. Minerva cleared her throat and turned to me. "He's likely just the ghost after Ray. We don't really know anything about him, but we know he's here somewhere."

I would have believed that if Constance didn't look so worried. They were hiding something from me, which seemed pretty stupid, because I was the one who they're stuck with for however long. They might as well be honest with me if they want me to trust them. Although I'm pretty sure Minerva could care less if I trusted her.

Constance's face lit up. "I have an idea!"

Minerva raised an eyebrow. "What is it?"

"Well," she said as she turned to face me, "it is safe to assume you lack experience with ghosts or fighting, correct?"

I slowly nodded. It's pretty obvious, but what's she planning?

"I think I know a way to get you...adjusted, to both of them." She looked towards Minerva. "The problem, however, is that Minerva would have to do it. I am not strong enough to do the training myself, so I must simply watch and interject if you two get at each other's throats."

I tried reading Minerva's expression as she considered it. While I may not enjoy Minerva's attitude, I thought it was a good idea, but my input would be useless if Minerva didn't want to do it.

"Well..." Minerva muttered. "I could, *in theory*, see the benefit of training. But how are we supposed to train in the time we have? Most training takes months, but I don't think Quigley would like to entertain that idea, and neither would I."

"Well then, I suppose we should start as soon as possible. What do you say, *Quincey*? Are you ready to start training to fight?"

I sighed and looked ahead. "Ready as I'll ever be."

I grabbed my robe and toiletries before making my way to the nearest bathroom. I turned the water to the hottest setting and stood in the steam for a few minutes before hopping in. Showers were always where I could think clearest, so it made sense to take one before I got started with training.

I felt the burning water hit my skin and wash away all of my worries from the day. When under the water, I could forget about the world outside where I had responsibilities that I wasn't even sure I could fulfill.

I started to hum a tune that had been stuck in my head for a week. I didn't remember where I'd heard it, or if I'd made it myself, but it sounded nice. It's like a song about not understanding anything, which was pretty accurate to how I felt. I wished that I could write down the melody, but I never really learned how to read notes. I could sing it, yes, but I couldn't tell you what the notes were.

While I worked through the song, I also worked my way through my rat's nest of hair. Having curly hair was no fun when you could barely take care of it. I ran my fingers through the curls to try and brush out the knots, and I got as much as I had the will for.

I had totally forgotten to bring a hairdryer, so I was stuck with a cold mop on my head for training. Great.

I didn't know what kind of training to expect. *Training to fight* didn't exactly reveal much. I knew that there were different types of fighting, but I had no clue what Minerva had in mind for me. I just had to pray it wasn't gonna be, like, jiu-jitsu or something.

If I didn't do well on this training, I could die. Minerva had almost killed me, but she had a gun. Maybe Ray would be easier on me.

Or maybe he wouldn't. Maybe he would go harder and kill me because I wouldn't be able to fight him off. What would happen then?

Shut up, me. I refuse to have a crisis in the shower.

I stepped out and immediately felt the rush of cool air. I quickly dried off and wrapped myself in my robe before heading to my room to change. I tossed my dirty clothes to the corner and changed into a tank top and shorts. As I threw my hair up in a ponytail and put on some tennis shoes, I reminded myself that this wasn't the worst that could happen before leaving to start the horror that was training with Minerva.

Chapter Eight

Minerva is Using Cheat Codes

The training was by far the most physically demanding thing someone's made me do since the fitness gram pacer test. Wait, no, this was way worse.

Minerva waited for me in one of the large but mostly empty rooms, and Constance stood by the side with a reassuring smile.

I had no clue how muscle strain worked with ghosts, but Minerva seemed completely unaffected by the different exercises she forced me to do. She found various methods of torture to put me through, like sit ups, push ups, and running. It felt like everything pushed me to the absolute limit despite the simple actions. My body screamed at me with every movement, which was as big of a sign as any that I needed to work out more. Minerva, however, kept going as if it were nothing.

I didn't think to bring my water bottle with me to the mansion, either, so Constance set up little water stations to make sure I didn't pass out.

Minerva stopped us after a half hour.

"Now that the warm up is done, the real training can begin."

Excuse me, that was a warm up?

There's no hope for me.

"Oh, come on. Don't tell me you're tired after a wee bit of exercise now, are you?" There was a fire behind her eyes that begged me to fight.

She was *taunting* me.

"I'm sorry, but I'm pretty sure that ghosts don't get the same aftermath as people who are still living and, you know, need oxygen." I gasped after every other word. I stood doubled over, my hands resting on my knees as I tried to regain my breath. My body burned and my side ached with so much pain I thought it would explode. I was reminded of all the reasons I had never done sports in high school.

"Just give it up, Quinn. Admit it—you're weak, and dumb, and you never should have taken this little 'project.' You seriously thought this was a good idea? No. You're going to die, and no one will remember you."

Anger boiled inside me, but I wouldn't give Minerva the satisfaction. "I don't care. Just because you're dead and don't feel anything doesn't mean you have to be an asshole about it."

I started coughing hard. It didn't exactly help me show Minerva I was a-okay.

"Queenie, *no one will remember you*. Let that sink in. If you die here because you are too weak, you'll go down in history as what? Just another nameless girl taken by misfortune."

I couldn't stand it anymore. Minerva was clearly just being an ass to get on my nerves, so I would give her what she wanted. I ran up to her and threw a punch at her jaw, sending a shock of pain through my arm as it hit her iron-like skin. She grinned.

"That's what I'm talking about! Feel that anger build and let it burst! You need to harness that energy for when and if you need to go hand-to-hand with Ray, or anyone else for that matter."

I kept punching and punching as she continued to throw smaller digs at me, looking at me with satisfaction. My punches kept getting more powerful until I hit my peak and fell backwards. I landed on my hip and felt a jolt of pain up my side. I hurried back up, not wanting to show much struggle. I could tell a little whimper had come out, but I hoped that Minerva couldn't hear it.

Minerva sighed. "You can't just keep going on adrenaline. You need to make sure your body is actually prepared to fight. We'll continue this later; that fall looked awful. Constance will help you, since she seems to have a knack for that."

I groaned, disappointed with myself. I ambled over to Constance, gently rubbing my hip as she greeted me with an ice pack and a smile. "You are doing wonderful for your first time, love."

I could see Minerva's attention drift toward us when Constance said 'love.' I ignored her. "Clearly not good enough, at least to Minerva's standards."

"Just give her time, she has to warm up eventually."

I raised an eyebrow.

"She is still skeptical about you, that is all. Give her time, and she will come around. Trust me, by the time you finish this, Minerva will have you under her wing like a baby bird."

I sighed. "I sure hope you're right, because this is awful."

I put the ice pack on my hip and sat down on a chair. The cold from the pack sent a second wave of pain, like a layered cake. If cakes were made up of various versions of pain, at least. It didn't take long for it to start helping, though. As I waited for it to help, I made small conversation with Constance, and before I knew it my hip felt better. For now, anyway.

"Thanks," I said as I handed the ice pack to Constance. She took it and set it on a small table nearby. Her eyes had a sense of sadness behind them.

"Do you really think I'll be able to calm Ray and the others down?"

"I would not have put this much faith in you if not, would I?" Despite the kind words, her tone matched the same feeling behind her eyes. Maybe she didn't have a reason to believe, but she had a reason to hope. She could only hope that I was the one who's supposed to help, or else who knows how long it'll be until someone else comes along? Assuming that Minerva didn't scare them off, Ray's still a threat. I didn't know what came after that, but it had to be absolutely terrifying.

"If not now, then with Minerva's training you will definitely be able to. I do believe that you will do great things, Quincey, even if you have yet to realize your true potential because of what others have told you. Do not allow yourself to base your self worth on what others think you can or cannot do—you yourself are the only one who can determine who you are."

Usually when I got the 'don't listen to what others tell you' speech, it made me feel awful. But something about this time's different. Maybe it's the warm smile that Constance gave me, or the fact that it's Constance telling me it. It's like there's a magic behind her voice that made everything seem better than it was.

I was about to go in for a hug until Minerva came up from behind me, looking me up and down. "How's the trainee doing?"

"Seems to be doing just fine, in my opinion. How about we ask her ourselves?"

"Hey, my hip may be numb, but it's better than the ache it had before."

"Alright," said Minerva, "now that we have combat done, any other ideas?"

Constance shook her head. They both turned to me, and I saw a glint from Minerva's belt. "Well, actually, I *do* have an idea, but I don't think you're going to like it."

"Oh dear Lord," I heard Minerva mutter, "go on."

"Gun training. It'd be smart to learn to defend myself long range, just in case. There is a slight problem, though; there is only one weapon in the mansion, and it just so happens to be that very gun resting at your side."

Minerva hovered her hand over the pistol like she was protecting a child. "No way. Nope. *Nada*. You are *not* laying your hands on Minerva Jr."

I bit back a smile, trying my best not to laugh as I spoke. "You named your pistol *Minerva Jr.*?"

"Did you have a better name idea? No? I didn't think so."

Constance cut in. "Actually, Quincey's argument is valid. Even if she may not need it for Ray, we do not know about the rest of them. I understand that you are wary to trust her with your gun—"

"—she's basically a toddler!—"

"—but I think Quincey's safety is more important than who you let use your gun. If Quincey handling your gun means that she will be safe if something happens, then I think it is worth handing it over, at least while she is with Ray. You can keep it on you all other times, and make sure that she learns how to use Minerva Jr. correctly so she avoids getting herself killed."

Minerva looked at me, debating whether or not she should hand it over. Eventually, she relented. "You break Minerva Jr., I break your mom, got it?"

"Yes, sir."

"Do I look like a *sir* to you?"

Thank God, Constance split us up before things could get worse. "Settle down. We need to get preparations ready. Gun training and combat sounds like it will be enough. Now, if you two can refrain from slitting each other's throats, that would be nice."

Minerva sighed. "I'm sorry, I really need to control my temper."

Hearing Minerva apologize didn't seem to fit her character. She technically apologized to me right after she calmed down, but she quickly became annoyed shortly after. At least with Constance, she seemed like she actually meant the apology.

Constance smiled with enough warmth to start a fire. "Thank you, darling. Now then, let us move on, shall we?"

Minerva stood rigid. It wouldn't have surprised me if she'd never been called anything so nice by anyone other than her mom. I thought I had seen the tips of her ears go red, but I could never be sure.

"Are you ready, Quincey?"

"Ready for what?" Minerva asked.

"The rest of her training, of course."

Chapter Nine

The Last One but New and Improved

I definitely didn't feel ready to start training right then and there, but I couldn't think of an excuse to postpone it. So, without much of an argument, we set up a target to continue on with the last of our training for the day: learning how to use a gun.

"Wash your greasy hands, you *bastard*!"

Unsurprisingly, I wasn't exactly on Minerva's good side at the moment.

"There are marks on Minerva Jr. you *disgusting*—"

Constance gave Minerva a glare that could have cut through steel, and Minerva shut up. Constance's nickname should be "Official Minerva-Shusher." People would pay some good money for that.

She took the gun before I could use it. "Now then, I can't lose it on you because our personal angel over there is watching with the eyes of a hawk, but I swear, if you leave so much as an itsy bitsy scratch on my pistol, you'll be leaving this room in a hospital stretcher."

I almost laughed.

I would have if the threat wasn't so terrifying, because I knew she would have no reservations on following through with it.

"So, we're going to use this random tool I found in the kitchen as your 'gun' right now, alright? I don't trust you with Minerva Jr. yet."

Minerva handed me a ladle, which I couldn't tell if she knew the name of. I didn't know how she expected me to use it; it didn't resemble a gun whatsoever. Either way, I had to do my best. I put the handle side facing outward and gripped onto the spooning side.

"You don't hold the gun from the barrel, dumba- ahem, Quink."

I barely refrained from whacking Minerva in the face with the ladle. "How am I supposed to know which side is which?" I muttered as I flipped it around.

She started to show me where all the hand placements were, when to pull the trigger, et cetera. It's pretty difficult, though, considering the ladle shared practically no anatomy with a gun. I looked over at Minerva, scared to ask if I could use Minerva Jr., but she seemed to understand.

"You better not leave a single mark on this baby or I will end you."

"Got it."

I could've sworn that tears had started to form in her eyes as she went for her side and handed it over to me. She took the ladle from me as I looked over the gun.

"Why do you like this gun so much, anyway?"

"No reason, dimwit," Minerva snapped.

I smiled as sweetly as I could. "It's okay Minnie, you can tell me."

"Never call me Minnie again."

"I'll keep calling you Minnie until you tell me, *Minnie*."

Minerva sighed, looking toward Constance. She seemed proud of the fact that we had lasted this long without blowing up. She looked down as she spoke.

"You wanna know? Fine. My brother gave it to me before he joined the army. Never came home, and I never saw him again. I hoped that when I died I'd see him again, but no luck there. I'm just stuck in this eternal damnation."

Minerva may not be the friendliest person I'd ever met, but it was clear that her brother meant a lot to her. Part of me wanted to hug her, but that definitely wasn't Minerva's style. So, I just waited in silence and handled Minerva Jr. with a newfound respect.

I got lost in my thoughts, and almost forgot that there's an upset Minerva who's currently holding a ladle. Not as dangerous as Minerva Jr., but because *Minerva* was holding it, I didn't want to take my chances.

Minerva cleared her throat. "Alright, you need to remember that the bullet will be loud. Don't think that I forgot about your reaction last time, and you were across the room. It's going to be even louder because it's closer to your ear. I can get you something to block out the noise if you need. I don't want you to be a seeping mess on the floor again."

Constance scurried over and handed over a pair of earplugs. How the hell did she even get those? I put them in, and everything became muffled. The sound of my breathing became clearer. Minerva and Constance were discussing something, but I couldn't tell what.

When they finished, Minerva came up behind me and rested a hand on my shoulder. "Ready, kid?"

"I'm older than you," I grumbled as I raised the gun.

Minerva took a step back.

I put my finger on the trigger.

Another step back.

I aimed. I took a deep breath.

I pulled the trigger.

I felt a force throw my arm back, hurting my shoulder. I tried finding where the bullet pierced the target, if it did at all. I found the hole sitting at the edge of the target, and my whole body started to shake.

Did I just use a gun? Like, actually fire a gun? I think I did.

Thankfully, the earplugs did their job. The sound was quieter, and while the vibrations caught me off guard, I had all my wits about me. My heart raced, but this time from excitement. I was finally learning how to do things.

Maybe I'd be able to do this after all.

I handed the gun back to Minerva, who looked relieved to have it back in her hands. The edges of her lips quirked as she looked over Minerva Jr.

"No visible embellishments." She looked towards the target. "Didn't hit the bullseye, but that was to be expected. Not bad for your first time, bigshot."

I grinned, trying to ignore the pain in my shoulder.

"How's your arm doing? The kickback can be pretty bad for first timers."

"So *that's* what that is."

Minerva chuckled, and not in the insane way she had yesterday. "It's not fun. Just make sure you don't make it worse."

I nodded.

"Now that we've got the beginning of gun basics down, how about we discuss hiding places? You weren't very clever yesterday. Everyone knows to look in the closet."

"No need to remind me," I said, remembering the fear from the day before.

Minerva gave Minerva Jr. one more twirl before tucking it away in the pistol holster by her side. She then motioned for me to follow her.

She guided me throughout the house, pointing out the best spots to hide if I got chased again. She added notes every now and then with tips on running and not getting caught if he got close to my hiding spot.

I was grateful for her help, don't get me wrong. She's just...overwhelming.

"This hallway has creaky floors, so avoid it if you can."

"The bathroom is always a great place to hide, but don't hide in the shower. If you can, try squeezing into a cabinet, if you can find one that fits you. You're pretty tall, so that could be a challenge."

"Don't be afraid to work backwards. Movement can mean life or death."

"Stay low; it becomes easier to avoid the person's eyes if you're lower to the ground. They're not going to go through the extra effort of ducking down if they're trying to find you quickly."

"Have something small you can throw at them, either in defense or as a distraction."

"You know," I cut in, "I won't be able to remember all of this. I already forgot which hallway I'm supposed to avoid because of the floorboards. Can we slow down a bit?"

"Come on, Queso. You've managed this long—can't you go a little longer?"

"You've been pushing me all day. You don't need to be a rocket scientist to know that I can't do my best after being worked out like that. All you have to do is give me a break! What do you have against me, anyway? You won't even bother to be nice to me if Constance isn't around."

"Maybe I just don't have time for you! You have no stamina, your body can be broken like a stick, and you lose your breath quicker than I can say hippopotamus! You'll never survive at this rate, so it's my way or no way at all."

I stared her down, even though the eye contact made me uncomfortable. It didn't seem like either of us were going to back down.

She noticed that, too, because she grumbled *unbelievable* and stormed off.

I huffed, staying where I was. Part of me wondered if this was another one of her tricks, but when she didn't come back, it became clear that it's a real fight.

I didn't care; she was being a prick anyway.

At some point, Constance found me standing alone in the hallway. She must have been looking for me; when we made eye contact, she looked relieved.

"There you are."

"Right where Minerva ditched me, forgetting that I don't know my way around the mansion."

Constance sighed. "Yes, she said you two got into a disagreement. I tried reasoning with her, but she is very…stubborn."

"Well, so am I."

"So I have gathered." She smiled. "How do you feel about lunch?"

Chapter Ten
Oh Look, I'm Seeing Things

I didn't have a clue what recipes they had in the sixteenth century, but *damn*, were they good.

Elias may not have bought much for fancy meals, but Constance worked her way around the kitchen. She could have been a world class chef; maybe she would have, if she had gotten to live long enough. Her passion for cooking was clear with every dish she made.

It felt strangely quiet without Minerva with us, throwing a remark at Constance or berating me somehow. I was actually starting to miss it, which was something I had never thought I'd say. But according to Constance, Minerva's isolated in her room. Which, thinking about it, why would ghosts even need rooms, anyway? They didn't need to sleep, at least I didn't think so.

Either way, I was grateful for the delicious soup. I finished quickly, likely leaving some stains on the sleeves of my sweatshirt. Constance looked at me with slight disdain as I wiped my mouth off with my sleeve.

Once I finished, I brought the paper dishes over to the trash. I heard the sound of footsteps and my heart raced. I forcibly reminded myself that I wasn't getting chased anymore as I looked over and saw Minerva, who looked awful. Maybe a vampire had come and drained her of all of her energy.

"I'm sorry, I shouldn't have snapped. I've been exhausted, and still a little pissed—"

Constance glared at her, and she sighed. "The thing is, I should do my best not to hold a grudge against you. You're only stuck in this mess because Elias was being a dunce and gave you a deal that anyone would have taken, and that isn't your fault. You don't even want to be here, especially now with Ray."

It felt weird to hear her apologize, but it sounded sincere, at least as sincere as Minerva could get. "Thank you. I forgive you."

"You better."

"That's the Minerva I know."

Minerva smirked, crossing her arms. Constance gave me a ghost of a smile—pun intended—and nodded to Minerva. I collected the rest of the plates and bowls and dumped them into the trash. We decided switching them out for paper ones worked better. I left a single bowl and spoon out for Minerva. She hadn't eaten breakfast, and I knew from experience that food helped with mood tremendously. She spooned some soup into the bowl and drank it, no spoon needed.

I quietly took the spoon and put it away as she finished up. Constance looked at her incredulously, pain in her eyes. I thought that she said *you both eat like savages*, but I couldn't be certain.

When Minerva put the bowl down, it was completely worth it to see the soup mustache. I brushed my finger across my upper lip to signal her the mustache, and she hurried to wipe it off, her cheeks tinted red. She gave me a glare, but I just replied with the lips-sealed motion.

Constance bit back a smile, and we were back to normal. Well, as normal as a household with only one person who's actually *alive* could get. It still felt weird to be with two ghosts, but it wasn't something I couldn't get used to. Even if it's only been a couple days, it was already becoming my new normal to have them around, now that the shock of it all wore off. They were starting to feel like a bizarre, slightly dysfunctional family of sorts.

That family would hopefully be growing soon, because Minerva had finished her food and was ready to start fighting.

"Rule number one—stay light on your feet. If you can, bounce up and down a bit. Helps keep you balanced and quick."

I had my fists raised by my chest, trying to figure out how to bounce on my feet without hopping like a bunny.

"No, not like that." She stopped and showed me her foot, pointing to a part behind the toes. "See this? This is the ball of the foot. You want to balance on that the whole time."

I tried lifting onto the balls of my feet, and it helped, but I almost fell over at least three times before I got the hang of it.

"There we go. Up next are those fists. They suck."

She grabbed my hand and showed me how to do a proper fist, thumb on the bottom. I tried recreating it on my other hand and grinned triumphantly when I got them.

"If you're proud of just getting the fist right, you need to raise your standards. You aren't even holding them in the right place!" She raised her own fists. "You have to protect your face. If they get a shot to your face, you've got much more to worry about than if your fists are in the right form."

I tried matching her, but she was getting more and more exasperated. "You have to be able to *see*, Quinlin. Put them a little above your chin."

Cautiously, I brought my arms to the spot.

Minerva threw a punch.

I ducked, yelping. "What the hell?!"

"You can't wait for a warning; he's going to come at you without so much as a second glance."

"I don't even know how to block!"

"Well then, it's a good thing you knew how to duck."

I really wanted to punch her, but she'd probably block me at a second's notice. "Do you want to, I don't know, *teach* me how to block?"

"Not really, but I will anyway."

We took a break from bouncing and focused on learning how to block. She threw a punch—which I learned was called a reverse punch—and I ducked. Without saying anything, she punched again. I held my arms in front of my face in an X.

"That *is* a block, but not for that punch. Here, I'll show you an upper block."

She asked me to punch her, and I did. She turned her arm to the side and slid it under the punch, raising it up. "This is an upper block, but you would do it faster than that. Do you want to try?"

I nodded. She threw the punch again, and I did my best attempt at an upper block.

"You'll want more force and more speed. But, you've got the general movement down, so that's good."

I put my arms down for a couple seconds, but in that small frame, Minerva tossed out another punch. I barely had enough time to block it.

"Really?"

"Another rule: don't *ever* bring your arms down, unless it's established among both sides that the fight is over. That's the easiest way to get your teeth bashed in."

"Why are there so many rules to fighting?" I mumbled, raising my fists again.

We went over a few more blocks, and she even taught me a couple punches. I kept confusing the reverse punch with the jab, though.

"Okay, you have the basics down. We should work on stances next."

"There's a specific way to *stand*?"

Minerva smirked. "Does that surprise you?"

"Not as much as I thought it would."

I took my best guess on how to stand, and I got bits of it right. It helped that I just had to think about how Minerva had done it earlier, so there wasn't much for her to nitpick. It was mostly about keeping my back straight, my head up, and staying on the balls of my feet.

"Ready to spar?" she eventually asked.

"Does it matter what I say?"

"No."

She counted us down, and we got started.

The match felt like it was done in a matter of moments, with my jaw sore from a hook. In the heat of the moment, I completely forgot everything I had been taught.

"Again."

Wrong block.

"Again."

Not supposed to duck.

"Again."

Forgot to punch back.

"Does this ever get exhausting to you?" I asked after the fifth lightning round.

"Constantly fighting or beating you? The answer's the same either way, but the distinction is nice."

I glared at her and was met by a cocky grin.

"One more round. I'll do better this time."

She shrugged and began the countdown. When she yelled *fight*, I threw the first punch. She blocked it easily, but the surprise made her falter. Satisfaction filled me, and it fueled me to keep it going.

Despite how hot I felt, a chill ran down my spine. The shape of a man appeared behind Minerva, catching me off guard.

I recognized him, but where…?

Those blue eyes.

He decided to stick around longer this time, so I got a good look at him. Chains curled around his arms and ankles, and he looked like a captive on a pirate ship, with outgrown brown hair and dirt all over him. He looked young, too; he couldn't have been older than Minerva or I. Something about his face was familiar, but I couldn't quite place it...

I didn't have much time to think about it, because I got knocked back from a punch.

"I don't know if I told you this, but you're not supposed to stare out into space randomly in a fight. I didn't think you'd need the reminder, but I guess not."

Had she not noticed him? I mean, he was behind her, but surely she would have noticed me staring at something behind her. When she looked over her shoulder, he was already gone.

"Despite the lack of attention span, that was better. I'll give you a few more rounds."

I sighed and ignored the panic in my chest as I brought my fists back up.

Chapter Eleven

What a *Ray* of Sunshine

A week and a half later of relentless training, they'd decided that I had made enough progress to make my first attempt with Ray. Personally, I would have given myself at least another six weeks, but we needed to get this done sooner rather than later. The sooner I could get out of this mess and calm down the ghosts, the better.

Constance told me all that she knew about Ray—he's fifteen, very aggressive, and just needed a bit of love in his life. So far, he's the youngest ghost, and the perfect age to want to reject any authoritative figure. It just so happened that I was the authoritative figure in this case. Great.

Best case scenario, he would listen to me and we would get this settled peacefully.

Worst case scenario, well, I might die at the hands of a teenager after two weeks in the mansion.

I hoped for the best case scenario.

My fighting skills had improved, and I could aim decently. On average, I could beat Minerva in a sparring match one of every five rounds. That may not have seemed very impressive, but if I was on the opposing side, one of every five against Minerva was a good statistic. Fighting her was like fighting a brick wall, except the brick wall could *also* beat you up.

Before I got sent off, Minerva pulled me aside.

"We've been training for days. You can throw a decent punch if needed, and you don't break down every time you hear a gunshot anymore, so that's an improvement. You've prepared for this, and now all you have to do is seize the moment, as well as Ray. The quicker you can calm him down, the less damage you'll face. And remember, fighting will only provoke him, so stay peaceful as long as you can. Try not to fight him unless it's absolutely necessary. Not that I think you would go out of your way to fight him." Her eyebrows furrowed with focus. "Are you ready?"

I looked Minerva in her eyes and noticed that a pale brown iris started to form.

"I'll do my best."

"Not what I wanted to hear, but I'll take it, Quink."

"Can't think of any more nicknames?"

"I could if I wanted to, but I've decided that Quink fits you best."

I grinned, and while Minerva would rarely give me a real smile outside of her own pride, there was a look of amusement. I nodded to her as she handed me her gun and passed me over to Constance, who had wanted to walk me down to the room where Ray would hopefully be.

"One cannot be too cautious. I will be right outside on the chance that something goes wrong," Constance assured me. It felt comforting to have Constance with me. Well, near me, at least. If anything went horribly wrong, I could dash out of there and Constance would be ready.

I took a deep breath, and Constance gave my arm a squeeze. Her touch brought reassurance. It reminded me of how Mom would take me to the doctors when I was younger, even though I was scared of them. This was way more terrifying, though.

We started down the hallways to the conference room. It had actually been my first time going there, so I tried to memorize the way there as we walked. If things went awry and Constance wasn't there, I'd need to find my way back on my own.

The closer we got to the conference room, the more panicked I felt. If Ray tried attacking me, would I be able to fight back? I was able to practice with Minerva, but she's around my age; Ray's younger than me. If it became life or death, could I actually bring myself to fight him? Let alone *shoot him* with a *gun*?

I pushed away the thought. I would try to calm him down with words first. No fighting unless absolutely necessary, like Minerva said.

We made it to the conference room just as I thought I'd suffocate. Somehow knowing that I was already there brought down the anxiety a bit. There's no turning back now; might as well go into it head on.

Constance whispered, "Are you ready?"

I nodded, even though I wasn't.

She quietly opened the door, staying hidden from the view of the inside. I hurriedly stepped in so that I couldn't try to convince myself out of it, and stopped when I saw Ray pacing behind a table angrily.

He looked...different from what I expected. I thought he would look like a war-torn young adult who lost everything, but he really just looked like a kid. A kid who had gone through a harsh life and needed help.

His outfit made me think of a newsboy, though all of the clothes looked a size too big and his shoes were old and worn. There's a dark stain around his stomach, but I couldn't tell what might have put it there. His blond hair, mostly hidden beneath a newsboy hat, was scruffy and unkempt, as though it had rarely been taken care of. His dull green eyes were tired and angry with dark circles underneath.

I looked around the room, trying to get a feel for the area. There was a large oval-shaped table with plenty of chairs surrounding it, but other than that, there wasn't much else. Maybe I'd be able to use the chairs as an obstacle between Ray and I, but that would also make it harder for me to talk to him.

A large whiteboard sat blank on the back wall, though it had clearly been used at some point. Remnants of black marker covered the board—I wondered what it was used for. There was one other thing on the walls: a small painting of a field and house. It was oddly peaceful in contrast to the anger that buzzed in the room.

Ray went on muttering to himself. He hadn't noticed me yet.

I worried about startling him, but I had to get his attention somehow. I mustered up my courage as best as I could before speaking. "Uhm, hi?"

'Uhm, hi?' That's what I say to someone who could kill me?

However stupid the phrase, it got his attention. He whipped his head around, making me jump. Although he's looking at me, his eyes weren't focused.

"Look, I don't know who you are or why you keep coming, but I *really* don't want to talk to you right now, no matter who you are."

I had forgotten that he wouldn't see me as myself. That was still something to get used to.

He had some sort of Midwest accent, and he sounded irritated, like he had dealt with me so many times before. Did anyone manage to find him before me? I couldn't imagine they would have stuck around for long, especially if they're trying to outrun Minerva. He was hard to look at; his skin's sickly pale, and he trembled with every motion. He could have been a ticking time bomb.

I hadn't noticed he had stopped pacing, his arms now crossed and facing me. "So? Are you going to go?"

How do I explain this? "Well, not exactly. My goal is to, uhm, help you. I can't imagine how angry you must be, trapped here all alone."

"At least it's better than dying!" he snarled. The lights flickered with his anger. "I'm perfectly fine on my own. I've lasted this long myself, and I don't need some...*guy* trying to act like he's been there for me. If you actually *cared,* why didn't you come before?!"

I winced, refraining the urge to cover my ears. There was so much pain in his voice...I couldn't imagine what he had gone through before his death.

"I may not have been there before, but there's no better time than now." I offered a hand to him and hoped it was somewhat realistic to say. He stared at my open hand in confusion, as though he couldn't decide whether to take it or not.

He shook his head as he walked around the table and towards me. His fist clenched, and I barely dodged the punch as he swung. Anger flashed in his eyes. He kept throwing punches, quicker than I could block. When I couldn't block, I ducked. Even then, I couldn't bring myself to fight back; he's just a kid. I knew he was strong, but the idea of hurting him wasn't something I liked very much. I shielded my face, receiving a strong hit towards the elbow that would definitely bruise later.

Constance sure is taking her sweet time. Either she ditched me, or she actually believes in me...

Who was I kidding? I was already failing miserably, so why wouldn't she come in? She definitely ditched me.

The bit of strength I had in my arms was starting to fade with every hit he landed. I still blocked a few of them, but not nearly fast enough to block the next. If I put my arms down, though, they wouldn't be the only part of me covered in bruises. Thankfully, Ray must have been tiring out, because his punches were weakening and slowing down.

I took a deep breath and decided to hold my hands up in surrender. Ray looked taken aback, frozen mid-punch. It looked like a paused action movie.

"Your clothes are cool."

Seriously? I wasn't sure why I said that. Maybe I needed to break the tension, maybe I needed a distraction.

Ray shifted at this, like a car sputtering out of gas. He dropped his arms at his sides and stared blankly at me, and panic flooded through me. Did I do something wrong? He stared at me, his confusion obvious, before he just...walked away.

He went back to pacing across the room from behind the table, as though I had never come.

Taking advantage of the moment, I silently slipped out of the room. Constance stayed outside waiting for me, and she smiled. "That is the most progress we have gotten with him. It appears that positive feedback helps. We should return to Minerva, and hope your health does not worsen."

We started walking back, my arms crossed. With the adrenaline gone, the pain felt even worse. I cradled my right arm, which had gotten the worst hits, with my left. Constance and I walked in comfortable silence until we reached Minerva in the kitchen, who was shoving a snack in her mouth. She stared like a deer in headlights before hurrying to drop her arms, like we caught a thief.

She finished eating before she spoke.

"So, I take it you weren't successful?"

"Well, *that's* a great question to start with," I grumbled.

"No, she may not have been, but we made incredible progress! We must not forget about that," Constance answered excitedly.

"He only fought me for a couple of minutes before a compliment had shaken him off. Maybe he just needs some encouraging words?" I suspected otherwise, but I needed what bits of optimism I could get.

Minerva spat out a laugh. "You *complimented* him? In the middle of a fight?"

"Don't judge me," I mumbled. "It worked. Briefly."

"If that's all he needed, *anyone* could have calmed him by now. No, clearly there is more to do than that. But hey, you didn't come back beaten to a pulp, so that's something."

"I'll take it."

"We have made such a breakthrough!" Constance exclaimed.

"I'm pretty sure you're overselling me at this point, but okay."

"Oh, shush, this is great!"

Constance went over everything she'd been able to see, and I piped in occasionally with details she missed. In the end, she made me sound way more heroic than I felt, but it felt nice to think someone had faith in me. Minerva raised her eyebrows, which I hope meant that she was somewhere along the lines of *pleasantly surprised*.

"Damn, Quink, I didn't think you had it in you. But next time, you need to actually, you know, *fight back*. Sometimes, the best way to defend yourself from a fight is by fighting. Ray won't go easy on you just because you go easy on him, and I hope that you understand now after that fight. So, will you actually fight him next time? Or will you panic like you always do?"

"I..." I thought to myself. I wasn't sure I could do it. "I'll do my best. To fight back, I mean." I took out Minerva Jr. and handed it back to her. "I definitely can't use this, though. I just can't."

Minerva sighed. "Well then, let's hope your best is good enough. Or else you could be finishing this 'project' as a ghost with the rest of us."

With that, Minerva walked away, leaving the air filled with dread.

Chapter Twelve
Teenagers Are Confusing

Why couldn't teenagers just stay consistent?

I knew I was still *technically* a teenager, only being nineteen, but we still sucked at being consistent about anything. I had been checking the conference room for days, seeing if Ray's there, but he must have decided that the intrusions were a nuisance, because he hadn't been there since. The chances of finding him in this huge mansion were slim to none. I wouldn't even know where to start.

My pillow—the same one I had thrown at Minerva—had taken the brute of it. I punched it, both as practice and as a way to get my frustration out. It started to have a permanent indent.

I felt weak and out of control. Not that I had much control to begin with, but not having *anything* that I felt like I understood still stressed me out. I tried my best to not lash out at Constance and Minerva, but Minerva's constant criticism of my abilities didn't exactly help. Sure, maybe I wasn't very confident in my abilities, but even that voice in my head wasn't as harsh as Minerva. I realized it's dumb to let her get to me, so I tried my best to let it go.

I had continued my training with Minerva, but after that last fight with Ray, my arms had become bruised in brilliant shades of purples and blues. It's like a toddler with a box of crayons came in and thought 'hey, that looks like a fun thing to color on.' It made me cringe to look at, and it didn't *feel* great either, but they weren't as bad as when they first showed up. My tolerance had built up, which became handy when a certain someone's ready to throw a punch at any given moment.

Thankfully, today I didn't have training with Minerva. She deemed it time for a break, as though it were unnecessary until that moment. Maybe she thought differently, but I would have thought that resting your arms after a fight like that would have been better. But hey, I never claimed to be the medical expert here. None of us were, but Constance was the closest to one. She approved of training, so that was good enough for Minerva.

Sometimes, if I distracted myself from it, I could ignore the throbbing. But most of the time it hurt *badly*. It felt more tolerable that morning, and since I had woken up early, I decided to finally surprise Constance and Minerva with breakfast. Obviously it wouldn't be as good as anything Constance could make, but I wanted to give her a break. She's been making food for all of us since they first showed themselves—she deserved to have a meal made for her once in a while.

I slipped on an oversized shirt, which wasn't fun to put on, and some shorts before walking over to the kitchen. My hair knotted into a tangled mess, but they had seen me in worse, so I stopped caring. I didn't have a plan of what I would make, but I could find something.

I looked over the pantry and fridge, which had been restocked recently with Elias' latest stop, to check what we had. I found a pancake mix, and we had the other ingredients, so I settled on that. I hadn't had them in a while, anyway. I hoped that neither of them were gluten free—or that gluten couldn't even affect them in the afterlife—and started stirring the batter.

My hands were covered in mix as I poured it into the pan. By some miracle, they turned out the right size before I saw a figure in the corner of my eye. I jumped as Constance came up behind me.

"My apologies, I did not mean to startle you."

I laughed awkwardly. "It's okay." I looked towards the pan, being wary of any sign of the food burning or a potential fire. "I *was* trying to surprise you, but I guess that won't work now."

"The thought is what counts." She sat down. "If it makes you feel better, I will turn away until you are ready to serve us, chef."

"Thanks," I said as I started to flip the pancakes. I had forgotten how much I loved to cook, what with how often someone else was making food. Though I wasn't the best at it, it still made me feel good to eat whatever I made.

Minerva came in as I started pouring the next batch with bags under her eyes. How ghosts even developed eyebags, I couldn't figure out. Her voice rumbled, rough and low, as she spoke. "Horrible morning, everyone."

Constance startled as she looked Minerva up and down. "Dear, what happened? Are you alright?"

Minerva shrugged. "Didn't sleep. Nightmares."

Constance walked over and rested a hand on her arm. "I know some remedies that helped me with my nightmares that we can try, if you wish."

I saw Minerva's cheeks flush a bit. It surprised me just how much Constance could sway her emotions like that. She covered Constance's hand with her own and squeezed it.

I longed for whatever they had going on, but I refused to be jealous of two dead women, so I settled on giving Minerva a thumbs up. The only thing I got in return was a glare, albeit a weaker one. Maybe it's the fact that she's tired, or maybe it's the loving touch that she's receiving, but the stare wasn't as withering as it used to be. I wished I had someone to care about me in the same way that they cared for each other.

The peace was nice but broke after Minerva pointed out how long they had been holding hands. Constance withdrew hers, cheeks turning pink. For how much Minerva had seemed to enjoy the touch, I was surprised that she cut it off so early.

All the happiness of the moment disappeared, even more so when I smelled smoke. I yelped and hurried to flip over the pancakes before it charred, leaving them a dark brown on one side and a golden on the other. I frowned and tried hiding it as best as I could by drowning them in syrup, but I didn't trust my own judgment. I prayed that they wouldn't make anyone gag too badly as I served the stacks to the others.

When I handed Minerva her plate, her face contorted with disgust. If the expression wasn't absolutely hilarious, I would have been terrified. Thankfully, she ate the pancakes anyway, albeit begrudgingly. I thought I caught her saying something about her dead grandma making better pancakes.

Constance, thankfully, had a bit more decency and at least pretending to like the pancakes.

I sat myself down and took a bite before spitting it right back out. "Oh God, those are horrible. Please don't eat them, I wouldn't wish those...pancakes, or whatever you could classify them as, on my worst enemy."

That got a chuckle from Minerva, which immediately boosted my mood.

"They aren't...*completely* horrible." She somehow managed to finish the pancakes, a true show of how impressive she was, while Constance politely pushed the plate forward.

I sighed. "I'm really sorry. I just wanted to surprise you guys."

"It's alright, Quillon."

"Are you ever going to use my real name?"

"Only when you prove yourself worthy of it."

How one could be 'worthy' of their name was beyond me, but I didn't even try to decipher it, so I just nodded and pretended to understand. "So, when should I check the conference room again?"

Minerva set down her silverware. "Actually, Constance and I had been discussing some things. Realistically, the odds of him coming back to the conference room are pretty low. We think it would be smarter to try and come back to him later. Trying to wait for him isn't worth wasting our time on. Maybe you could start looking for that other ghost—"

"What?"

"Did you not understand me? I said—"

I shook my head. "No, I understood what you said. I just don't get why you could *possibly* think I'd do that."

Minerva raised an eyebrow. "What?"

"I *mean* that Ray isn't just some…I don't know, *math problem* that can be skipped over. You think trying to help him is *wasting* our *time*? *He* is wasting our time? Well too bad, because I'm stuck here whether you like it or not, and *I* say that I'm not giving up on him!"

Minerva spoke cautiously. "I think you're misunderstanding what I mean. Besides, that isn't the smartest—"

"You can't change my mind. I can help him *right now*. You know what, I'll even show you that he's there."

I slammed my hands down on the table and pushed myself up before making my way towards the conference room. I could hear Minerva and Constance following behind me, telling me to come back, but I was on a *mission*. I was *determined*. I kept going anyway, even though I knew he wouldn't be there.

Which made it even more surprising when I got there and he *was*.

I skidded to a halt, not wanting to scare him off. Minerva was prepared to yell at me until she noticed who stood in the conference room. We stood frozen, unsure of what to do.

Minerva pushed me into the room, whispering *go*. I hadn't actually thought that he would be here, so I had no clue what my strategy would be going into this.

Ray turned to face me, looking me up and down with a critical stare. He must have decided that I was worth his time, because he walked up to me.

"I still remember you, you know. You keep coming back, on and on, like you can't get the idea inside your head." He tapped his temple with his finger. "When will you learn that *I don't want you here*, and I never will. All you are is a reminder that I lost *everything* because of you. Would you just leave me alone?!"

His volume kept rising until he started screaming. He cornered me, and despite the fact that I was taller than him by a good three inches, I couldn't find a way around him.

"I'm not who you think I am," I tried saying in a calm voice.

"That's what they all say! *I* don't even know who I think you are! What part of you thinks that I *like* the mystery of not knowing who killed me!"

He doesn't even know who killed him? I thought to myself. *That's awful.*

He seemed to suddenly realize how close he stood to me, because he took a step back and inhaled, trying to maintain whatever cool he had.

"Oh, so *now* you can calm down."

I spoke the thought aloud, but it wasn't doing me any favors. Ray whipped his head around, causing me to jump back a bit.

"What did you just say?"

Well, if I want to try and help him, maybe he needs to get some real anger out on me. It's like what Minerva did with me to get me fighting. "Yeah, you heard me. You're so stuck in this loop of fruitless anger that you aren't even paying attention to how dumb it is. At least you have a bit of common sense to not blow up *every* time. That would just be useless."

He took another step closer to me. The lights started to flicker again. "You don't get to *tell me* what is *dumb* or *useless*. You have *no idea* what I've gone through."

"Sure I don't. But what does it really matter? If this is one of those 'what doesn't kill you makes you stronger' type things, it doesn't seem to do much. Besides, would that even be true at this point?" I gestured towards him. Did he even know what the phrase meant?

I felt bad for how I spoke to him, but I needed to try *something*.

"I may not be the strongest, but I'm stronger than you'll ever be." He threw a punch, and this time I managed to block it. He kept pushing towards me, but he restrained from hitting me as many times. Definitely harder though. Was the anger helping?

I needed to get him angrier. I started to fight back. I shoved him, kicked him, slapped him. He hit harder than me, but I landed hits on him now, too.

We fought harder than before. He nicked my jaw, I got the side of his head. The rush of the fight was getting to my head, making it hurt. Or maybe it was a punch that I hadn't felt hit.

My lungs were burning, but I had to ignore it. I wanted to stop right then and there, but I kept going. Maybe there's a small part of me that liked the pain, the thrill of the kill.

What am I doing? The thought crashed down on me. *This isn't helping.*

I grabbed his arms and stood. The pain started to settle in.

"Okay, okay, no more fighting. At least right now."

He seemed to accept the truce, because he pulled his hands out of my grasp but didn't continue the fight.

I kept trying to talk to him, but he always either cut me off or ignored me. If I was this hard to handle at his age, I felt bad for Mom. He just kept getting angrier and angrier, and eventually I realized that it was my time to go if I wanted to leave without more bruises. I whispered a goodbye and slunk out of the room to be greeted by a confused Constance and Minerva.

"At least you are not...badly hurt?" Constance said, trying to find a bright side.

The tips of my shoes were the most interesting thing in the hallway. I couldn't stand to look them in the eyes after that miserable attempt. "Let's just go. I'll try again tomorrow."

Chapter Thirteen

Ouch!

It had been almost three weeks since I started, and Ray still refused to listen to me. I knew it would happen, but that didn't mean I felt happy about it.

I began to lose hope on him, but I told myself that I would keep a positive attitude. I knew that if I went in a downward spiral, I might have never stopped. I would repeat affirmations to myself in the mirror, and they weren't helpful most of the time. But I knew the longer I said them, the more I'd start to believe them, so that was something.

Every day the question stayed the same: *would he be there today?* The moment that he decided to leave the conference room for good, we were screwed. This mansion's huge, and there's no way I'd be able to find him again unless by some miracle I found a map of this place. I really doubted that, though.

Yesterday, I left the conference room with the start of a bruised cheek because I couldn't keep my arms up. Even after I had finally found it in me to fight back, a majority of the time he's too quick to do so. He definitely learned how to fight from someone, but I wasn't sure what type of fighting they did in the thirties.

It's a good thing that I had my own lessons. It didn't help that they weren't as consistent as they used to be, though. At that point, they're only after I got my ass handed to me on a silver platter.

I got up earlier than usual that morning, which surprised me. I looked out the window and saw the sun peeking up, barely risen. I hadn't gotten the chance to watch the sunrise in a long time; I forgot just how beautiful it was.

With extra time, I decided to try contacting Mom again.

I hadn't had much time to talk about the mansion, but I couldn't bring myself to tell her what's really happening. I had settled on telling her about how creepy the mansion was but avoiding Minerva and Constance. Even if I did somehow explain it in a way she could understand—I could barely understand it myself—would she believe me? I knew she believed in the paranormal, or was at least open to it, but this whole thing's insane. Some days I didn't even believe it myself even as I lived through it.

I typed out the message a few times, trying to figure out what to say. We hadn't talked in a few days, and there hadn't been much more than the constant fighting with Ray. Eventually I found what to say.

Morning. How's home base holding up?

I'll explain it to her later, I told myself.

I put on some lightweight clothes and my tennis shoes, which somehow weren't completely demolished. My toe came close to peeking out, and the sole of one shoe started to break apart. I might as well have been running thirty miles every day, but what I actually did was much worse.

I got hit by a wave of cramps as I walked around my room and quickly took some ibuprofen. As much as cramps sucked, they weren't as bad as the pain I had been dealing with for the past three weeks.

When I made it to the kitchen, I was surprised to find that Constance was already there.

"It's really early, what are you doing up?" I asked in a tired voice.

"I was hoping to try remaking those pancakes that you made. I was unable to find the recipe, however, so I decided to recreate it as best as I could, adding a few of my own touches."

I didn't have the heart to tell her the 'recipe' was just a premade mix, so I just smiled and thanked her. I knew hers would be better, anyway.

I sat down at the table and rested my arms on the surface. Something seemed off. I put them down again, and looked under the table.

Huh, I thought to myself. *It's uneven.*

I fiddled around with it for a bit, releasing and pushing down again, unable to take it off my mind. *That's* going to be annoying when we try to have conversations.

Minerva sat down next to me as Constance finished making breakfast. She smiled when she noticed Minerva and set down their plates before mine. Constance found her spot on the other side of Minerva and started to eat herself.

As usual, the food's amazing. It always was when Constance made it. I finished it quickly, as did Minerva. I took the empty plates and tossed them.

"Ready to check in on Ray?" Minerva asked.

I grabbed a towel and started to dry them off. "Almost. I just want to stretch before I go in case there's another big fight."

Minerva nodded and stood up. I looked at her quizzically as she began stretching herself.

"Why are *you* stretching? You're not the one about to fight someone."

Minerva looked up as she began to touch her toes. "To show you how it's done, Quizzard."

I laughed. "I'm pretty sure I know how to stretch for myself, thanks."

We continued to stretch together anyway, despite the fact that I was certain that Minerva had no reason to. Having someone to do it with me made it easier, though. I mimicked what she did for most of it, though she seemed confused by some of the things I did.

"No, you should be doing *this* instead."

"Where do they teach you these?"

"Please tell me you're making that up."

"How does that make *any* sense?"

After a very harsh critiquing of the school's physical education system, we were finally ready to go to the conference room again. Well, *I* was ready to go to the conference room again. Minerva was ready to stand outside and make sure I didn't die.

I felt like a soldier marching into a battle as I reached the conference room. Thankfully, Ray was still there, pacing like he always did. He talked to himself in a hushed voice, but I could never figure out what he said.

I went over the plan in my head.

Keep my cool.

Make him feel safe.

Calm him down.

Try not to die in the process.

That last one was very important.

I stepped into the room, and Ray immediately whipped around. As much as he's stuck in his head, he's still very observant.

"Oh, welcome back! Well, you actually aren't very welcome. You know, you're getting *really* annoying, and in case you haven't noticed, I don't have very much patience. So if you're done trying to reason with me even though *you* were the one that screwed up, I'd like you to leave."

He inched closer to me, and I tried to skirt away from him.

Keep my cool.

"I understand that you're annoyed with me, but I'm not here to hurt you. I'm just here to help."

Make him feel safe.

Laughter broke out, an insane laugh that reminded me a bit too much of Minerva's. "'Not here to hurt you'? *'Just here to help'*? Really? That's the dumbest excuse you've made yet. In case you don't remember, you were the one who put the *bullet through my stomach*. It must not have mattered much to you, though."

That's what the stain is, I noted. *It's where he was shot.*

He walked around the table, shoving a chair out of the way for no apparent reason. I walked backwards, hoping to stay out of his reach.

"Come on, come at me. You know you want to. Or are you too scared of a teenie weenie teenager?"

You aren't that teenie weenie.

He suddenly sprinted at me, and I didn't have time to get out of the way. I slammed into a chair, stumbling to find my footing. I clung onto the chair and slid it in front of me, using it as a blocker between Ray and I as he tried hitting me.

He grabbed onto the chair and threw it to the side, which gave me enough time to get myself back up. I blocked and dodged his attacks, trying to stay light on my feet. As hard as Minerva had drilled the bouncing into me, it's harder to remember that in the middle of a fight. If I get one bad hit, it's over. I wouldn't be back for another few days at least, and he could be gone by then.

I got a couple of punches in myself, but I couldn't hit him hard. Even when I fought for my life, I still wouldn't throw a serious punch. When I did hit, he retaliated swiftly and hard.

During the fight, I still tried to talk to him calmly. I wasn't sure how effective that was, though, considering he continued to fight and I continued to defend myself. Time slowed down, and I lost track of time quickly. I pushed another chair towards him, but it only hindered him for a few moments before he moved it out of the way again.

Any moment now, I thought to myself. *If you two can come in here and do something, that'd be great.*

Despite my mental beckonings, Constance and Minerva continued to wait outside. It was one of those times where I wished I had telepathy, because my throat was too dry to say anything. The lights wouldn't stop flickering—this was the worst it had been.

Every attack felt more powerful than the last.

Pow! Hit to the bruise on my cheek.

Bam! Kick to the hip.

Woosh! Hair tugged.

Soon enough, he had me cornered.

He grabbed my shirt and tried to lift me up, but that didn't exactly work. For once, being tall had an advantage.

Sadly, he realized the flaw in his plan and switched gears. He whirled me around with surprising strength, slamming me to the ground. I landed directly on my tailbone and pain shot all the way up my back. I tried to get back up, but the pain that came from that was overwhelming.

I was losing and losing hard.

For being a teenager, he had a surprisingly strong grip. He grabbed me again, and I couldn't break free. He dragged me up to my feet, giving me just enough of an advantage to break free from his grasp. I almost made it to the door when he knocked my feet out from under me, sending me back down.

He didn't seem to remember what happened a few moments before, because he tried bringing me back to my feet again. I couldn't get out of his reach that time.

He froze when he had me, and for a moment I thought I could get something out of him.

That moment didn't last long though, because he promptly threw me into the nearest wall. The air got knocked out of my lungs. I gasped for air.

My head throbbed, and I felt something warm and wet at the back of my head. I reached back with a trembling hand, and when I put it in front of me, it was stained red.

"That's not good," I mumbled, not really processing what that meant.

My vision blurred. I saw the silhouette of someone next to me, but I couldn't tell who. A dark hand squeezed my own, turning it red as well. When I looked up, I saw the red of Constance's dress. She spoke to Ray in a hushed tone.

I wasn't sure what happened. Someone said something, and then before I knew it, everyone else surrounded me, too.

The world spun. Everyone spoke at once. I didn't know what was being said.

Minerva yelled at Constance, who ran out of the room. Ray stared down at me in panic, though I couldn't figure out why. Was he calmed?

Did we do it?

I said something, but I couldn't process what.

My brain's too fuzzy for this.

I closed my eyes, and I faded out of consciousness.

Chapter Fourteen
Ray's Perspective

Why couldn't I just be left alone?

Shadow Man had been plaguing me for a long time now. I couldn't remember exactly when he first came, but I remembered the anger. The tingling in my fingers. The boiling in my blood. The bite of my words.

It didn't take me long to figure out he was the one who killed me.

As of lately, he decided to become a prominent part of my afterlife, or whatever I was in. He came almost every day, and no matter what I did, he wouldn't leave me alone.

Ignoring him didn't work.

Telling him didn't work.

Even fighting him didn't work.

He kept bumping his gums, saying things that couldn't be true with his weird distorted voice. *I'm not trying to hurt you. I'm here to help you.* Couldn't be further from the truth.

I tried not to think about what I'd miss from my life too often. The fact that I'd never get a girlfriend, get married, or start a family. The fact that I'd never get to work a job, or say goodbye to Rowan or Riley. Not even Ma. Whenever I did, it never ended well, so I just elected on not thinking about it at all.

I didn't remember much about what I actually *did* get to do during my life. There was never enough food for everyone, so Ma and Pa would usually go hungry so that we could eat.

The one time I try to help my family, I end up with a bullet in my stomach.

I laughed bitterly at the thought. That shopkeeper must have had the gat ready in case a kid like me came along. Selfish jerk.

I had stolen before, but it was always small stuff—a broach in a woman's pocket, a lighter in the hands of a drunk. Even my good luck charm: an old coin, the first thing I had ever stolen. I had given it to Rowan the night before I died. Maybe I should have kept it.

I recognized the voice of the Shadow Man as the same one that shouted as the bullet pierced me. I never knew him by name, though. It didn't matter either way, because I would still be the same level of dead.

Angry tears started to build in the back of my throat. I coughed, trying to get the tears to go back to whatever pit they came from. I didn't have time to let emotions overwhelm me; I had more important things to do.

My list was short: find out who killed me, and get revenge. If my family had to go hungry because of him—

I interrupted myself. *Without an extra mouth to feed, maybe Ma and Pa got to eat. I gave them a better chance to make it through.*

I just wished that chance included me.

When the man died—he better have—did he get stuck in the endless purgatory like me, or did he descend? I wished that I could have seen his face the moment he realized his fate. Alas, that fantasy would never come true.

I wondered if Shadow Man had known who me or my family were before that horrible day.

Maybe he would have let me go if he had.

I may not have known who he was, but when he began showing up more frequently, I decided to do what I could. Every day he came, we got into a fight; every day I would win. He's either extremely brave or extremely stupid to keep coming back after every losing fight. I assumed the latter.

That last time, however, was different. I couldn't tell you why, but I knew that something would change. He came in with his usual calm demeanor, like he was talking to a toddler. Every sugar coated word that came out of his mouth sent a flash of anger through me. I had gone through one hell only to be sent to this one; I deserved more credit than I had been given.

I was ready to finish him off. If he wanted to keep torturing me, he'd have to find me in whatever came after this.

The fight didn't last long. He scrambled around the table, stumbling constantly. I picked him up only to throw him back down again. I felt *powerful*.

I kept going, powered by the adrenaline and euphoria, and then—

I did it.

All it took was slamming him into a wall, and then I finally did it. It may have made a mess, but I couldn't resist the grin.

The crash was loud, but I didn't care.

I didn't even bother to cover my ears.

This was *my* victory. I *won*.

The body of Shadow Man crumpled, and two women I had never seen before came bursting in. One appeared in a long maroon gown, the other in a man's suit. The suited one shuffled over to Shadow Man's side, and the one in crimson came up to me. They both looked fancier than anyone I'd ever met.

"Are you alright?"

I stared blankly at her. I just threw a man to the wall, and she's worried if *I* was alright? That felt bizarre to say the least.

"I—" I thought about that. Seeing the man—or the vague, crumpled shape of him—wasn't as satisfying anymore. I thought that if he's gone, I'd finally feel better, but I just felt empty. My chest felt empty. "I guess not."

"Why is that?"

"I thought—" my voice started to crack— "I thought if he was gone, this would all be over. But I'm still here…Also, who are you?"

Instead of answering the question, she silently wrapped her arms around me. My body tensed up at the touch. When was the last time I had been hugged? I couldn't remember.

All the feelings of home I had yearned for all this time came flooding back. I saw Riley and Rowan, laughing like they were just told the best joke. Even while we struggled, they were always laughing. Ma and Pa were hugging each other and smiling, and everyone was *happy*.

I melted into the hug, hoping that if I just squeezed my arms tight enough, I could keep the memories forever.

I stayed like that for a long time. I felt all the anger seep out of me, until I became nothing more than a sack of bones. The anger poured into the cracks of the floor and sunk into the room, a reminder of what I had been while confined in here. The anger left my body, and all that remained was exhaustion and ache.

The woman let go. "Are you feeling any better?"

I nodded.

"If you two are done being all affectionate, I'd like some help with the person who's about to die in my arms, thanks!" the one in the suit yelled. I looked over, wondering why they were helping Shadow Man.

Except Shadow Man wasn't lying there anymore.

There's another woman in his place, with curly brown hair and casual clothes. Blood trickled down her shirt and chin, staining them a dark red.

That wasn't him.

I froze in shock: had *I* done that?

The woman who had hugged me grabbed my arm with a firm grip and brought us over to her. The dark one started to panic, shaking the body of the nearly unconscious woman. "Quincey! Quincey, oh God, wake up, wake up!"

My hands trembled as I looked at her. *I couldn't have killed her, could I?*

I sat beside her, trying to figure out what to say. "I- uh- I- I—"

Quincey looked up at me, her eyes a startling gray. "I'll be fine, don't worry."

She then proceeded to pass out.

I could have laughed at how ironic that was if I wasn't so scared for her life. The dark woman slung Quincey's motionless body over her shoulders and motioned to the other. "Constance, get on her other side. I can't carry her all on my own."

I didn't know how Constance would help as she's significantly shorter, but she somehow managed. I wanted to help, but I didn't know how, so I just stayed behind them awkwardly.

"Ray, can you open the door?"

I sped ahead of them and held the door open as they walked through, Quincey's blood leaving a small trail. I tried not to gag at the sight and followed behind them, praying that she would make it. She had to make it.

"Do we have anything we can use as a wrap before we get back?"

I looked around, and quickly tore off a bit of my worn sleeve. The fabric was thin, but it's the best I could do.

I handed it over to Constance, who wrapped it around Quincey's head. While she did that, I went ahead of them and held up Quincey's legs. I never realized how hard it would be to carry someone, even with the help of two other people.

We hurried our pace, though it was hard to run backwards. I could see Quincey shaking, her breathing labored. If we could get her some help quick enough, she might be okay.

When we got to the kitchen, I let go of Quincey's legs and swept everything off the table. I didn't even know there was more outside of the conference room, let alone three other people here with me. The two women lifted Quincey's body onto the table, limbs hanging off the sides. Her skin had started to go sickly pale. There had to be more blood loss than the injury on the head.

This wasn't good.

I began throwing open cabinets, not knowing where anything was, in search of a first aid kit. I paused in shock to see how much food there was.

"Minerva, could you find the bandages while I treat this with tap water? This must not get infected, or else it could become worse."

The woman—Minerva—nodded and joined me in looking through the cabinets and drawers. My hands shook and fumbled with the handles as I searched, mumbling to myself.

I wanted to hurt him, *not her. She didn't deserve this. If only I'd known, I wouldn't have—*

"Found it!" Minerva exclaimed, holding up a small kit. She ran over to Constance, and they switched out my sleeve for a wrap bandage. When the wound had been properly cleaned and dressed, Minerva bridal carried her to her room.

I tried reaching out for a blanket to put over her, but Minerva blocked me with intense eyes.

"You've done enough damage, kid."

Those words sent a sharp pain through my chest. I looked over to Quincey, who's breathing slowly returned to normal.

Please be okay.

I crossed my arms in front of my chest and followed Minerva out to the living room, where Constance waited.

"How did she look?"

"As good as someone who got slammed into a wall could look." Minerva side-eyed me. I shriveled under her glare.

Constance sighed. "We have nothing to do but wait. I will prepare something for us to eat, and all we can do is hope that she will make it through the night."

Chapter Fifteen

Elias Sucks at Apologizing

The moments before the crash played in my head over and over again, each time adding new details. I couldn't be sure what was real and what wasn't.

The red stains on my body and clothes.

The rattling in my head.

The ache in my bones telling me to give up on everything and let the darkness overcome me.

When I finally woke up, I still felt that same pain. It felt a bit better, but I put it on the backburner. I had to find the others.

I sat up, resting against the back of the bed. I looked across my room; when did I get there? I knew I hadn't gotten back myself.

Even sitting up caused a rush to my head. I cursed under my breath as I turned to the side. I slid off, holding onto the bed, and my knees buckled beneath me. I let out a yelp as I fell to the ground, waves of pain rushing over me.

Someone threw the door open: Minerva. She looked at me in alarm. "You're awake?"

I stared up at her. "I sure hope so."

"Don't be cheeky with me, you gave us a heart attack." She grabbed my arm and brought me back to the bed, surprisingly gentle. "You shouldn't be out of bed any time soon if you don't need to be. Rest is just as important as the training it took to get here."

I groaned as I eased back into bed.

"Exactly."

Once I was in a comfortable position, I turned to Minerva. "So how long was I out?"

"Only a few hours. I was honestly surprised to hear you wake up. It's dinner time."

My stomach grumbled.

Minerva snorted. "Hungry there?"

"A bit," I answered reluctantly.

"I'll bring you something to eat. The food should help you regain some strength. You nearly died on us, and we need you here."

Minerva shifted uncomfortably, not looking at me. She didn't necessarily seem guilty. Maybe she was confused.

"Can I get the food?"

"Oh, right, yes." She shuffled out of my room, and I saw a shock of blond hair from behind her as she left. I heard her scolding Ray, but I didn't know what she said. I couldn't see his reaction, because she closed the door behind her.

Ray must be calm. We did it.

I smiled at the small victory. If I already had two ghosts calmed, who knew if it would take much longer to calm the rest, especially since now I have all that training under my belt. I could be out of here in another month.

The thought brought a surprisingly melancholy feeling with it. I mean, wouldn't it be better if I was out of danger and safe again? I could see Mom again. Rachel and Kayden, too.

But then I'd never see any of the ghosts again.

With all that had happened, I didn't expect to be so sad at the idea. Going into this, I hadn't thought that staying here would be anything I'd want to do. Nonetheless, maybe even despite myself, I somehow managed to get close to them. Even Minerva, who wasn't that likable.

As though summoned, Minerva opened the door to bring in dinner. "Hope you like chicken, because that's what we have."

She set it on my lap. "Need any help?"

"I think I'm strong enough to cut my own chicken, thanks." I meant it as a joke, but Minerva still looked down.

"I'll be okay, you know."

"I- I know that. You aren't dead yet, so clearly there's something here left for you yet." Minerva stammered. I knew she cared about me deep down, and that brought a satisfying smile to my face. She brushed off her clothes and walked out without anything else to say.

I ate happily, ignoring the weakness in my arms. The brunt of the hit may have been my head, but all the fighting had worn down my arms. It would take a while to get them back to their old strength.

The chicken tasted like heaven in my mouth. In only a matter of seconds, the plate was empty.

I set the plate on the table beside me. I didn't want to bother them any more than they needed to be, so I decided to wait until the next morning for them to grab it. A dirty dish wasn't the end of the world, anyway.

I pulled the blanket over my head, enveloping myself in darkness and warmth. I didn't need to look at the bruises all over my arms, or the bits of blood still underneath my fingernails. I could just rest.

I didn't know how long I hid under the covers, but the light had been turned off at some point. It must have been night.

I took a slow breath and eventually, sleep found me.

It had been five days since I got to walk across the house. The most I had done was go to the restroom to clean up, but I couldn't even do that without a struggle. Constance had found something I could use as a makeshift walking stick, but it felt awkward to bend down so that it'd work.

Minerva had gone from slightly uncomfortable guardian to overprotective mom. She hadn't let me see Ray yet, though I've been dying to meet him since he calmed down, and only lets Constance in occasionally. Having someone who tried to kill me only a month before watching over me wasn't very comforting.

"You have to stay in bed until your head's all better, you got that?" She would constantly remind me.

"I know," I'd assure her.

It got tiring; I was ready to get out of bed for longer than a few minutes. I needed to remind myself I was on Earth, not some weird dream land.

That morning, we were eating French toast yet again. It became an easy meal, as well as a boring one. But the memories that came along with them outweighed the repetition. Mom made them whenever there was a celebration, and the nostalgia flowed through every bite.

Minerva set down the plate and sat by my feet. "How's your head holding up? Are you feeling okay?"

I nodded. "Other than the gash on my head, I'd say I'm doing good."

"No need to remind me. It's still nasty to look at."

I sadly agreed. I did my best to ignore it, but the scabbed skin near the hairline stayed persistently present. It took everything in my power not to break it open; scabs always bugged me.

I sat up, putting the plate on my lap. "Got anything else to say? Any sarcastic remarks or jokes at my expense?"

"Don't get funny with me. I'm the one bringing you food."

"I could get Constance to do it, too. Who would say no to the dying girl?"

"The people who are already dead."

It was hard to remember that they were actually *dead*. I knew they were ghosts, but the fact that they died just felt...surreal to me.

Minerva looked me in the eyes, causing me to squirm. "Seriously though, is there anything you need?"

"I don't think so. I've been feeling pretty comfortable here in my fuzzy palace. Maybe a bit coddled."

"You said it yourself. You're the dying girl, and we need to keep you further from that line."

Constance called out for Minerva, and she stood up. She looked down at the plate and tapped the side. "Make sure you eat. It'll boost your energy, and maybe we can get you out of this bed by next week."

That was enough of a seller. I started to eat as she left for the kitchen.

I didn't even get to finish before there was another knock at my door, much softer. Exactly four knocks. No one in this house knocked other than Constance, so I decided to just welcome the visitor in. If Minerva hadn't gone into a panic, they couldn't have been bad.

Elias opened the door and stepped inside.

It shouldn't have surprised me that he came here, but it did anyway. It slipped from my mind that he would have kept coming with the food, what with all the training. Constance must have been getting the food. Was this his first time here since Ray got calmed? Seeing three of the ghosts calmed already must have been a fun surprise.

I hadn't realized just how angry I would be to see him until now. The least he could have done was give any sort of warning that I would be fighting for my life every other week, but that wouldn't have helped his case, would it? I refrained from throwing the slew of choice words that I wished I could have said.

How many people before me had felt this way? Did he tell them, or did he hold back that piece of information, knowing that no one would come if he didn't? Maybe they didn't even get the chance to get angry before Minerva shot them. I shuddered when I thought about how many people could have stayed in this very room that never got to leave the mansion. Would they have become ghosts, too?

Elias walked in with a nervous gait, as though he felt guilty.

I hoped he did.

"Before I continue, I'd like to say that I'm sorry about all of this."

"I sure hope you are. Because of this damn mansion, I probably have a concussion, and I'm flirting with death with every new room I find!"

"You must know that I truly mean it—"

"How many people have you said that too? How many people did you not? Do you remember their names?"

He sighed. "Yes. Every single one. They fill my head when I try to sleep at night. I mourn for them every day with the constant reminder that I'm the reason they aren't here with us now."

"Then act like it! Stop luring people in and refusing to tell them that they're going to *die*. See if they still want to do it so badly."

His brows furrowed. "Well then, if you hate this job so much, then why do you still do it? Why not just quit?"

"In case you never realized before, I'm *stuck here*. I tried leaving when I found out I had to fight a *kid*—another detail you failed to mention—and found myself right back at the door. Did you ever figure that out, or were you not paying attention?"

Elias stood there for a moment, processing what I said. "What?"

"You seriously didn't notice? Why wouldn't anyone have bolted out the door the moment Minerva pulled the gun on them?"

Elias fumbled, trying to figure out what to say.

"Wow. Now I see why you suck at this so badly. You're such a coward."

"I- you're right. I am a coward. I won't deny that. But don't say I didn't try."

I stared at him in confusion. "What do you mean?"

His eyes drilled into my soul more and more with every word he spoke. "When I first found the mansion, I had tried to free them on my own. Did you seriously think that I wouldn't even bother to try it myself? I wasted a *year* of my life just trying to help them. No matter what I tried, nothing worked. I needed to find someone else to do it for me, despite how much I didn't want to bring other people into this. That was why I started looking five years ago."

I sat there in shock. *A year?* I couldn't imagine dodging Minerva for that long. It's a miracle this man wasn't dead yet. It could explain why Constance wasn't someone to worry about though; even if she didn't need to be calmed, he might have helped with the process.

All of my anger dissipated. "I...I never knew that."

"Of course not. I hadn't told you much more than the basics."

"If you couldn't do it," I wondered, "why let a *teenager* do it?"

"You're the first one to do so. Before you, everyone was at least thirty. They all failed, so I realized that maybe a new set of eyes would be helpful. You know, perspective." He gestured towards the door where the ghosts waited on the other side. "Just based on the progress so far, it seems I was right."

I could see where he was coming from, sort of. He could have picked someone a bit older, probably someone at least twenty five, but he had faith in me. I'd take faith.

"Do you understand my struggle now?"

"You really think I can help?"

Elias smiled and gestured outside the door. "Look what you've done thus far. It wouldn't be impossible."

"You speak like an old wizard."

He feigned panic before laughing. "Oh dear, you've found me out! Now I must lock away in my secret tower, never to be seen again until the next prophecy comes to me."

I would have laughed along, but doing so only hurt more. I clutched my side, as though that could help the pain.

He looked at me sympathetically. "Get well soon, Quincey. I have a feeling you'll need your strength now more than ever."

With that cryptic message and not even a goodbye, he left me to decipher what that could have meant.

Chapter Sixteen

Homeless Man Threatens Me

I stared at the spot Elias had been, my mind stuck on our conversation. I still felt a bit annoyed, but not nearly as angry as when he first came in. There was a sense of understanding between us now, however small.

Once again, Ray had been waiting outside the door. I saw him with Minerva hovering at his side before Elias had shut the door. He looked into the room, and his eyes lit up when they met mine. Minerva tugged on his shoulder, leading him back to the kitchen after he tried to walk towards me.

I wanted to talk to him. Now that he's calm, we shouldn't have to worry about him attacking me. It seemed like he wanted to see me, too. Minerva wouldn't let him, though. Maybe I should ask her to just let him in this once.

I shut my eyes, taking a deep breath. I had been sleeping a lot, which just made me even more tired when I was awake.

I almost fell asleep when I heard someone come in and felt a rush of cold air. I peeked my eyes open, planning to pretend to be sleeping if it was Minerva.

Instead, my eyes met a pair of blue ones.

I frantically sat up, trying to put as much distance between us. I tried calling for help, but no sound came out. My eyes widened when I noticed his finger to his lips, telling me to be quiet. The chains wrapped around his wrist clattered together as he moved, ringing out.

"Your words wouldn't be helpful, now would they?"

I moved my mouth around, trying to speak. No words came out.

"No one will be able to help you now."

My eyes flit around the room in a panic. I didn't think I had enough strength to run across the room, let alone fight. Could I get myself against the wall?

"Don't be alarmed. I came today with only a warning."

What? That shut off my thinking. What could his warning be? I cringed thinking about how curious I was about it.

"Let me ask you a question, Quincey. If you got the chance to leave all of this behind, would you take it?"

I paused. I'd thought of it before, but I didn't think that was even a possibility. I shrugged.

"I can give you that opportunity. All you have to do is listen to me, and you can leave all of this behind."

Where had all his anger gone? I thought to myself. *He went from being furious to peaceful just like that? Something isn't right.*

I gestured toward my mouth, reminding him I couldn't talk.

"Oh, right." He swirled his wrist, and I could talk again.

I didn't trust where this was going. "As tempting as that offer is, I'm sticking this through. I've made it this far, and I don't know if anyone else will do the job."

"No, the point is that *no one* else will do the job."

I raised an eyebrow.

"Have you ever wondered how the ghosts got here?"

Before I could answer, his head thrust forward. From behind him, Ray grinned triumphantly.

"Who did that?!" Blue Boy whipped around and locked eyes with Ray. All the victory disappeared from Ray's face as the bigger ghost towered over him. He started to back into the door, but the door was shut.

He was cornered.

Screw it. I shakily stood up, leaning heavily against the bed. My legs were about to collapse below me, but I still shoved my shoulder into his back. "Hey, homeless!"

He turned to look over his shoulder. "What?" he snarled.

"You wanna fight? I can fight. " I raised my fists, feigning more confidence than I had. I had to get him away from Ray—he may be strong, but this guy had some kind of magic, and I didn't know what he was capable of doing to the ghosts.

He stared at me and restrained his anger. "I'm staying to my word. No fighting; at least this time. All I want you to do is *leave*. I'm not out to hurt you."

Without anything left to say, he disappeared. Ray and I looked at each other in confusion before he grinned ear to ear.

"I don't know who *that* was, but that felt good."

Minerva, with the worst timing she's had yet, came in at that moment. The moment she saw me standing up and Ray beside me, she glared at Ray. "Did you hurt her? You knew that you weren't supposed to be in here yet."

"No, no, Ray didn't hurt me," I cut in, "we just had a weird encounter with a new ghost."

Minerva gaped at us. "You saw a new ghost? What was he like?"

"Uh...angry."

She sighed. "Was it the one with blue eyes that you mentioned earlier?"

"Yeah. Do you think he's a ghost, too?"

"It's the only thing that would make sense. He certainly isn't alive if he can just appear and vanish like that. Though why *we* can't do that, I don't know...but that's besides the point. Did you learn anything else about him? Something that could help us?"

"Well," I started, "he seems convinced that no one should help the ghosts. He dissociates himself from you guys, but is completely aware of your existence. Does that make sense?"

Minerva shook her head. "No, not at all."

"Can I just say something *please*?" Ray snapped. We turned to face him; neither of us had even noticed him trying to speak.

"Sorry. I had to get your attention somehow."

Minerva motioned for him to explain.

"He's been here for a while. I remembered that he would bug me about Shadow Man—" I looked at him in confusion— "who was actually just Quincey. When he showed up, he did what he could to make me angrier when you left. He never actually tried to help me, which makes a lot more sense now that I know he's not actually a good guy."

Could he have been the same one that made Minerva go into that breakdown?

There was an emotion behind Minerva's face as he talked about Blue Eyes that I couldn't decipher. Finally, she spoke again. "Well, what matters most is that you're safe. Now, get your ass back in bed before I make you, got it?" Instead of glaring at me, however, she threw a look at Ray.

"I already told you it wasn't Ray's fault. He actually tried protecting me."

Minerva crossed her arms, looking at Ray with clear skepticism. "Really?"

Ray rocked from side to side. "And then *she* actually ended up protecting *me*. I tried fighting him, but he's...big. She only got up to get him off my back."

She looked back at me with an exasperated expression. "Damn you and your good heart. That heart of yours is going to be what gets you killed if you aren't careful."

She looked down at my plate. "Your chicken's likely cold by now. Want me to grab you some more?"

I prodded at the chicken with the fork. "Eh, it's fine by me."

"Come on, Ray. We shouldn't bother her while she eats."

He exchanged glances between Minerva and I before setting something in my hand and scurrying out behind her. I opened my palm and found a small caramel, wrapped in a thin layer of plastic.

I smiled, feeling the wrapper beneath my fingers. I began to eat the rest of my chicken as I set it to the side, saving it for later. It felt weird to eat alone again after eating almost every meal with one of the ghosts. It's like I was in middle school again, before I became friends with Rachel or Kayden.

Oh God, I haven't called them this whole time. They didn't know where I was, or what I was doing, or even that ghosts were real. A sense of panic rushed through me, but I pushed it aside; they had their own lives, just like I had mine.

Theirs just happened to not be filled with psycho ghosts. Or near-death experiences. Or fighting. Or being taught how to use a gun by a girl from the 1950s.

Part of me wished I was with them still and that I'd never called Elias about the mansion. The more I thought about it, though, the more I realized how much I regretted that part of me. I had experiences I never thought I would—for better or for worse—and met some of the best people. If none of this had happened, I would have never met Constance, or even Minerva. I would have continued thinking I didn't have a purpose in life.

It didn't matter if my purpose was for the greater good of the world, because I was making changes right here. That gave me enough of a reason to be here.

Minerva came back in. "I know you're still recovering, but I think we should start talking about the fourth ghost. Have we talked about him at all?"

I shook my head.

"Good, because there's not much to go off of, anyway. He's some New Yorker, which begs the question of how he ended up here. I'm from Washington, and they're on opposite sides of the country. I don't know what kind of rules there are when it comes to ghosts, but it doesn't make sense. Where are we, anyway? You don't sound like you're from Washington."

What? "We're in Arizona."

"And Constance isn't even from America! What kind of weird geography is this?"

I was thinking the exact same thing.

"That's besides the point. With what little information we have, there isn't much training we can do to prepare you for him. We aren't sure where he is, what he's like, or even his name. It'll be up to you to figure that out."

"Does that mean I can get out of bed?" I asked hopefully.

"You get to do all of that in at least a week. You're not nearly strong enough to walk long distances yet; did you even notice how reliant you were on the bed when I had come in earlier?"

"I- I guess not."

"Maybe you can start walking around the room to build the strength back up, but you aren't leaving this room unless it's an absolute emergency. Got that?"

"Yeah," I lied. I couldn't stare at these same four walls for another *week*.

"We just have to hope you won't need to fight him. If you do, we're all doomed."

I wanted to argue, but I knew she was right. I wasn't sure if I could bring myself to get into an actual fight with anyone else, kid or adult. No matter how much physical training I went through, I still couldn't change my thought process on that.

Constance and Ray were at the door, waiting to be welcomed in. I waved for them to join us, and they either stood or sat on the bed. Constance traced her thumb over the back of Minerva's hand. "I may not have said it like *that*, but we would need to make some improvements. Possibly some more training with Minerva and mental training with me. Do you think that would help?"

"I doubt it."

Constance nodded sympathetically. "Yes, I understand. I could never imagine fighting anyone until I had my children. Although they must have passed a long time ago, I still liked to believe they had the fighting spirit of their father. His temper got him into trouble on more than a few occasions." She smiled as though thinking of a fond memory.

"Are we just going to ignore the fact that there is a ghost who has it out for Quincey that we have no idea who he is?" Ray cut in. "Like, if she dies, what happens to us?"

Everyone waited in silence.

"Do we go back to being angry, or is she just replaced again?"

"Yeah, I don't really want to die quite yet- no offense to you guys."

"None taken," Minerva said, "Ray's got a point. Not only do we have the actual fourth ghost, we also have the angry one. Can you describe what he looks like, other than his eyes? I think we've gotten the picture with that."

I did my best to describe him, and with every new detail, Minerva's eyes widened with recognition.

"So it *is* him! That's the same bastard who kept messing with my head before you came along. We have to find out how to take him down, because he clearly isn't like either of us. He can leave if he wants, yet he chooses to stay. What could that mean?"

Constance didn't give us time to think. "Well, I believe Quincey should be completely out of bed in two weeks. That sounds reasonable to me. Quincey?"

I pretended to agree as I already groaned at the thought. Another *two* weeks? I was going to combust.

But now we have some things established about the angry man. He isn't like the rest of the ghosts, and if he decides to make an encore appearance, I'd need to be ready.

Chapter Seventeen
Ouch! Part Two

Before I came to the mansion, I thought that staying in bed all day would be the pinnacle of life. I wouldn't need to go to school or do any work. Now that it was actually happening, though, it just turned out to be extremely boring.

I would sleep for long hours, which felt nice, but when I did wake up I couldn't do much. I barely had enough attention to try reading the books I had brought, and nothing on my phone could keep my focus for long.

It just turned into a whole lot of nothing.

While Constance maintained the balance in the house most of the time, Ray and Minerva made sure to visit me frequently. Minerva changed my bandages and brought me food, but Ray started to open up to me. Now that he calmed down and didn't have the anger of a thousand suns, he's just a regular teenager again, goofing off and cracking himself up. Having that kind of energy was refreshing, even if it could get draining.

I made sure to constantly ask Minerva about my progress, but she would just shake her head, as though I would never get out of bed. It didn't do much to boost my morale about the whole situation, but that wasn't her job, so she refused to do that. I could respect that in most cases, but when you could have died, that wasn't exactly what you wanted to hear.

Every now and then I would get the urge to run around the hallways like a madman just to stretch my legs. I slowly needed the makeshift cane less and less, but if I tried walking much farther than the bathroom, I still needed something to rest on. I couldn't deny that I likely hurt my legs much more than I thought I had. Even with the laps around my room, there wasn't much space to regain their strength. Since nothing was broken, they should have been better; it had been a little over a week since the battle with Ray. I couldn't imagine that I was hurt *that* badly—I was still able to stand, albeit with some help.

If I'm not better soon, I might not get better at all. Not without proper treatment.

I decided to put that to the test; I would sneak out whenever the ghosts made their leave for the night.

First, though, I needed to make it through dinner.

There were three primary dinners in the mansion; chicken, soup, or breakfast. Tonight, we had a whole breakfast buffet set up. Did Elias bring more food again, grabbing things that even ghosts could make? Which brought up the follow-up question that's been there since the beginning, how were ghosts able to touch things?

Would Elias know about Mr. Angry Dude? If he had been helping the ghosts for that long, it would make sense. Although, when he first told me about the ghosts, he hadn't done so much as mentioned him...

He probably just didn't want to scare me off, I reasoned. *If someone said that there would be a guy actively trying to stop you, it wouldn't make people want to do it. Not that death was very inviting, either.*

Why didn't he want me to help them, anyway? He asked me if I knew how they ended up here, but I hadn't given it much thought, other than the occasional confusion. They all came from different places around the country—or even outside the country—so far. Could someone have somehow brought them here? Or maybe all their deaths were connected in another way entirely?

"I ask too many questions," I muttered to myself.

"What was that?" Minerva scolded, holding a plate with a bit of everything.

"Nothing," I lied. "Thanks for the food."

She set it down. "I wasn't sure what you were in the mood for, so I grabbed a bit of everything. You better be okay with it."

I thanked her for bringing it to me and started to eat. She sat down in her usual spot, looking downwards.

"I know that being on bedrest isn't fun for you. It's very boring, and you want to get started on Mr. Beatnik—"

"Is that his name?"

Minerva's face contorted with what seemed like an unreasonable amount of disdain. "What? No. Do you seriously not know what a beatnik is?"

I shook my head. "Probably some older slang."

"I keep forgetting that you're from the future, or the present, or whatever it would be called for you. A beatnik is someone who likes music, booze, and all those other things. They weren't good influences."

"Were *you* a beatnik?" I asked with a raised eyebrow.

"That's not the point. What I'm saying is that the best thing you can do right now, however unentertaining it is, is to *rest*. You can't get to him if you can't get out of this bed."

"It's just really *boring*—"

"Do you want to know what's boring?" Minerva snapped. "Spending eternity in a mansion that you've never seen before, and your life purpose meaning nothing anymore, because you didn't go to heaven or hell, if those even exist. You're stuck in an endless cycle of anger and nothing else. *That's* boring."

I shut up, feeling the irritation from Minerva like the heat from a fire. "You're right, I shouldn't be complaining."

"Damn right you shouldn't."

I wasn't sure how to comfort her, but I knew that being hugged by Mom always helped, so I did just that. I sat up and wrapped my arms around Minerva. She stiffened with the contact. The fact that she didn't push me away right off the bat had to mean something, though.

After a few awkward seconds, she finally relaxed and held me tight. Her nails dug into my skin as her body started to shake. I could easily forget that she's technically younger than me, what with the tough front she put out.

Tears started to slip, soaking my shoulder. It took me by surprise—this was Minerva, after all. She never let herself show happiness, let alone sadness. But I didn't say anything; I knew how hard it was to let yourself cry in front of people if you had a choice. I let all the emotions come loose, waiting for her to finish. When she did, she took a deep breath to recollect herself and motioned to my pillow.

"Lay back down, you little rebel." She rubbed her nose, voice shaky. "We need you better. And don't tell Constance, okay? She can't think I'm weak."

I didn't think Constance would actually care that much, but I nodded anyway. "My lips are sealed."

When she left, I felt a bit of guilt for still wanting to sneak out. But I needed to move. I already made a plan, and I wasn't going to go back now. I hadn't even been inside the kitchen since the fight, and I missed being able to get my own food without having to worry about annoying somebody else when they brought it to me.

I looked at my plate, the food having gone cold.

Sometimes you need to ask for forgiveness, not permission.

I just had to pray that it was one of those times.

I snuck out in the middle of the night. I didn't know if the ghosts really had a sleep schedule, let alone if they needed sleep at all, but they knew to leave me alone at night because *I* still did. If I just made sure to avoid their rooms, I could probably get away with a bit of exploring before getting back into bed.

The wood creaked under my feet with every step and every move with the cane. I tried to be as quiet as I could, but everything felt magnified. Even my breathing felt too loud.

I kept my free hand up to act as a guard. I knew the mansion well enough to not ignore the possibility of something bad happening while I walked about, but I didn't think that anything was a serious concern, even with my paranoid thoughts. There weren't any maniac ghosts in this hallway that *I* knew of.

This was my first time around the mansion after the usual time I went to bed. I certainly never got up and moved around at one in the morning, but there's a first for everything. Between the sudden lack of familiarity and noise, the mansion became much eerier than usual.

As I turned a corner, I came to a hallway dimly lit by several wall lamps and the moonlight from the windows. It would have been beautiful in any other context that *wasn't* a mansion filled with murderous ghosts.

One of the wall lamps flickered off suddenly, catching me off guard. I almost whipped my makeshift cane at the wall, but there was nothing there. Strange.

Slowly, the rest of the wall lamps followed suit. I tried to turn around, but instead I got greeted by a dark creature, like a shadow peeled right off the wall.

It had long tendrils of appendages but a vaguely humanoid shape. I couldn't make out any features, and I didn't bother to try; I wanted to get away from it as soon as possible.

I backed against the wall, feeling my way around. That tactic usually worked for me, but the walls were completely smooth. No hidden knives or sharp rocks I could use as one.

The creature made the first move. It sliced my thigh open with a dagger-like hand, making me yelp. I tried whacking it away with the walking stick, but it did nothing; my stick just passed right through.

Leaning against the wall, I adjusted my grip on the cane, jabbing it at the creature. It passed through, but I finally made contact at the neck. Well, the equivalent of a neck on whatever creature this was.

I shoved the stick as hard as I could, and it sent the creature shrieking. It disappeared to whatever hole it crawled out of, but there was something in its place. It looked like a folded piece of paper.

As I bent down to pick it up, I heard footsteps from my left. I shoved the paper in my pocket as Constance ran up to me, breathing heavily. We both spoke at once.

"How long have you been there?"

"What are you doing out of bed?"

"My question first, mama bear." I carefully brought my now-empty hand out of my pocket, hoping she didn't notice me putting something in there.

"I have been here since…whatever that was had appeared up behind you. I tried warning you, but you had already seen it. You will want to hurry off to bed. Minerva might have a fit if she finds you out of bed, let alone fighting."

I motioned to the cane. "I'm not sure how much physical toll is caused by an oversized stick, but it's a good thing I had it. Looks like it does more than just help you walk."

"Yes, dear. Now then, let me see your thigh. The blood is staining your leg."

We walked back to the kitchen to give me a place to rest my leg. Elias must have known what had been happening, because we had a full medical kit. She did a quick job of cleaning and wrapping it, but I knew the wound couldn't be that serious.

"That should be enough for now. Let me know when you need another change. Just make sure Minerva does not hear you."

I nodded and made the rest of the trek to my room. With a racing heart, I curled back under the covers. I heard the crinkle of paper and pulled the folded piece out of my pocket.

As I unfolded it, it began to grow in size, until I saw what it was; a complete map of the mansion.

"Why would that get left behind?" I whispered to myself. "This seems pretty valuable, at least to me. Who knows what would happen if it ended up in the wrong hands."

I hit it under my sack of books, not wanting the others to see it yet. For all I knew, it could be faulty, if faulty maps existed.

That's a problem for Tomorrow Me. Tonight Me needs sleep.

As much as I had been sleeping for the past ten days, fighting a shadow—or whatever I should call that—became draining real quick. Once my heart calmed down, I was asleep only a couple minutes after I closed my eyes.

Chapter Eighteen

Under A-Rest

I woke up much earlier than usual, and I immediately began studying the map. If it's accurate, the mansion was much larger than I had thought. It's hard to tell, though; the map looked distorted, and some rooms weren't labeled accurate. I knew that the conference room had been where it now said 'casino,' but I couldn't figure out for the life of me how a casino could fit inside of a mansion. There's obviously a chance that something got mislabeled, but I didn't know how someone could honestly mess up that badly. And it only took two seconds to look at the conference room and deduce that it *wasn't* a casino.

There's a whole section towards the right of where we were at, but there wasn't much to see—a couple bathrooms, though something that intrigued me was an artifact room. It didn't make sense to focus on it, though. Not like I would get to see it, anyway.

In the back, there's a large area labeled 'garden,' and it's the only way to get to that second half. I hadn't seen it from the outside that first day, so I assumed that it's an indoor garden. I wasn't good at transposing things to scale, but it didn't seem possible for a garden inside a mansion to be that large.

I almost dozed off a couple times while figuring out the map, but the images of the shadow kept startling me awake. I tried—without much success—to convince myself that it wouldn't come back just because I left myself more vulnerable. If this was the struggle Ray had gone through, I could see why he wanted to get rid of me so badly.

I was sprawled out on the bed when Minerva opened the door. I hurried to shove the map underneath the blanket as she stared blankly at me, holding a bowl with curls of steam hovering above it. I had forgotten about the bandage on my thigh, so I just had to pray that she didn't notice it.

"Constance said that you mentioned not feeling well, so we made you some soup. Well, Constance did. It may not be the most breakfast-like, but it should help."

I took the soup as Minerva took up her usual spot. I sipped the soup, feeling the warmth go down my throat and heat up my chest. I wasn't sure why Constance had said I wasn't feeling well, though; save for the cut on my leg, I was feeling pretty good at the moment.

"The soup is great, as usual," I said as I shifted my leg.

Minerva eyed it suspiciously. I knew I couldn't hide it, so I just let out a sigh of defeat.

"Quinkly, what is that?"

I avoided eye contact as she connected the dots.

"Did you seriously sneak out last night? Is that why Constance said you weren't feeling well? And what happened to your leg? Why didn't you just tell us?!"

"Constance knew," I said quietly.

"Then why hide it from *me*?"

"Because I knew you'd blow up like this."

Minerva stumbled, trying to figure out what to say. "I- uh- I'm not *blowing up*. I just don't want you to hide things from me, because that makes it really hard to take care of you."

"Constance wrapped it. I already have her. Besides, when did you decide that you cared for me?"

"When I thought you were going to die!"

The weight of the sentence was hard to miss. Guilt passed through me, and I sunk further into the mattress, wishing I could somehow become submerged. At least then I wouldn't have to deal with the hurt that I saw on Minerva's face.

"This whole mansion is a hell of its own. And you may be the one risking your life, but what we've gone through leaves a connection, even if you didn't think so."

I had been thinking the same thing, but it was totally different to hear the ever-stoic Minerva say it out loud. Hearing the words made it feel a thousand times more real.

I slowly pulled out the map, which now looked a bit crumpled. "I found this last night; the same thing that hurt my thigh had dropped it when it disappeared. It looks like a map of the mansion, but some of the details are wrong. Like, that's where the conference room is supposed to be, but it says 'casino.' Isn't that weird?"

Minerva examined the map, bringing it closer so she could see. "You're right, that's really weird. Have you shown Constance?"

"Nope. You're the only other one who knows about it."

"Gambling was prohibited when I was alive, so most establishments had to shut down. If there's a ghost and they're from around my time, we could be dealing with another criminal." She said it so easily, as though we were talking about a coworker, not a ghost.

"Wait, another?"

Minerva smirked. "Oh, I definitely had my fair share of law breaking. Not sure how much of it is *still* illegal with how much time has passed. It's been a long time, according to Elias."

That didn't come as a surprise to me.

"Could this be the New Yorker you brought up? I would think that NYC would be a pretty big spot for illegal gambling."

"You could be onto something. Should we have you check it out once you're *actually* out of bed?"

"I think so."

We fell into an awkward silence, neither of us sure what else to say. Eventually, she stood up and walked out. When she got to the door, she began talking quietly to someone I couldn't see. I tried moving my head to see, but the person was perfectly blocked. Finally, she walked away, and Ray stepped inside, holding his cap against his chest.

I grinned. "Hey, there."

He returned the smile, though it didn't have the energy that it usually did.

"Is everything alright? You don't seem as upbeat as usual."

"Minerva told me you snuck out last night. Because you hated being trapped in here. It's just- I still feel bad, you know?"

I cut him off before he could continue. "And I still forgive you. It may suck, but it's not your fault that you thought I killed you. I'd be pretty angry too if my killer kept showing up with, like, a mask on or something so I couldn't tell who it was." Up until I had moved into the mansion, I never thought I would have to say anything like that.

"Do you really forgive me, or are you just saying that to make me feel better?"

"Of course I really forgive you. I'm not usually one to lie about that stuff."

Ray smiled and pushed some caramels into my hand. He had begun to do that more and more frequently, and I began to think it's a type of peace offering. I wasn't sure how to tell him that he didn't need to do that, because I tried, but he continued bringing them anyway.

"Do you know how many more of us there are? Other than the one who looks homeless. I think Minerva said there's a guy from New York!" His eyes glittered as he mentioned New York with the same excitement Rachel would have whenever she talked about it before her trip. Was she back now?

"He's the only other one we know for certain about." The reminder of the mystery sabotager wasn't a pleasant one. He hadn't bugged us since that one day of bedrest, but it couldn't be for any good reason. He's probably plotting what's going to happen when he decides to attack us next. The shadow probably did him a favor. Unless...

Could that shadow have been *sent* by him?

I wasn't sure about whatever he was, but he seemed to have a pretty good influence on the mansion, as well as the ghosts inside. He'd been a problem even before I had come along. What would happen when he became violent? It was sure to happen.

I hadn't realized I was shaking until Ray grabbed onto my shoulders. "Woah, steady there. Can't have you exploding on us."

I took a deep breath. "Thanks."

I looked down at the handful of caramels in my palm. "How do you keep sneaking these in here without Constance noticing?"

"I just move the bag around so it doesn't look like any are missing. I'd say it's pretty brilliant on my part."

I bit back a smile. "You must be a pro at stealing food then."

His smile faltered. His eyes went glassy before he blinked away any tears that had been there. "I mean, I had tried."

"I- I'm sorry, but can I ask what happened?"

Ray motioned to the bullet wound with a dry laugh. I gasped, covering my mouth. I knew he got shot, but I never knew why. "That's horrible."

He shrugged. "I try not to talk about it too often. Makes it easier to tolerate." Despite his nonchalant approach, it was obvious that it still hurt to think about after all this time. There probably wasn't much else to think about in an endless purgatory, or whatever weird plane of reality the ghosts were on.

"Do you like music?" I eventually asked.

That got his attention. "Uhm, yes, but I don't think you have a radio in here."

I smiled and pulled out my phone, much to Ray's confusion.

"What is that?"

"This is a cell phone. It's sort of like a landline, except you can carry it around and do more things on it. You know what a landline is, right?"

"Uh- yes. What does that do?"

"You can play games, call and message people, find information, and," I said as I pulled up a music browser, "you can play music. Just tell me what you want."

Ray stared, stunned. "I- that's amazing. Can it play anything?"

"Pretty much."

I played a thirties station, and his face lit up as the music started. He swayed, tapping his fingers on the bed, and began to quietly hum along to a couple of the songs. He got up and started to dance by the second song. I thought the music was cool. Not really my style, but the excitement on Ray's face made me want to play it over and over again. He'd never looked so happy.

After a few more songs, Ray leaned against the wall, grinning silly. "That was amazing. It's been so long since I heard music. I haven't gotten to *dance* like that in so long."

I smiled back at him. "I bet."

"When you're out of bed, are you going to dance?"

"I would love to, but my dancing skills are on an impressive level of horribleness."

"You don't need to be good at something to do it, as long as you're doing something you love. Besides, you don't have to do it in front of anyone. You can just do it here."

"I'll have to take you up on your offer."

"It's a deal then. When you're out of this fluffy prison, the first thing you're going to do is dance your heart out. Safely, of course."

I laughed softly, glad that it no longer hurt to do so. "It's a deal."

Chapter Nineteen

A Free Man (Or Something)

My little 'escapade,' as Minerva liked to call it, sent my progress back by a few days.

"Seriously, what were you thinking?" Minerva grumbled as she changed the bandages, both on my thigh and my head. "If you had died, I wouldn't have been able to help you, and you would never get to see my marvelous face again."

"Unless I become a ghost with you."

"Neither of us would want that."

I stifled laughter, even though she was right. As much as I loved the ghosts, I couldn't imagine spending an eternity with them.

I had been training on walking again, and I could walk pretty far without pain anymore. I had ditched the cane a week before, whether or not I should have. It didn't matter at that point, though, because I was almost walking normally again.

Constance knocked on the door, and I called her in. Constance's red skirt flowed behind her in waves, like ripples in water.

She asked me to walk around and smiled when I showed her my progress.

"You have improved immensely since your fight with Ray, even with the setback. I believe that Minerva and I are in agreement when we say that you are finally ready to continue."

I was about to explode in a passionate flurry of sparks. It had been almost three weeks of not much more than my room, and I was finally able to leave.

"When will we start looking?" I asked Minerva excitedly.

"Slow your roll, kid. We're going to do some training to get you back in shape before you do so much as *look* for him. You'll need a refresher lesson from fighting and—" Minerva sighed— "using Minerva Jr."

It didn't matter how often I used the gun, I guessed that Minerva would always be reluctant to hand it over. I grinned, refraining the urge to jump around and yell. The excitement brought a sudden burst of energy that I hadn't felt in the whole time I had been cooped in my room.

"I have a feeling that this adventure will be going by much quicker for Quincey than it had been," Constance said with a smile.

"In that case," Minerva cut in, "we should get started as soon as we can. Quink here has got to get dressed, though; those clothes aren't anywhere near appropriate to fight in."

I looked down at my sweatshirt and sweatpants. I had been wearing them for the past few days, not having enough energy to get changed. They definitely wouldn't work to bounce back into training.

When neither of them had left, I gave them a motion to get them out of my room. "I'm not changing with you here."

Minerva's eyes widened. "Oh, uhm, yeah. Sorry."

Constance grabbed Minerva's hand with her own and led her out of the room, giving me a knowing look. I bit back a smile as they left.

I changed into a pair of shorts and a tank top, trying to find my gym shoes. When you looked at them, you would have thought that the wearer had just gone through hell, and I used to think I had. Not anymore, though; I was riding on the high of not being confined to my room.

I was just about done when Ray came in, just as excited as I was. "How does it feel to be a free man?"

I laughed. "Pretty good."

"Have you lived up to the deal?"

I tried remembering what deal he was talking about. "Huh?"

"You know…" He gave a little shimmy.

"I already told you, I can't dance. Training with Minerva will have to be good enough, however treacherous it is."

"Not even a little?"

I tossed a jacket at him, smiling. "Give me a break. I still have to go through Minerva's berating. I have a hunch that all that *oh so generous* kindness I had is going to mysteriously disappear. I'm enjoying my last few moments of happiness until I have to face her."

Ray caught the jacket easily, tying it around his shoulders. "I think I look pretty good in this, don't you?"

"You look *amazing*."

Ray posed dramatically. "I knew I should have been a model."

I cackled. "I'm gonna need that back."

Ray took it off and threw it back to me. "Alas, my modeling career was not meant to be."

"What a shame. You would have made a fine model."

Ray tipped his newsboy hat at me. "*More* than fine, my dear Quincey."

A silence fell between us until I sighed. "Well, I guess it's time to start training, isn't it?"

We decided to start off with Minerva Jr. since that would be less physically demanding.

"Though it's true that you didn't need to use this with Ray, that doesn't mean that you won't need to with the rest of the ghosts. Maybe you can even use it on that bastard that won't leave us alone—"

"—assuming you ever give it to me when he comes—"

"—yes, assuming that. We have no clue what to expect for the rest of this journey, so it's better to be safe than sorry."

I gave her the side-eye. "You say that as though I didn't know that already."

"The reminder doesn't hurt."

"Just hand me the stupid gun."

Minerva reluctantly handed the pistol over. She's clearly still unhappy about the idea of anyone else handling it, but she didn't threaten to attack Mom, so that's an improvement. I looked at her expectantly, waiting for further instruction, but she just twirled her wrist.

"What are you waiting for, Quink? Shoot the damn thing, and we'll make adjustments from there."

My heart flared to life with a newfound panic. I hadn't worked with Minerva Jr. in a while, and I was still worried about every time I did so much as make contact with it.

What if I forgot how to use it?

What if I miss?

What if I accidentally shoot something else?

All the 'what-if's ran through my mind at a million miles an hour. I forced myself to push out every nagging question as I adjusted my grip and aim.

Shut up, me.

Before I could hear any other bombardment from my anxiety, I locked my position and pulled the trigger. It sent a shock through me, making me jump. It took a bit to calm my down heart after that shot, but it wasn't as bad as the time she nearly blasted my face off. How long ago was that, a month? Jesus, I had been here a long time.

"Alright, you didn't quite hit the mark we were hoping for, but you got close. You were on the right, so you'll want to shift your focus to the left."

Minerva cautiously grabbed my hands and moved them to a better spot. I aimed as Ray slammed open the door, causing me to pull the trigger in surprise.

The bullet had thankfully been closer to the *bull*seye and not *someone's* eye.

"How's training going?"

Minerva stared at him in astonishment. "Because of your little surprise attack, she could've gotten herself killed! You shouldn't startle someone who's holding a gun."

Ray looked towards me and his eyes turned into tennisballs. "Oh."

"It's fine, just a simple mistake."

"It could have cost you your life!"

"Simple mistake."

Ray watched the gun with a bit of disdain. I remembered the wound on his stomach and tried angling the gun away from Ray's line of sight. He looked at Minerva with an unreadable expression. "Can I watch?"

"Are you sure?" I asked nervously. I didn't think that he would have been comfortable with anything surrounding guns, for obvious reasons, but maybe he's trying to get better. I had no way of knowing, but I wasn't sure if he would want me to ask him while Minerva was there. I gave him a look, hoping it portrayed the silent question behind it.

"I'm sure."

Minerva must have seen the look between us, because she let out a sigh of defeat. "Just be quiet, and whatever you do, *don't distract her*. We don't want another surprise shot."

Ray sat down against the wall, resting an arm on his perched knee. I could see the discomfort on his face, but anger was even more prominent. I couldn't think of why he would put himself through this, but he clearly wanted to watch. I just had to pretend he wasn't there.

"So, that shot was closer. Next time, we want it to be just a bit closer still, and not just when you're caught off guard. If you can get a shot like that consistently, you'll be good to go. And don't expect to have perfect aim every time, especially since you're someone who just started doing this recently."

We kept going with the shots, the noise catching me off guard less and less. Ray watched with a mix of resentment and curiosity. My shots slowly became closer and closer to the target until I had hit a couple bullseyes consistently.

"We're finally making some progress with you. As much as I'd like to keep you working for another few hours, Constance won't let me go that hard on you for the first few days. Don't want to risk overworking you until you get back into the swing of things."

Ray pushed himself off the ground and walked over, his eyes flitting back to the gun every couple seconds. "I'm no expert on how to work a gun, but I'd say those were pretty good. How long has she been doing this?"

"I think I started…I don't even know how long ago. Time has become irrelevant. Over a month, at least."

"Considering Quink is…well, herself, she's doing really well."

I had no clue what *that* implied, but since Minerva's the one saying it, it's safe to assume that it's an insult. "Thanks for the vote of confidence," I grumbled.

Minerva rolled her eyes. "It's as good as you're getting. Now if you'll excuse me, I'm going to go lay down for a bit; you two can do whatever. I don't really care right now."

She put a hand to her head and briskly walked out. I looked over at Ray.

"What do you think that was about?"

"Probably a migraine. She looks like she would get those a lot."

I wasn't sure what made someone look like they got migraines, but I wasn't about to question the teenager about that.

"Why'd you decide to watch? I could see you struggling over there."

Ray shrugged. "I don't know exactly. It just seemed…therapeutic, maybe. I'm not sure how to describe it other than that."

We both gazed upon the target, the bullets withering it away.

"I hope you make it out of here," Ray eventually said in a hushed tone. "You don't belong in a dark place like this."

I inhaled sharply. "I hope so, too."

Chapter Twenty

A Glowing Staircase and a Gambler

It didn't take long to get back into the rhythm of training. The sessions were shorter, and there wasn't much change on my end. After a few days of refresher lessons, they finally decided that I was officially ready to start the quest for the fourth ghost.

I felt excited to start looking again, but there was that terrified voice in the back of my mind that never knew when to shut up. There's a difference between the rational fear that should be coming along with this and whatever my mind had going on.

When the day came to start the search, a thousand emotions coursed through me. It wasn't like Minerva, who had come and found me, or Ray, who we already knew the location of. This time, I actually had to go out and *explore*. It took everything in me to pull myself out of bed and get ready.

I looked over at the map, folded on the side table. It could be useful to bring along, but I didn't want anything to happen to it. I unfolded it and laid it on the floor, snapping a quick picture with my phone. That way I could still use it without the risk of damaging it.

The others were waiting for me in the living room with a range of expressions. While Minerva looked solemn and perhaps a bit nervous, Constance had a look of pride that a mother would have for her child. Ray, however, looked surprisingly excited.

"Minerva said I could go with you!"

"I did *not* say that *once*."

They started to bicker, quickly forgetting that I was even there.

Constance walked up to me and put a hand on my shoulder. "You will do perfectly fine, Quincey. Just remember what you have learned from Minerva, and I trust that it will go well."

"At least one of you seems to care about my safety," I mumbled as I looked over to Minerva and Ray, who were still in a heated argument.

"You may want to leave before they finish, just in case Ray elects to ignore the heedings of Minerva."

The two were starting to close the distance between them, Minerva looking down on Ray. Although it didn't seem like the same anger that Ray had before, he still seemed upset.

"Yeah, I think you're right."

I bid Constance goodbye and began the route to the conference room. If the map wasn't faulty and there really *was* some sort of casino there, however unlikely, it could be a lead to wherever the fourth ghost hid.

No matter how many times I looked into the room, it's the exact same as it was when I had been in here last.

At first, I thought that I must have just misread the map, but the picture on my phone still showed the word *casino* in bold letters. I made my way through the list of possible gateway openers, in case the casino's just hidden.

I walked through the doorway more times than I could count, trying to ignore the blood stained wall from where I had been thrown. It still looked like the same unsettling room.

My next strategy had about the same success rate.

"Open sesame."

"Alakazam."

After going through the main wizard words, I just began shouting anything that came into mind, including 'defenestrate' for some reason. It may not have been the most logical, but I was starting to run out of ideas. When faced with a blank room, there were either a lot of possibilities or very few, and it leaned more towards the latter.

Either way, I was stuck in this stupid conference room...

Trying to find a casino that shouldn't exist...

Man, my life had taken a weird turn.

"He's probably just somewhere else. No use wasting any more time here."

As I turned off the lights, I finally noticed something; where the table had just been now sat empty, a square of light marking off a staircase. I wasn't sure where the staircase led, but I could hear the sounds of talking and drunken laughter.

The casino.

"How the hell does a casino even end up there?" I muttered to myself.

I flipped the lightswitch, but the box disappeared the moment that they flickered on, placing the table back to where it was.

"Okay, *this* is some weird stuff."

I hit the lightswitch a few more times, and it stayed consistent; when the lights were on, there's a conference room. When the lights were off, the entrance to the casino opened.

"Guess that now's as good a time as any." Even as I spoke to some imaginary force, it helped ground my thoughts and determination. I kept the lights off and walked down the steps to the casino.

As soon as I stepped onto the stairs, I got hit by everything at once. The sound of multiple different songs playing and drunks blabbing on about whatever. So many figures passed by me. It's all *too much*.

I had to fight the urge not to immediately run back to my comfort zone. This mission didn't care about my thoughts on the matter, however, because that's when I spotted the fourth ghost.

Despite the bustling of the casino, I could still easily tell which one I'd been searching for. He's the only one who looked human. I hadn't noticed it before, but everyone else there was less...lively. They might as well have come out of a grayscale painting. All their features had been wiped away, leaving only vague shapes. I could make out certain bits of facial structure; dark oval shapes where the eyes would be, a line in the spot of the mouth. Why did they look so different from the rest of the ghosts? I wasn't sure who to ask, if an expert existed for these kinds of things.

I was sucked into the world of the casino until one of these gray shapes passed right through me, leaving a sharp pain on my side. I swore under my breath and clutched my rib, looking back at the fourth ghost, who was chatting up one of the silhouettes. I couldn't make out their conversation, but it looked like they were laughing about something. I decided to walk over, hoping to learn a bit more about him.

As I got closer, I noticed more about what he looked like. He was dressed in nice clothes; a white button up shirt with the top button or two open and a tie loosened, black suspenders with matching black pants. His pale blond hair pulled back in a small ponytail that rested at the nape of his neck. Everything about him radiated confidence. He's smiling, which didn't seem to fit the rest of the mansion.

He wasn't angry like the others; he actually looked *happy*.

"Lyle, my guy, do you ever lose at cards?"

"Only when I let you win," he said with an exaggerated wink.

Lyle.

Minerva was at least right about where he's from. He had a heavy New York accent, speaking quickly. It's hard to tell what he's saying, especially with all the other noise around us.

I didn't think he noticed me yet. Could I sneak a spot by him at the bar before talking to him?

Despite the fact that he's working at a casino, he didn't look that much older than me. I didn't know how old you had to be to serve alcohol, especially in whatever time period he's from, but there was no way he could have been more than twenty-five. Were *all* these ghosts going to be so young?

I was almost to the bar when he locked eyes with me. I groaned as he threw his hands in the air, cheering. "Enzo, get over here!"

For a moment, I thought that he might have been talking to someone else. I never remembered that none of them will actually see me for who I am until after I calmed them down.

Nonetheless, I put on my best smile and sat by him. "Hey there, uh...*bud*."

I internally cringed, but I didn't know how to act like this Enzo guy. I just had to hope that Lyle didn't pay close attention to me, or at least not close enough that he'd notice I wasn't him.

I avoided making eye contact with Lyle until that moment. As youthful as the rest of him seemed, his eyes were clearly drained. They weren't too tired to beckon me in for a game, however. Without breaking eye contact, he began shuffling cards.

"I know it's been a while, but do you still know how to play?"

Oh God, do I have to beat him in poker?

It's better than having to fight him, but that brought up a worse realization; I had absolutely no idea how to play. I saw bits on TV, but I never bothered to learn, and it wasn't something that I had done in my training with Minerva.

"Don't tell me you're too scared for a little friendly game."

I swore under my breath before looking back. "You're on, pretty boy."

Lyle let out a hearty laugh. "There's the Enzo I know."

He motioned for the gray man he had been talking with to leave, who did so gladly. Without anywhere else for me to go without it becoming awkward, he patted the now empty spot. "You don't need to stand."

I laughed nervously and sat myself down in the chair, trying to drown out all the other noise. I didn't know how to play, but I would have to make my best guess if I wanted to make my way through the night.

He tossed in two chips. "I'll be big blind, you'll be little blind."

I awkwardly slid two of my own chips in as well. He laughed and pushed one back to me. "Don't be giving out your chips that quickly now."

What the hell does this mean?

After shuffling, Lyle passed the cards out between us. "I trust that you won't need a reminder of how to play."

"It could never hurt." I tried to play it off as a joke, but if I could get him to give a rundown—even a quick one—that would help greatly.

Instead of explaining anything, however, he just finished with the cards. "If you end up *really* needing help, I can guide you through. I don't doubt that you should be able to make it through by yourself just fine, though."

Two cards? I thought to myself. *What am I supposed to do with two cards?*

I was going to find out soon enough, because the game had already started.

Chapter Twenty-One

I Guess I Don't Like Poker

To start us off, he put in two chips. "Let's start this off light, huh?"

Even though I didn't have any idea what he was talking about, I nodded along anyway and put in two chips as well. I may have been completely oblivious to the game, but I did know that you wanted to have the most chips at the end. I looked at my cards; it didn't look like anything special. I'd never played before, but I didn't think that a seven and a four could do much.

He must have noticed my grimace, because he raised an eyebrow. "You couldn't have seriously forgotten how to play. It hasn't been that long, has it?"

"Uhm, no, it hasn't. I'm good."

You idiot, I thought to myself. *You could have gotten him to explain it but you didn't? You're a moron.*

I already know that, me.

He flipped over another card and placed it beside the one that was already face up. A king.

He looked right at me with piercing blue eyes that poked at me and a knowing smirk. "Do you want something to drink? It'll help you loosen up a bit."

I pretended to examine my cards with a critical eye. If I didn't answer, maybe he would drop the question.

"I'll take your silence as a yes. Want the usual?"

Damn it. "Why not?"

Let's pray he doesn't give me alcohol poisoning.

"Give me two seconds, and maybe a laugh for good measure."

When I didn't, he frowned. "Wow, you've really become a grump. I guess that becoming a dad does that to you."

Just my luck. He's a dad. I don't know jack about kids, let alone taking care of one.

Despite being in the middle of a game, he disappeared to make me this mystery drink. If it didn't taste fruity, I wasn't sure I'd be able to down it.

"Is my first sip of alcohol really going to be from *this*?" I sighed under my breath.

"What was that?" Lyle called from a few feet away.

"Nothing!"

My leg bounced from beneath me like a sewing machine. The anticipation started to build up, and I didn't think I could handle being in here much longer. If Lyle didn't come back in the next few minutes, I might just ditch and come back after a quick search of how to play...whatever type of poker this was. Weren't there multiple kinds?

I hadn't even noticed that he came back, holding a drink in a small glass. It looked like some weird tea; maybe I could down it in one gulp if I pretended it's something else.

"Are you gonna drink this, or did I waste time for the both of us?" A playful smile danced across his lips, egging me on.

"No, no, I'll drink it." I carefully took the glass from him and took a deep breath before taking a sip. It burnt the back of my throat and tasted insanely strong. Despite that, it could've been worse. I still didn't know how people could drink that stuff regularly.

"There we go. Now that we got some booze in your system, wanna keep playing?"

If that glass was enough to change my thinking, I didn't know, so I just nodded. He put in three more chips, and I matched him. He placed another card.

More chips.

More cards.

After there were five laying face up, he announced that it's time to reveal our hands. I threw my cards on the table; it didn't look like anything.

Lyle *tsk*ed and put his cards down. One of the cards in his hand matched a card that was face up. "Looks like I won this round, Ezzie. Your poker face really has gotten much worse since we played last."

He grabbed the cards and began to shuffle again. "That was a warm up; ready for round two?"

Even if I wasn't confident, I had to at least fake it. I grinned at him. "Hell yeah."

"That's what I'm talking about. You better beat me this time."

I bit the inside of my lip. *Was Enzo good at this? I mean, probably, if he regularly played with Lyle.*

We continued playing, and I slowly started to learn more about hands. There's a pair, two pairs, three of a kind...the names of the others kept mixing around in my head, but they were less likely to happen, so I decided to cross that bridge when I got to it.

I started to feel comfortable enough to talk while we played. "How've you been holding up? It's been a while."

"You know," Lyle said, "helping with the casino is always tiring. It doesn't matter how long I've been doing it for, at the end of the day, the best thing is when there's no one here. I don't remember how long it's been since I've had that, though. I've been running on little to no sleep as of recently. Glad that someone I actually like finally decided to come along." There was a sense of longing in the way he said that last sentence, accompanied by a bittersweet smile. It didn't make me feel better to know that his joy came from a lie.

"How's your family been? Still feeling the effects of the war?"

Finally, some useful information. There were only a few major wars I could think of that we as a country were involved in, and they had to have been within the last hundred years or so based on other clues around the area. If the rest of the casino hadn't hinted towards it, at least now I knew that he must have been pretty recent.

"We're doing as good as we can." That was vague enough of an answer that I shouldn't need to worry about further pestering.

We laid down our hands, and I had a winning hand.

"About time you beat me. I was starting to worry that you weren't going to," Lyle said jokingly.

I felt a flush of pride run through me, but it quickly got stifled. "That was only one round, though. You're still losing by, oh I don't know, around eighty chips. You don't have much left."

He gestured to my stacks of chips, which didn't have nearly as much as his stack did. I sank into my chair.

"Don't look so disappointed, big guy. You can still win the next game. We have all the time in the world here."

It didn't take much longer for him to take the rest of my chips. How long had we been playing, an hour? I started to lose track of time as everything began to blur together. We continued talking, but he started to push more and more with questions about Enzo. Apparently, not only did he have a kid, he also had a goldendoodle named Larry and a wife with cancer, who he was trying to divorce. Not only that, but I guess that he had been raised in a gang of sorts. If I had the chance to talk to him, I would probably send him straight to therapy.

If Lyle had thought I was Enzo at the beginning of this, he must have been starting to seriously doubt that.

"Ay, you look like you're about to pass out right here at the table. How about you just go home and rest. You got that kid to take care of, anyway."

Something felt off about the way he said it, but I was ready to leave as soon as I could. I simply nodded and stood up, pushing the drink towards him.

"You barely drank it. And here I was, thinking that my drinks were special." He tossed me a quick smile, but it didn't have the same joy as earlier.

"Just tired, man. I gotta get home."

Lyle shrugged. "Suit yourself. You better come back, though. Would be a shame to leave on a losing game."

I agreed, knowing that I needed to come back anyway. Something about this whole scenario seemed too easy. If I just needed to beat him in a game of poker, all I needed was a quick tutorial and I could just hope for the best. No, there had to be something more to him. I just couldn't figure out what that thing would be.

I went up the staircase and back into the dark conference room. The sounds of the casino faded away, leaving me in a suffocating silence. I pulled out my phone to use as a flashlight and walked through the halls of the mansion. It's already dark out. How long had it been inside the casino? It felt like an hour, maybe an hour and a half.

I looked at the time on my phone; it's a little after six. I left at eleven—was I seriously there for seven hours? It certainly hadn't felt like it, but I had never been good at time management. Even then, I couldn't have been *that* far off.

I found the others in the kitchen, with Constance and Ray preparing a meal while Minerva paced back and forth by the dining room table. I knocked on the wall, warning them that I was there. "It took me a while, but I'm finally back."

Minerva saw me first and stopped in her tracks. "Oh, good, you didn't die. I was starting to get worried there." Despite the lack of enthusiasm in her voice, I could see her relax.

Ray turned to face me with batter-covered hands and an excited grin. "Welcome back! Constance is letting me help her make dinner. Look!" He spread out his fingers, showing off the dough.

Constance laughed and placed a clean hand on his shoulder. "Please refrain from making a mess. I would not like to clean that."

Ray nodded quickly, becoming extra cautious of where he was going. He's finally starting to act less like an angry war-torn vagabond and more like an actual teenager. It warmed up something in my chest, and almost made me forget about what I still needed to do.

"Well, I've got good news and bad news. The good news is that I know where the fourth ghost is."

"Let me guess," Minerva cut in, "you have to get your ass beat again."

"Actually, no, my pessimistic ghost friend. I just have to beat him in a game of poker."

"That should be easy enough…" Minerva muttered. "What's the catch? That can't be all to it. There has to be *something* else."

"Exactly what I'm thinking." I slouched into a chair, sprawling out. "I can't figure out anything else that would make sense, though. Even if it *is* just that, it's still going to be a while; I don't know how to play."

Minerva stared at me. "Seriously?"

"Just because you're basically a dead teenage mob boss doesn't mean that everyone is."

"I'm not a *mob boss*, I just did stuff that was actually *fun* as a teenager, unlike whatever your boring life must have been before this. Do you need me to teach you that, too?"

I wasn't sure how much more of Minerva's training I could put myself through before I snapped. "I could just find a video online—"

"No, I'll do it. I don't trust whatever you're going to learn from to teach it to you the right way. We start tomorrow morning, before you go to see him again. Did you catch his name by chance?"

I groaned, but part of me was surprised that she had actually offered. I thought that she would have been elated to not being required to deal with my amateur skills, but maybe she didn't care. "His name's Lyle."

Constance put whatever bread she'd made into the oven. How had she even learned how to use the appliances? Maybe Elias had taught her. "Is there anything else we need to know?"

I tried to remember what the casino was like, but I was starting to shut down. "Uhm…oh, there's one thing. It's really weird. Lyle is, like, the only one there who looks like you guys."

"Huh? What does that mean?" Ray asked.

"There were more ghosts there but they were all kind of shapeless. They looked more like gray shadows than actual people. And they could pass *through* me; it was just really weird. Any idea what that could mean?"

They sat in silence, thinking.

"Maybe it's something simple: they could just not belong here. I don't know what classifies who belongs where in the ghost world, but if they're not supposed to be here, that could explain why they don't look like they fit in," said Minerva.

I shrugged. "I think that's as good an answer as we'll get."

Constance frowned. "Dear, you look exhausted. You should try getting decent sleep before going back to the casino. Would you like me to bring you some food later?"

I nodded, feeling the fatigue starting to weigh me down.

I dragged myself to my room, quietly slipping under the covers. All the energy left my body the moment I was settled.

Let's pray that the only thing to it is a little game. Maybe I'll have a chance to make it out of this alive.

Sleep had never found me quicker.

Chapter Twenty-Two
Fake It 'Til You Make It

Sadly, life had never found me quicker, either.

I had woken up to Minerva hovering beside me, glowering. I jumped, almost hitting my head against the back of my bed. I ducked under the covers; maybe she hadn't noticed that I was awake.

"Time to get up, it's almost noon."

I let out a long sigh, burying myself deeper into the blankets. "Gimme five more minutes."

"Nope. You need to learn how to play, and that doesn't involve you getting seventeen hours of sleep. How do you even sleep that long?"

I poked my head out so I could give Minerva a proper glare. "It's called being *tired*. Ever heard of it?"

"Sounds like an excuse to me, so you better be ready by the time I come back in ten minutes, or else I'll drag you out of that bed myself."

She turned away with a huff and walked out of the door, giving me a quick backward glance before closing the door. I sank into my bed, contemplating if I should actually get out of bed or if her words were an empty threat. I decided not to take my chances with an angry Minerva and pushed myself out of the cushions of my bed.

I hurried to get dressed in appropriate clothes—a Northern Arizona University sweatshirt that Mom got for me and jeans—and walked out to where Minerva was waiting, tapping her foot impatiently. "Took you long enough."

"I just woke up and was greeted with annoyance, don't test me."

"Oh dear, what ever should I do? The small kitten is hissing!" Minerva said dramatically. I made a crude gesture involving a particular finger and was met with laughter. "Its paw is *so* intimidating! I may never recover from the sight."

"Let's just get started before I actually punch you in the throat."

"Do you want to try, kitten?" Minerva looked at me with a smirk, and I ignored the brief flush of my cheeks and racing of my heart.

When I didn't say anything, we came to a silent agreement that it was time to go practice.

I was surprised to find a deck of cards waiting for us at the table. "Where'd you find these?"

"Constance found them on the table of the conference room this morning. It seemed like a bit of a weird spot, but they'll work."

Lyle, that sly bastard. He was taunting me. That led to a different horrifying thought.

Does that mean he knows that I'm not Enzo? The moment that he can be certain is the moment my life gets put into jeopardy. Who knows how he'll react to some sort of imposter impersonating his best friend.

We sat down across from each other, and Minerva began shuffling the cards with surprising energy. "Can you describe what the game looked like? We'll just have to assume you play the same kind every time."

I described what I could remember of the game, which wasn't much. There were chips, blinds, two cards—there wasn't much else.

She figured it out pretty quickly and filled me in on the details that Lyle didn't do so much as to allude to. She described different hands and what would win against other hands, and my mind began swirling before we even started playing.

By the time I had the two cards in my hand, I already started to lose focus.

"Did you hear anything I just said?" Minerva eventually said.

Minerva sighed when I just looked at her in confusion. "I *said* that you're going to learn to bluff. I don't know how good you are at acting, but that's primarily what it is; you're acting as though you have a better hand than you do. You could also use reverse psychology and try convincing another player that they have a *better* hand than you so that they bid more, leaving you more to gain. However, we won't go into that yet; first, we need to teach you how to hide your anxious tendencies."

"I can't just *not* be anxious. Trust me, I already tried."

"I'm not saying you can't be anxious. You just can't reveal it."

"What does *that* mean?"

"Are you trying to write a book? Just try for this first game, and I'll explain what you can do better. Have you figured out how betting works yet?"

I shrugged. "Somewhat? I know that you can't go less than what the opponent puts down, but that's about it."

"That's right. You will usually start with one, and your opponent can either meet your one, or they can raise the bid. If they raise the bid, you must now meet theirs. If you don't want to, or you can't, you drop. Once everyone's either matched the bet or dropped out, those who are still in will reveal their cards. Easy enough?"

"We'll see."

"Okay then, this is what we'll do. I'll do a practice round with you right now while asking you questions about yourself to see how well you can bluff. Sometimes, bluffing isn't directly lying; it could be as simple as *avoiding* the truth. Are you ready?"

I nodded and looked at my pair of cards for the first time. I was starting to line up for a flush…or was it a straight? Whatever the name was, I had two of the same suit, as well as the first card that lay face up.

My thoughts hit me before I could even get asked a question by Minerva.

Does Minerva have a better hand?

What if I'm horrible at bluffing and she bets more than I have?

Am I actually going to lose money?

The questions that attacked me on the inside didn't give me a break from Minerva's, either.

"So, how's the family? What are your parents like?"

I avoided looking Minerva in the eye. "Well, my dad isn't really there all the time. My parents got divorced when I was four, but they're still good friends. He and his girlfriend visit us on holidays and other celebrations, like birthdays and such. I also go see my mom's family a lot for the holidays—my *abuela* always insists we go at least once a year. There are a *lot* of people there who only speak Spanish. I live with my mom, and she's the best mom I could ever ask for. She works as a manager at a local fast food place. I had actually worked there with her, but when I started looking for colleges to attend, I dropped my job so I could focus on that. If you couldn't guess, that plan didn't work very well for me, because I'm here in this stupid mansion and not in a college dorm. Oh, and I also have a dog named Oliver."

"Cute. What breed?"

"A curly-coated retriever."

"Yes, very cute."

"*You have a dog?!*"

I almost threw what little cards I had at Ray from the scare. He grinned with such excitement that it felt hard to ask him to leave so I could focus.

Minerva, however, did not have the same problem. "Ray, we're doing things not regarding you. Leave us alone."

"I live here too, you know. I'm pretty sure most of this involves me now."

"Well, this doesn't, so *leave*."

They fell into a back and forth banter, as their interactions usually did. It was always so awkward when I was around arguments; they always made me want to curl up into a ball and avoid everything.

I wasn't sure when Constance had come into the room, but she stared intently between the two. I could see the restraint that kept her from curling into herself as well. Maybe I could silently leave the table to help ease Constance's own anxiety—

I jerked back as Ray slammed his hands on the table, causing everything to tremble. That's when they remembered that I was there, and that I still needed to learn how to play. Minerva gave Ray one last glare before turning back to me. "He can *watch* in *silence*. If he becomes too distracting, he will leave, *right*?"

Ray hastily nodded, pulling up a chair beside Minerva.

We continued through the game, and she asked more about my family. I hadn't talked much about them outside of a few people—Kayden knew a bit, but he was always closer with Rachel, so we didn't hang out much on our own. Rachel and Adrianne heard about my struggles with Mom a lot, but it was always one-on-one. Even with Ray being completely silent, his presence there made everything about it feel weird.

I may not have been the best at bluffing, but I got better at hiding my small nervous habits. I think she called them 'tells' at one point, but I didn't remember. It just mostly meant that he went from 'can obviously tell I'm lying' to 'probably knows but can't confirm it.'

We played a couple of rounds, and by the time we decided to end, Minerva had been in the lead. I started to catch up, but I wasn't quite there yet.

"I don't expect you to beat Lyle on the second day, but that should be good for now. It will only take short training sessions to get you good enough at acting to bluff against him easily—you seem to already have experience with acting, so that's good. You just have to make sure that he doesn't kill you before then. Simple enough."

There still wasn't any sign of anything beyond the game for calming Lyle down. I may have gotten some luck with my current ghost, but I didn't trust life that much to say I'll be fine for the rest of this. There's *always* something that's ready to go wrong, especially in places like this.

"Is there anything else I need to do?"

Minerva shook her head. "Don't die. That's all we're hoping for right now. Everything else comes second."

I sighed, looking at the watch on my wrist. It wasn't even close to the right time anymore, but I couldn't bring myself to take it off. "I should find something to help me keep track of time down there. That casino takes the 'time flies while you're having fun' thing a bit too seriously."

Minerva paused for a second before she began pulling things out of her pockets. She had a lot of business cards, but eventually, she handed me a small pocket watch.

"I don't know what the rules of time are inside the casino, but this should be able to help. Be careful with it, though. My mother gave that to me in 1953."

I nodded and put the watch in my pocket. "I guess it's time to find him now."

"Be careful. Don't die."

"Thank you for the encouragement," I muttered as I made my way towards the conference room.

Chapter Twenty-Three
Candles Are Annoying

The speed at which the table disappeared when the lights were turned off still caught me off guard. I didn't know where it went, but the chairs had disappeared with it. The room was empty except for the glowing staircase in the center, beckoning me towards the casino.

I tried to remember everything Minerva had taught me as I walked down the stairs. It's easier to handle the noise this time, but it still made my head hurt. With all the overlapping voices and other noises, I hadn't even noticed that there was another man talking to Lyle. This one, however, I recognized instantly.

I shiver ran down my spine as I found the unnaturally blue eyes of the angry man. He didn't give me much more than a sideways glance, but it's enough to make my blood run cold. Did Lyle see him as he was, or as someone else? Someone who looked like that wouldn't blend in very easily. I cautiously walked towards the bar as they continued their conversation.

"Wick, I've told you *repeatedly* to leave the casino."

Wick? That's an...unusual name, to say the least. Having a name for him made him feel much more real.

"I can't just leave an amazing environment like this, now can I? It's just so impressive. So many people bustling around, having the time of their lives." Wick smiled wickedly, enjoying the look of annoyance on Lyle's face.

Lyle gave a quick glance before motioning toward me. "Could you leave us to our game? My buddy Enzo has been waiting for who knows how long."

Wick gave me a longer look this time, taking me in. I could feel the question that he's urging on; *how long until he finds out?*

"What if, instead," Wick slid beside Lyle, "I joined the game?"

Absolutely not.

Lyle hated the idea as much as I did. "No, no, really man. We need to talk about some rather important matters that we would prefer to have privacy for."

"It'll be fine, Lyle, calm down. This is a place for fun."

Wick's voice sounded unnaturally relaxed, his usual anger nowhere to be found. I wasn't sure what scared me more: the rough yelling or this calm before the inevitable storm. Everything about Wick set me on edge, and the sudden calmness only irked me more.

Lyle grumbled under his breath and began shuffling the deck. His laid-back demeanor must have been waiting wherever Wick's anger was, because his body tensed. I found a spot to sit in front of both of them.

Lyle passed the deck to Wick, who passed out the cards.

"So, what did you say this fine *gentleman's* name was?"

I *knew* Wick knew my name. This was just a ploy to play into Lyle's delusion. I guessed that it was better than him revealing me, but what was his ulterior motive?

"His name's Enzo, what's it to you?"

"Ah, *Enzo*. Such a unique name, don't you think?"

"Tell me, what is *your* name, Mr. Tough Guy?" Two could play at whatever sick game Wick was playing.

"Wick."

"Wick sounds much more stupid than Enzo," Lyle piped in.

"Like a candle! Can I call you candle boy?"

Lyle started to grin, and Wick's anger started to show again. I saw it flash up for only a moment before he regained his composure. For how angry he had always acted when I saw him before, he was surprisingly good at keeping calm.

"Yeah, like a candle." Lyle pulled out an old styled lighter, sparking it on. "Do you melt like one, too?"

Wick put a bit more distance between them, and I stifled laughter. He whipped around and gave me a glare before standing up, pushing his pair of cards in.

"Alright, be that way. I'll leave you to your game. Maybe I'll serve some of the other customers."

"How about you leave the casino entirely?" I said hopefully.

"Oh, no, I won't be doing that."

There was something about Wick that set me on edge every time he spoke.

When Wick wandered around to a different part of the bar, Lyle let out a sigh of relief. "Finally, the bastard's gone. Can never seem to get rid of him for good. Now then, let's play, shall we?"

We hadn't even gotten one round in before Wick had slid back over to us. "I made you two drinks. I hope you don't mind."

His chains clinked against the glasses as he placed one in front of each of us, looking almost identical. I had already had one taste of alcohol, and that was enough to last me until I was thirty. Besides, it's never good when someone angry suddenly begins acting kind with no context. There had to be something behind his surprising change of heart.

"You better not have spiked this drink, my guy."

Wick only answered with a shrug.

After setting our drinks down, he winked at me and walked away, pretending to take interest in something towards our left.

Lyle stared down at the drink. "If I die in the next ten minutes, beat that guy to a pulp, got it?" Without a second though, he took a swig of the glass, downing it in one gulp.

"Got it, sir."

Without anything else to worry about, we started playing. It started in silence for the most part, other than the occasional remarks from Wick as he walked by. As hard as he made it to ignore him, we had come to a silent agreement that no matter what, we wouldn't give Wick the satisfaction.

Lyle noticed that I hadn't tried the mysterious drink Wick had made earlier. "Y'know, you don't gotta drink whatever the hell he made. I don't trust it either, and it tasted horrible anyway. Want me to make you something?"

"Why not?" The drink he had made me earlier wasn't bad, albeit strong. Maybe that's just an experience of someone tasting alcohol for the first time. Besides, I wasn't sure if I could get away with saying no anyway.

Once again, just like that first game, he stood up and went to one of the bartending stations to go make a drink. Were bartenders usually playing with the customers, too? I didn't really know how casinos worked.

I looked over at Lyle, who was making the drink with great showmanship. It was impressive but also didn't feel necessary.

When I turned back towards the front, Minerva stood where Lyle had just been. I startled, opening my mouth to yell before Minerva shushed me.

"Not so loud. Don't get his attention when we don't want it."

"Why are you here?" I whispered through clenched teeth. "You're supposed to be with the others."

"I could smell the booze off of you after yesterday. I wanted to pop in and say hi."

"Now is *not* a good time, unless you're looking to get me found out." I kept throwing nervous glances to Lyle, who hadn't noticed Minerva yet. "If you want me to ever leave this casino, you're going to have to leave first."

"As much as I want to see your pretty face again, I need a quick swig before leaving." Minerva looked down the counter and settled on one of the drinks of a gray silhouette. It looked like the silhouette had gotten angry, but it was hard to tell without much of a facial expression.

Lyle, by some miracle, had come back after Minerva left. "Sorry 'bout that, there was a small problem. Nothing to worry about now. Drink up, bud."

He made himself a drink as well—it's starting to look like he had a drinking problem—and clinked our glasses together before finishing his in a matter of seconds. I was more hesitant to start on mine, but in the end, I just took a smaller sip. It wasn't as bad as the first time, but still not something I would drink often.

It started to look as though we never should have begun a game in the first place, because our favorite homeless man came back again. "You couldn't *seriously* expect me to stay away for long, now could you? Come on, now, that's just foolish on your part."

If one more dumb thing came out of his mouth, I may need to beat the stupidity out of him.

Lyle enjoyed this about as much as I did. He snapped at Wick. "My man, we have some rules here. We've asked you politely, you didn't leave. We ignored you, you didn't leave. Rules aren't going to be relevant much longer for you, so tell me, how would you like this to go: would you like *my* fists to leave you black and blue, or would you like a few extra hands to join that fight?"

"I would much rather enjoy my time here, but clearly you don't like that."

"No, I only don't like it when you're being an asshole. The two are not mutually exclusive."

They continued bantering back and forth as I watched from my seat. It didn't take long for them to forget I was there, which seemed to happen often when I watched arguments, but that's fine by me. I didn't want to get dragged into whatever was going on if I didn't need to be.

What started off as a small discussion with sharp words turned into full yelling, both of them standing. The anger that Wick had was all too familiar, but seeing Lyle angry didn't seem to fit. As angry as the rest of the ghosts had been when I worked with them, Lyle's the only one who wasn't. The only reason he's mad now was because of Wick, that snake who refused to leave well enough alone.

A few of the gray people around me noticed the shouting match, but all they did was watch for a small while before continuing on with their day. While Wick tried to get into Lyle's space and tried to be the bigger guy, Lyle stayed quiet. His eyes may have been afraid, but the rest of him seemed determined.

"Why aren't you saying anything?!" Wick said eventually. "You've just been standing there!"

"At least I have the decency to wait for privacy before starting an argument. Now then," Lyle looked at me, "could you please leave so that no one may witness what I am about to say to him?"

When Wick got angry, he exploded like a firework. When Lyle got angry, he became as silent as an empty cave.

I nodded and walked away, pulling Minerva out with me. There's no way that I would let her in here without supervision.

"Why not just let me play ten more minutes?"

"Ten minutes will turn into ten hours. Just be glad it wasn't Constance who found you, or you'd be a twice-dead man."

Minerva grumbled with reluctant agreement as we walked up the stairs. I looked over my shoulder and saw more of Lyle's colors showing. Wick tried to look unaffected, but you could see less confidence in his pose.

"Go get him," I whispered. I didn't know what they were saying, but if it was shooting down Wick, it was good enough for me.

"Will you be okay on your own?" I asked Minerva. "How did Constance not notice you were gone?"

Minerva shrugged. "Said I was napping or something. I don't remember."

"You better pray that she's feeling forgiving."

"It's Constance. She'll *always* choose peace over fighting, which includes forgiving people."

If only it were that easy now.

Chapter Twenty-Four
Can You Not Do That?

The walk towards the kitchen felt longer than usual with Minerva next to me. The silence was pressing down on us like an invisible weight. Our footsteps fell into sync by the time we turned the corner towards Constance and Ray. They were already eating dinner, with two plates of food set out for Minerva and I.

"Minerva, there you are," Constance crooned. "I was looking everywhere for you. Did you go to meet Quincey at the conference room?"

"Uh, you could say that."

I elbowed Minerva, who cursed under her breath. Constance looked between us with confusion before deciding to drop the topic.

"So, how did the journey for today go? Did you learn anything new?"

"Actually," I started, "there is one pretty big thing."

I told them about Wick's identity and what it was like having him there. We may not have gotten much playing in, but the information about Wick had more of an impact. If we learned more about Wick, maybe we could learn how to win this fight against him.

"Wick? What an unusual name..." Constance eventually said.

"Does everyone here have weird names except for me?" Ray asked. "I think Ray is much more normal than anyone else's."

"Excuse you, Minerva is a perfectly normal name."

"It can't be more normal than *Ray*."

Surprise, they got into another argument.

Thankfully, most of their fights weren't much more than those siblings would have, but I could see the toll they had on Constance with every petty fight they got into. She had become less strict about arguing since Ray calmed down, probably just because of how often it happened, but it still made Constance nervous. I saw her playing with the fabric of her dress anxiously, eyes flitting towards the two every couple seconds with an unspoken and secretive fear. Maybe it was just her being a mom, but I wondered if there was something more behind her fear of yelling.

"Minerva, Ray, can you two stop fighting? It's clearly stressing Constance out, and it's stressing me out, too," I snapped. They both turned to look at me, then at Constance. All of the fire in Minerva's eyes disappeared.

"I...I'm sorry." Her gaze averted.

"Me too," Ray added.

While Constance was still a bit tense, she visibly relaxed. She wrapped her arms around Minerva, squeezing her tight. Minerva held Constance in her arms until Constance's breathing slowed down.

"Thank you," I heard Constance whisper. Minerva nodded, and they let go.

"So, we got some work we need to do. You may know the general rules of poker now, but you need to learn how to bluff and ask indirect questions to learn more about Enzo. The more you can learn about him without revealing yourself, the better your odds will be of staying...'undercover,' if you will."

"Okay then...how do I do that? Do you have like, a list of questions, or—"

"Quill, you gotta learn how to do this stuff. I'll help this time, but you need to learn how to do this in the future, I'd reckon."

"Trying to fake being a guy who's probably been dead for a long time because I'm trying to win a game of poker against a ghost who believes I'm his best friend? Yes, I'm *totally* going to do this again. It's my favorite pastime." I crossed my arms.

"I meant *asking people questions*, Quink. Not *why* you're asking the questions."

I didn't think that I had ever felt so dumb before. I hoped that they would forget I said anything. "That makes more sense."

"Of course it does. I'm brilliant."

"You sure do have a lot of confidence, don't you?"

"I have to. You won't go very far without it."

I decided to take what she said to heart. I sat up straighter. If I wasn't actually confident, I could at least pretend. "You're right. If I have to play the role of Enzo, I better play it damn well."

Minerva gave me a small but proud smile. "That's the spirit."

Ray had been surprisingly quiet. I couldn't tell what he was looking at or if he was just spacing out. "Ray, you alright?"

He startled, looking up at me.

"What? Oh, yeah." He stood up and yawned. "I'm just going to go hit the hay. Haven't been sleeping well." Without anything else to say, he walked towards the direction of the bedrooms. I still didn't know which ones the ghosts actually slept in.

Minerva followed shortly after him, until I was left alone with Constance. She had also been quieter than usual, though she wasn't much of a talker to begin with. "How about you? Are you feeling alright?"

"Yes, I suppose. There have just been many things to think about. How are you, however? *You* are the one in danger here."

I sighed, resting my arms on the chair in front of me. "If I'm being honest, I don't really know anymore. Like you said, there *are* a lot of things going on. I don't feel like I'm prepared enough for this. Like, I *know* that I've made it this far, but I don't know how I did. Why am I the one who's able to calm them down where everyone else failed?"

"I am not the one to answer that question for you, Quincey. That may be something you need to ask Elias. However, what I can do is give you encouragement. There must be something special about you if you were the one to succeed. Do not forget that."

That made me feel better, at least a bit. "Thanks, Constance....Real quick, I have a completely unrelated question for you."

"Hm?"

"How do you know English? I don't really know how old the English language is, but you were from France, right?"

"Yes, that is correct. I learned simple words when I was younger, but Elias taught me how to speak more fluently. He has been teaching me for a little over...five years now. I have had time to get better. It took quite a bit of time to teach, though. He knew very little French."

How much had Elias actually done with the ghosts before me? I know he didn't start looking for people immediately, but he took the time to teach Constance English. It's kind of confusing how he could come in and out of the mansion just fine while I'm stuck.

"I'll let you go to bed. You must be tired."

Constance squeezed my hand. "Do not think too much about what has happened. The mind is a...*fickle* thing."

She glided away to wherever she slept, and I was left standing alone in the kitchen. Again.

I looked down at the table; the plates for Minerva and I had been left untouched. I sighed and put them in the fridge. I'd probably eat them later, if I didn't forget they were there.

I grabbed the other two plates and threw them away. I was glad that Elias brought us the disposable dishes and utensils after Minerva's little episode. He didn't question it—his biggest problem was the waste of nice dishes. Constance hid them somewhere in case Minerva had another breakdown.

The song that had been bugging me for the past month came back into my mind. Once again, there was nothing else except for that vague idea for a melody. Maybe a couple lines, but not much more.

I looked over my shoulder every couple seconds, not used to the feeling of being alone. The last time I could be this alone outside of my room was those first few days at the mansion. Now it felt forbidden.

I hastily scurried to my room. At least I felt safe there.

Just as I settled into bed, I felt a weight shift at the foot of my bed. I poked my head out from under the covers and saw Ray.

"What happened to 'hitting the hay'?"

"Didn't work. Maybe I just needed to have some alone time."

I let out a quick laugh. "It was only fifteen minutes."

"What can I say? I'm a social man. I need people."

I turned over so I could look at him without hurting my neck. "You sound like you'd get along with my friends Rachel and Kayden. Kayden is off at college right now, but he's always been more outgoing than me. One time he made friends with an entire school group on a field trip to the theater. And I can't even begin to *describe* Rachel. She's beautiful, funny, smart, actually *social*...I still don't know why she wanted to be friends with me. She could've been with the popular kids easily, but instead she looked at me and said 'I want the loser.'"

"Oh, come on, Quincey. You're not a loser."

"Maybe not now, but you should've seen me when I was in middle school. My anxiety was worse than it is now, and my social skills were off on vacation in Jamaica or something."

Ray laughed, making the bed wobble.

"Now that I've made you laugh, can I go to sleep? You may not be tired, but I am, and I need my sleep."

He slid off, still smiling. "Sorry about that."

He paused, his hand in his pocket. His smile slowly faded.

"Uhm, are you okay?"

He pulled out his hand and opened it. In his palm was a single coin.

When I looked up at him, tears were in his eyes. "It's my lucky coin. I don't know how I didn't notice it before…I had given it to my brother Rowan, the night before I was shot. I guess he snuck it back without me realizing." He met my gaze, trying to smile as tears started to spill over. His voice cracked as he spoke. "I guess it didn't do me much good, now did it?"

Oh my God, now I want to cry.

I slowly closed his fingers over the coin again, holding his hand. He watched me for a second before running up to wrap his arms around me. He clung onto me tightly, and I hugged him back. I rubbed my hand up and down his back.

"I'm so sorry," I said quietly.

He sniffled and slowly let go of me, backing up.

"You know," he said as he wiped off his face. "We may not have known each other that long, and it may not be for much longer, but I'm really glad you're here. I'm gonna be really sad when you're gone…" He looked up at me, smiling sadly. "You're kind of like a sister to me now."

I smiled back at him, trying not to get overwhelmed by all the emotions I was feeling at that moment. "And I'm glad to have you as a little brother." I lightly pushed him, making him laugh.

"I guess I should let you sleep," he eventually said.

"And *you* need sleep, too, mister."

He smiled and started making his way towards the door. He didn't make it very far, however, because soon someone was standing in between us. That familiar cold breeze passed through the room. I pushed myself as far up against the bed as I could and Ray hid by the door when Wick appeared, adjusting the chains by his sleeve.

"Oh, hello again, Enzo! Or should I say Quincey now that Lyle isn't here?"

"What do you want, candle boy?"

"It isn't so much what *I* want as it is what *you* want. You see, what *you* want to do is calm down the ghosts—" a sick grin danced across his face— "and that doesn't exactly go along with my plan."

"What *is* your plan? You're so vague with your answers, it's not like it will make me want to help you. Who pissed you off so badly that you don't want to help them?"

Wick clenched his fists. Clearly he had *someone* in mind, but I couldn't figure out who it could be. There weren't many people that were relevant to the situation, so unless it was one of the ghosts, no one came to mind. The only other person was Elias, but how they were connected, I wouldn't know. However, there's something familiar about Wick that I couldn't quite place...

"That...*person* is none of your concern. Besides, my initial goal has changed a bit. I need to get a bit more...aggressive." *Seriously, what is it with the vague answers? Come on, people.*

He raised his fists to fight, but before he could, I got a nice hook across his face.

He scoffed, holding his jaw. "What was that?"

I grinned. "One satisfying punch."

"Oh, you're going to regret that—"

Not before I shot off the bed and got another hit. I jammed my foot as hard as I could against his, which didn't do much damage, but it still made him angrier than before.

He shoved his hand around my throat, slamming me against the wall. I clawed at his fingers, but they didn't let go. My head hurt. My eyes filled with angry tears. I couldn't breathe. I couldn't breathe. I couldn't—

Wick buckled as Ray kicked the back of his kneecaps. I knew firsthand how strong his hits could get, and Wick definitely received that strength. "Don't hurt her!"

He pulled Wick's arm away from my throat with as much force as he could muster. I stood there gasping for breath as I realized Ray's downfall.

"Ray, you can't kill him!" I yelled out hoarsely.

"What?"

"He's dead too!"

Ray yelled out a word that no one should be saying at his age and put all his weight behind his hold on Wick's arms.

Despite Ray's small height, Wick had a decent struggle against his grip. Wick wasn't that much shorter than me, but he had much more muscle. I froze in shock. I wanted to help him. I *needed* to help him.

It didn't take him long to break out of Ray's grasp. He got one arm out, and then he pried away Ray's fingers one by one, shoving them far back. Ray yelled out in pain with every finger that pushed back, but his eyes were only filled with fire.

Wick looked down at Ray's hand, which he clutched. "I hope you know now that I *don't* like to be touched."

The threat didn't sit very well, though, because Wick still limped slightly with the leg that Ray had kicked. It may not have done much, but it did enough.

Wick turned to me with an annoyed look. "I'll have to find you at a time a bit more...private. You may not have gotten too hurt this time, but all I need is one vulnerable moment and..." He squeezed his hand shut. "Well, I think you know what I'm implying."

My mind thought of all the worse things, but they all ended in one thing: death. Wick must have known the effect that had, because all he did was smile and disappear. How did he just disappear like that?

Ray looked at me. "That guy's a real pain in the ass."

"Tell me about it. I'm the one he's trying to attack." I paused. "I'm sorry I couldn't help after he started going after you—"

"Eh, I'm fine. Just like *he* can't die, *I* can't die. It's better that I take some damage than you. We still need you here." His eyes were fixated on my neck, the skin still sore.

"Are you going to go to bed now?"

"I think I'll just walk around a bit, actually. That fight really got my blood pumping; I don't think I could sit still if I tried."

I was inclined to agree, however much it sucked for me. With all the panic in my chest, I didn't think I'd be going to bed anytime soon.

Ray left to wander the halls of the mansion, and I was all alone.

I realized my hands were shaky as I pulled the covers over my head. The silence had never been so loud.

Chapter Twenty-Five
A Bar Fight in the Basement

I had been ready to go back to the bar and try my chances with Lyle again, but that didn't happen as life would have it. I woke up with a wicked cold that had me stuck in bed again. Just what I needed.

It felt pathetic to lay down all day, but there wasn't much else I could do. Every time I stood my head would start throbbing, so that left me confined to my bed or the couch. The others brought me food throughout the day, which was nice. We had a theory that ghosts couldn't truly get sick, so they didn't bother to distance themselves from me. Other than feeling the occasional exhaustion, they didn't seem to feel effects on the body, just like how Minerva didn't get overworked during all of our training sessions.

Even while in bed, Minerva and I worked on my poker skills. Minerva still took any chance to nag me about how I could do better, but positive feedback wasn't her strong suit.

Maybe it's the fact that I was sick or that I didn't have enough energy to be anxious, but my poker face had gotten better. I actually remembered all the hands, which came as a surprise to both of us. I would win a few rounds of the game, which may not have been enough to beat Lyle, but would start pushing me towards that.

Wick didn't bother me, which also came as a surprise. It would have been the perfect opportunity: I was sick, weak, and confined to one space. Either he really didn't care as much as he claimed he did, or he's planning something much worse than before. Just the thought of it made my stomach knot. I just had to hope that I could do at least a bit more before he came at me again.

The cold only bested me for a couple of days. By the end of the week, I was ready to get back to the casino.

That morning, as I walked to the kitchen, Constance and Ray were waiting for me, with Minerva nowhere to be seen. It's still early in the morning, but I was still surprised. I cautiously sat down where she usually did; it had the comfiest chair. Even as I sat down, I thought she would magically appear to cuss me out just for sitting in her spot.

"Has anyone seen Minerva?" I asked.

"We have just assumed that she is inclined to stay in her room."

It made sense to me. All that snark must be tiring.

Ray couldn't be still for the life of him. I was starting to get dizzy just by watching him walk around the kitchen so much, practically dancing. "You sure have a lot of energy."

"What can I say? I'm a morning person!"

I groaned and put my head on the table. "I'm not."

Ray chuckled and ruffled my hair. I resisted the urge to slap him right across the face with as much force as I could muster. Instead, I quickly pried his hand off my head. "The hair is *not* to be touched."

"But it's so *curly*—"

"Ray, I love you, but *no*."

Ray sighed and sat down in the spot next to me. His leg bounced from under the table, drawing my attention.

Constance balanced one plate in each hand and set them gently down in front of Ray and herself. "I did not believe you would be awake at this hour, so I only made eggs for Ray and I. Would you like me to make you some?"

I stood up, worried that I'd fall asleep if I sat for much longer. "You just eat, I'll make some myself."

By the time I was done making the eggs, the others were already done. Constance grabbed their plates and tossed them herself as I quickly ate.

"Are you planning on returning to the casino?" Constance asked as I shoveled a bite of eggs in my mouth.

I nodded before swallowing. "I'm tired, but I might as well get back. If I can finish up with Lyle, then maybe I can take a break."

I doubted that I'd actually be willing to take a break once I had him calmed, especially if he wasn't the last one.

This could be the end of my time at the mansion.

I knew Elias had thought there would be only a couple more ghosts after these three, but the reality hadn't hit me yet. As much as I didn't like the near-death encounters, there's still some part of me that knew I would miss it when I left.

I blinked away the tears. I didn't want to think about leaving them yet. They had become like a second family to me, and I wasn't sure I'd be able to let them go when the time came.

I jumped, noticing Ray suddenly beside me. "How long have you been there?"

"Can I *please* come with you this time? I promise I'll be good."

I wasn't even sure if he could get in there without getting kicked out. He was only fifteen and definitely looked the age. Besides, I already didn't want Minerva going, so she'd get mad if I let Ray in. "We'll see about next time, okay?"

That was good enough for him. He nodded and happily skipped away.

"You are not going to let him come next time, are you?"

"Definitely not."

Constance smiled softly. "I believe that it is time for you to go. As you said, once you accomplish this, you can rest. You deserve it."

I tossed the plate and sighed. "Time for another day at the casino."

I had thought that the constant sounds and sights of the casino from before were too much. Everything before me now was absolute *chaos*.

Stools were tipped over. There were several shards of broken glass littered across the floor, various alcohols staining the floor. I heard chanting and yelling coming from a group of ghosts huddled around in a circle.

I had no clue what I should expect. This was a casino in the basement of a magical mansion; you didn't exactly prepare for this. Maybe it's another shadow spirit like the one from earlier that had come to attack. Maybe it's some sort of ghost animal rampaging through the casino with damage in its wake.

It turned out to be neither of those.

Two people were in a fist fight, and who they were shouldn't have surprised me as much as it did.

"*Minerva?!*"

Despite how loudly I yelled, I didn't think she heard me, between the chanting of the other ghosts and being preoccupied with throwing hands at Wick. Minerva definitely wasn't sleeping in like Constance thought.

Loud cheers rose from the crowd as Minerva toppled Wick to the ground with the occasional boo. Blood trickled down from an area close to her head wound. I hadn't been paying much attention to it until now, with the blood now turning it a brilliant red.

Wick's in much worse condition. I didn't know how long they had been fighting, but dark red marks were beginning to form around his arms. Minerva's clearly the winning side of the fight, and as proud of her as I was, I was much more terrified.

I debated whether or not I should put myself in the middle of the fight to stop it myself or try finding someone else. I noticed Lyle to the side by himself, watching it with an entertained look, and decided that I wasn't ready to die that day.

I shuffled over to Lyle, keeping an eye on the fight. Constance was not going to be happy when Minerva went back.

"Shouldn't you try stopping this?"

"I dunno, this is the most exciting thing to happen in a while. And I like seeing Wick get his ass beat."

"I have to admit, it is very fun to watch. But what happens if this, like, I don't know, gets bad reviews?"

"Are you kidding? This could *help* the reviews. Free entertainment, right here at the bar."

"Until customers are too scared to come because they think they'll be attacked."

I crossed my arms, looking up at him. I had a point and he knew it.

He sighed. "You're right, as always. Let me go break the busters up."

I grinned triumphantly as he went over to settle the fight.

I couldn't tell what he said, but whatever he did worked. Wick disappeared from the casino and Minerva ventured further into the games, much to the crowd's disappointment. The circle that had been there only moments before dispersed like scared bugs. Without worrying about Lyle finding me, I followed the path Minerva took until I eventually found her

"Now I know for a fact that you shouldn't be allowed out of Constance's sight."

Minerva sighed dramatically, as though it's unreasonable for me to ask her not to beat people up. "He was being annoying, what else was I supposed to do?"

"Walk away? Ignore him? Do anything *but* fight?"

"That's boring."

I was pretty sure she had something to drink, so I led her towards the staircase, praying that she wouldn't make a fuss.

And she didn't...for the most part.

She flailed around a bit, groaning about how this wasn't fair, and how come *I* get to go to the bar when I don't even *want* to go. All that jazz. I tried muttering back some replies, ignoring the stares from the gray people, but eventually she became unintelligible.

I made sure that she made it out of the conference room and shut the door behind me before going back. Lyle waited at the bottom of the stairs with a knowing smirk. "Are you ready for another game?"

I smiled back at him. "As ready as I'll ever be."

Chapter Twenty-Six
Poison and Other Party Drinks

Lyle grabbed my wrist and brought me back over to the bar with newfound energy. Now that he didn't have to worry about Wick for a while, he began to relax again. He led us to our usual spot and wrapped around to where he stood on the other side of the counter.

He got us set up, but by then I already knew how the game worked. I put in my blind and got more comfortable in my seat. I didn't have anything in my hand, but this game could go anywhere. We talked as we played.

"So, how's your little Ralphie doing nowadays?"

"Y'know, about as good as a kid his age can be." I had no idea how old Enzo's kid was, but he was younger, so that answer felt safe enough.

Lyle's ice blue eyes narrowed slightly, and I gulped.

"Wouldn't he be going to school soon?"

"I, uh, try not to think about him growing up that much. I've gotten attached, I don't know what else to say." At least part of that sentence was true—I had absolutely *no clue* what to say.

"Is Helen's treatment going good?"

I quietly cursed. I had totally forgotten about his wife. "As good as it can be. Having cancer is bad enough, but it's good that she's getting treatment, even if it sucks." They probably didn't have that good of treatment in whatever decade he's from. Maybe the forties, if a war had just finished. "She's feeling miserable."

"I bet. That new stuff they'd be trying must be hard on the body."

I agreed, despite having no idea what this 'new stuff' was. I only really knew about chemotherapy, but maybe there was something else at the time.

"The hospital trips must be rough for the both of you."

For the first time in this whole experience, I could relate to what Enzo went through. I remembered Mom having a heat stroke when I was in eighth grade. All the hospital visits with Dad, wondering if she's going to ever live a normal life again. Dad hadn't lived with us for a long time, but he took care of me when Mom couldn't. Tears pricked my eyes.

"Yeah, you're right."

Our attention to the game had been diverted until Lyle threw down another winning hand. "Yet another win."

"Screw you."

Lyle laughed, which just annoyed me more. Did he seriously expect me to win against him, who actually *worked* at a casino? I didn't care if Enzo's the second best poker player in New York, that's just unreasonable.

He must have seen the frustration on my face, because he made a *tsk* sound. "Guess you've gotten a bit rusty over the years. Would've thought that this practice would make you better at it, but I guess not."

"Shut your face," I said with a scowl.

"You'd like me to, wouldn't you?" he taunted. I wanted to punch him for being so insufferable, but I wasn't sure how much that would help my situation.

"Hey, it's *impossible* to win against you."

He grinned, shuffling the cards. "Not impossible, my friend. Improbable, yes, but not impossible."

I gave him the bird, which only made him chortle. "Good to know that you still have your feisty side."

We continued playing like this for hours on end, going at each other with retorts. I knew that I had won some rounds, but I started to lose track of how many. I sure didn't keep track of the chips either of us had anymore, although our stacks looked pretty balanced. I thought that I could see Minerva out of the corner of my eye every now and then, but I was more focused on the game at hand. If she's still there later, I'd deal with her then.

Towards the end of the rounds, we went back into silence. It wasn't as uncomfortable as it was at the beginning; now there's an air of challenge around us. We still exchanged glances every so often, occasionally holding them longer than necessary to read the opponent.

Lyle, however, was impossible to read. I didn't care what he said about impossibility versus improbability, impossible's the right word. I had no idea how long he'd been playing this, but he definitely had a lot of practice. All that practice under his belt compared to me, with no previous experience before this, made going against him a real pain. Some days I could enjoy his company as much as I could with the constant threat of danger because of his stupid charming self. Other days I wanted to slap him across the face so that he'd take me seriously and *stop taunting me.*

Right now was one of those times on the latter end of the scale. He's just toying with me for his enjoyment at this point. I could tell by the way he smiled after everything I said, as if he's luring me away into a trap.

The upper hand had been going back and forth between us for a long time. He had the lead for a while, but then I'd win a couple of rounds and gain it again. Either I was extremely lucky, or I was starting to learn how to play this well. Considering my previous experiences with the mansion, it's easy to say that it definitely *wasn't* luck.

It definitely wasn't him going easy on me, either. Based on what I knew about him, he wasn't someone who gave pity points.

Then again, how well did I really know him?

After an hour of more playing, we were both too exhausted to continue.

"Y'know what? I think it's time we tally up our chips. We've been playing for hours, it's about time we see our results. Whoever has the most chips wins. Good match, buddy."

I relaxed in my seat, glad that he thought the same thing I'd been. We counted in silence, ignoring my humming. Lyle didn't seem to mind, thankfully—I didn't think I could handle getting yelled at this late at night. If it felt like hours in the casino, who knows how long it actually was.

I took a sneaky look at the time on my phone since the watch didn't work, praying that no one else noticed: *3:48 a.m.*

Jesus, I'd been here a while. I had come at, what, ten in the morning?

I shoved my phone back in my pocket and continued counting, curious how much I had gotten. I was pretty sure that we had each started off with fifty chips, so I guessed that I had *maybe* forty at most. Lyle still would have had the winning stack, even with how long we'd been playing. I had only been playing this for...what, a week? It had been one of the longest weeks of my life. I might as well have been the one stuck here for centuries, not the ghosts.

Alright, that may have been a bit dramatic on my part.

"You done counting?" He eventually asked.

"I mean, maybe? I think I miscounted. I might try again."

"Before you go on to do that, I got something I wanna try." He stood up and walked towards a different part of the bar, his face solemn. I wondered what he was doing until he came back with two glasses that looked nearly identical.

He placed both drinks in front of me and stared at me with an intensity I had never seen before. "One of these has a tasteful drink that would make any glitterati excited. The other has secretly been laced with a special poison just for you. They have a very faint smell difference, and only the real Enzo would know that difference."

This is the catch.

Panic shot through me. It must have been obvious on my face, because Lyle sighed. "You're not the real Enzo, are you?"

There was no use hiding it, and the pain on his face hurt. "I'm sorry."

We waited in silence, even though we had both finished counting our chips.

Eventually, he leaned against the counter. "I've got to say, Mr. Fake Enzo, that was the most fun I've had in a long time. I thank you for that. I can't wait to find out more about you. The real you this time."

Maybe it's what he said, or the way he said it. Maybe it's even the soft smile he gave me. Either way, something about that made my chest flare up with emotion.

Then again, that emotion might still be the fear of the poison sitting right in front of me.

He noticed me staring at the two glasses and moved them to the side, giving me a small smile. "Neither of them had real poison, y'know. Unless you're allergic to grenadine. The real Enzo had always loved drinks with grenadine, and we joked that it would be the death of him. His *special poison*. He could always tell when a drink had some."

I laughed quietly. "You two sound like you were good friends."

"We were. We really were."

I hoped more than ever that I had won this time, because I didn't know what would happen if we kept playing now that he knew I wasn't Enzo. Would there be any consequences from the mansion, or would the worst thing be the awkwardness?

"I don't think you need to check your counting."

"What?" I asked.

"You got fifty-one, right?"

I stared at him with wide eyes. "How'd you know?"

"We each had fifty to start. I only have forty-nine, which could only mean one thing."

I counted my chips again as quickly as I could. He was right—there were fifty-one chips.

I stared in awe between the two piles. "I won."

Chapter Twenty-Seven
Lyle's Perspective

Even from the moment that Enzo had walked in, I knew that it wasn't really him. Whoever this was may have looked just like him and spoke with his voice, but the way he walked and the way he talked gave it away.

It didn't matter to me, though. Having a familiar face in this world of blaring music and strangers was enough for me. It's better than being stuck with Wick for all eternity, that smug little bastard.

I had to admit that even though I knew this guy wasn't Enzo, I still held onto some naïve hope that it had been him. He's one of the only people in my life I had left, one of the only people who understood when I told him my struggles and didn't judge me for them. No one else would listen, and I was desperate to cling to whatever I could get of him. It was pathetic, even for me. And I'd done some pathetic things.

Casinos were designed to muddle your sense of time. Without any windows or any way to tell the time of day, it's easy to get trapped in the glitz of the world of gambling. I had never asked my family why we continued the business, especially in times like the one we were in. It's a miracle that people still came when I couldn't even go to school. Even in the aftermath of a war, my family still sucked the money out of the poor people who came into the casino.

Where was my family? They should have been here with me. I knew I wasn't the only one working that day, but I was the only one here. Wherever 'here' was. As much as this place *looked* like On The Rocks, it couldn't have been. There were almost always people here—no closing time. Sometimes I fell asleep at the bar, but the people were still there. I never got a break. I knew that time felt different in casinos, but it was physically impossible for it to be this busy all the time. It felt like one day was lasting decades.

Maybe I was just starting to lose it.

Usually, I loved structure and routine, but at that point I was ready for change. Anything would have been enough. That had to have played a role in my willingness to welcome this mysterious clone.

We played a few games, had a few laughs. Sometimes they looked like they were ready to slap me, but that's a look I received often.

They intrigued me—they were someone trying to be someone they weren't, like an actor without a script. That situation was all too familiar to me. There were always girls who put on a fake smile and fake laughter if it meant they could spend a night with me, even if they always ended up leaving me in the dust as though I was worth nothing else.

Though I supposed that this was a different situation.

The pretending didn't stop with the women. I remembered the neglect of my father in favor of my other siblings. The family was big, and times were hard. I was older, so I was expected to be more mature and more prepared for the world than my younger siblings. After he figured out my...problem, he stopped caring. I never had a chance to be a child, and I wasn't sure I'd be able to recognize it if given the chance.

I kept my trap shut. If I didn't, my father would let out his anger in more ways than one.

Even in death, I felt as though I disappointed him. The sense of shame may have been more frustrating than what was causing the shame itself.

I pushed away those feelings when playing, however. Poker had always been a means of escape, and it worked well. I had to focus on reading the opponent more than whatever guilt my father pushed onto me.

'Enzo' and I had been playing for who knows how long when I cut it short. That hope I had earlier started to fade away bit by bit, and I didn't know how much longer I could go without bursting. Instead of deciding by the whole pot, I decided we would elect the winner by majority. After a small test, I knew for certain that it wasn't him. I had known that would be the outcome, but I still felt the stab in my chest like a twisted knife.

The stranger had barely won. Winning by only two chips was a feat in itself.

I stared at them as they transformed before me.

His shortly cropped black hair turned into a thick bush of brown curls.

His tan skin paled and became sprinkled with freckles.

His brown eyes, warm and dark, were traded for a pair of fierce gray ones unlike any that I had ever seen.

I had to admit, the woman in front of me was *quite* the pretty girl.

"Pleasure to meet you, miss. Shall we try this again, with the real you this time?"

She sighed with relief and smiled brilliantly. "We *shall*." The way she said it was strange, as though a new word on her tongue. She held out her hand and I shook it, impressed by her firm grip. A lot of gals had dainty handshakes, so it's a nice change.

"I don't think I caught your name during that endeavor," I said when she didn't introduce herself.

"I didn't throw it." I saw a small smile that she completely failed to hide with the joke. Why she wanted to hide a smile like the one she had, I wouldn't know.

"Then can I steal it?"

"Quincey."

That wasn't a name heard often. "Well then, *Quincey*, what happens now?"

She gazed across the casino. "I guess that we just go back to the others."

Others? Other what? More dead people stuck here?

She motioned for me to come around to her side, and I did so. She didn't utter any explanation as she led me away from the casino and my comfort zone. Towards the entrance.

However, I couldn't see it anymore. The entrance was blocked by a large staircase. Had that always been there? It's rather noticeable.

My head started to pound as we walked up the staircase, but I ignored it. I had dealt with much worse, and I didn't want to bother Quincey.

She already seemed much more comfortable than she had before. Her arms were still crossed over her chest, but it looked more relaxed. I fell into stride beside her, her pace slow. Silence hung between us; what was there to say in a situation like that?

"We're almost there," she said eventually.

The walk was much shorter than I previously thought. Were there really people living just above me, only a few minutes' walk away? It's hard to believe, especially with how long it had felt inside the casino.

The moment that we made it, though, I was glad that I stayed in the casino. At least I knew what to expect there.

Blankets were thrown over various pieces of furniture. A chair or two were turned over. A little boy with a shock of blond hair ran out of a nearby room, holding a long stick. A woman in a suit—the same one that had gotten into the bar fight with Wick—wore something indistinguishable on her head, also bearing a stick. Unlike the temperament she had during that fight, she wore a wide smile now. I looked over to Quincey, hoping that she could explain, but she seemed even more confused than I was.

"*En garde!*" yelled the woman from the couch.

They were in some sort of fight, but it looked to be nothing more than playful. Another woman stood off to the side, this one in a burgundy gown. She had a gentle smile on her face as she watched the warriors.

"Is that my walking stick?" Quincey asked. I turned to her in bewilderment.

The sparring woman startled, dropping her stick with a clatter. The little boy made a final strike, knocking the dark skinned woman over. He grinned at me victoriously, but my energy started to fade, so I only returned it with a small closed-lip smile. The headache continued getting worse, but it felt disrespectful to bring it up at that point. This lot didn't seem to mind disruptions, however.

"*Hi!*" the little boy exclaimed, rushing over to me. Beside me, Quincey let out the briefest laugh, similar to the way Enzo would while telling a joke. The memory of him ached my heart. The last time I had spoken to him was in the heat of an argument. I couldn't even remember what it was about. It's too late now—I'd never see him again.

I looked down at the boy, trying to distract myself. "Hey there."

"I'm Ray! You're Lyle, right? How did you die? How long have you been here? Do you know what year it is? I don't even know what year it is—"

He continued rambling, overwhelming my mind. I could not figure out how so many words came out in one breath.

Quincey cut him off, much to my gratitude. "One at a time. I know you're excited, but he's literally never been outside of the casino before. Give him some time to adjust before the question tornado."

"You said your name was Ray?"

Ray's eyes sparkled as he nodded.

"We should be getting to bed," Quincey said. "It's four in the morning, and I don't know about you guys, but I've had a long day."

Ray groaned. "Do I have to?"

"Yes, please," said the woman in the crimson dress, the first time she had spoken. Where's that accent from, France?

"*Fine.*" He huffed, crossing his arms, before leaving.

Quinccy looked at me and sighed, her pretty smile gone. How disappointing; it's a welcome sight. "I'm sorry about him. I forgot how...*excited* he can get. He's probably just ready to have another guy around."

"No, no, it's alright. No need to apologize. I think I'll be inclined to get some shuteye soon, though. Y'know, tired."

It wasn't completely true, but she bought it. "Then I'll make the next couple introductions quick." She led me over to the two women. "So, the one in the dress is Constance. And the one in the suit—"

"Ay, I remember her from the bar fight."

The woman in red, whom I had learned was Constance, glared at the other. "You were in a *bar fight*?"

"A mighty entertaining one, too."

The black woman looked away, though her face still beamed with pride.

"You said you ran into a door!"

"...whoops?"

"The one who's about to get strangled by Constance is Minerva," Quincey said with a chuckle.

Minerva stood for only a few moments before scrambling away. Constance chased after her with surprising speed, despite the thick skirt. Their footsteps echoed down the hallway as they went farther and farther away, leaving me alone with Quincey again.

Quincey looked around. "Ugh. I forgot to get Ray to clean this up."

"Would you...like some help?" I didn't know where anything went, but I could make an attempt.

"No, *you* need to rest. Based on what I've learned, it's pretty important after getting calmed."

I couldn't figure out what she meant by 'calmed,' but that's a problem for a different time. Calmed or not, I did need to lay down, if only to help the pounding of my head. "Where do I sleep?"

Quincey blanked. "I actually have no idea. Usually you guys decide your own rooms, but I don't even know where most of them are. Do you want some help looking around?"

Having someone with me would be enjoyable. "I don't see why not."

She walked up beside me. "I can clean this later, anyway."

I didn't have any idea where to go, so I let Quincey lead the way. We walked down a different hallway than the one Constance and Minerva had gone down, opening up doors as we went. A lot of the rooms were empty or filled with seemingly useless things.

"What exactly are you doing here?" I asked. "I don't think you just happened to move into a mansion with multiple ghosts."

"I mean, that *is* kind of what happened. I'm the only *living* person here—those three are ghosts like you. I got asked to help you guys, and I agreed. Sometimes I still ask myself if I should have signed up for this mess."

That wasn't much of an explanation, but I couldn't complain. "Do you know how many there are?"

Quincey shrugged, opening another door. "There shouldn't be too many more after you."

"What does that mean for y—"

"Found a bedroom," she interrupted, gesturing to the room inside. "Is there anything else you need?"

I got the impression that she didn't like the continuous questions, so I stopped. It wouldn't be polite to annoy the person who helped you, I suppose. "Outside of a nap, I think I'm good for now. Are you sure you don't need help cleaning after the mess in the parlor?"

A look of confusion spread over her face for a brief second. "Oh, the living room. I'll be fine on my own, but thanks. You need sleep."

"It looks like you do as well," I noted. There were circles rimming the bottom of her eyes, however faint.

"We don't talk about that."

I smiled. "Goodnight, Quincey."

"Make sure you get some sleep. These first few days are the worst." She turned to go before looking back over her shoulder. "Oh, and goodnight."

She scurried away, presumably to clean up the mess in the parlor. I continued looking in the spot where she had been long after she had left.

She seems like a sweet cookie, though I can't say much for her friends yet. This is going to be interesting, that's for certain.

I closed the door behind me to my new bedroom, curious as to what she meant about the first few days. I decided that I'd have to find out in the morning and pulled myself to the bed, embracing the comfort.

Chapter Twenty-Eight
Hangover Cure and Caramels

Thankfully, it didn't take long for the living room to get cleaned. Despite how messy it had seemed at first glance, there wasn't actually much to clean up—a couple chairs here and there, blankets to be folded, and the two sticks. I knew immediately which one had been used as a crutch only a couple weeks ago. There's a swell of satisfaction as I put it away, hoping that I'd never need to see it again.

By the time I was done, I was about ready to fall asleep on the floor. I made it to my room and crashed as soon as I hit the bed. I was pretty sure that was the first time I had ever fallen asleep so quickly.

I woke up the next day with a surprising burst of energy. Maybe it's because I wasn't terrified for my life anymore, but it had been the best I had gotten. Even the long naps I had taken in bedrest weren't very helpful.

It was already well past noon when I woke up. Minerva, Constance, and Ray were having casual conversation at the table, but Lyle was nowhere to be found.

"Lyle hasn't come out yet," Minerva said when she noticed my searching. "It'll likely take him some time to get used to being away from the casino."

I sat down beside them, a bit disappointed. "Yeah, you're probably right."

"Would you like to check in on him later?"

"Eh. I'll let him rest."

The rest of the day went on normally, however much left. When Lyle didn't come out the morning after, though, I started to get worried. I knew that it was just my anxiety being stupid, but it still took a bit to keep convincing myself that he's fine and calmed.

"Quink, if you're that worried, just knock on his door. You know where it is, and he's probably awake now." Minerva rolled her eyes like it was just common sense.

"What if I'm botheri—"

"He's been dead for who knows how long and only had Wick's annoying ass to keep him company. You can't be worse than Wick."

She had a point.

"So are you going to go? Or are you just going to stand there?"

"Come with me?"

Minerva sighed and walked over to me. "Underneath all of that sarcasm you are the most awkward person I have ever met. Come on, let's get you going before you back out."

I started the way to Lyle's room, vaguely remembering where it was. I knew it's on the right side…maybe it's by the room with the closet I had hid in? I couldn't remember, but I'd hopefully know it when I got to it.

I had a good feeling that we had found the room—I recognized the room across from it. I took my chances and knocked on the door.

I was met by a loud groan on the other side. "*Go away.*"

"Maybe a hangover?" I whispered to Minerva.

"Definitely a hangover. Give me five minutes and I'll see what I can do."

It didn't surprise me that Minerva knew how to treat a hangover, despite the fact that she probably wasn't even of legal age. I had no clue what the legal age had been in the fifties, but I couldn't imagine it being much younger than twenty-one. I also didn't know how helpful remedies would be if they were from the fifties, but it's a good place to start. Even if it's outdated, she still had more knowledge than me.

I wandered back to the dining room, where Constance waited with an exhausted look on her face, rubbing her eyes. I had never seen her look so tired. "Didn't sleep well?"

"No. I worried that something may happen."

"What?"

Constance went quiet, looking towards the kitchen. "Do you remember when Minerva was first calm and she had that fit you mentioned? She was yelling and throwing dishes at the wall, hence why we switched to paper plates?"

It's hard to believe that was only a couple months ago—I had almost forgotten about it. "Yeah, I do. What about it?"

"What if that was Wick?"

I had thought the same thing before, and it made more sense the more we learned about him. He had been bugging Minerva in the past, so it wasn't out of the picture.

"I thought that it was going to happen again with Lyle, and that he may attack something...or someone."

"I think we might be in the clear for now. He's a bit...preoccupied at the moment."

"How so?"

"He's hungover!" Minerva called from the kitchen.

"Ah, I see." I didn't think Constance actually knew what it meant, but I didn't want to be the one to explain it to her.

I tried thinking about what I could do next. As tempting as the idea of taking a break was, I worried that Wick might start interfering more now that I got close. There should only be one or two more ghosts, if Elias' prediction was correct. I wasn't sure what kind of recognition there would be when I had helped them all, but I thought I'd feel...something. Maybe some glorious light from the heavens would shine down on me, or at least Elias could acknowledge that I was done with a little trophy or something. It could say "Congratulations! You Stayed Alive!"

"Maybe I should start looking for the fi—"

"*No.*"

I was startled by the intensity of the word. "No?"

"No. You are *not* going to risk your life further without a break."

"I would hardly count playing poker as 'risking my life.'"

"What I *mean* is that you have been overworking yourself. You have yet to take a willing break since you arrived here, and that was nearly two months ago. You forget that you have needs as much as the rest of us, perhaps even more so. You need to give yourself time to relax before continuing on!"

I could barely tell what she was saying. "Constance, *slow down*."

She took a deep breath. "I apologize. I just hope that you understand what I am trying to say."

"I think I do." Just because I understood it didn't mean that I liked it.

"I agree with Constance," Ray said from behind me, making me jump. When did he come in?

"Okay, okay." I didn't know how to tell them that I just couldn't bring myself to take a break. I needed to be useful; I didn't care what I was doing as long as I helped. I needed to be in control of something, or else everything in my life would unravel like a ball of yarn.

At the same time, part of me didn't want to tell them. They were my friends—at least *I* thought so. I trusted that they knew how to help, however stubborn I was about what they were suggesting. They cared about me.

"Quincey? Are you alright?"

I pushed away my thoughts. "What? Yeah, I'm fine. I just...is there something else I can help with? Anything at all?"

Constance smiled. "I am certain we can think of something."

Lyle's hangover lasted on to the next day. And the day after that. And the day after *that*, too. If he wasn't already dead, he probably would have died from alcohol poisoning.

Minerva had to have been doing some sort of witchcraft, because he improved a lot every day. She didn't seem to enjoy it, though. I was pretty sure she's only helping him to make sure I didn't try to myself. There's a good chance I would mess it up if I did, anyway.

I stayed away from them most of the time. The most I did was check in on Lyle when Minerva needed a break and make sure he had everything he needed. We had started to have regular conversations without him snapping at me towards the end. Well, as regular as you can get with someone who's from the forties.

Finally, after four very long days, he was back to normal.

"Sorry for all that," he said. "Hangovers are a pain."

"I guessed so. Can't say that I know first hand, though. That was my first time having a taste of alcohol."

Lyle laughed. "I could tell by the face you made when I gave you Enzo's drink."

I hid my face in my hands, groaning. "Oh God, was it that obvious?"

"Painfully so."

"Ugh." I fell back onto the couch, and he sat beside me. I could practically feel his eyes tracing all over me like he was trying to solve a puzzle. I resisted the urge to curl up into myself—I didn't like feeling analyzed. "What are you doing?"

"Trying to figure out what kinda struggles a gal such as yourself could be dealing with nowadays," he said nonchalantly.

I resisted the urge to ask him the obvious question: *why?*

"Do you want to entertain the notion and explain?"

"Considering the fact that I thought you were going to kill me less than a week ago, I don't think we're quite at that level yet." I said it with a bit more venom than I intended, but I wasn't too keen on explaining all my problems to someone I just met. I may have known him for a bit already, but that was different.

He averted his eyes. "Sorry."

I sighed. "It's not your fault. It's this damn mansion's fault. In case you haven't realized it yet, the constant paranoia of being killed hadn't really been a part of my life until I moved in."

He leaned his head against the back of the couch. "I would hope not. A life like that isn't one for someone like you."

I bristled. "What's *that* supposed to mean?"

"I mean that your heart's too kind. It's soft and warm, and it ain't built to withstand the craziness of the life you have now."

He acted like he had known me for years, not days. Even then, it felt nice to hear that. Well, I was pretty sure it was a compliment, but I couldn't tell.

Lyle turned to look at me again, now curious. "What's it like now? So much time has passed since I've been…well, *alive*."

"Well," I started, "a lot has changed. We still have some problems as a country, but things have gotten a lot better." It felt bizarre to talk about the present with someone who hasn't been around since the forties. Even though so much has changed, I couldn't figure out what to say. "More people have rights now, which is good."

We sat in an awkward silence.

"What about your family? Do you mind telling me about them?"

"Uhm, it's just me and my mom. She divorced my dad when I was four because they both realized they basically just married their best friend and didn't love each other that way. He moved to the U.S. when he was…seven? Eight? I don't remember. He still visits us a lot with his girlfriend, Mimiko, like for celebrations and holidays, but I only live with my mom. I don't think she's dated in, like, a year. Always says she's 'waiting for *Señor Perfecto*.'" I paused. "Oh, and I was named after my grandpa on my mom's side. He disappeared right before I was born, so that's kind of interesting. Said he was going to visit some island and never came back."

He watched me with curiosity. I felt like I just sounded weird, so I changed to a more normal topic. "Uh, I don't remember what my dad does, but my mom works at a diner as a manager."

"What diner?"

"Uncle Driver's Pizza."

Lyle's eyes glittered. "Ay, I remember that place. We had one in the neighborhood. Very popular place because it was one of the few businesses that *didn't* go bankrupt. They kept their prices at just the right place to keep the people coming."

"Really?" My voice jumped an octave, startling him. "Sorry, I just didn't know there were any buildings outside of town. I guess that ours is the original, built almost a hundred years ago and redone."

"That's fantastic."

"Pizza is disgusting," Minerva said, making a *blegh* sound. I hadn't even realized she had come in. "It's so greasy."

"Go away," snapped Lyle. He had been calm for not even a week and they were already at each other's necks?

Though, to be fair, it happened to Minerva and I after less than a day.

"Hey, what's with the attitude? I didn't do anything wrong."

"I just don't like you, you idiot."

"Oh, *I'm* the dumb one? That's coming from the guy who thinks that bananas are disgusting."

"Because they are. Haven't you ever had one?"

"Of course I have, you idiotic *bastard*."

It didn't surprise me that Minerva had already found something to argue about with him. I tried to hold back laughter at their petty argument, but it wasn't enough to stop a small snort. I quickly covered my mouth when I saw them turn to me, but it took a bit to stop shaking.

"Wow, Quincey, I didn't know you were a little piglet," Lyle said with a grin.

"Oh, shut up."

"And what if I don't?"

"Then I'll tape your mouth shut myself."

"Looking forward to it."

I rolled my eyes despite the smile that started to creep up on me. I was glad that we were getting along so quickly—it's much easier to start off on a good note than a bad one, like how I had started with Minerva.

I leaned back into the couch, loosening up a bit. I hadn't realized how tense I was until I finally gave myself the chance to relax. I looked to my right and saw Lyle sprawled out comfortably, his arm resting on the back of the couch. Minerva's still watching us with a discerning look, as though trying to solve a puzzle.

Lyle turned to face me. "Tell me more about them. Your family, I mean."

"Well—"

"She has a dog!" Ray chimed in. Was he there that whole time, too? "She brought it up earlier when she was practicing with Minerva!"

Lyle sat up straighter, raising an eyebrow that begged to know more. "Practicing what exactly?"

"In case you hadn't noticed," I said, "I *suck* at poker."

"We practiced *nun-ya*, pretty boy," Minerva chastised.

"Aw, you think I'm pretty," Lyle rebuked, winking towards me with a grin.

"Pretty damn stupid."

Lyle gasped dramatically, standing up quickly with a hand over his heart. "The pain. It's real. And here I was, really thinking we had a connection."

Minerva whipped her head towards me, her eyes practically bulging with anger. When did they start to turn brown? "Quink, I'm going to strangle him."

"I'd rather you not."

"*You can't stop me.*"

Lyle was spared by chance because that's the moment Constance walked in. I may not have been able to stop her, but Constance could every time. "Minerva, dear, please calm down. Now is not the time to get angry with him."

Constance must be some sort of siren, because Minerva relaxed instantly.

"Thank you. Shall we go on a quick walk?"

Minerva reluctantly agreed, and I was left alone with Lyle and Ray. Lyle had awkwardly sat himself back down on the couch, and Ray sat on the floor in front of us.

Out of nowhere, Ray pulled out a handful of caramels. "I have some more. Want some?"

"Where do you keep getting these?" I took one anyway and immediately popped it into my mouth. Lyle cautiously grabbed one as well, unwrapping it and placing it in his mouth gingerly.

"Constance still hasn't noticed that I am taking them."

Considering how many he must have taken over the past month, I was starting to think that Constance *did* know and just chose not to bring it up.

Lyle picked up another few, shoving them in his pockets. "I don't care how he got them, they're *good*."

I sighed and sank farther into the couch. I pulled a folded blanket off the side and wrapped it around myself, feeling a sudden chill. My eyes naturally went in search of Wick, even though nothing else would have suggested he was there at all. My heart raced in my mind at the mere thought of him showing up.

"Quincey, are you okay?"

"Huh?" I chewed the caramel and swallowed it. "I- I'm fine."

Lyle frowned. "You certainly don't *look* fine. What's—"

"I said I'm *fine*," I snapped. I immediately regretted how harsh I sounded when I saw Lyle's hurt expression, but I also didn't want to talk about Wick, so I ignored the guilt in my chest and left it at that. Besides, that wasn't exactly a polite thing to say, anyway.

I checked the time on my phone and briefly looked at the date, ignoring the confused look on Lyle's face.

"Oh."

"What?" Ray asked.

"It's Halloween."

I adored Halloweeen, so I was surprised that I hadn't even noticed it coming up. I had been hoping to spend the day with Rachel, but clearly that wouldn't work. A wave of guilt flowed through me. We had been talking about it since the beginning of August and even had some matching costumes picked out.

I glanced back at my most recent conversation with her. There wasn't much to it; just her asking about any bizarre encounters and how I was doing in the 'rich oldie's' mansion. That was what she called Elias. I didn't bother to correct her.

I missed her so much.

"Well then," Ray said as he pulled an unreasonable amount of caramels out of his pockets and began to divide it into piles, "it looks like we'll have to do what we can with what we have. I hope you guys don't get sick of caramels easily."

I raised an eyebrow. "What?"

Ray motioned for us to join him on the floor. I scooted down, and Lyle did shortly after. He pushed one pile to Lyle, one to myself, and kept one. "We may not be able to do trick-or-treating, but we can still eat some candy."

I knew I was going to get sick of caramels soon, but at that moment I just wanted to hug Ray as tight as I could. After a brief thought, I realized that would be weird and settled on enjoying the sweet goodness of the caramels.

We went around the circle telling jokes and funny stories. As dark as life in the mansion had been, it was a relief to have something good happen for once.

Lyle and Ray both went from telling either funny anecdotes from their lives to making up scary stories. They both definitely had a knack for storytelling. I laughed alongside them, throwing in my own occasional stories.

The mansion was scary, but right now, we were *happy*.

For the first time in what felt like an eternity, I let myself enjoy the moment without worrying about the problems of the future.

Chapter Twenty-Nine
You've Missed a Lot, Dude

That moment of joy was only that: a moment. I got brought back to the harsh reality of what was really happening when Minerva and Constance had returned. Lyle and Ray were laughing at something, but all of my attention had been turned towards the two behind us.

"...truly think that she is prepared to take on someone else?"

It didn't take a genius to figure out they were talking about me. It wasn't like there were many other options. I sank down, hoping that I hadn't heard them correctly but knowing that I had.

"She *has* to be ready. We've been training her for two months, and she's made so much progress. I know how important rest is, but too much can make her lose what she's got going so far. If she loses that, she'll be in even more danger than before."

I hadn't noticed Lyle and Ray had stopped laughing until they were looking at me with pity.

"Quincey? Are you okay?" Ray asked.

He took my silence as enough of an answer. He leaned in, lowering his voice. "Does it have to do with..." He rolled his eyes over to Minerva and Constance, who were still talking. "You know."

I glanced over at Lyle, but he seemed just as worried as Ray. I wasn't exactly thrilled at the idea of Lyle hearing my problems after knowing me for less than a week, but I didn't think I'd get away with hiding it from Ray, so I just sighed. "Yeah."

"Well..." He never finished his sentence.

"Can I add something?" Lyle asked. I turned to him, not realizing until then how close he had gotten. I moved back slightly, careful not to hit the edge of the couch. He waited for me to nod before continuing.

"I know that we ain't known each other for that long, and I don't have a *single* idea of what you've gone through. Based on what I've heard, it's a lot. But I trust that you'll make it through this. Clearly there's something about you that makes you strong enough, because you've made it this far already. It doesn't matter if you take a month-long break or no break at all—you'll be fine either way."

I wasn't sure how much he knew about what I was doing here or what it meant, but he sounded so confident. How anyone could have that much confidence in a person, I didn't know.

"That's what I was gonna say," Ray quickly added. "Definitely."

I laughed quietly. "Thanks for the encouragement guys."

"Of course," Lyle said with a smile that warmed my chest.

I sat up straighter and felt a buzz coming from my pocket. I pulled my phone out again and saw a message from Mom: *did you find any ghosts yet?*

I smiled down at the screen. *Only a couple. Some of them are mean.*

I hope they aren't too bad. Can't have you leaving too soon.

I doubted that she knew I was being sincere, but at least telling her the truth felt like a weight lifted off my shoulders. It made me feel bittersweet; as much as I wanted her to know what's going on, I didn't know how to tell her without her thinking I got a brain injury. I'd explain it to her when all of this was done and I could leave the mansion behind.

If I leave.

It was hard to forget the constant threat of death that hung over my head, but I somehow managed to for a brief moment. It didn't make me feel any better about the whole thing.

"What is *that*?" asked Lyle, pointing to my phone.

"Oh, this." I looked down sheepishly—I had forgotten that he wouldn't know what it was. "Uhm, this is a cell phone."

"Huh?"

"It's like a landline that you can carry in your pocket," Ray filled in. "Did I get that right?"

"Basically, yeah. There's a few more things it can do other than calling people, but that's the big one."

I fiddled around with it, hopping back to my music browser. "I really like to listen to music, so I use this a lot. It can play pretty much anything, as long as it has been published. Sort of like a radio, except you get to choose what you want to listen to."

I remembered explaining it to Ray however long ago, but it's still weird. Being the only one who knew about anything modern was a weird experience in itself. Was there anything from when they were alive that they thought was going to stick around but didn't? How much was there to learn?

"What would it have been like if I hadn't come here?" I didn't realize I had thought out loud until Ray answered.

"Boring. Maybe safer, but definitely boring."

I couldn't argue with that.

Minerva and Constance had stopped talking. I stood up and turned over my shoulder to see them looking at me with the same pity Lyle and Ray had just given me.

I don't need pity right now. I need a break.

"Why are you looking at me like that?"

"Just...wondering about some things," Constance said, her voice uncertain.

"What is it with you and being more ominous than you need to be?"

"Life is simply more entertaining that way." She smiled. "Now then, would any of you like to help with dinner?"

I thought I had dealt with torture from Minerva's relentless training, but the awkwardness at the table was an obstacle I hadn't accounted for.

We sat there in silence, unsure of what to talk about. I sat between Lyle and Ray, with Minerva and Constance sitting across from us. I was surprised that there were more chairs; we still had three that sat empty. The food was delicious, sandwiches and salads, that made me feel like I was eating from the deli.

"I really thought you guys would be more entertaining than this if I'm being honest," Lyle said to fill the awkward silence.

Usually we found something to talk about, but something must have changed from the conversation that Minerva and Constance had earlier. Between that and the fact that we had someone new at the table, there's a lot going against our usual routine.

Suddenly, I noticed Minerva starting to bristle in her seat. I couldn't figure out what would have made her tense, though. Maybe she's still frustrated about what happened earlier, but it's impossible to tell with her.

"May I be excused?" she asked through gritted teeth.

"You've barely eaten—"

"May. I. Be. *Excused?*"

Constance sighed. They exchanged a look with some sort of telepathic communication before she relented. "Go. Come back when you are ready." Did she know what's going on?

Minerva stood up and walked away, though it looked more like marching with how stiff she was. The anger felt as though it had come from nowhere; there wasn't much that could make her that angry that quickly anymore. The last time she had been like this without a reason was that first day, when she was throwing the plates and someone was bothering her...

Wick.

I hadn't seen him in a few days, but he managed to creep into my thoughts every day despite that. I thought about Constance's theory about him bothering the other ghosts. If they were angry enough, could that undo all the progress I had done?

197

"Not only do I have to find a way to calm down another ghost, I also have to find out how to defeat Wick. Whatever that means."

Part of me wondered if he *was* the fifth ghost, but he seemed different than the others. He's clearly angry, but he still saw me as myself, and he could disappear and reappear at will. Not only that, he definitely had at least a bit of magic...did *magic* exist? Other than Wick and the mansion itself, there wasn't any solid proof, but it's the only way to describe everything I had gone through.

"Who's Wick again?" Ray asked.

"The angry ghost you keep having to fight when he comes into my room."

"Oh. *Him.*"

"Woah, woah. Hold up. The child did *what*?" Lyle turned to Ray. He sounded shocked, if not a bit impressed. "That guy's a real menace, and the *kid* of all people tried to fight him?"

"You got that right!" Ray beamed. "I scared him off, too."

Lyle rubbed his temples. "Are you *asking* to get killed?"

"I can't die a second time," Ray said, motioning to his bullet wound.

With how lively all of them were, it's hard to remember that they weren't *actually* alive. Anytime I thought of ghosts or zombies, it's obvious that they were undead. But other than Ray with his wound and Minerva, who even then slowly started to look more normal with her eyes starting to show color, they all appeared just as alive as I was.

I heard the sound of a knock, faint from the distance. I recognized the knock; he always knocked exactly four times. "I think that's Elias."

"Who's *that*?" Lyle asked.

"He's the reason I'm here in the first place. He comes every few days to make sure we don't run out of food." I hurried to the door and opened it, greeted by the anxious smile of Elias. I hadn't had fresh air in so long. It was surprisingly cold. I looked down at Elias' hands, which were each carrying multiple bags, and then back up at him. I wasn't sure how, but he looked older than when he had last come.

"Hello Quincey, it's a pleasure to see you. Constance has been the only one answering the door lately. I see that you're out of bed?"

"Yeah. I'm feeling great. We actually got the fourth ghost calmed down."

Elias' eyebrows shot up. "My, that is impressive."

It felt awkward to not let him in, so I stepped to the side. "We're eating dinner right now. Do you want to come in?"

He laughed nervously. "Oh, no, I really shouldn't. You seem to have everything all figured out. Besides, I have to go home and…well…tend to my cats. They're nasty little devils."

If he's lying to me or not, I couldn't tell. I didn't care either way. It's much easier to think about him having a life outside of this mansion than if he spent all of his time wondering about what happened inside.

I stared at the distance between us. It was only a few steps, and I couldn't even take them. I'd just end up back to where I was right now. Then again, I hadn't tried since that first time, when I first learned about Ray…

I must have spaced out, because by the time I looked up I stood alone, holding all the grocery bags that had just been Elias' hands.

"Weirdo," I muttered as I headed back to the others.

"Ay, would you look at that? The lady has come back with gifts!" Lyle called out when he saw me.

"And finally, more food than just chicken and breakfast food!" I set the bags down, glad that they weren't very heavy. "Can I get some help putting stuff away?"

Lyle stood up immediately and began taking food out of the bag, occasionally asking about and judging Elias' food choices. As long as it didn't require a lot of effort on my end, it's good enough for me. Constance could spice it up if she wanted.

With his help, we got done pretty quickly. When I walked back to the dining table, I saw Ray sneaking some of my food onto his plate. He froze midway through a transfer, like a robber being caught in the middle of a heist.

"Take as much as you want. I'm not really hungry."

Ray's eyes sparkled as he pulled the plate closer to him and continued eating. Constance had finished her plate and put Minerva's in the fridge.

I yawned, my eyelids starting to droop. "Man, I don't know what's up with me. It's like I never sleep anymore, or I'm always sleeping too much."

"Just go to bed, you'll be fine. We'll try not to miss you too much," Lyle said jokingly.

I rolled my eyes and bid them goodnight before escaping to my room. Going to bed right after dinner had become a regular occurrence, but I wasn't complaining.

My anxiety loved when I laid down, because that's always the best time for it to sneak up on me. Many thoughts went through my mind, but I managed to push out most of the ones that weren't relevant or didn't make sense. Adrianne taught me some tricks to filter my thoughts, like the memory cabinets.

How long had it been since I last saw her? My last appointment was early August, I think. Maybe late July. We had been talking about college and how scared I was for it, but she said it's okay to be scared. When thinking about the future, I still needed to stay grounded to the present.

I tried to stay grounded, but my thoughts kept drifting. So, instead of staying tethered to the real world, I decided to push myself away from it. I plugged in my headphones and put on a relaxing playlist, falling asleep to the soothing melody and soft words.

Chapter Thirty

I Need a Break (Feat. Gary)

We didn't do much for the next week; Minerva had relented to Constance's pestering and agreed that an extended break was necessary. She would still put me through small tests—from throwing random things at me to 'test my reflexes' to asking me random riddles, much to my confusion. I loved riddles, but the riddles from the fifties were a bit weird. Even with the break that I knew they wanted me to have, I still felt guilty about taking it. Why should I be resting when I could be helping them?

I'd brought up that concern a few times, but I was always met with some variation of the same answer: *you deserve it*. It didn't matter how many times they said it, though. No matter how they said it or how many times they did, it still wasn't enough to make me believe it.

I had been spending most of my time with the others, which I was glad about. After Halloween, the awkwardness between me and Lyle died down—I was surprised with how comfortable I could be around him. Being around everyone was great, but I needed some alone time without it being in the middle of the night.

I shut myself in my room and grabbed a pencil and my notebook. Originally a diary filled with the angsty thoughts of my fourteen-year-old self, it had slowly been turned into a songwriting journal. There were pages and pages of lyrics, but not a single note to be found. When looking at some of the older ones, I could still remember the tune to a few of them, but most had been lost to time.

There were a couple decent lyrics from my early years, but a majority weren't amazing. I even noticed whole pages that were crossed out; damn, how long had it been since I looked through this?

I knew I wanted to write *something*, but I didn't know what. Usually I found inspiration in what happened around me, but there's not much to go off of when you're stuck in a weird mansion with dead people. Either that, or there's too much to go off of but not nearly enough things that actually made sense.

Just when I thought I had some inspiration, I heard a knock at the door. I groaned, the thought disappearing with my alone time. Thankfully, there was only one person who stayed here that knocked, so it's easy to guess who stood on the other side.

"You can come in," I said, shoving my notebook to the side.

Constance gently opened the door, just as I thought she would. "Hello, dear. I know that you wanted some time to yourself, but I had an idea that I wanted to speak to you about."

I moved over to open a spot for Constance, motioning for her to sit. "Ask away, my lovely friend."

Constance sat in the now empty area, leaning on her arm. "Well, I know that you have been very stressed as of recently. You want to get going on the next ghost, but we need you to take a moment to relax. I am starting to believe that all of this relaxation has become too…" She stopped mid sentence. "What is the word again? When there is too little going on that you become overwhelmed?"

"Boring?"

"No, not that," Constance waved away the idea. "It is boring but more…stressful?"

I shrugged.

"That is not important. What I am trying to say is that perhaps we should do something that still gives you something to do *without* risking your life. It would not be stressful, just entertaining enough to bring you out of this drift you have put yourself in. We will do something that is actually *fun*."

I wasn't sure what she meant by *drift*, but I was open to the idea…whatever she'd meant. "Any ideas?"

"Perhaps something like a party?"

I thought for a moment. A party *could* be fun, but how would you throw a party for people with nearly five hundred years of culture between them? "What kind of party? There isn't much that we all know."

"Whatever you would like. I may not understand what they all do, but I will do my best to learn."

"No, I want you to have fun, too..."

I glanced back at my notebook and had an idea. "How do you feel about a dance party? At least a party themed around music, anyway."

I may not like dancing in front of people the most, but I was slowly starting to get more comfortable with the idea of it. It wouldn't need to be anything too fancy, anyway—I could just use my phone and speaker and play some music. Everyone likes music, right?

"That sounds delightful. Shall I tell the others to plan on it being this evening?"

"If you wa—"

I got cut off by the sound of a loud, high shriek. At first I thought there might have been a little girl, but I didn't know where it would have come from.

"GET THAT DEMON SPAWN AWAY FROM ME!"

"AWWWW, IS THE TOUGH GUY SCARED OF A LITTLE SPIDER?"

Between the yelling and Minerva's loud and wicked laughter, I was more than a bit scared to leave the room. But I also didn't want them to kill each other—again—so I just sighed.

"We're going to have to break them up, aren't we?"

"I suppose we are."

I rolled up my sleeves and ran out of the room, Constance following close behind holding the skirt of her gown in her hands.

"AY, PRETTY BOY, YOU'RE GONNA MAKE MY EARS EXPLODE!"

I needed to cut this off before it escalated more. "Can everyone *shut up*?!"

They turned to me in dead silence. I hadn't seen so many emotions in the same room before. "Jesus, I haven't had to yell like that in a long time."

Ray excitedly held up a spider. "I found a spider! I want to name him Gary."

"If you love that...*thing* so much, why don't you just marry it?" Lyle spat out, scrambling to put distance between him and the spider.

"Oh God—I never thought—Lyle would be—this *terrified*—of spiders." She cackled between every few words.

I personally loved spiders; the idea of people being scared of them usually seemed comical to me. Still, I felt compelled to defend him. "Hey, my mom's scared of spiders, too."

Ray grinned. "I'm certain that Lyle isn't your mom."

I gently reached for the spider, much to Lyle's horror, and led him onto my hand. "Gary's going outside now."

"*Noooo*," Ray booed.

Lyle's face changed from horrified to thankful, and I gave him a small smile as I brought it to the front door and let it out. I came back shortly after, hearing Constance explaining the dance party to Lyle and Minerva. Ray stood deflated in the corner, so I had no idea if he heard anything that Constance said.

"It ain't gonna be a...*formal* dance, right?" Lyle asked. I would have thought he was nervous, but that wasn't an emotion I associated him with. The whole 'nervous energy' thing was more of *my* thing.

"Not at all. I doubt that Quincey wants that, either. Think of it as something more casual."

I joined them, standing beside Constance. "Oh, definitely *not* formal. I think Constance here is the only one who would know how to dance for that."

Lyle looked relieved.

"Well, I've certainly had my fair share of sock hops. I have nothing to worry about." Minerva turned to look at me. "You, on the other hand, may need to learn how to dance."

"You haven't even *seen* me dance."

"I don't need to. You can barely keep up a good stance when fighting, I can't expect you to look graceful while dancing."

"I'm pretty sure fighting and dancing are two *very* different things."

"Besides," Lyle cut in, "I bet that she's an *amazing* dancer."

I definitely didn't think I was *that* good, but I also didn't want to give Minerva the satisfaction of knowing she was right. I crossed my arms and grinned triumphantly at Minerva. "See, *someone* thinks I can dance."

"He was just screaming like a little girl over a spider; I don't think his standards are that high. He also hasn't seen you fight *or* dance."

Lyle narrowed his eyes. "You've clearly never had a giant spider crawl up your leg in the middle of the night and try to lay eggs on your stomach."

I shuddered just thinking about it. "Damn, glad to say I haven't either."

Minerva rolled her eyes. "It doesn't matter anyways. I'm just saying that we will all *clearly* know who the best dancer there is."

"If you say so," Constance added with a small smile. "Just refrain from showing off your dancing *too* much, or else we might learn from it and become better than you."

"You are absolutely right."

Nothing Constance just said made sense, but Minerva would agree with it anyway. Constance must have known that, too, because she gently grabbed Minerva's hand. "Would you like to go warm up? You must not have gotten the chance to dance in quite a while."

Minerva flashed a rare genuine smile. "I haven't. I'll be back soon."

With that, she retreated in the direction that I assumed led to her room. Constance turned to us with a loving but exasperated look. "She really can be a handful."

"Tell me about it," I mumbled.

"Well, I ought to rehearse my dancing as well. Let us hope I still remember what I learned when I was younger." Constance curtsied and left.

I looked around for Ray, but he's nowhere to be found. Probably off looking for another spider to torment Lyle with.

I fell back onto the couch, and Lyle crossed his arms, looking down at me. "Don't sit quite yet, Quincey."

"What?"

"Minerva's right—I haven't seen you dance, so I have no idea if you can. I also don't *like* it when Minerva's right, so let's prove that I put my faith in the right thing."

I turned to look up at him with a raised eyebrow. He held out his hand to me with a sly smile. "What do you say, princess? Shall we dance?"

Chapter Thirty-One

Don't Ruin Our Dance Party

I took his hand and he hoisted me off the couch, continuing to hold on after I was up. "Have you ever danced before?"

"Obviously I have. But if the question is 'have I ever danced *well* before,' I can't guarantee anything."

"Well, we're changing that today."

I rolled my eyes with a smile on my face. "What are you, a dance instructor?"

"Only a gentleman."

He took a small bow, looking up to me with a brilliantly confident smile. When he stood back up, he put the other hand on my back, pulling me closer. I could see his chest rising and falling. We were so close—I hoped he couldn't tell how fast my heart was beating.. Mine wasn't usually so...fluttery.

"You'll want to look down at my feet to start. I'll go slower right now, but it goes much quicker when you're in the moment."

He released his hand off my back and grabbed my other one, looking down. He shuffled his feet around, pausing every couple seconds when I tried to recreate it. I felt like a giraffe on roller skates, but he still gave me encouragement every time. Soon, we were blending multiple steps together and going quicker.

"You're doing fantastic. Are you sure you've never done this before?"

"Positive."

"I never would have guessed. But learning the foot movements like this is the easy part. Now you have to do that while being tossed out and pulled back in."

I groaned, making him chuckle. I glared at him with annoyance and gave him a light shove. "I'm glad my displeasure is entertaining for you."

"It's not your displeasure, it's the cute face you make when you're frustrated."

"Oh, shut it. You're just flattering me at this point."

His only response was a smirk and a raised eyebrow. "You may never know. Do you want to try the steps while moving now or later?"

"Might as well get started now."

He counted us off and we started dancing. I fumbled around a bit, stepping on his feet repeatedly, but he didn't complain once. He just smiled and told me to try again. How he had this much patience with me, I didn't know.

"You'll get it eventually, it just takes time. There are a couple things you'd need to learn to do it the proper way, but it doesn't matter with you. We can call it...the *Quincey way*."

I laughed. "The 'Quincey way' is just incredibly failing and someone ending up with an injury. It's a good thing that the Quincey way isn't real."

"I find the stumbling quite charming."

He didn't need to be so polite and nice all the time; it made it hard to tell when he's being serious or when he's joking. That distinction's pretty important.

We continued practicing. I finally started to get the hang of it, even if it took a million tries to get that far. Once I was confident enough, I asked him what kind of songs you were supposed to dance like this to.

"Swing, mainly. It's very jazzy."

I stepped aside and played the first playlist that showed up, which was thankfully from the forties. He held onto my hands as the music started.

"You better tell me when to start."

"Not to worry, cookie."

It wasn't as fast as I thought it would be, which made it easier. I struggled to not step on any feet—both mine and Lyle's—but I got into the swing of it (pun intended) after a couple songs. I was surprised at how gentle he could be.

"Okay, Quincey, you gotta tell me something."

I was confused and automatically a bit scared. "What?"

"That first day after you 'calmed me down' or whatever. When we came back, Minerva and Ray were doing that duel, and you said something about your walking stick. What happened? You certainly don't need it now."

I glanced down. I didn't want to think about it much. "I just got hurt pretty bad the day I calmed Ray down. Made it hard to walk for a bit."

I could see Lyle's face processing what I said. Before he could say anything, I cut him off. "I'm fine now, though. It just took me some time to get my strength back after being stuck in bed for a majority of the time for the next couple weeks."

He slowed down a bit. "Are you *sure* you're okay?"

"Yeah, I'm sure."

Even as I reassured him, the way he looked at me changed. I couldn't quite describe it; it might have been pity. Or maybe even frustration. To whom though, I wouldn't know.

By the time the next song came on, it was as though our conversation had never happened. I felt more comfortable that way, more safe. I was perfectly fine with not talking about it, but it still felt like it put a border between us. I didn't want borders.

Hopefully he'd just forget he asked.

"Quincey?"

I hadn't realized we'd slowed to a stop. His hands were still holding mine. "Sorry, what?"

"The music stopped."

I looked at my speaker and saw the light that signified the battery flashing red. I cursed under my breath as I let go of him and walked over to it, double checking. "Looks like the speaker died. I'll go plug it in—I'm pretty sure I brought the plug. It should be ready by tonight."

He tried saying something, but I was already heading towards my room in search of the plug. I felt his eyes follow me as I left. I wrapped my arms around myself, trying not to think too much about the dancing. I went into my room and quickly plugged in the speaker after a bit of scouring for the charger. We didn't *need* to start the party at any specific time; I could just grab my speaker again in a few hours. It'd be fine.

Everything would be *fine*.

I took a deep breath before leaving. When I got back, Lyle was right where he was when I left.

"Sorry about that, what were you trying to say?"

"I was trying to say that we don't *need* music to dance. We can make the music ourselves." He started to hum a bit, though I couldn't tell what song. He grabbed my hand and spun me around. He didn't make it much longer before he started coughing.

"Eh, maybe not that. I'm better at guitar. Besides, there's gotta be some dances from the present that you can teach me."

If our talk from earlier was still on his mind, he's good at hiding it.

"I promise you, you do *not* want me to teach you how to dance. I only know basic moves that probably won't even make sense to you. They look kind of weird, anyway."

In reality, I just didn't want to make a fool of myself in front of him. It wasn't like I was trying to *impress* him by any means, but I was a total wreck. He always acted so...put together. I was as far from it, and I didn't want him to see that, even now.

"Alright then, if you're oh so inclined to avoid teaching me your mystical ways, I suppose I'll just have to guess."

"What?"

He stood for a moment, contemplating his next move. Just as I thought he started to space out, he grabbed my arm and pulled me back to him, catching me off guard.

He must have noticed my startled expression. He quickly let go. "Sorry, I should have asked. I don't want to scare you. But you can't expect me to become an expert dancer of the present when you're all the way over there."

"No surprise grabbing." Even as I glared, I realized I hadn't actually been scared. I rarely let guys that were anywhere near my age close to me; Kayden's the only one, and that's because he had a girlfriend. Usually I didn't want to get that close, but I actually found myself drawn to Lyle—both metaphorically and literally.

Even as I thought it, I didn't like the sound of it.

"You're not going to let this go until I show you something, are you?"

"Definitely not."

"Okay, fine, you win."

I stepped back a bit, putting enough room between us to move and calm my nerves. Despite all the simple dance moves that I knew, not a single one came to mind the moment I had to use them. Of course they came at random times of the day but not when I actually had to *show* someone them.

"Come on, can't be getting cold feet now."

"Well go on then, big guy. Show me what *you* think it'll be, and I'll work from there."

"*You're* supposed to be showing *me*, not the other way around."

"I think it's time you figure out that I absolutely *suck* at trying to explain something. I can learn easily enough, but the moment I'm trying to teach someone else, all of my knowledge goes out the window." I looked over to the nearest window. "Oh look! There it goes, flying away!"

"Well you taught me you're bad at acting, so that's a start."

"That's different! I had no script or any basis for a character. I'm actually a pretty good actress."

"Not important. Just add some dancing in there and you're all set."

"Are you saying that I'm a bad dancer? Because I thought you were trying to prove to Minerva that I wasn't." I started smiling a bit.

"God, no- I- you know what I meant. Just give your best."

I sighed dramatically, trying to think of what to do. Everything was either embarrassing because it's easy enough for a nine year old to understand or embarrassing because it's too complicated for me to even try. I bobbed around a bit, resembling something like a buoy.

"If that's what dancing looks like now, I've lost faith in humanity."

I stifled an awkward laugh. "I promise it's not."

"Then *show me*."

I gave up, admitting defeat. It would be awkward to not do it at that point, so I started doing some simple moves. "I guess you just copy what I do?"

Lyle didn't even try. "Wow, you really are a bad teacher."

"Rude."

"Can't say I'm the rude one if you said it first."

We were both laughing, and I grabbed his hands to pull him closer. There's one *actual* dance I knew, albeit a short one, but it required two people. "Ready for a partner dance?"

Lyle smiled, sending a weird feeling in my chest. If I needed to live with him I'd need to get over whatever anxieties I may feel around him. It's starting to freak me out.

"Now we're getting somewhere. Give me your best."

I guided our arms, putting one behind our heads and pulling apart, our fingertips barely touching. It took a few tries for him to get the movement right, but it helped that we were close to the same height. I wasn't sure how to explain the spin, so I just led his hands to where they were supposed to go.

He didn't stop smiling. "Maybe you can't explain things well, but you can demonstrate them just fine."

I wasn't sure how we kept ending up so close together, but we did. His face felt so close to mine, and it's hard to look away despite the way it made me nervous. His blue eyes searched my face for something I couldn't figure out. Wait, was his left eye always a shade lighter than his right?

We waited there for a few heartbeats, our breathing falling together. There's no one else around us, nothing dangerous to keep an eye out for, and the physical contact's suddenly much more noticeable than before. My heart pounded loud enough to follow me up to my head. How did I manage to feel so scared yet so safe?

He opened his mouth to say something when I heard the sound of running. I quickly put distance between us without thinking. In only a couple seconds, Ray ran into the room. He skidded to a halt when he saw us.

"What were you guys doing? It's been two hours."

"Nothing," I said at the same time that Lyle said "dancing." We glanced at each other for a brief second.

"I don't think *dancing* is the same thing as *nothing*."

Ray took one more glance between us and shrugged. "You're acting weird, but I don't care as long as you're done now. I want to get the party started."

"Minerva and Constance aren't here yet," Lyle pointed out slowly.

"Well, they better hurry. I wanna dance!"

Right on cue, Minerva and Constance joined us, holding each other hand in hand. Minerva looked uncharacteristically happy—well, as happy as she could look with her naturally angry expression. Whatever they'd been doing had gotten Minerva in a better mood, which was good.

Ray grinned from ear to ear; he must have noticed it, too. "Now that everyone's here, who's ready to start the party?"

The party was only really a party to start. We weren't immediately in the mood to dance, but I hurried to get my speaker from my room and started playing music. I stuck to a playlist I saw that had jazz with some rock and roll. Constance was confused when it first started, but she found her footing quickly. Ray was happy to dance by himself, and that left me with Lyle or dancing by myself. Not wanting to look pathetic, and maybe something else, I chose to dance with Lyle. For some reason, however, I couldn't bring myself to. I had just been dancing with him only minutes before—why did it suddenly feel so hard?

After a few awkward minutes of us looking at each other then looking away, I finally gathered enough courage to go back up to him. Even though I knew everyone else was doing their own thing, it still felt like there's someone watching us.

I pushed away the thought. They were doing this to help get my mind off things. I should be enjoying it instead of worrying about…I wasn't even sure what I was worried about. There's the constant feeling of anxiety I usually felt, but it's something else…

"Shut up," I whispered to myself.

"I didn't say anything!"

"Sorry," I muttered. I'd forgotten that I was still standing right in front of Lyle, not even doing anything. I reached over and grabbed his hands, fiddling around. Nothing's happening, but my eyes still drifted towards our hands. Just like before, every bit of contact I had with him had suddenly felt much more obvious.

One of my favorite songs came on, though I could never remember the name. It's a random song from the seventies. I liked the other songs we'd been playing, but I knew the reason this one stuck out: it's one of the only songs I actually knew choreography to. It's the song that had the move I taught Lyle earlier.

"Want to try that move?" I asked.

Lyle beamed. "Of course."

I tapped my foot until the part came, and whispered *go*, just loud enough for Lyle to hear. We tried the move, and I got hit in the face with his elbow, but it still sent a wave of euphoria. I'd originally earned that dance with Rachel, and doing it made me feel a bit closer to home.

Lyle chuckled. "You seem surprisingly happy for someone who just got elbowed in the face."

"Shh, don't take this away from me."

"Take what away?"

The joy I feel. The sense of safety. The comfort of being with people I care about. The feeling of being so clo—

"Nothing." I interrupted my own thinking. The thought made my cheeks burn. Despite the warmth in my face, I felt a cold breeze pass through the living room.

I froze in panic, my heart jumping. My breathing hitched. I clenched Lyle's hands until they turned white at my fingertips.

"Woah there, what's got you so—"

He stopped mid sentence. His expression changed from concern to fury.

"Come on, did you think you could throw a party without me?"

I didn't need to turn around to recognize Wick's voice from behind me. "I've always thrived in environments like this. Music is truly the way to the heart, wouldn't you agree, Quincey?"

"Don't turn around, don't acknowledge him. Keep your eyes on me," Lyle whispered. "He can't hurt you when I'm here."

I knew what he said wasn't true, but the words eased my mind, if only a bit.

Lyle snapped his head up, looking in the direction that I assumed Wick stood in. "If you want to lay a *finger* on her, you're going to have to get through me."

Wick shrugged. "Easy enough."

I didn't see what Wick did, but in a matter of moments my hands were empty. Lyle was no longer in front of me; he slammed against the wall to my left. I resisted the urge to yell right there. I wanted to run to him, but I couldn't.

An invisible force confined me to a small square. I couldn't figure out how to break free, and soon, I stood face-to-face with Wick.

"Let me go!" I fought against the invisible cage, my arms stuck to my side. The others stood frozen in fear, or maybe they had been confined, too. Constance and Ray were terrified, but Minerva looked ready to whoop Wick's ass in another bar fight. I still couldn't see Lyle or know if he's okay.

"Clearly words weren't enough." Wick pushed back his sleeves, the chains trembling, as a wicked smile spread across his face. "I didn't want it to come to this, but I don't think getting you to *leave* is working anymore. Now, I just need to get rid of you for good."

He walked up to me, but I had lost all movement. All I could do was watch this unfold like a movie instead of being the main character that lived through it. When he got close enough, I spat in his face. "You're sick."

Wick huffed, wiping off what got on his cheek. "Then you better pray you don't feel ill."

He clocked me square in the jaw, throwing my head. The chains hit me with a second slap of hard metal. Everything in my head was sore, but I didn't have much time to think about it, because I was getting hit again in the gut. I inhaled sharply with every jab. He may not have been hitting much, but he knew how to make it *really* hurt.

I may not have been able to move my body, but I could still move my neck. As he got close to my face to make a taunting sneer, I slammed my head as hard as I could against his nose, ignoring how much it hurt.

He stumbled back, holding his nose. I couldn't see through my tears, but it clearly did something.

With more fury than before, he threw more punches, each one knocking the wind out of me. The whiplash didn't help, either. I stopped keeping track of what happened around me.

He got a hard hit that made me double over, but before he could punch again, he fell on the floor. I rubbed my eyes, glad I could move again, but my vision's too blurry to see much. It's still easy to tell who's on the floor with Wick, though.

"*Don't. Touch. Her.*"

When my vision cleared, I saw Minera getting Wick hard. Constance stood to the side in fear. Ray came by me and looked over the spots that he had been hit, making sure there's nothing too horrible.

I heard Wick grunt with every hit. Lyle had scrambled over to help Minerva, the first time since he had calmed down that they worked together. He held Wick down as Minerva kept making hits.

"GO—" *Punch.* "AWAY—" *Punch.* "NOW!"

Wick stopped fighting. For a second, I thought he was dead.

But then he opened his eyes and smiled, his smile bloody. Before disappearing, he said one thing:

I'll be back.

Chapter Thirty-Two

Try Not to Die

I ran up to Minerva and Lyle and wrapped my arms around them tightly, ignoring the growing ache at my side. My head pounded, but that's something I could worry about later; all that mattered to me was them.

"Are you okay? Did he get you bad? Oh God, how could he hurt—"

Minerva cut me off before I could continue rambling. "We're fine, nothing more than a few hits and scratches, but you probably got the worst of it. How are you?"

I reached up to my face and felt something wet. When I pulled my hand back, there's a mix of tears and blood at my fingertips. "Oh. That's new."

Constance and Ray scrambled over to us, both of their arms filled with various medical supplies. Ray, looking a bit nauseous, threw his stack down on the ground when he reached us, and Constance handed me a box of tissues. "Here. For the blood."

I laughed then groaned from the pain. I grabbed a handful and wiped off my face, staring at the stained tissues. Were bloody noses usually that...bloody?

Lyle's breathing heavily but didn't look too hurt. His cheek looked red from a hit, but there wasn't much else. He looked me up and down with worry, but his fists were clenched at his side. "That prick got what he deserved. Look what he did to you."

"I mean, it wasn't much worse than Ray's fighting. This is just the first time I got hit in the face, which is *not* fun."

Lyle reached for my shirt, and I instinctively tugged it down.

Minerva pushed my hand away. "We've had to revive you from near death, a little bit of tummy isn't gonna do anything." She lifted my shirt just enough to notice the large red mark where I guessed a bruise would form.

"I don't think I've ever seen a human punching bag before, but here we are," Minerva muttered.

Despite the pain I was in, I still managed to give her my best glare. "Stop it."

"When you stop getting beat up all the time."

"For the first few weeks, *you* were the one beating me up!"

"Not relevant."

I didn't have any more energy to fight her on it, so I just relaxed. Constance handed me an ice pack and I held it against my stomach. My nose still throbbed, but we only had so many ice packs, so I decided that the hit on my abdomen was the bigger issue. I actually didn't know if we had any more ice packs, but it wouldn't make sense to have more than one. It's just like home; we only had one, which I was now realizing wasn't very smart.

I got hit by a sudden wave of homesickness. I wanted to be with Mom and Oliver. I wanted to be with Rachel—she would have been back from New York by now. Kayden would still be at college, but maybe he'd be visiting for the holidays. Even if I did make it back home, would I be able to go back to the life I lived before?

My hand started to burn from the cold of the ice. I squished the ice pack into the crook of my arm and covered my hand with my sleeve before putting it back. At least it wasn't as painful to touch anymore.

"So," Constance said slowly, "we see now that Wick is beginning to become more volatile."

I hadn't mentioned the encounter with Wick where he had tried choking me, but I guess that's different—*I* had initiated that fight. This was out of nowhere.

Constance continued. "As much as I regret to admit it, I believe that we know what is to happen next."

We waited in silence, but we were all thinking it: *time to risk my life again.*

I took a long shaky breath. "You're right. We need to keep moving. If Wick is getting this dangerous, we need to get to the next ghost before he gets to me. Is there anything we know?"

"Quincey," Lyle started, "you just got attacked, give yourself time to relax."

"Doesn't mean I can't learn what I can in the meantime. Do any of you know anything?"

None of them said anything, but that's enough of an answer for me. "Well then, I guess it's time for me to start exploring."

"You're sure as hell not going alone," Lyle interceded. "I'm coming with you."

"Can I come too?" Ray added.

"You'll clearly need backup if Wick comes again, and—"

"Okay."

Lyle was ready to keep going but froze. "Uh, just like that? No fighting for help?"

I sighed. "Yeah. You're right, I'm gonna need all the help I can get. You're offering, so what's the point of saying no?"

"When are we gonna go?" Ray asked excitedly.

"*After* Quincey gets the chance to rest up a bit. I don't care if it's five minutes or five hours." Even Minerva's in agreement, which was rare to come across. I guess that had to be some sort of sign.

I fell back onto the couch in defeat, knowing that any fight against Minerva would be a losing one. "Alright, fine. I'll wait here for...an hour. That's it. Then I'm going to start exploring."

"I suppose it's better than nothing."

Minerva rolled her eyes and walked away, bringing Constance along with her. Ray sat on the couch beside me, and Lyle paced in front of me. He didn't seem very attached to reality at the moment—he's muttering to himself with *lots* of hand movements.

"Can you please stop pacing before you wear a hole in the rug?" I asked in a lighthearted tone. "I don't know how old it is, but it looks nice."

Lyle stepped off the carpet and sat on my other side, an arm on the back of the couch. "How do you resist the urge to slap Wick across the face every time you see him?"

I thought back on the encounter where he tried choking me and smiled. "Eh, can't say that I have *every* time."

He looked at me with a tired grin. "I wish I had your level of patience. Even that much would be an improvement to what I have right now."

I pulled out a small rubber ball from my dress pocket—I *loved* dresses with pockets—and fiddled with it. I'd forgotten it was in there, but it gave me a distraction.

I tossed the ball against the floor, catching it as it came back up. "Oh, trust me, there isn't much to long for. I'm just usually more focused on trying not to die than worrying about how annoying Wick's ass can get."

My eyelids started to droop. I leaned against the couch, turning on my side. I didn't want to ask them to move, so I just hoped that kicking them could work.

I wasn't even fully down when Lyle stood up. "You probably want the couch, don't you?" He tapped Ray's shoulder, who hadn't stood up yet. "Come on, kid, let's give sleeping beauty some time to nap."

Ray sighed and pushed himself off the couch.

"Want me to wake you up in an hour?" Lyle asked.

I nodded, already feeling sleep starting to cling to me. I felt more vulnerable than I was comfortable with, but my exhaustion overpowered me. I pulled a blanket over myself and drifted off to a deep sleep.

I woke up slowly. I instinctively reached to turn on my bedside lamp, forgetting that I was on the couch. My back rested against the armrest as I heaved myself up. It certainly didn't feel like I'd only slept an hour. "How long was I out?" I muttered to myself.

"A few hours."

I startled, looking down at Lyle, who's laying down on the floor. "How long have you been there?" I narrowed my eyes. "Were you watching me sleep?"

"Not *watching*. I had tried waking you up after an hour, like you said, but you didn't. So I decided to wait here until you woke up. Besides, you look cute when you're sleeping. Talked a bit, too."

I threw the blanket over my head and tried not to die of embarrassment. "Please don't tell me I said anything stupid."

"You said a lot of very smart things."

I pulled off the blanket and looked down at him. "Oh really? Like what?"

Lyle spoke in a higher and obviously mocking voice. "*Lyle is amazing, Lyle is hot, Lyle is so perfect—*"

I threw the pillow I had been resting on at his face as hard as I could. "I would not have said that. And I definitely do *not* sound like that."

Lyle caught the pillow before it hit him and tossed it back, laughing. "It was worth a shot."

I ran my fingers through my hair, hoping to get out at least some of the tangles. I didn't even want to think about the horrible bedhead I must have at the moment. If Mom were here, she would have taken a picture instantly.

I relented—the curl gods had won today. I grabbed a hair tie from my wrist and tied my hair up in a ponytail.

I sat up, dangling my legs over Lyle's chest. "You might want to move before I kick you."

He pushed himself up, but not before tickling my feet. The tickling didn't work much in his favor, though, because that just prompted me to kick him even harder anyway. He barely dodged a blow to the face as he finally sat up, leaning back against his arms. "You're ticklish?"

"You say that like it's surprising."

"It is. Only because *I'm* not."

I had a hunch that he's lying, but I didn't really care. "Sure you aren't. Come on, I need you to get Ray. We've got stuff to do."

He stood. "So, you're actually letting us come with you?"

"If you don't take a century to start *doing something*, yeah. Now help me up before I melt into the couch."

He smiled and pulled me up. He hollered for Ray, who came shortly after.

"That was *not* an hour," Ray grumbled.

Without much more thought, we started our way through the mansion without a single idea and praying that it wasn't going to go completely, horribly and utterly *wrong*.

Chapter Thirty-Three
Another Evil Shadow Thing?

Something told me it was, indeed, going to go completely, horribly and utterly wrong. But there's no voice from the heavens or versions of me from the future telling me not to do it, and that's good enough for me.

I had almost forgotten that I was still in a blood stained dress until I looked down and startled myself. We put the adventure on a brief pause so I could go back and get changed.

While looking for something else to wear, I had some time to think. *Am I really ready to start looking again?*

It didn't matter anymore if *I* thought I was ready; I would need to be no matter what, both for myself and the ghosts. If I didn't finish this, they might never get freed. Besides, I didn't even know if I *wanted* to leave them—they were my friends now. Maybe even family. Would it be worse now, knowing they were so close to...whatever came after this? Or would they go back to how they were before, angry and dangerous?

This was either the end of my life, or the end of the ghosts.

I wished there was a way so that neither could happen.

I put on the same shirt I had worn on my first day here. The stain from the hot sauce's still there—had I just forgotten to wash it? I thought my life was a bit weird before coming here, but now it looked like a paradise where the most I had to worry about were the awkward conversations I'd have with Mom's friends.

I met Lyle and Ray outside of my room. "Okay, *now* let's go."

We started towards one of the many hallways of the mansion that I'd never gone down. I didn't think I'd ever explore the mansion in its entirety. It's off the path to the ballroom, which I hadn't even gone to since the very beginning. I couldn't remember where the trigger to the secret room was, but I knew it was there somewhere.

We walked in silence, not having much to talk about. Silences were rarely comfortable for very long. Well, it was mostly silent—Ray had gone up ahead, talking happily to himself. Lyle and I were just following behind him, because he seemed to know where he's going.

"What's your shirt about?"

I looked down instinctively, even though I knew what I was wearing. I felt somewhat embarrassed, though I didn't know why. "Uh, it's this rock band I really like."

"Rock band? Do they play with rocks or something?"

"Uhm, okay, I'm not really brushed up on my music knowledge, but I'm assuming rock music hasn't started yet in your time. Well, I don't know how long ago the electric guitar was invented, but it has a lot of that. And drums. It's not a super popular music style anymore, but I still like it."

"You'll need to show me sometime. If you enjoy it, it has to be worth a try."

I'd never had anyone who wanted to try something I liked *just* because I liked it, and it sent flutters in my heart. Even Rachel hadn't shown much interest in the few things we didn't already have in common.

"What about you? What kind of things do you like, other than beating everyone at poker?"

Lyle shrugged. "There wasn't much to do when I wasn't working. I liked listening to the radio, when I could. I learned a few songs on my guitar."

"Oh yeah, you mentioned that earlier. Do you play it often?"

"Not much. It belonged to my mother, and she taught me how to play notes and chords. After that, she left it up to me to learn whatever songs I wanted to. I couldn't do much without having someone to actually *teach* me, though."

"Huh." My mind whirred with a million thoughts that refused to stay still, but *that's* the only thing that came out?

"Do you do anything musically? Other than dancing, of course."

For a second, I contemplated telling him about my journal that sat on the bedside table. I decided against it; not even Mom knew about it, and I didn't know if I was ready for anyone to know yet. "Nothing big. I listen to music, sing sometimes, but not much more than that. I know some basics on the piano, but I was never that good."

"We may just need to duet sometime. If I could find a guitar here."

I laughed. "I doubt it, but the thought's still nice."

"How much of the mansion have you explored, anyway? You've been here for nearly three months, yet you still don't seem to know the layout that well."

"That's because I haven't done much exploring. There isn't anywhere else I need to be other than the areas I know already."

"Alright, then how'd you find the casino?"

I thought about what to say carefully. "Well, there's this map I...*found* a while ago. I thought it was broken at first, because it said you were in the same room that Ray had been in." I pulled out my phone to show him a picture.

He grabbed my phone and held it close to his face like an old man, making me crack up a bit. If he had a regular life, he *would* be an old man by now, if he was alive at all. "How do you see anything on this thing? It's so *bright* and *small*."

I shrugged. "It's just like a supercomputer, but much smaller."

"What's a supercomputer?"

There's so much history I needed to teach without any knowledge. "I'm not even going to try explaining it. Maybe Elias can."

"Ah, *Elias*. The man who signed you up for this mess, correct?"

I nodded slowly, confused. Lyle seemed almost angry at Elias, but I couldn't figure out why. Last I had checked, other than being annoyingly vague with the job description, he hadn't done anything wrong as of recently. He brought food and drinks so that I wouldn't die of starvation before being killed by this psychotic mansion.

"What's got you so worked up about him?"

"'Cause," Lyle started, "he's the reason you're always an inch away from death. He's the reason you're stuck with us, and Wick, and whoever the hell the others are. And don't get it in your head that that means I'm not glad I met you. As a matter of fact, I'm *elated*. You're wonderful. I just wish that seeing you didn't also require seeing you throw yourself at the next dangerous thing. I wish we could have met in better circumstances."

Unfortunately, he had a point; there were a *lot* of dangerous experiences in the past few months, way more dangerous than what I should be facing. With everything in mind, it's surprising to remember that Wick wasn't even the one who attacked me most of the time. That's the first time he had ever gotten physical without being aggravated, and while I couldn't say I was happy about it, it just meant I would have to work twice as hard to keep myself and the people I care about safe. Because now it wasn't just myself I had to worry about—it's the ghosts, too.

Before the dance party, I wouldn't have cared what Wick thought. He couldn't even bring himself to be much more than a nuisance. Besides, I didn't think he would do much since I had the ghosts with me. But something about the party had changed my mindset; now he's not just an annoying teen trying to mess around. Now I hesitate in front of every corner, afraid I'd run into him.

I hadn't realized that my breathing had hitched until Lyle reached out to give my shoulder a quick squeeze. "You don't look so good. How can I help?"

Not 'tell me what's wrong.' Not 'it'll get better eventually.'

How can I help?

Lyle's willing to help without even knowing why. It's such a small detail, but it meant a lot more than I thought it would. I may not have known him long, but he already reminded me of Mom; wise, kind, and fun. When everyone else as a teenager hated their parents, I could almost always able to talk to Mom, and sometimes Dad, too.

My chest felt like it'd burst into a flurry of butterflies, which kind of annoyed me. I would need to grab some insecticide if my heart kept going like this.

I didn't even know that I had begun to spill everything out until there was nothing left to spill. I talked about the stress from Wick, the anxiety of having to leave them, everything. Ray's far enough ahead that I didn't need to check if he could hear.

I was out of breath by the time I was done. I hadn't gone on that much about...well, *anything* after Rachel had left for New York at the end of June. I might as well have been talking to her and not a ghost.

"Anyway, that's been bugging me for the past two and a half months now." I tried smiling and playing it off as a joke, but Lyle saw right through it.

He didn't say anything, though. He just watched me, and I stood still right next to him. Ray's footsteps were fading into the distance, but he seemed to be fine for the time being.

Suddenly, Lyle wrapped his arms around me in a tight hug.

Usually I was the one who initiated the hugs, and getting hugged by someone else with no warning was *not* a fun surprise. Especially not Lyle, with his curious eyes and laid back personality. He's so confident and relaxed; both things I could never be. If *he's* worried, something had to be wrong.

Still, something's different about this. I didn't really know how to respond.

He must have noticed my tension, because he started to pull away. "Sorry, I forgot about the 'no surprise grabbing' thing, I should have asked—"

I cut him off by pulling him back in, clinging to him tighter. I hadn't been hugged like this in a long time, I didn't realize how much I needed it until that moment. I rested my head on his shoulder as he wrapped his arms around me again.

People didn't usually hold me this way. I couldn't tell if it scared me or made me feel better. It just seemed like there's something about Lyle that made me feel like I would be safe no matter what happened.

"No, it- it's okay," I whispered. It surprised me even as I said it.

The moment shattered like frozen glass at the sound of Ray's voice.

"Uh, guys? You might want to see this…" His voice sounded far away, but the panic's still obvious.

I pulled myself away from Lyle, still holding his arms. "That can't be good."

Then there was a scream.

Any self preservation I had went out the window, and all instincts took over. I bolted down the hallway as adrenaline rushed through me. *I needed to get to Ray.*

Lyle followed shortly behind me, but I was already starting to feel the pain from the sudden sprint. Even with all the training, I still got winded quickly. But I ignored it, because if Ray's this scared, it had to be *bad*.

When we reached Ray, he was being strangled by another shadow.

I skidded to a halt. The memory of my last encounter flooded my brain, and my feet were cement blocks. I still had the scar on my thigh—I could just hide it most of the time.

The shadow had its dark tendrils wrapped around Ray's entire body, gagging and strangling him. I could see him struggling to break free with what little mobility he had. He knew he was trapped. His eyes were the only things visible, wide with fear. He tried to scream, but there was only a muffled sound.

The shadow snarled at Lyle and I, reaching out his black limbs.

Lyle frantically looked back and forth between myself and the shadow before shoving me off to the side, making me fall to my knees. My kneecaps stung as they started to bleed, but I still pushed myself up.

Lyle fought off three tentacles, but at the same time two more came at me the moment I was on my feet. Right now I really wished I had Minerva. Jr. with me, because yet another tentacle formed beside me. Come on, how many times can this shadow-monster-human-whatever-it-is create random arms out of its body?

I swerved out of the range of the shadow and ran right to the heart of the creature, where Ray's being held captive.

"Quincey, what the hell are you doing?!"

"Trying to free Ray, now ignore me and keep fighting!"

"YOU'RE GONNA GET KILLED!"

I ignored him and ripped at the tentacles, surprised that I could actually grab a hold this time. With the last one I had faced off against, I couldn't even get a grip.

But I had a different problem; *how am I supposed to defeat this one?*

I had forgotten what I was doing for two fateful seconds and was given the absolutely *brutal* reminder when a limb swept across my stomach, knocking me to the side. Its tentacle wrapped around my waist as I struggled to break free. I have no clue if this was the same shadow as before, but this thing's *strong*.

"I knew something would go wrong…" I grunted as I pushed against its grasp.

I glanced over at Lyle and saw he's holding his own, which gave me a bit of confidence. Before I knew it, I got whipped across the room by the dark appendage. Lyle yelled my name as I hit the wall with enough force to knock the wind out of me. What was it with me and getting slammed into walls?

After a bit of squirming, I found my way out of its hold. The one advantage of being lanky was that I could get myself out of tight spots, which wasn't relevant most of the time but saved me here.

I looked at Ray, who's getting weaker and weaker. I put as much distance between the creature and my body as I could without worrying about getting attacked. My neck's starting to ache—it must have been from the slam.

The neck.

That was the weakness of the last shadow, and I prayed it's the same with this one. How would I be able to reach it, though? Ray's right where the neck appeared to be, and there's no way I was going to hurt Ray.

Lyle's now on the floor, kicking away the tentacle.

"Lyle, how are you holding up?"

"Absolutely *amazing*, thank you! No help needed *at all*!"

"Okay, thanks!"

I ran over to Ray. If Lyle had enough energy to use sarcasm in a time like this, he would be fine on his own for another few minutes.

"Ray, I'm sorry in advance."

I pushed against him as I tried to reach behind to the creature's neck. Ray winced, but if I could get the creature, he wouldn't have to worry about it much longer.

I managed to find what I assumed was the neck, and I dug my fingers into it as hard as I could. The creature hissed and let out a foul screech before releasing Ray. The shadow melted back into the wall. Ray panted heavily as we both fell to the ground.

The fight's over.

"Are you guys okay?" I breathed hard, but it's better than not breathing at all.

"Other than the fact that you ditched me, yes, I'm perfectly fine."

"I knew you could handle yourself."

"*Still*. A little help would have been nice."

Lyle gave me a bit of a side-eye, and I crossed my arms.

"God, you two are acting like my parents when *they* get into fights. Can we just get back to the others before I pass out on the floor?"

Lyle's gaze wavered, and he eventually sighed. "Yeah, let's just head back."

With that, we started our trek back to the others, hoping that nothing would try to kill us on the way back, either.

Chapter Thirty-Four

A Library Tries to Kill Us

We made our way through the labyrinth of the mansion, not sure which way we had gone. I had let Ray take the lead again, hoping that he remembered the way back and wouldn't collapse in the process. His walking was slightly staggered, but he wasn't complaining. When I had asked him if he wanted help, he just brushed me off.

I fell into stride with Lyle again as Ray walked a few steps ahead. "I really am sorry for leaving you back there. Are you okay?"

"I don't know, Quincey, am I?"

"Now isn't the time for sarcasm. Are you *injured*?"

"The only thing that's *injured* is my trust." He sighed dramatically, acting as though I had just insulted his entire family.

"*Wow.*"

"If I was with my family right now, you would have a black eye."

"Well then, I'm glad that they *aren't* here right now. I think I've had enough bruises to last a lifetime since coming to this stupid mansion."

"You should be glad. They've done some pretty bad things to avoid the law. Running an illegal casino is one thing, but *keeping* it running is another."

That sent a chill down my spine. I thought of all the things they could have done; how come I'd never thought of it before? They probably had it running for a long time, obviously they would need to do some other things to keep it going.

Lyle must have noticed the panicked look on my face, because he was quick to assure me that he's safe. "I promise that I've never done anything really bad. Only my father did. I never had the heart to, unless it was to protect someone I cared about. I didn't enjoy it one bit."

That eased my nerves.

"He used to tell me about how I was weak for not letting myself do that. It never really bugged me, though. He thought of other work for me to do, like working the bar. You know what they say, *chi dorme non piglia pesci*."

I turned to look at him. "What language is that?"

"Oh, it's Italian. The literal translation is 'who sleeps does not catch fish,' but it means the same thing as 'the early bird gets the worm.'"

I smiled. "Huh. You learn something new every day. Just like I didn't know you knew Italian."

He let out a nervous laugh, rubbing his hand against the back of his neck. "Saying I *know* Italian would be a bit of an overstatement. My father had tried teaching it to me and my siblings since he had grown up in Italy, but most of it wouldn't stick for me. I didn't know a lot before I died, and I remember even less now."

"I still think it's cool. I always wanted to learn Italian, but I never had the time to try picking it up."

"I guess I'll just have to teach you then," Lyle said, looking at me with a wide smile.

I smiled right back at him. "I would love that."

We fell into silence again, continuing to walk. Every now and then I'd think he was glancing at me, but it was probably just my imagination.

Lyle broke the silence. "Have *you* ever had to do anything like that?"

"What your dad did? Oh, of *course* I have. Daily dose of fighting in the morning really gets my day started." Even though I was just being dramatic, it wasn't much of an exaggeration.

"What is it with you and your sarcasm?"

"Coming from the man who- uh—"

Lyle crossed his arms with a raised eyebrow that begged me to challenge him. "Go on, then. Name *one* time I've used sarcasm against you."

"Literally two minutes ago!"

"That doesn't count."

"Of course it does!"

I huffed, and Lyle did, too. The flash of anger didn't last very long, though—it's hard to stay annoyed with him. No matter how hard I tried, I couldn't stay mad at him. It's like my mind just refused to.

I hadn't even realized we had gone off path until we were standing right in front of a library, doors wide open. I vaguely remembered seeing a library on the map, and it definitely *wasn't* in the direction we were supposed to be going in.

"Ray, I thought we were going back to the others."

"We *were*, but then I missed a turn, and now we're here! Doesn't this look cool?"

I looked in, and I had to agree with him; it made me feel like I was in a university with the sheer size of it. I knew the mansion was big, but I didn't realize it was *that* big.

"We're gonna need your help getting back to the others, you do know that, right? Can't have you overworking your leg."

Ray threw his arms down. "It's *fine*. Besides, who doesn't like an old library?"

"It smells like must, dust, and depression," I heard Lyle grumble beside me.

I lightly shoved his arm. "Oh, lighten up."

"Hey, I'm lighter than this place."

I quickly tapped his nose, ignoring the confused look on his face. "Not unless you're talking about your paleness." I crossed my arms, smiling. "You look like a ghost—pun absolutely intended."

Lyle must have realized that this would be a losing battle, so he just sighed and gestured towards the doors. "Come on, now. If you two are going to somehow have fun in a place full of *books*, might as well get it over with."

Ray grinned and ran in, quickly getting lost in the shelves. Lyle joined me as we walked in.

Ray's right; other than Lyle, who *didn't* like an old library? It's like being brought straight into a fantasy novel. The smell of old books was overwhelming, but it was still a scent that I loved. All they needed to do was find a way to bottle it into a perfume, and I'd buy the whole store.

As I walked through the shelves, I was surprised at how many books were even here. So many of them looked ancient, like they'd crumble to dust if someone touched them. I gingerly picked one off the shelf and examined it; the cover's a dark maroon with yellow lettering. The pages had deckled edges, which I always loved.

I held it open and skimmed through the pages, coming across some older names like Elizabeth and Tom.

"Wow, how long have these books been here?" I said to myself in wonder.

"At least a few decades," Ray chimed in. I had no clue how he had even heard me, considering he's over by at least two bookshelves. "I bet some may even be a few *hundred* years old."

"Do books like these even date back that far?"

I didn't need to see Ray to know that he had shrugged. "Maybe."

My foot fell behind me as I took a step back, looking at the books in wonder. I wish I could have taken a few to read, but that felt disrespectful to…whoever owned these books. I nervously put the book with the maroon cover back to where it was.

I walked right into Lyle. I jumped, turning to see him smiling softly at me.

I crossed my arms, smirking at him. "What's got you in a happy mood? I thought this place was too *depressing* for you."

"Oh, nothing."

That's a nonanswer, but there wasn't much else I could do. I just turned to look at all the books again, hoping I hadn't missed one.

As I continued looking, I noticed the sound of whispers in my head.

I couldn't tell what they were saying, what with all the voices overlapping each other. There were multiple adults, a few younger kids. Some were talking about the 'birth of darkness,' while others talked about the rise of a false prophet in darkness, whatever that meant. There weren't many voices I could hear clearly, but one pierced through the others like a bullet.

That voice belonged to a young girl, wrecked. *Please help me.*

I whipped my head around, trying to find where the voices were coming from. All I found was Lyle, covering his ears with his hands to push the sound out. He's yelling, and I could see tears beginning to form.

"Make them stop! It hurts!"

His voice broke more with every word, desperation filling his pleas. From a few shelves over, Ray was screaming, too. Whatever they were hearing must have been the same thing as what I was hearing, except worse.

I ignored the taunting whispers in my mind as I grabbed onto Lyle's shoulder, squeezing him tightly. I yelled his name and different reassurances, but the most that did was give me his attention for a few seconds.

Without warning, the ground began to shake under our feet.

"What the—?"

The shaking got worse with a sudden jolt. I got thrown into a bookcase, and Lyle landed on the floor beside me. I thought for a second about Mom and if she was okay, but it didn't make sense. There weren't many earthquakes where we were, and they certainly weren't this bad. This wasn't an Arizona thing—this was a *mansion* thing.

I ignored the pain as I landed on a bruise. I reached an arm out to Lyle, who clutched onto the bookshelves.

"We have to go!" I screamed to be heard over the noise.

I saw him mouth *one, two, three* before pushing himself off the bookcase and into my hold. I grabbed his wrist and held it as tight as I could, turning the skin around it white. There was a brief moment of stability, and I used it to make sure we were okay before continuing to look for Ray.

"*Ray!*" I screamed."*Where are you?!*"

I heard the sound of the first bookshelf falling, and I started to run, still holding onto Lyle. I was desperate to find Ray. I refused to lose either of them. Not now, not later, not ever; they weren't going to leave me yet. Could ghosts somehow die again? I didn't want to find out, but I was getting close with Ray.

I almost got crushed by a bookshelf when I froze, torn between which direction Ray's voice may have come from. Lyle barely managed to pull me out of the way before I would have become a Quincey pancake on the floor.

"Quincey, we need to *go*!"

"I won't leave without Ray!"

"Ray's gonna make it through; you don't have that same guarantee. Now then, let's get your ass out of here before you die."

Everything about me churned. I wanted to go in and help Ray, but I also wasn't sure how helpful I'd be if I was dead. "Okay, fine. But we'll be looking down the aisles."

Lyle nodded and ran with me following close behind him. Tears streamed down my face as we ran out of the library; my mind ran at a million miles an hour, my heart felt like it's going to explode, and I'm pretty sure my hands were going to cramp up with how tightly I had been holding Lyle's hand.

We made it out just as the last few bookcases fell, closing off the entrance to the library.

No one else came out.

Chapter Thirty-Five

The Deadliest Game of Hide and Seek (Reprise)

I screamed.

Lyle came up from behind and wrapped his arms around me in a tight hug. He turned me around as tears started to stain his shirt. I didn't even care that I was crying in front of him—if Ray was gone...

"I- I'm sorry, I was so sure he was gonna make it out..."

That only made it worse. Until a familiar voice came out from the sound of my sobs.

"Wait, who's 'he'? I don't *think* there was anyone else with us."

I whipped my head around to see Ray, who's coughing but definitely alive. Well, not dead again. "Aw, did you miss me that much?"

I broke away from Lyle and ran over to Ray, holding him as tight as I could. I had to remind myself that he's actually *there*, in front of me, in my grasp, not an illusion. There's something hard pressed between us, but I couldn't tell what it was.

I tried to speak, but my words were all slurred together. "Oh my God, Ray, I thought you were gone. I was so sure you were gone. How are you not gone? Are you okay? Pleasetellmethatyouareokay—"

Ray laughed as tears ran down his face as well. "I'm fine, I promise. Don't worry, and please stop crying or else I'm going to cry even harder."

"Sorry to burst the happy mood," Lyle cut in, "but Ray is *not* fine."

He motioned toward Ray, and I looked down for the first time, which was when I noticed Ray's leg being crushed by a bookcase. I didn't know how the rules of magic worked with ghost injuries, but if ghosts could get hurt, his leg had to be broken, if not completely shattered.

Ray shrugged. "The pain hasn't hit me yet, so that's good."

"God, okay, uhm. I'll get you out of there."

I did my best to lift the bookcase but to no avail.

Lyle came up to us, crouching down beside me. "Quincey, I know you're strong, but not *that* strong."

"Do you think you could hold it up long enough for me to pull his leg out?"

Lyle nodded and prepared to pull the bookcase up. He waited for the cue to lift, because even he couldn't hold it very long.

"Ray, once the pressure is off, this is gonna hurt like hell. I need you to do your best not to pass out or whatever from the pain. Are you ready?"

He took a deep breath before nodding.

"Three...two...*one*."

Lyle's arms were shaking from the force, but he managed to get the bookcase up high enough for me to pull Ray's leg out. Ray bit his lip so hard it looked ready to bleed, but he didn't make much more than a grunt. They were both much stronger than I gave them credit for.

In a matter of seconds, Ray's bad leg was free from the bookcase. Lyle dropped the bookcase with a thud and scooped Ray up in a bridal carry.

Lyle turned to face me once he had Ray adjusted. "We need to get back to Constance and Minerva. Maybe she can make a cast, or a splint, or..."

I groaned. "Sounds like the walking stick is making an encore."

"Good thinking."

"I'll quickly tell Elias to bring some supplies."

I pulled out my phone and found Elias' number. I hit the call button, and he answered after two rings. "You haven't called me in quite some time, Quincey. Is everything alright?"

"Not exactly. Can you bring stuff to make a cast? And maybe some crutches?"

"What? What happened?"

"I'll explain when you get here. Just get the things."

I hung up the phone and put it back in my pocket. Out of the corner of my eye, I noticed a single book where Ray had just been. I bent down and grabbed it, dusting off the cover. "Ray, did you bring a book with you?"

"Huh?" He looked at the book in my hands. "Oh, that's what I was holding. I ran too quickly to put it back."

I looked at the title: *La Surnaturelle*.

I began turning it over to examine it. "Woah, this looks, like, *really* old."

The back pages had all fallen out, leaving a small gap between the pages and the leather cover. The worn book felt soft in my hands from years of handling. The title was engraved in the front cover in silver, but there's nothing else on the cover. The pages were yellow and crisp with age. The ink faded in certain places, too.

As I flipped through the pages, there's a lot of text in a small font. It almost seemed like a textbook, with bits of annotations written in the margins in a language I didn't know. I couldn't read most of the handwriting, but I could decipher the signature on the first page. It's the same name as the author:

Beatrix Moreau.

"I *think* that this is French. Do you think maybe Constance would know anything about this, or Beatrix Moreau?"

"I doubt it, but it wouldn't hurt to ask."

"Can we hurry this up a bit?" Ray groaned. "My leg is mashed like a potato."

How I had forgotten about his leg, I didn't know. But I knew it must have been pretty bad, so I tried leading us back to the others. Ray wasn't in much of a state to guide us, so I was grateful that there weren't nearly as many turns as I thought there were.

Ray was helpful at the beginning, but soon he became too frazzled to do much more. In only a few minutes, he fell limp in Lyle's arms.

I started to panic, despite Lyle's insistence that everything's fine. He tried convincing me not to panic, but for once, this was a reasonable time to.

We were lost in the mansion carrying around an unconscious ghost kid with a broken leg, which in theory shouldn't even be possible. I thought that was definitely a good enough reason to panic.

Lyle took charge once Ray was out of the picture, despite the fact that neither of us had been paying attention to the way back. I tried getting out the picture of the map, but my phone had died at some point after I had called Elias.

Lyle acted like he knew where we were going, if only to keep me from having an anxiety attack right then and there. It didn't take long for him to start hesitating when we got to a fork in the hallway. Who the hell designed this mansion, anyway?

Just as I started to lose hope, I finally started to recognize my surroundings. There's a painting that I knew was close to the living room, and relief flooded through me. "We're almost there."

Lyle nudged Ray awake, who's still groggy.

We made it to the living room and saw Constance wrapping a bandage around Minerva's ankle, which was resting on the coffee table. Minerva winced with every movement. When she noticed us, she put on a neutral face and tapped Constance's arm.

Constance turned around and her eyebrows shot up when she saw Ray. We spoke in unison.

"What happened to Ray?"

"Is Minerva okay?"

Constance glanced furtively at Minerva, who didn't look very happy to be in this situation. "Answer my question first."

"Long story short, a bookcase fell on his leg. Now, what hurt Minerva?"

Minerva straightened, shooting me an annoyed look. "That's none of your concern, Quink. You have your own problems to deal with, so stick to them."

She pushed herself off the couch to prove the point, but it didn't help that she grimaced the moment her ankle touched the ground. She quickly hid the wince, but it had clearly been there.

It was no use trying to get the story from her, so I turned to Constance. "Do *you* want to tell me what happened?"

"We were attacked by a spirit, similar to the one that had attacked you a few weeks ago."

Lyle awkwardly maneuvered Ray in his arms. "Ay, we got attacked by some sort of spirit, too. Was it all black and had these weird tentacle thingies?"

Constance nodded. "Yes, ours was like that as well. It appears *someone* does not wish us to continue exploring, and I believe we all know who it is."

We all knew who she was talking about: Wick.

Who else would have sent them? Scratch that, who else *could* have sent them? It's not like they were just waiting for us to show up—no, someone had to have known what we were doing. Someone who would do anything to stop us.

I heard a groan from Minerva, who was grabbing her head as though having a terrible migraine. She leaned against the chair, holding her head with the other hand.

"I need to go…" She turned to leave, but I stopped her. I was tired of her hiding away every time she suffered—she may not have liked it, but we were in this together, and that means I deal with her struggles just as much as she deals with mine.

"Minerva, you need to *tell us* if you need help. We want to help you, but we can't do that if you keep disappearing without giving us the chance."

"This is none of your concern, now leave me alone and *let me go*."

"Actually, I think it became my concern the moment I calmed you down. You've spent all these weeks trying to take care of me, so let me take care of you. Even if you don't think you need help, *I* do, and you're my biggest aid. We need you here to help, and it's no use if you're suffering."

"I *said* I'm *fine*, Quincey." Her using my real name without me being on death's door stunned me. Something had to be *really* wrong if she wasn't using some sort of taunting nickname.

I was just about to let her go off and sulk—any kind of support would be useless if she didn't want it—until Minerva doubled over, crying out in agony. Constance muttered something along the lines of *not again*, much to my confusion, before rushing to get Minerva to a separate room. Minerva had a different idea, though.

"*Don't touch me!*" Minerva snarled, whipping around to Constance. We were all taken aback; Minerva had never been so harsh to her.

Her voice was the same as it was when I had first met her, dripping with insanity.

Oh, this can't be good.

"Oh, I see how it is!" Minerva grinned wildly, looking between us. "*All of you, right here. To do what? Torment me?*"

I saw her eyes, which were fuschia. A deep red that faded into the shade of blue I had become all too familiar with. Those same eyes shifted between us with suspicion.

"*Nothing will ever be enough for you! What will it take to get you to leave me alone?!*"

She fell to her knees, digging her nails into her scalp.

"*The voices are too loud! GET OUT OF MY HEAD!*" Tears streamed down her face—she's *crying*. We were all stunned into silence.

Suddenly, she froze like a statue. "*It's you, isn't it? You're making this happen. And since you won't leave on your own,*" she said as she stood, "*I'll show you the door.*"

Her hand, which had just been empty, now held Minerva Jr. She shoved it towards me, laughing with the same psycho ring as she did that first day. "*This will be just like that time my brother took me hunting! Except this will be much more satisfying.*"

Everything in me screamed to run, hide, get away, but I knew I couldn't leave Minerva alone like this. She's in so much pain, and she didn't seem to have much control over whoever was harassing her.

Constance stayed close beside her, being careful to stay out of her line of vision. Thankfully, Lyle's still holding onto Ray, but that made it harder for the two of them; there's no way that Ray could fend for himself, but it also put Lyle in danger. I certainly couldn't carry him, though, so there weren't many other options.

"So NOW you look down on me with pity! Well, since I'm so nice, I'll give until the count of twenty to run as far as you can." Minerva cocked her gun. "*That's when I start chasing.*"

"Damn it, not again," I muttered. I knew I was supposed to be running, but I was frozen.

"*Again?!*" Lyle exclaimed in disbelief.

"Oh, come on, you shouldn't be surprised."

"GO!" He got a steady grip on Ray. "You're the only one here who can *die*, you need to stay ahead!"

Constance began whispering what I could only assume was comforting words to Minerva as I rushed back down the hallway. Lyle followed close behind me but was much slower with the extra weight. I prayed to whoever's there that Constance would stay safe—if Minerva snapped and attacked her, there wouldn't be anyone around to help. It made me nervous, but if I couldn't trust anything else in this mansion, I could trust Constance.

I couldn't hear Minerva from behind us, which was a good sign. It had definitely been twenty seconds, so either Constance was working her magic, or we put enough distance between us for now. I didn't want to assume we were safe quite yet, so I kept running despite the pain.

"Any good hiding places from the first time?"

I responded back between staggered breaths. "I think I know one, but it might be a tight squeeze."

"Anything is better than running for eternity."

"Welcome to my life!"

I knew Minerva had given me some tips earlier on the best places to hide, but I'd already forgotten most of it. I just prayed that she wouldn't be paying much attention.

I couldn't remember exactly which hallway it's in, but I just had to hope I'd recognize the room when I saw it.

Good news: I had. I saw the room with the closet I had hidden inside on that first day. It looked much smaller than the first time, though. "That's the closet—do you think you two can fit?"

"We'll have to try." Lyle, pressing Ray close to him, somehow managed to fit inside. "Wait, what about you?"

"I'll be fine. Just trust me."

Lyle looked at me longingly for a few seconds. I was about to close the door when I heard him whisper. "Go, find somewhere to hide. Stay safe, princess."

I gave him a quick squeeze on the shoulder before closing the door. I continued through the mansion, hoping to find a place to hide from Minerva. That had taken some time, and she could have caught up by then.

If things went my way, I would have found a perfectly convenient hiding spot right as I turned the corner. Alas, life didn't like me that much. Instead, I continued to run for what felt like another five hours, although it was probably only five minutes. It's a miracle when I had found another piece of furniture I could try fitting myself into; this time, it was a pantry.

By pure luck, one of Minerva's tips came to my head: hide in a cabinet, if I can fit in one. The pantry would have to do.

I had to pull out the shelves, but I managed to clear out enough room to fit myself. I hid the shelves before squeezing in.

I wasn't usually claustrophobic; I had been just fine in the wardrobe. But this was a whole new level of fear. I might as well have been sealing myself in my own coffin, and the smell of old, musty wood didn't do much to help.

With how much anxiety I've had since living here, it's impressive I hadn't been hit by a heart attack yet.

I didn't know how long I was there, but eventually, I heard Lyle's voice calling out for me.

"Quincey! Where are you? It's safe to come out now!"

I was still terrified, but I cautiously opened the door. I wasn't sure if I could come out yet. I yelled his name, trying to grab his attention; he could have been five feet away or five miles.

When he found me, he ran up to me and pulled me into a tight hug. I didn't hesitate to squeeze him back.

"You're okay," he whispered into my ear, almost breathless.

"So are you."

"I don't think I've ever been more scared in my life."

I laughed quietly, still trying to calm down my racing heart. "Sad to say I can't say the same."

"It doesn't matter." He held me tighter, like he was scared I would disappear. "I'm just happy to see you safe."

My heart fluttered, and I hoped that he couldn't feel it, even though we were definitely close enough. I wrapped my arms around him as tight as I could. "Does this mean Minerva's back to normal? What happened?"

He pulled back so he could look at me. "I don't know exactly. I heard nothing for a while, so I just assumed it was safe to come out. When I got back, Minerva was a bumbling mess, rambling on more apologies than I think she's ever said in her life. She seemed more mad at herself than anything."

Minerva showing remorse didn't add up with her usual character, but neither did going psycho out of nowhere. Something, or someone, had her twisted up in knots, and I had a hunch about who it was.

And If *he's* worried about what I'm doing, so much so that he tried to use Minerva to get to me, I must be doing something right.

"Wait, you thought it was a good idea to just *go out*? With no real sign of safety? Oh my God, you are such a dumbass."

"Maybe I am, but you still decided to keep me around, so that's on you."

I laughed. "Can't argue with that."

Minerva was in the middle of an apology to Ray, who's lying on the couch with his leg on a pillow. When Minerva saw me, she ran up and hugged me. *Definitely* not like her, but I wasn't complaining. I was getting more hugs today than I had in the past two and a half months.

She began to spit out an apology, but I cut her off. "Shush, it's okay. You weren't in control."

"That was most definitely *not* okay," Lyle interrupted.

"It's not like she willingly did it!"

"Because I didn't!"

Minerva's voice was so shaky, so broken and filled with fear. I'd never seen her so shaken. It's like she was a different person. "Quincey, I would never try to hurt you."

"I know. Can you explain what happened?"

She inhaled sharply. "Can I not?"

I pushed her far enough away that she could see my face clearly. "Technically, you don't have to. You could never talk about it again and let it bother you the rest of your…afterlife. *Or*, you can explain it and get that weight off your shoulders. But, if it means that much to you, you don't have to say anything. I won't push you to do anything that you really don't want to do. That's a decision all for yourself."

Minerva thought for a moment before relenting. She let go of my arms and hugged herself, avoiding eye contact.

"You remember when I had thrown all the plates at the wall, correct?"

I nodded hesitantly. That was a long time ago—what did that have to do with what just happened?

"I believe that Constance mentioned some of your theories about why that happened."

I turned to Constance, who nodded silently. So we *were* right about Wick.

"That first day was horrible. Wick kept...I don't know, *harassing* me inside my own head. I felt so...powerless. He told me all these lies—I *knew* they were lies—but he was so insistent. Sometimes it felt like everything he said couldn't be anything *but* the truth." She paused. "There was a lot about my brother and my mother. He also talked a lot about, well, you guys. When you weren't looking, I would have these...episodes. He would overcome me, if only for a matter of moments, but Constance was always there to help me. She's the most...wonderful person I've ever met."

She gazed lovingly at Constance, who softly returned a smile. She motioned for her to continue.

"It got worse, the longer he was there. The episodes became more frequent and longer. They were easy to hide at first, but the more they came, the harder it got to act like I was fine."

I remembered all the times Minerva had excused herself from the table with what had seemed like sudden anger. So much made sense now, and I just felt horrible for not knowing about it sooner.

Minerva didn't continue. "I- I'm sorry, I don't think I can talk about it anymore."

I nodded, giving her a quick hug. "That was enough. If you ever need anyone to talk to, I'm always here, and I'm sure Constance is, too."

"I know that was a heartfelt moment, but we also got something on our hands," Ray said, pointing to the book we had grabbed earlier. I had set it down before running, but it had already slipped my mind.

"Not the greatest timing, but he's right." I picked it up and handed it to Constance, who caressed the spine. "It looks like some sort of textbook—I didn't really read it, though. I think it's an author's copy, because it has the signature and some annotations in French. You're French, so I was hoping you might know something."

"Well, that *is* my aunt. Beatrix Moreau, correct?"

I gaped at her. I had been hoping Constance at least knew *of* her, but what were the chances that she would have been related?

"How long ago was this written, then?"

She flipped through the pages. "If this is an original, it must have been sometime close to when I was alive, which was quite some time ago. It would make more sense for this to be a kind of remake of the original, however. Possibly the newest edition with her original notes. I believe the most recent was published...sometime in the past fifty years. It had been edited when more information was found, but she was close to a lot of things."

"About what? And how do you know all that?"

"Elias told me all about it when I had first calmed down. There seems to be a group of people who still enjoy the book, though they believe it's fiction."

I took the book back from her. Now that she had mentioned it, I did remember a girl in my high school talking about it a lot. I forgot her name, but she'd really enjoyed it. I opened the first few pages and skimmed the introduction. "Does this mean that magic...?"

"The direct translation *does* mean 'the supernatural,' so it is a safe guess."

I stared in awe. The book I was holding in my hands could explain everything that had been happening here, and maybe help me figure out what the hell I'm supposed to do next.

"Well, guess I've got some reading to do."

Chapter Thirty-Six
The English Language Sucks

It had been a few days since Minerva's episode. I confined myself to my room in hopes of getting through *La Surnaturelle* faster. Instead, it just made me burn out because I refused to do anything to help myself in the meantime. I needed to keep my focus or else I would lose all my attention and would never get to it again.

I was running on a little over an hour of sleep for the past three days, boosted by four cups of coffee. The headaches were starting to get unbearable, and I almost fell asleep while trying to read it many times, but I was too determined. I had trained for this when it was exam week—if I could handle it in high school, I could handle it now.

Constance would bring me food and coffee, but didn't talk to me much. The few times she did was when she tried convincing me to take a break, but she must have realized that it wouldn't do anything, so she stopped. I knew I probably started to sound snappy, and I really wished I didn't, but I needed to get this done.

Instead of bothering Constance, I settled on using a translator app for the annotations. I wrote down what they said in my notebook, but most of it wasn't very relevant. There were a lot of unusual facts that would probably never be useful—I mean, when would I need to know how to solve a feud between a siren and a human?

I hadn't had that much alone time since before I met Minerva. Even when I was in bedrest, they always tried talking to me. The solitude felt much worse than I thought it would. Part of me hoped that someone would ignore my attitude and just come sit with me, but the other part of me knew that they were being completely reasonable by ignoring me. I wouldn't want to deal with me, either.

Even then, I still felt so alone. And I was having one of those lonely episodes when I heard a knock at the door.

"Who is it?" I asked in a tired voice.

"Only your favorite person."

"Mom?"

I heard Lyle's offended gasp even through the door. I laughed to myself before calling out louder, quickly making myself look more composed and less like a zombie. "I know it's you, Lyle. Just come in already."

He opened the door and looked me up and down. "Woah, you look like you haven't slept in days."

I motioned to the collection of coffee mugs scattered on my floor, the only regular dish we kept. "That's because I haven't."

The only times that I had gotten decent sleep since moving in was when I had nearly died, but for some reason my body decided against it that time. I rubbed my eyes, but even as I closed them, I saw the vivid images of the shadow spirit and the falling library. Both times felt like a nightmare.

Both times I had almost lost Ray.

Lyle sat down beside me, and I could see the look of concern on his face as I opened my eyes. "It'd be smart for you to try and get some sleep."

"No," I said, harsher than I intended. "Sorry. I mean that I can't, not now. With Wick getting more dangerous, I need to find and calm the fifth ghost as soon as possible, and if this book can help with that, I've got to do everything I can."

Lyle paused for a moment. "I could- err- I could...help?"

Usually, if it were anyone else at any other time, I would have said *absolutely not*. Getting help from others when I knew I could do it myself wasn't something I enjoyed very much. But I was exhausted. And it's Lyle—I couldn't argue with him. "If you want to. How's Ray doing?"

Lyle shrugged, suddenly fidgety. "He's been resting his leg and hasn't moved around much. That Elias guy came by after you vanished with the book, and Constance explained everything that happened. He had the things for Ray's leg, and taught

Constance how to wrap it. May not be as good as a doctor, but that woman can really work miracles." He paused, looking at me again. "Are you certain you don't want to rest? I wouldn't judge you."

"No, let's just read. I guess if you're really that concerned, I can try sleeping afterward. Deal?"

"Deal."

I showed him where I was in the book and noticed his eyebrows furrow. His eyes flitted around a bit, but he didn't actually say anything.

"Do you want me to start?"

He swore to himself. "Yeah, sure."

Instead of facing the page, however, I turned to him. "Okay, something's up. You didn't need to offer help if you didn't really want to give it."

"No, it's not that, I just—" he sighed, covering his face. He mumbled something, but I couldn't tell what between how quietly he said it and his hand covering his mouth.

"What?"

I heard him the second time, blush creeping up his cheeks. "I can't actually read all that much."

"Oh."

"I know I *should* know how to read, it's just- I never learned how. I can say things just fine, yes, and I can work my way around numbers like it's as easy as breathing, but I was too busy working to help the family to go and figure it out. And when I *did* try, it was like all the letters jumped around. I just couldn't figure out how to do it."

He noticed my silence and started to twist into himself. I could practically *see* him spiraling. "My father always told me it made me weak. Maybe that's why he stuck me to the bar—he didn't have to look at me. Barely even acknowledged me unless it was to yell at me. Because I'd always be a disappointment." He paused again, hugging himself. "I'm sorry, you probably think I'm weird, and- and *stupid—*"

"I can show you how."

Lyle looked up at me. "I- what?"

"Well, I'll do my best, at least. I don't know what it's like reading like that—it sounds like dyslexia, based on how you're describing it—but I can try at least matching the spoken words to the written ones. Reading isn't actually that important when you're dead, believe it or not."

"Dyslexia," Lyle said slowly. "Huh. So...you *don't* think I'm a dunce?"

"Lyle, look at me. Why would I care if you can read or not? If there's anything where reading is *that* important, you can always get someone else to help you. And there's no spelling bee in the afterlife that *I* know of."

His face slowly relaxed, and soon he was smiling that smile that could make anyone's heart skip a beat. "Can we start with the easier ones?"

"Of course. I'm gonna warn you, English spelling is absolutely horrible, and I can't imagine it being any easier with dyslexia."

"Bring it on."

I pointed to where I was in the book. "Okay, we'll start with words that actually make sense."

The good news was that he could figure out most of the short words pretty quickly. It made sense; less letters in need of rearranging. But the longer the words got, the harder it became. Especially when they weren't spelled phonetically.

"So you're telling me that *a-u-g-h* makes an *ah* sound?"

"So does *o-u-g-h*?"

"*Only sometimes?*"

I would point to a word, spell it out, and say it. After I did it, he would repeat. His strong accent didn't help when there were words we pronounced differently already, like water. Hearing him trying to pronounce some of the harder words may have been the best part of it. He butchered half of them, but he's giving it his best try.

"Quincey?"

"Yes?"

"Why the *hell* is *island* spelled like that?"

I burst out laughing. "Just wait until you try *Wednesday*."

"Wouldn't it just be spelled *w-e-n-z-d-a*?"

"Oh God, you couldn't be further from the truth."

A look of horror spread across his face—I hadn't seen anyone look so scared over spelling a word before. "How is it spelled?"

"We'll save that for a different day."

We moved on, and I started reading along with him. His eyebrows furrowed as he read along, sounding out each syllable and trying to spell it as best as he could. He looked so determined and refused to move on from a word until he got it right. To make it easier to read, we had moved closer together. His shoulder brushed against mine, and all I could think about was how cute he looked when he's focused.

What? Why did I think that? He's Lyle. He's dead, for Christ's sake.

My cheeks started to go warm. Impulsive thoughts were weird. I was probably just exhausted, anyway—I was too tired to be thinking clearly, and that's definitely *not* something I would have thought normally.

"How drunk was the guy who invented the English spelling?"

I was pulled from my thoughts, which was probably for the better. "On a scale of one to ten, I'd say approximately 32."

"I think that's an underestimation."

It didn't take much longer for Lyle to want a break. "I don't know how much longer I can handle this, Quincey. Now I know why people hate this stupid language so much."

"Now imagine this, except everyone's names are spelled weird, too."

"How is *your* name spelled?"

I spelled it out for him, and saw his confusion. "Don't ask me why it's spelled with an *e-y* and not just a *y*. That's what everyone asks. I don't know either."

He gasped dramatically, holding a hand over his heart. "I was *not* going to ask that. Assumptions like that are very harmful."

I leaned back and smiled. "Then what *were* you gonna ask?"

He thought for a few moments, obviously trying to think of a different question that would still make sense. "How do you spell Wednesday?"

I gave him a playful shove. "That wasn't what you were going to ask and we both know it. I'll just take over reading for a bit and give your brain a break."

I grabbed the book as Lyle laid down beside me, his hands behind his head. I traced the words until I found the next paragraph and started to read. Luck must have been on my side—we were starting to talk about ghosts.

"'While *ghosts* is the common word for any undead apparitions, it is only an umbrella term. If you want to get more specific, there are two types of ghosts you can encounter: spirits and souls. There is a very distinct difference between the two. Spirits are the psyches of the departed that remained on Earth, balancing on the plane between the living and the dead. Not every person who dies becomes a spirit. Souls, on the other hand, are psyches of the not yet departed who were forced into the same plane as spirits. Only those with a high experience in magic can send a living person's psyche into this bridge between worlds, and this action cannot be undone by the magicfolk who performed it.'"

"What the hell?" Lyle muttered. "Who would do that?"

"I don't know, but they must be real assholes. That's a horrible thing to do, and anyone who can do that must be…a sociopath or something. But the wording is weird. It's like someone else can undo it, but how would that even work?"

Lyle made that *I don't know* sound. "Just keep reading. Maybe it'll explain it."

I nodded and continued from where I left off.

"'Ghosts began getting attention around the first century A.D., when a Roman author described a very notable ghost sighting. The first sighting of a poltergeist—a spirit or soul that can cause physical disturbances—was in 856 A.D. in Germany. There are people who may spend their entire lives devoted to helping ghosts pass on.'"

"Isn't that what you're doing, princess?" Lyle asked.

I fell back so I lay beside him before I sighed, holding the book against my chest. "Unfortunately."

"Well, I don't know about you, but I find it very fortunate that you're the one who got stuck with us." Lyle turned to look at me with his curious eyes. "I don't think I'd enjoy anyone else nearly as much as you."

My heart leapt to my throat for a brief second. "If only it didn't involve almost dying all the time."

"Ain't that the truth."

I held up the book, though the lighting wasn't great anymore. I skimmed the rest of the section, but there wasn't much more information that could help; it's mostly the history of ghost stories and which ones were accurate or not, a majority of them I didn't recognize. There were a few popular ones that I did recognize, which made me wonder just how old these stories were.

"There's nothing else that is actually useful here." I tossed the book to the side.

Lyle pushed himself up with a groan. "I think it's about time you get some sleep. You're in desperate need of it."

I yawned. "Yeah, you're right. And hey, if you want to keep doing our lessons, feel free to stop in. I still don't think you really need them, though; if there's anything where the spelling is *that* important, you can get someone's help. But if you really are set on learning how to write and spell, I can try teaching you how to remember the spelling of words. And I don't care what the hell your dad told you; you're not a burden, or a disappointment, or anything else he said. I think you're amazing just the way you are."

He smiled at me. I thought I might have seen tears in his eyes, but I wasn't sure. "Thank you. And yeah, I'd like that."

He bid me goodbye, but only after a few rounds of reassurance that I was actually going to bed. He shut the door behind him softly as he left.

I laid there for a few minutes, just thinking about everything that I had just learned about ghosts. I tried remembering the differences between a spirit and a soul—which one would all of them be?

Ray's the only one who actually remembered exactly how he died, at least that I knew of. Lyle hadn't explained how he died yet if he knew, and there wasn't anything obvious about him. That's something I'd need to ask him about later.

But even if some of them *had* been sent to…wherever ghosts were, who would have sent them? The only person that made even a hint of sense was Wick. He clearly didn't care about the ghosts, what with the drastic measures he's going to take in an attempt to stop me. But what would they have done to him to make him want them here so badly? Besides, I had already calmed them down, which begged a different question: why hadn't anything happened yet?

"Man, I need to shut up," I whispered to no one. I forced my mind to empty itself, and the exhaustion did its work. I fell asleep faster than I ever had.

Chapter Thirty-Seven

I'm an Insomniac (But So Are You)

I ended up sleeping the rest of the day and well into the night, waking up unreasonably early the next morning. My body didn't seem to care that it's four and still dark outside, because it gave me more energy than I had in my entire childhood.

I stayed still, hoping I could convince myself to fall back to sleep for just a few more hours. Sadly, I had no such luck, and I was stuck feeling like a caffeinated ten-year-old that was forced into time out.

I sighed and pushed myself out of bed. It seems like I needed that more than I thought.

I put on my NAU sweatshirt and some shorts, debating whether or not to leave my room. I doubted that anyone else would be awake, except for maybe Minerva, but I also didn't want to be cooped up in my room with so much energy.

"Maybe I'll do a quick lap..." I muttered to myself.

I grabbed my headphones and put my exercise playlist on shuffle; I really had a playlist for everything, didn't I? My tennis shoes were one foot in the grave—pun intended—but they would have to work, because I didn't bring a different pair.

I didn't make it very far, though, because when I reached the kitchen I almost walked face first into Lyle.

I popped an earbud. "Jesus, it's four in the morning. What are you doing up?"

He hurriedly hid something behind his back, and I heard the sound of crinkling paper. "Drugs."

"Nice try, there aren't any here."

He sighed, and I leaned around to try peeking at what he's holding. All I saw was one piece of paper and a pencil. He must have been practicing. "Aw, are you writing a *love letter* confessing your *undying love* for me?"

Even though I said it as a joke, my heart still went in a loop. Or three.

Lyle laughed, his head tilting back. He had such a great laugh; I would never get tired of hearing it. "Not quite."

"Then can I see it?"

I reached for the paper, and he held it as high as he could, just out of my reach. Despite the fact that he's only an inch taller than me, he still managed to keep it away. He smirked at me as he saw my frustration—damn his long arms. "Only if you can reach it, princess."

I stared him down for a few seconds, thinking of a battle plan. If I tried to reach for it now, he just had to move his hand and I'd end up flailing around like a moron.

I narrowed my eyes, and he grinned triumphantly at me. "I win."

"Alright, if you say so…" I began to walk away. I counted to three before whirling around and snatching the paper out of his hands, surprised it didn't rip. "Ha!"

All of Lyle's confidence drained, and he averted his eyes as I opened it. As I read it, I was hit by a wave of confusion. "Why is it just my name written over and over again?"

"I- err- well…"

"Lyle, *please* don't tell me you were putting some sort of weird curse on me."

"No, it's not that, uhm…" He's usually so put together and nonchalant, and his sudden wave of nervousness made *me* nervous. "It- it's going to sound really weird."

I crossed my arms, careful not to bend the paper. "It can't be weirder than thinking you were trying to curse me."

He glanced between the paper in my hands and myself before sighing again in reluctance. "It's just- you already know that I'm not the greatest speller in the world, heh…"

That wasn't much of an explanation.

"I wanted to…" The rest of his sentence became too quiet to understand.

"What?"

"I wanted to make sure I knew how to spell your name, that's all."

It's such a simple sentiment, so why did it make me feel all warm and fuzzy? As I looked closer on the paper, I could see a few times that lines were crossed out, or remnants of words that had been erased. In front of the *Quincey* in the center, there were lots of eraser marks. I wondered what it said before being slaughtered by the eraser.

I handed it back to him. "I think that's…"

I didn't know what word to use. *Thoughtful? Endearing? Adorable?*

"Weird?"

"That wasn't what I was going to say."

"Then what?"

I hesitated before eventually saying *nice*. It wasn't nearly close enough to how it made me feel, but everything else sounded way too cheesy. "Nice. Yeah, I was going to say it's nice."

Not just nice, I thought.

He folded up the paper and put it in his pocket, along with the pencil. Where did he get that stuff, anyway? And why were men's pockets so big, even then?

Lyle threw his arms in the air. "Well, we're both awake at four in the morning, and no one else is. What do we do?"

"Master karate?"

"I like your thinking, but alas, I think that may take a bit longer than the time frame we have."

I shrugged and walked around to the cabinets. "We *could* try making a fancy breakfast for everyone. Who knows, maybe we can actually make a whole meal without burning anything. And," I said, pulling out my phone, "I can get some music playing. Time to bring back those amazing dance moves."

Lyle joined me by the cabinets, and the feeling of his hand brushing mine sent tingles up my entire arm. "You may not want my help. Drinks I can do—anything else is like navigating a maze with a blindfold on. There's a reason I never went into the kitchen."

"I think it'll be fine. If anything goes *too* badly, you can think of some epic story of how we fought Wick or something," I said teasingly.

"In a baking competition?"

"Who knows, maybe he has a talent for making pancakes."

Lyle cackled. "For some reason, I find that hard to believe."

I unplugged my headphones and shifted to yet another playlist, this one just having a mix of my favorite songs. Part of me was worried about what Lyle would think of my music, but I pushed the thought aside. He would have to deal with it since I was the only source of music around here, save the record player.

I reached for a boxed pancake mix instinctively before hesitating. We had *hours*—they could be made from scratch. But did I want to go through that effort, especially if they had the chance of turning out like they came out of a wildfire?

Lyle came up behind me and reached over my shoulder for the mix. "If you needed help reaching it, you could have just said so."

I didn't have the heart to tell him that wasn't the problem. It didn't help that the feeling of his body being so close to mine always seemed to set off fireworks and distract me from whatever I had been thinking. I ignored the feeling and pushed past him to get the milk and eggs needed.

Despite the fact that I had music playing, I wasn't paying much attention to it. Lyle kept cracking jokes and trying to get me to hug him despite his hands being covered in batter, but all I could think about was how much more comfortable I felt. I could almost forget about the whole reason I was here every time I was with him.

Jesus, what's wrong with me?

After getting him to wash his hands for the fifth time, he suddenly pulled me away from the oven where I was making eggs, almost making me drop the pan.

"You can't just do that!" I tried sounding mad, but a damn smile still crept across my face, sneaky as ever. That little bastard.

He paused for a moment. I saw him tapping his foot. "What are you doing?"

"Waiting."

"For what—?"

Just as I asked that, he pulled my arm behind his head and drew it back out again before spinning us around, exactly like the dance that I had taught him only a few days before. And this time, I didn't get whacked in the face.

Did everything happen only earlier this week? It felt like it had been an eternity since everything went down with the shadow, and the library, and Minerva's psychotic episode.

"That *was* the song, wasn't it?"

I listened closely. "Yeah, it is. How did you remember that?"

Lyle put a finger to his lips, making a *sh* sound. "I will never reveal my secrets."

"Admit it—you just liked the song."

He gave me a quick twirl. "The song wasn't the best part of it."

"Then what was?"

Before he could answer, I started to smell something...off. In a matter of seconds, I caught on and yelped, running over to the eggs. Sadly, by the time I realized they were burning, it was already too late. They had made their trip to the fiery pits of hell and back up again.

"Damn it," I muttered angrily. "I knew it was going to happen. I *knew* it."

Lyle grabbed my hands, bringing them away from the pan. "Ay, don't cry over spilt milk. It happened, and we still have quite a bit of time until the others wake up. We can make some more."

He carefully held the handle of the pan as he dumped the burnt eggs in the trash. I took a sharp breath—why was I getting so worked up about some bad eggs? I made my way over to the fridge and pulled out the carton, getting another batch set up.

We finished making breakfast in only a couple hours, which may seem like a long time if one didn't take into account how many mouths we had to feed and our resources. We had exactly one pan and managed to get a whole buffet set up, with eggs, bacon, hash browns, pancakes, sausage...

We started setting it up as Minerva walked in. Even with her pessimistic attitude, she still seemed genuinely impressed as she walked in. "Did you really make all of...t*his*?" She flailed her hand around as she spoke. "How long have you been up?"

"Since four."

"Well, these better taste *heavenly* if you've been making them that long."

Constance and Ray joined us shortly after, despite the early hour. Breakfast didn't last very long; there were a lot of leftovers, so we would be stocked on breakfast for at least the next few days. My cooking wasn't nearly as good as Constance's or Mom's, but considering I hadn't made breakfast in a bit, I'd say I did pretty good.

Once we were done eating, I quickly secluded myself in my room again. I could get so much more done in the book now that I had gotten some sleep and ate early. With this newfound energy, I had high hopes.

Lyle sat in most of my reading sessions while I taught him the spelling of different words. He's already doing much better than he had only the day before. I didn't expect him to take a spelling test or something, but the knowledge could still be helpful later. Even with his reading slowing us down a bit, we still got done in a week.

I grinned triumphantly as I read the last sentence. "Only took a week."

Lyle beamed back at me. "Probably would have been quicker without me constantly looking over your shoulder."

"It's okay," I said with a shrug. "I liked the company."

I looked over some of the notes I had taken between the translated annotations and notes about ghosts that could have been helpful. There were some other details, too, that I was surprised to learn, like the fact that people could become immortal just by performing some sort of spell. It was advanced magic, but that begged the question: how many people in my life had magic? For all I knew, Rachel could be magical. According to the book, it only took around a tenth of magical blood to learn magic, assuming you weren't born with it.

"What's up next?" Lyle asked. "You've read the book, I hear you've done the training. There isn't much else to do now other than push forward."

I closed my notebook. "Guess it's time to look for the next ghost."

Ray and Lyle decided to join me again, despite Ray's injured leg. Elias had thankfully brought not only supplies to make an effective cast but crutches as well. Minerva was already walking normally on her ankle again, which gave me hope for Ray. Whenever ghosts got hurt, however infrequent, they healed much quicker than someone living, such as myself, would.

I made sure to keep my phone charged this time so I could keep the map up; we didn't want to lose track of where we were, or it could be a wreck. We decided to take a different route than before, but Ray still led the way with a direct place in mind, though he refused to tell us where. I just made sure that we didn't get completely lost.

There were a few times when I asked Ray where he's taking us, but he didn't let up. There wasn't anything distinguishable roomwise on the map, so maybe there's a secret hallway or an underground room like the casino. I had thought the map was faulty earlier, but that was before we found the casino, and consequently Lyle.

As we started to get closer and closer towards the back of the mansion, the temperature started to drop. I hugged myself and tried not to shiver.

"Are you cold?"

I looked Lyle dead in the eyes. "*No*, it's a *heat wave*."

"Must you always be so sarcastic?"

"What can I say? I'm currently living off of sandwiches, sarcasm, and spite."

Lyle looked forward, his arms crossed. "Well, I find your sarcasm to be quite adorable."

Any chill that I had felt earlier disappeared as heat flared my cheeks. I turned away from Lyle, praying that he wouldn't notice. "Thanks, I guess."

Ray's called from over his shoulder. "Hurry up! We're almost there!"

I glanced down at the picture of the map. There weren't many other places we could be going other than one spot: the garden. My standards weren't very high for what could have been deemed as a *garden* for this place. For all I knew, it could just be a room with a few plants in it.

That idea couldn't have been further from the truth. When Ray finally stopped, we were standing in front of the most beautiful garden I had ever seen.

The vibrance of the garden immediately caught my attention—it was almost *too* vibrant, like someone turned the saturation up. All the flowers and leaves were brighter than most of Rachel's clothes, and that was saying something. The sun glared down at us through the glass ceiling, snaked with intricate beams. There were white cages that held various types of exotic-looking plants. It looked like it came straight from a painting.

"This is it!" Ray was shifting around excitedly with what mobility he had. I was impressed with how much he could still move.

Lyle stood beside me, scoping out the garden. "Have you actually been *inside* it?"

"Well, not yet. I wanted to wait for Q! It looked like something she would enjoy, and I wanted to see her reaction first."

He's so sweet.

"Can we go inside now?" Ray looked ready to fizz over with anticipation.

I laughed and nodded. Ray hobbled over to the side, motioning with his head. "It only makes sense for you to go first."

My eyes nervously flitted to Lyle, but he seemed to agree. I wasn't sure how comfortable I was with the idea of going alone if needed, but this was a journey I would have to make myself. Constance may have been the one to calm Ray, but that's starting to look like the only exception to the pattern.

I took a deep breath and stepped through to the garden. Fresh air hit me the moment I stepped foot inside the garden. It had been so long since I had fresh air that I had almost forgotten what it's like. I kept breathing it in; I couldn't get enough.

I jumped at the sound of a thud.

When I turned around, Ray was being stabilized by a fumbling Lyle. It's good that Lyle's strong enough, or they would have both gone toppling down.

"What the...?" Ray's voice was distorted, as if he were underwater.

Lyle secured Ray before trying to go through himself, but something stopped him from crossing over.

"Is it some sort of force field?" Lyle called out.

"I think so!" I yelled back, trying to be heard.

I walked over to the bridge between us, but nothing looked different about it to me. It just looked like a regular doorway. Ray and Lyle met me in the middle so that we didn't have to yell at each other anymore.

Ray tried reaching out one more time, but there might as well have been a glass wall separating us. "I think you might need to do this alone!"

"What? No! When did her doing things alone ever turn out good?"

He had a point, but I didn't have many other options. If there's something stopping the ghosts from coming in here, then it had to be something worthwhile. "I've got this! Go back and give Minerva and Constance a heads up."

Lyle crossed his arms. "I'm not leaving until you come back in one piece."

I knew he was just worried, but I had to prove that I could survive on my own. "I'll be fine, I promise."

I tried giving him my most reassuring smile until he reluctantly agreed.

"Fine. But if you get hurt, we *will* find a way to make sure you're not in there alone, got it?"

"Got it!"

Ray tugged at Lyle's sleeve as best as he could, and Lyle sighed. They slowly walked away, with Lyle looking nervously over his shoulder. I kept my smile up so that he knew I would be okay.

As soon as they were out of sight, my smile dropped. He was right: things never turned out good when I tried things alone, and this was definitely a bad idea. But if this was the only place the ghosts couldn't cross, there had to be something important. I ignored the rational voice in my head telling me to go back and faced towards the garden again.

"It's now or never," I reminded myself as I carefully walked into the depths of the garden.

Chapter Thirty-Eight
A Giggle in the Garden

The garden's stunning, that's for sure.

I saw various flowers, some of which I recognized from when I had taken up gardening for a summer, like hibiscus and zinnia. The fumes from all the flowers were strong, almost to the point of being overwhelming, making it hard to focus.

I saw a babbling creek of dancing water underneath my feet as I walked across a small bridge. Vines snaked across the sides, wrapping themselves around the railing. I grazed my hand over the plants, feeling them underneath my fingers.

There were so many flowers, more than I thought could be possible. Flowers and other plants covered every inch of every surface I came across. It's a challenge just to avoid stepping on the flowers and crushing them, even on the stone pathway. It made me feel like I was in my own greenhouse, or like the botanical gardens had been condensed into one smaller space.

It's so peaceful, so different from the rest of the mansion. When I was in the mansion, it felt like there was danger lurking across every corner. Here, however, I could have been as far away from this damn mansion as possible, with everyone I care about, even the ghosts.

I imagined walking through here with the ghosts in a completely normal situation, but I quickly pushed the thought out of my head.

Stop getting distracted, I chastised myself. *I have stuff to do*.

I sped up, hoping I could leave that fleeting thought behind. It's useless to think about, and it could never happen, anyway. It's better to not think about it at all then dwell on an impossible idea.

My feet took me farther when my mind wasn't paying attention. In front of me were a cluster of blue flowers, a very pale but nice blue. The color felt familiar, but I couldn't pick out where. It wasn't Wick's eyes, which were practically glowing and unnaturally vibrant.

I looked on my left and right before bending down to examine the flower closer. That's when I caught on as to why they were so familiar—they were the same color as *Lyle's* eyes.

"Jesus *Christ*, can't my mind just calm down for two seconds? I don't need to think about Lyle every damn second," I grumbled to no one. Still, having something to remind me of him, however vague, helped ease my mind.

The world must have hated me, or maybe it's just the mansion, because right at that moment was when I heard a fit of creepy laughter.

I pushed myself up faster than I ever had, almost making me fall back down again from the speed. I spun around, trying to find where the sound was coming from. I couldn't see anyone, and trying to find the source wasn't going to help, either; it sounded like it was coming from nowhere and everywhere at once. For a terrifying moment I thought it might have been Wick, but it's too high—it sounded more like a little girl than a grown man. Though maybe 'grown man' was too mature for Wick—more like 'a boy who just finished puberty.' Either way, it couldn't have belonged to someone older than thirteen.

My body immediately went into panic mode. The echo of the laughter still hung in the air like a smothering fog. My legs propelled myself forward, though I had no idea where I was going. I wasn't going back to the entrance. I was pushing myself deeper into the foliage.

I slowed myself down as I got hit by a wicked cramp in my side. I put my hands on my knees and took deep breaths. Those bursts of energy didn't last very long, and they had gotten me farther away from where I *should* have been going, which was the way back to the others.

"I really don't have stamina, do I?" I panted between gasps.

Once I was stable again, I decided to save whatever I had left of my energy for when I was in immediate danger. Being afraid of the chilling laughter could wait until after I found whoever it belonged to.

My head must have worn itself out, because everything was starting to look the same as before. Had I passed those bushes of flowers already? And was it just my imagination, or were the colors more dull than before? It's getting harder to remember where I was.

The giggling came back multiple times, getting louder and louder each time. I thought I was getting closer, but something inside me told me I wasn't.

I didn't know what to do.

I was starting to lose hope, energy, and maybe some sanity.

I froze, looking around. It *wasn't* just my imagination; the garden was starting to lose its color. The luscious green of the bushes had started to fade. Roses turned to the color of dried blood and the temperature dropped even more. The pleasant rustle of the leaves disappeared, leaving a deafening silence. Even the laughter had disappeared, as though I had suddenly hit the mute button.

As I turned to the left, I found what must have been the center of the garden. All the color had been drained from the garden, leaving it looking like a grayscale picture. When I looked behind me, I could still see bits of the vibrance at the entrance over the shorter bushes. But as I stared in front of me, all the color had been sucked out. I looked up, and even the sky looked gray despite the sun glaring down at me, bright and pale.

"What the hell?" I whispered.

Everything about this garden was unnatural, whether the vibrance of the entrance or the dullness of the center. I started to shiver again, and my breath made small clouds in front of my face. Most of the time, I liked the cold, because it's rare for it to become legitimately cold in Scottsdale.

This was not one of those times.

I took in my surroundings. There's a small pond with dark waters and lily pads floating on the surface. How did the garden stay maintained? Clearly the ghosts weren't taking care of it, and Elias was too busy. It was doubtful that Wick was, either.

Could it have been the little girl? I didn't know much about her. If I was being completely honest, I didn't know *anything* about her. She could have been this sweet little child, but this damn mansion didn't like me that much. I just had to hope that she wouldn't be like how Ray was.

I distractedly sat down at a bench by the pond. As I stared into the waters, I couldn't help but imagine what would happen if I walked in and just let myself get surrounded by the waters. If I was at such peace, would I ever want to leave?

I moved the bench back, distancing myself from the pond and the thoughts that surrounded it. There's a reason for me being here, and I couldn't forget what it was—finding the fifth ghost.

"Hello?" I called out, not expecting an answer.

Unsurprisingly, I didn't get one.

I held my breath. Maybe if I was quiet enough, the mystery girl might show herself.

My breath released as a headache started to come on. This wasn't going anywhere, whatever *this* was. Sitting around, doing nothing, hoping she shows up? That's the most useless plan I'd ever come up with.

Can't be that much worse than trying to talk to a ghost trying to beat you up. Or trying to beat one at poker when you didn't know how to play.

I sighed and pushed myself off of the bench. The pond would make this spot easy to remember, and it definitely felt like a good place to check frequently. Trying to find it again would be the hardest part. And not getting attacked by a little dead girl, I guess.

I pushed forward through the garden, my legs and arms getting scratched by thorns. I wasn't ready to give up yet, but my faith in finding her was still dwindling. Either way, there's still a job to do, and I needed more progress than just *hearing* her.

The color slowly returned to the garden as I found myself farther and farther from the center. What happened that made the center start to lose its color? Was it something about just the magic of the mansion, or could it be because of the girl?

As I started to emerge from the denser part of the garden, I noticed something that looked like a shed. White paint covered the door, chipped and peeling. The rest of the building was in similar condition; it's the only place in the garden that didn't look taken care of.

There's an exit on the other side that leads to a hallway like all the other ones in the mansion. I pulled out my phone and scanned the photo of the map. If the map was accurate, then I was in the back of the mansion, but there's more to my right.

"Now isn't the time to keep looking," I reminded myself. "Let's just focus on the ghost in here before anything else. One ghost at a time."

I carefully walked over to the door. The grass was so thick that when I looked behind me, I could see the path of my footsteps. If I didn't know any better, I would have thought that the grass was fake.

My hand grabbed the cold brass knob. I took a deep breath, counted to three, and turned it sharply.

Part of me expected to be grabbed from behind, or maybe pulled into the shed, but nothing happened. I opened the door and peered inside, but I only saw darkness, as though there was a black hole on the other side. It shouldn't have been that dark.

"I better not get killed," I muttered as I stepped inside.

The good news was that I did not, in fact, get killed.

The bad news was that the girl wasn't anywhere to be found.

The *confusing* news was that I somehow ended up standing in front of the garden, right where I'd been before.

For a moment I thought my mind was just playing tricks on me, but when I felt around, everything felt the way it should. Somehow, through magic or some other type of interference, I was brought back to the other side of the garden.

"Not the weirdest part about this mansion."

I wasn't sure who I was talking to, but I was still grateful to be out of the garden. Even if I didn't get the chance to actually *see* the child, now I knew she was there, and that's more progress than we had before.

Now, the next problem: trying to figure out how to explain it all to the others.

There'd been far more unusual things in the mansion in the months that I've been here, so I didn't doubt that they'd believe me. But what would we have to do to actually get ahead? It's no use knowing that the girl's there if I couldn't ever talk to her.

That's a problem for them to help me solve, whether they liked it or not. I took a deep breath and tried remembering the way back to the others.

Chapter Thirty-Nine
Elias is Finally Helping

Despite the fact that they told me they were going back to the others, I found Ray and Lyle waiting for me in the hallway. They hadn't gone much farther from where they left my line of sight at the entrance. Ray looked bored, sitting with his back against the wall and his leg out in front of him, while Lyle was pacing. When Ray finally pointed out my arrival, Lyle didn't make much of an effort to hide his relief.

"I told you guys I'd be fine," I chided. "You didn't have to wait."

Ray slowly brought himself back up. "Well, I *was* going to lead us back, but *someone* wouldn't stop complaining." He posed as dramatically as he could with his crutches, switching to a terrible New York accent. "*Will she be okay? What if she gets hurt? What if—*"

"She gets the point," Lyle said, cutting him off.

Ray grinned, speaking normally again. "Just telling her the truth."

"What, that she could have died? I think she already knew that."

"No, not *that*. The *other* thing."

I looked at them in bewilderment, but neither of them expanded further. Lyle wouldn't look at me, which hurt me more than it probably should have. I tried thinking of what they could have meant by *the other thing*, but the only answer I thought of was a bit weird to think about. And near impossible anyway, even if I wished it wasn't.

I didn't even realize that my cheeks must have been going pink until I felt the heat rushing to my face. Hopefully I could blame it on the chill from the garden.

I tried explaining what had happened in the garden as best as I could, which wasn't very well considering I didn't really know myself.

"Well, it was...a garden. Obviously it's a garden, you knew that, you were right there. And like, it was *super* bright, and when you were inside it felt like you were outside. It was weird, breathing fresh air again after being inside for so long. And when I was getting closer to the middle—at least I'm pretty sure it was the middle—it completely lost its color. All black and white. And really cold, too."

"But did you find the fifth ghost?" Lyle asked.

"Sort of?"

Ray's face twisted with confusion. "How do you *sort of* find a ghost?"

"Well, I didn't *see* her, but I heard her. She was laughing and it was *very* creepy. It was super loud but I still couldn't find where she was. And she sounded, like, really young. There's no way she's a teenager. I'd guess around eleven?"

"Damn," said Lyle. "Must have died young."

"Oh, what must have led you to *that* conclusion?" Minerva's sarcastic remarks could have been heard from anywhere. I hadn't realized how close we were until we walked into the living room.

"Shut your trap."

Constance bit back a smile watching the two bicker. Minerva and Lyle weren't quite enemies anymore after Wick's attack, but they most certainly weren't friends, either. They were still constantly at each other's throats, but at least it wasn't literally.

Constance stepped between them, resting a hand on Minerva's arm. "If you two are done quarreling, would someone like to explain *who* died young? I doubt you were discussing Ray."

Ray went rigid beside me. No matter how much we talked about ghosts, talking about his death specifically would never be easy. It couldn't have been particularly easy for *any* of them, but it seemed to hit him the hardest. "We were talking about the fifth ghost. She's in the garden."

Constance raised an eyebrow. "The garden, you say?"

I relayed everything that I had told the guys on the way here, from the disembodied giggling to the bright colors, as well as the lack thereof.

"That's...disturbing," Minerva said. "Didn't you also hear creepy voices when you were in the library as well?"

"Yeah." I hadn't even realized the possible connection until then, but it could make sense. There were two voices that I heard more than the others: one belonging to a small child and a deep, rough voice. I still couldn't tell what they were saying because of the chorus of voices behind theirs, but it wasn't really something I wanted to hear, anyway. Whatever they were saying, it couldn't have been anything good.

"Well," Constance said slowly, connecting her thoughts, "if it *is* a little girl, she is probably wanting some entertainment. Could she be playing a game?"

I ran a hand over the side of my face. "Good Lord, not again."

"*Not again*?" Lyle asked.

"I had to play some sort of mix between hide and seek and tag with Minerva when I first met her, and then I had to learn to play poker with you." I groaned. "Why is it always a game?"

"Because we like messing with you, sweetcheeks." I glared at Minerva, who was batting her dark eyelashes at me and smiling innocently, something I hadn't thought she could do.

"That was a rhetorical question and you knew that."

Minerva shrugged, a helpless smile on her face.

I returned the smile while giving her the finger, and anger flashed across her face for a second. She took a step towards me, but Constance stepped between us before she could get much closer.

"Darling, I know how much you love to irritate people, but now is *not* the time to do it. Quincey has a lot on her hands, and we need to help her any way we can."

Constance's stare was steely as Minerva finally relented, scoffing. The former turned to me with a relaxed face—it was scary how quickly she could go from stern and slightly intimidating to happy and warm.

"It is quite helpful that we realized that, because with this new information, we know how to *play*. All we have to do is figure out a way to find the child, and then we can work from there."

"See, that *sounds* easy when you say it like that, but it's way harder when you're the only one looking."

Minerva immediately whipped around to glare at Lyle and Ray. "Did you two leave her to explore the garden *alone*? After we've clearly determined that she *can't survive on her own*?"

That last bit stung, but she was right. Still, I came to their defense. "Hey, it's not their fault. There's some sort of barrier that wouldn't let them pass. I think it only lets living people through somehow. The problem is, I'm the only living person here."

Almost perfectly timed, there was a knock at the door. It may have been more accurate to say *four* knocks.

"Actually," I mumbled, putting my thoughts together, "there may be one other person who can help."

"Who?" Lyle asked. He's the only one here who hadn't met him.

"There's only one other person who's stepped foot inside of this mansion and walked out of it unscathed—"

Another four knocks.

"And I think you're about to meet him."

"Quincey, what are you talking about—"

I was already walking away before I could give him an answer. I couldn't risk Elias trying to run away before I got the chance to catch him up on everything. There's so much he's missed since he came last, but I didn't know how much time I'd have before he would try escaping.

I swung the door open and saw Elias, his hand lifted to knock one more time. "Oh, you finally answered. I was starting to worry."

"Well, there are other things to worry about. You wanna come inside and hear about it?"

Elias' nervous eyes flitted on either side of me. "Are you sure they are ready to see me? I hadn't truly talked to them when I had come the previous time—"

"If they aren't now, too bad for them, they're gonna have to be. We have stuff to do, and I think there's a way you can help us with this one. Now get in here so I can catch you up."

I was so close to the outside, but I knew that I wouldn't make it far. With the door open and my eyes out on the open road, even with the cold, I was still tempted to run right out. Maybe there's a chance that it would work this time, but there were clearly still things to do here, so those odds weren't in my favor.

Elias waited outside the door, fiddling with his fingers.

"I'm not gonna wait all day for you."

He sighed in defeat and cautiously took a step in. If I was able to walk in and out but still knew there's a chance I'd be trapped, I'd be wary, too. But that didn't change the fact that he could finally help as he had tried so hard to do all those years ago.

It didn't take long for us to get back to the others, but the short trip was filled with uncomfortable silence. I hadn't realized just how weird it must be to meet the people you had been trying to save but couldn't. Did any of them remember? I was pretty sure Constance mentioned it before, but the others might not have a single clue.

The others had barely moved from where I left them, though Lyle now had his arms crossed. "I don't appreciate being cut off."

"That's not important. Lyle, this is Elias."

Lyle had relaxed for only a moment before sizing up Elias and crossing his arms again. He narrowed his eyes, and despite how much he had played poker, the skepticism found its way onto his face easily. "*This* is Elias?"

Elias nodded hesitantly, avoiding Lyle's eyes.

"Looks a lot younger than I thought. He's got an old name, and he certainly doesn't look like he's this strong guy who should be dealing with this."

I didn't like where this was going, and neither did Constance by the look on her face. "Lyle, maybe tone it back a bit—"

Lyle wasn't done. He pushed closer to Elias, who's clearly wanting to escape. "Why didn't you just do the filthy work yourself?"

"What?" Elias said incredulously.

"I meant what I said."

"*Lyle.*"

He whipped his head toward me, and I mouthed *quit it*. He seemed to soften a bit, but it wasn't enough to get him to shut up.

"What I *meant* was why didn't you try 'calming us down' yourself, or whatever the hell it is! Quincey's an amazing person, and she didn't deserve to be stuck in a situation like this. She's constantly scared for her life because of you."

"If we're being technical here, she's scared for her life because of *us*—" I was proud of Minerva for trying to help, however ineffective it was. Constance was beside her, clinging onto her arm, her eyes watching Lyle with nervousness.

"She wouldn't even be in that situation if *Elias* had told her what the job implied! Or if he *tried* doing it on his own—"

"*Lyle!* Shut up for *two seconds!*"

He finally shut his mouth. As nice as the sentiment was that he's trying to stand up for me, he didn't need to do it. I could stand up for myself. Besides, he didn't even know what's happening. "Elias *did* try. For a long time. It just didn't work for him for whatever reason. We don't really know."

I could practically see the gears in Lyle's mind whirring as he processed what I said. When it finally clicked, he let out a long sigh. He still didn't seem that happy, but at least he wasn't about to explode in Elias' terrified face.

He took a step back, but something still bothered him about Elias. What it could be, I wasn't certain. Could Elias' vague instructions be annoying? Absolutely, but Lyle didn't need to be bothered by that.

"I'm sorry, I guess."

I wasn't sure how much more I would be able to get from him, so that's good enough for me. It's better than not having any apology at all.

"If Lyle is done being Quincey's guard dog, I think we need to settle some things." Minerva rolled her eyes in Lyle's direction as he huffed. "First off, Quincey, what do you even think Elias will be able to help us with the kid?"

"With *what*?" Elias started to back away, putting his hands in front of him. "No, Quincey, you already know I can't help—"

"In this case," I cut him off, "you're the only one who can."

Elias hesitated for a couple seconds. "What?"

I gave him the quickest run down of the situation with the fifth ghost as I could. "That's what we need your help with. If my theory is correct, you're the only other person who can pass through that border."

"What is your theory?"

"Only living people can go through the border. At least that's what it looks like."

Elias thought for a moment. He seemed surprised that there was a border at all, but maybe he just hadn't gotten that far in the mansion. It'd be kind of hard with all the other things in here that are trying to kill you. "Alright, I will help you as best I can. But I need some time to prepare. I have an idea for something that could help."

He bid us a hasty goodbye before scurrying away and out of the mansion.

Chapter Forty
Coffee Confessions

A week passed with no word from Elias, save the silent grocery run. I didn't have any idea what he meant by 'something that could help,' but this was the same guy who didn't tell me anything about what would happen when I moved in, so I was hesitant to put too much faith in him.

Minerva made it her personal mission to try searching through the rubble of the library for any more books like *La Surnaturelle*. She would be gone for hours of the day, pouring through all the books that were still intact and could be reached. We had left that place pretty wrecked.

I could tell that the stress started to take a toll on me, but I wasn't sure what to do. I was stuck in a mansion with ghosts and magic and death around every corner—there wasn't much I *could* do. The days were starting to blur together without much time outside of my room.

For the most part, no one had come to see me for much more than a quick 'how are you?' before leaving again. And the few times I did leave the room, it was just to grab a snack—they were all doing their own things, too. I wasn't sure if I was grateful for the alone time or disappointed.

I looked towards the stack of books on the bedside table. My mind had been wandering a lot recently; maybe a good fantasy's all I needed to ground myself again. I grabbed one about some sort of war—with what I've learned about the real magical world, that could happen in real life. I shuddered at the thought; I could never survive a magical war.

I tried reading it, but the words barely passed my mind. It's as though I was seeing them but not reading them. My thoughts were somewhere else entirely. Sometimes it was about Wick, sometimes it was about the others. A lot of the time it was Lyle, frustratingly. It didn't help that he's the only one who made an effort to see me every day, even if the conversations didn't last very long. Every time I saw him, all I could think about was the way that he always knew what to say. The way his blue eyes glittered when he's excited, or the way his head tipped back when he laughed. The way that he hugged me tight and I could feel him holding onto me...

Even just thinking about it made my stomach flip. I smacked my head with the book, groaning. "Jesus Christ, I'm never that cheesy. Why can't he just get out of my head? I'm not in some romance novel—I have more important things to focus on right now than some *guy*."

I opened my book again as I heard a gentle knock on my door. I groaned and set the book to the side. "Come in."

Constance practically glided in, finding a spot on my bed. Her fingers traced over the cover of the book, which was lying on the bed. "This looks intriguing. What is it?"

"Uh, nothing." I knew it was a fantasy world with a war, but that's all I could remember. My brain was really starting to give out on me.

Constance's brows furrowed. "You do not appear well. Is there something you wish to discuss?"

There *was* something bothering me, but I did *not* want to talk about it. Maybe if I could ignore it, it would go away. *Out of sight, out of mind.* "I just...had a nightmare last night, that's all."

"That is unfortunate."

I noticed the cup of coffee that had been set on my bedside table, next to the books. Steam curled off of it. "Is that for me?"

Constance followed my gaze and gently cupped her hands around the mug. "Yes. Your exhaustion has not escaped my attention, so I thought it best to bring something to help energize you. I am unable to tell if it is lack of sleep or if the sleep is simply unsatisfying, but this should help you stay focused for now." She handed me the coffee, which I took thankfully.

"Is it that obvious?" Just by my voice, I could tell it was. I hadn't even noticed how dead inside I sounded. I made a quick apology to Lyle for every time the past few days that I probably sounded like I wanted to kill him just for existing.

I took a sip and was instantly hit by the warmth. I wasn't usually a hot coffee drinker, but *damn*, this was good. Better than anything I ever had at the cafe Rachel waitressed at, no offense to the baristas.

"Did you add some sort of magic touch to this? It barely even tastes like coffee. Not that it's bad, it's great, it just usually tastes bitter." I drank some more, feeling the caffeine already starting to wake me up.

"Unless you count *motherly love* as magic," she teased.

I continued to drink. "Hey, this might seem weird, but I just realized I don't actually know that much about you. What was your life like before the mansion?"

She looked to the side. "There is not much to tell. I grew up in a noble family with my parents. We lived in a big house with the staff and my dogs. Occasionally we would walk into town, but I was not allowed to be with the other kids. I was told that I was *above them*, not to be associated with them. But that did not stop me." She beamed. "I often snuck out at night when I was younger to play with the other kids."

My jaw dropped. "I never imagined *you* to be a rebel."

"You would be quite surprised." Her smile faltered. "My father was often yelling at me or my mother, so leaving at night was a pleasant escape. Sometimes I would bring small bags of coins to give to the children I saw on the street. I also had a garden, though I would always insist to the gardeners that I would take care of it myself. But if they did not work, they would not get paid, so I gave them small things that they could do to help out. I had to say goodbye to all of them when my father married me off at sixteen. I met my husband, and I had my first child not long after."

"You seemed *so cool*. Damn, I regret not asking about it earlier."

She smiled yet again. "I am happy to talk about it."

Comfortable silence fell over us. I peered over my cup to look at her tracing her hand over my bed. I couldn't help but think about how well she would get along with Mom, if they could ever get the chance to meet. I knew it could never happen, but it's still nice to imagine a different world, one where I had gotten to meet all of the ghosts in the present. Maybe I'd see Constance at the library, or Ray at the high school football games. Minerva could have been graduating. She could have been *in my class*. I could have met Lyle at Uncle Driver's, just enjoying his food, and we could exchange glances from across the restaurant...

I swore as I pushed that last thought from my mind, ignoring the brief rush I got from it. It's dumb to think about what could have been—what *had* happened was we had all met because they all somehow ended up in the same place after they died and *I* somehow ended up finding it. And even then, I didn't know how much longer I'd be with them. I was brought here to calm them down, and we have to be nearing the end.

So what would happen when they were all calmed? Would they just disappear? Move onto the afterlife, if that exists? Or worse, would they just stay in the mansion forever? I didn't know which possibility I hated the most. But what did it matter what *I* cared about? They were the dead ones.

My heart constricted at the thought of never seeing them again. I knew it was going to happen, I *knew* it, but I didn't think that saying goodbye to them was going to be so hard. I wish that I could just bring them to the real world with me.

"Constance?"

"Yes, dear?"

"What do you think is going to happen when everything's done? When all of you guys are calmed down or whatever, and we finally defeat Wick, and there's nothing else for me to do...what happens then?"

She set down the book she'd been holding and looked up, thinking her answer through. "You ask plenty of questions, but some of which I do not have the answer to. I may be a mother and the oldest here, but that does not mean I always know what is going to happen. Could we disappear? It is always a possibility. The question is, are you ready to move on if we do?"

"No." I answered before I could even think. It's true, though; I wasn't ready, and I might never be. Knowing that didn't make it any easier.

"Darling, people come and go as they please. Is it safe for me to assume that you do not talk to your friends from childhood? Think of it that way with us. We were good while we lasted, but we will inevitably have to say goodbye, and you will need to be ready for that. Everyone says goodbye eventually, some sooner than others. One day, you will have to say goodbye to *your* mother, just as she will have to do with hers, and the way *she* did with *hers*."

Tears were starting to build up, and I tried rubbing them away before they could spill, but it only made them pour out more.

I kept silent, though. I didn't want to stop her.

"This should not stop you from becoming close with people, however. Enjoy it fully while it lasts, for it does not do well to dwell on the future to the point where you can not enjoy the present."

Damn, that was poetic as hell.

I still didn't feel great, but the despair wasn't as bad as I thought it was going to be. I was able to blink away the tears and by some miracle my throat wasn't scratchy. "Thanks. That helped. A lot."

"It was my pleasure. I will help you in any way I can. And Quincey?"

"Yes?"

"I have really enjoyed your time here with us. You are a wonderful girl who will grow up to be an even better woman. *That* is something I can be certain of."

I almost wanted to cry again, but I told myself I wouldn't, so I just smiled. The consistency that came with Constance was always comforting. In a world where everything changed all the time, having something reliable was much more valuable. Even if that reliability came from a person, which was very rare. I wanted to hug her, or do *something* to show her just how grateful I was, but I couldn't figure out what.

So we just waited in that comfortable silence again.

My mind was never quiet, and now was no exception. I thought about the ghosts—they were all really young, so chances were they didn't get to say goodbye to anyone. I couldn't imagine never saying goodbye to Mom or Dad, or Rachel, or Kayden. Did they have people they cared about but never said goodbye to? Constance obviously had her children, and I could guess that Ray and Minerva probably had families. I didn't know much about Lyle, though; he had Enzo, but he rarely mentioned his family, other than his ass of a dad. Maybe the rest of them would have been nicer. What would they have been like? Would they have liked me?

Why do I care if some dead family would have liked me? They're dead. *Not like I'd ever get the chance to meet them, anyway.*

Lyle needs to get out of my head.

I exhaled sharply, as though it would push out any thoughts of him. Constance's gaze flitted toward me, and I went rigid. There was no way she didn't notice.

"You didn't see anything."

Constance smiled, clearly planning something. "Quincey, the months we have spent together have made it hard to hide your feelings. Something else is on your mind, and I have a feeling as to what may be bothering you...the instinct of a mother, if you may. May I ask about it?"

I shifted a bit before nodding. I didn't think it was *that* obvious, but maybe she thought it's something else, something easier to talk about.

"I have noticed that you behave differently when you are around Lyle. Is there any particular reason for that?" I wasn't oblivious to the twinkle behind her eyes.

"Nope," I said quickly. Too quickly to go unnoticed by Constance's discernable eye.

"Darling, ignoring your feelings will not make them go away. It may be...beneficial to try explaining them."

She reminded me so much of Adrianne in the way she spoke to me, but I knew she was right. But how could I explain what went on in my head whenever Lyle did so much as walk into a room? The brain's bad enough as it was, but mine's just plain stupid.

"I mean, I can try. I was never very good at that, though."

"Then do your best."

"Well," I started, "whenever I see him, my...chest starts to hurt, and my stomach feels like I'm riding a roller coaster. It's such a happy feeling, but also scary as hell, like I'll fall right off if I do one thing wrong. I'm balancing on a tightrope every time I'm with him, and every time he brushes against me it's like lightning strikes every part of us that makes contact. It's even worse because I have to *live* with him, and I can't get away. Every time I see him he's just so...amazing. I mean he's confident, and smart, and just absolutely astounding in every way."

I took a deep breath, running out of air. I didn't realize I had so much to say, but now I couldn't stop. "But at the same time, I'm terrified that he doesn't see me the same way. I *really* wish I didn't think this, but I *want* him to. I want him to get the same butterflies, the same shock with every bit of contact. It's horrible, because I know that when this is done I'll never see him again and I *still* feel this way. I tried my hardest to push the feelings away so I won't get hurt when this is over, but I just *can't*."

I began to sink into the bed, slowly covering my face as I noticed how warm I was getting. "Everything about him is so...perfect. Maybe not the perfect person overall, but as close as I'd get. Like, have you seen the way that he smiles, and it just lights up a whole room? If I could live in a world where I could take all his sadness and throw it off a cliff, I would give anything to go there. To a world where he's happy, and I can stay with him for the rest of my crazy life. Even in this nightmare where I'm constantly trying to escape death, he still manages to make me feel *safe*. *Safe* in a mansion where it feels like there's something trying to kill me around every corner. Even as I say this, I still can't tell what the hell I'm feeling!"

Constance gently moved away the blanket so she could see my face. "It will be alright, dear. I too have felt this uncertainty before. And I do believe you know what this feeling is, if only you can admit it to yourself."

She's right. I did know what this stupid feeling was, but it didn't make me like it any more than I had before. "Oh." A pause. "*Oh.*"

"Hmm?"

I groaned, falling back into the bed. I could barely speak above a whisper, as though saying it quietly would make it less true. "I think I might love Lyle."

Chapter Forty-One
People Like to Fight Me

Constance smiled triumphantly, pulling me up. "You finally said it out loud. Did that make you feel any better?"

"Not really. It just made me feel like a dumb thirteen year old with a crush."

I shoved a pillow in my face, which probably didn't help. Even as I said it out loud, I felt wary about using the word *love*. It felt too strong for how short of a time I'd known him, but I couldn't think of a different word to describe it without sounding even more childish. Besides, it's probably a bit different timewise because I was stuck living with him and seeing him all the time.

I sighed loudly into the pillow before realizing what she said. "Wait- *finally*?"

Constance laughed. "Even if you were unaware of it yourself, it was *very* transparent to the rest of us."

"Oh God—do you think he noticed?"

"It is truly a miracle that he has yet to."

I tossed the pillow at her, which she caught easily with a sly smile. It's easy to forget that she wasn't much older than me, but right now I felt like I was talking to someone actually close to my age. Not the mature Mom persona she always put on.

"And what did you mean I was 'behaving differently'? Was I making a total fool of myself and I just didn't realize?"

"Quite the contrary," she said. "You have been appearing much happier while around him. I was starting to worry about your heart and your soul, but he seems to have helped lighten the weight that you have been carrying."

She's completely right, I realized. I wasn't sure if it was his helpfulness or just *him*, but something about him always managed to make me feel a bit lighter. Like there wasn't complete despair at the end of this, no matter what happened.

"Now that you *do* have the thought in your head, what are you going to do?"

"I honestly have no idea. What I am *not* going to do, though, is *tell him*."

Constance feigned a dramatic gasp, her hand on her chest. "My, why not? What could *possibly* be the worst to happen?"

Before I could answer, however, a yell came through the door.

"Constance? What are you doing in Quink's room?"

I swear, if Minerva heard any of that conversation, I will personally send her to the afterlife. Again.

"I brought her a cup of coffee! Would you like me to make you one as well?" Constance turned to me with a finger to her lips. My stupid secret was safe with her.

I felt a buzz by my side and instinctively glanced over. A message from Mom: *How's it going? Any real ghosts yet?*

I picked up the phone and stared at the message. We talked pretty often now—whenever I had downtime at least, even if it didn't come up very often. Even in those conversations, I hadn't told her everything. To her knowledge, there's just some weird stuff going on, but no *actual* ghosts. The 'weird stuff' was enough to keep me interested, and that's the only reason I haven't left yet.

I had phrased my last few texts just ambiguous enough that she didn't question it without flat out lying to her. I couldn't bring myself to do that.

I started to type out a message.

They've always been real. No, that sounded weird.

They're still being mean. Eh, they'd gotten better. But no.

Only the ghost of my sanity. It's been gone a while. No, I wasn't sending that.

Yep, and I happen to really like one of them. No, I *definitely* couldn't send that.

I sighed and settled on answering her later, if I remembered to. As much as I wanted to tell her everything that's happened, I didn't want to drag her into this. Knowing her, she'd march right into the mansion and personally curse Elias out for the lack of communication and then maybe curse out the ghosts for nearly killing me. I didn't know if I'd be able to handle it if she were stuck here with me.

The sound of the door creaking pulled me from my thoughts. Constance was already on her way out—I hadn't even felt her get off the bed. I felt a tinge of guilt, hoping that she hadn't tried saying anything that I missed.

I tossed the phone on the bed behind me as I pushed myself up. I'd been wearing the same sweatshirt-sweatpants combo for three days in a row, but now I actually had motivation to get dressed. I didn't want to look like a mess, even if my mind felt like one.

I settled on an easy outfit—I didn't have *that* much motivation.

I slammed my right foot into the sneaker, not wanting to bend down. After a bit of shuffling I finally managed to get it and made my way out the door.

Once in the kitchen, I was greeted by a variety of surprised faces. Despite the relatively early hour, everyone was in the kitchen.

Minerva eyed me from her spot at the table, holding a cup of coffee identical to the one Constance had made me. "Look who finally decided to leave her room and do something instead of moping around."

I went rigid, my mind already spiraling. *They don't want me here, I don't want to be here, Idon'twanttobehere—*

"Ay, stop being an ass," Lyle said with a side-eye, receiving an eye roll from Minerva.

Constance came up behind her and rested a hand on her shoulder, which seemed to help her mood a bit. Her gaze softened ever so slightly, but it's better than the hard steel it had been before. Now it's more like a rock.

Lyle smiled at me, making my heart flip. "We're *all* glad you're feeling better."

I couldn't help but smile back as I tried pushing Minerva's snide comment from my mind. "Thank Constance's coffee. It's a small piece of heaven in a mug."

"Can I have some?" Ray asked innocently, batting his lashes. "I promise I'll be calm."

"The fact that you needed to add that tells me the answer is definitely a *no*." The idea of Ray on caffeine was too much for me to handle. If he's this energetic with none, I couldn't imagine how crazy he was with any in his system.

I didn't want to wait in the awkward silence. "So, Minerva, how's your book hunting going?"

"It would have been coming along much better if *someone* hadn't wrecked the library."

My anxiety changed to annoyance. *God, was her goal just to piss me off? If it is, it's working.*

I tightened my grip on the chair in front of me, my knuckles turning white. "Maybe I didn't clarify the first time I told the story, but *I* wasn't the reason the library collapsed on us. I don't know what happened; the ground just began to shake like an earthquake and that's when the books started falling. I was a bit preoccupied trying to get out to pay attention to what caused the library to collapse. Which, by the way, *almost killed us.*"

Minerva rolled her eyes. "Ghosts can't die a second time."

"Oh, I'm sorry, it almost killed *me*. Sorry that I wasn't specific enough for you the first time."

"One day you'll get past your petty sarcastic stage and learn how to handle the truth when it's given to you."

I almost stormed over to her just to give her a nice smack in the face when I felt a hand rest on my shoulder. I whipped around, ready to shove it off, when I was met by Lyle's ice blue eyes.

He spoke quietly, just loud enough for me to hear. "Don't let her get to you." He glanced over at Minerva for a brief second. "She's been in a bad mood for a couple of days now. I know what that anxious little voice in your head is saying, but it can shove off. This isn't your fault."

My breathing hitched. As I slowly exhaled, the frustration went along with it. I gave him a small smile, and he returned it. I needed Lyle to teach me his ways, because he's great at clearing my head in a way no one else could. Except I couldn't tell if it's the words or because he's the one saying them.

I heard someone clear their throat, and I turned to look at Minerva. Her eyes flitted to Constance, who just smiled and urged her on.

Minerva sank back into her chair, crossing her arms. "I...I shouldn't have said that. I just haven't been feeling the greatest lately, that's all."

Not quite an apology, but it's probably as good as I'm gonna get from her. "It's okay, I get it. Bad days are no fun."

That seemed to be enough of an effort for her, because she didn't care to dwell on it further. "Okay, now that we have that settled, we should start talking about going into the garden again."

At least I didn't disagree with her this time—I shouldn't have been wasting that time just waiting for Elias to come back. If I wanted to have any closer sense to what I was supposed to be doing for when he does, staying cooped up in my room wasn't going to do anything.

"Do you think you're ready? I mean, it's just going through a garden, so it can't be too bad, right?"

She had a point. "Yeah. And the fresh air will probably do me some good."

"Then it's settled. You'll be going...?"

"After breakfast," I concluded, forcing a sense of finality into the words. If I didn't give myself a strict time, I knew I'd never get around to it. At least not soon enough. My ADHD didn't like me when it came to actually getting some work done unless I was hyper fixated on it, like with *La Surnaturelle*.

Constance made a quick breakfast, bacon and eggs. We ate in silence, save the occasional compliment towards Constance's cooking. Even though we told her how great she was after everything she made, it never went to her head. All she did was smile and thank us.

After breakfast was done, I was still wary to get going, despite the promise I had made to myself just minutes before. It's such an easy task, so why couldn't I bring myself to do it?

Girl, you're better than this, get yourself together, cried the little voice in my head that sounded vaguely like Rachel.

"I guess that worked," I muttered under my breath. I stood up, pushing my chair in behind me. "I'm heading out. Wish me luck."

"Good luck," Minerva said without looking up from the book now in her hands. *She must have found an interesting one at the library if she's reading it.* "Don't die."

"Thanks for the confidence, everyone."

A chorus of 'good luck's rang out from around the table, though Ray's was a bit muffled through chewing food. I gave them a quick salute and started down the path towards the garden. I still wasn't great at navigating all the hallways, but that map of the mansion helped.

I kept my gaze down on the picture of the map, only looking up to make sure I wasn't about to walk into a wall. With the emptiness of the mansion around me, my thoughts started to pound down on me.

I could die. I'm wandering the mansion, all alone, and if I get too far the others wouldn't be able to hear me.

What if there's a freak accident?

What if the ghost in the garden wasn't actually a sweet little girl but instead someone who can play tricks with their voice and kill me slowly once they reveal themselves?

"My anxiety really needs to shut up," I muttered even though I knew no one would hear me.

A sudden chilling breeze swept through the hallway. I froze in my spot, not looking up from my phone. I didn't need to, though—I already knew who was going to be standing in front of me once I did.

"See, that *would* be ideal for you, but it makes my job all the more easier."

I groaned despite the racing of my heart as I stared up at Wick. My breath shook as he stared back at me with his unnaturally blue eyes. "What, you didn't think I was going to just *let* you walk to the garden now, did you?"

"Why would it matter? This other ghost has an opportunity to kill me, and isn't that the goal?"

In a second, he's right next to me, stroking my arm. The chains were cold against my skin. He leaned close to my ear. "I wanted to feel the satisfaction for myself."

Even with the cold air from earlier, that sent a deeper chill down my spine. I tried ignoring it as I glared at Wick, slapping his arm away. "What do you actually want? I know the whole spiel of '*oh, I want you to leave*' stuff, but *why*? What does it matter if I help the ghosts or not?"

Wick stepped back so he could pace properly. "Well, originally I had just wanted you to leave all of this alone. I meant it when I said I really wasn't planning on hurting you. But there's been some changes in the plan. I don't just need you gone anymore—" he whipped around to face me. "I need you *dead*."

I took a step back, a sudden burst of anxiety shooting through me. "Woah, woah, woah, you don't need me dead. I'm just fine in my living and breathing self, thank you very much."

"I don't care what *you* want. There's something different about you, and *he* must have seen it, too. Getting rid of you would help both of my problems—removing you from the equation and leaving Elias hopeless *again*."

He was getting closer. I took another step back—I couldn't let him near me. "What does Elias have to do with this? Sure, he's extremely frustrating. And he is annoyingly vague. But why are you mad at *him*? I thought your issue was with the ghosts." I started to trace my hand against the wall. I didn't think there were any turns—I shouldn't end up cornered. But it's Wick; he could probably change the hallway with magic or something.

Wick sighed. "Sadly, I don't think I could say anything to make you understand without giving too much away." *Seriously?* "Now if you want any chance of dying peacefully, surrender now."

He locked eyes with me in a challenge, and I could take in every bit of his face. It was very punchable from what I'd distinguished. If only he would come a bit closer again and *bam*, I could sock him square in the jaw.

Don't be dumb, I thought to myself. *Wick has magic, you definitely don't.*

When has that ever stopped me? I thought back.

I crossed my arms with a sudden—and likely unwarranted—confidence. "And what if I didn't?"

He shrugged. "Dying painfully it is."

He started to raise his hands, and in the moment I did the only thing I could think of—I decked him right then and there. I knew it was stupid the moment I hit him, but by then I couldn't just go back and un-jump. I was on top of him now; I could give him that solid punch.

His smirk had dropped. I grinned down at him; the element of surprise had worked in my favor.

I reeled my arm back for a mighty blow, but he caught it as I slammed down. The man who had been haunting my nightmares grinned up at me wickedly and rolled me over. I tried spreading his arms farther so it would be harder for him to hit me, but that only left me as an open target.

He easily broke free from my hold, pinning my chest down with one chained arm and giving me a hard punch to the jaw with the other. I got another hit to the sternum that left me gasping for air.

The surprise hadn't been enough to get an actual hit on him. He smirked as he went for another blow just as I kneed him as hard as I could. His grip loosened just enough from the hit that I could squirm out from beneath him. I stumbled back, rubbing my jaw, and backed myself against the wall.

He pushed himself up, keeping one arm where I got the hit. "You've gotten stronger, Quincey! Too bad you'll never be able to defeat me. I have *magic*, and last *I* checked, *you don't*." He started to laugh maniacally. "And this time, you don't have your little friends to protect you! Not that they'd stand much of a chance, anyway."

"You never answered my question. Why are you doing this?"

Wick suddenly stopped in his tracks, the laughter getting abruptly cut off. The deathly quiet may have been scarier than the cackling. "I don't owe you an explanation. All that *you* need to know is that life isn't fair. It takes and it takes and it takes, until you have nothing left. And sometimes, you want to take something back."

I stared at him incredulously. "Is your motivation literally '*life's not fair*'? I was expecting a dramatic villain backstory, like your parents died or something."

"Oh, no, I have a backstory, I'm just not stupid enough to tell you it."

This conversation is going nowhere. "Okay, if you want me dead, why didn't you let the ghosts kill me?"

"*I'm* not the one who wants you dead. Your fate truly doesn't matter much to me as long as you're gone. I'm just doing what I need to do. But that's besides the point now." He paused. "Tell me, Quincey, do you ever regret taking Elias' offer?"

There was so much to unpack with that. *Who wants me dead, other than the ghosts? Why is he doing this if he doesn't care?*

Do *I regret taking his offer?*

That's when I remembered that I was literally talking to the classic fantasy villain. I didn't owe him anything, just like he didn't owe me an explanation, which was still kind of confusing. So I just walked away.

I could feel Wick staring at me, stunned. "What? No. You can't do that. Don't just walk away."

I turned around to give him two birds. "You don't tell me what to do."

I had no idea where this newfound confidence came from, but it had the effect that I hoped it would. He was too annoyed with my seemingly lack of effort that he just huffed and stood there.

I started to walk backwards, still flipping him off without breaking eye contact.

"You may be leaving this fight with merely a bruise, Quincey, but you must believe me when I say I can do far, far worse."

With that, Wick took a bow and disappeared.

Even with the sudden surge of strength, I was still relieved when he was gone. I rubbed my jaw—there's definitely going to be a bruise later. By the time I see Mom again, I'm gonna look like I got dipped in a rainbow.

"There goes my quick garden expedition," I muttered as I started the walk back to the living room.

Chapter Forty-Two
He Brought a Bear?

"Again? Really?" Minerva said after I explained my interaction with Wick. "What is *wrong* with that guy?"

She had been pacing the floor since I came back, clearly roughed up from a fight. None of them would even let me explain what happened before Constance got a chance to look me over. After she deduced that I wasn't going to die, they finally let me describe the encounter in the hallway.

As I described it, I thought about what Wick had said. *There's someone else who wants me dead. But who?*

"My guess is that he's bluffing. Trying to reason with himself to try and...I don't know, convince himself that he isn't doing anything wrong. If not that, he's just trying to freak you out."

Minerva's explanation made sense. Wick had said several times before that he didn't actually want to hurt me, but then again, he has gotten significantly more aggressive. Maybe he's just trying to back up his claims without needing to actually kill me. At least not yet.

After that, Minerva's been trying to come up with ideas to get me to the garden without the risk of running into Wick. If not that, then she was making stupid comments.

"If he's going to attack you, the least he could do is leave more than a stupid bruise. He claims to be all-powerful or whatever, yet he can't get much more than a few bruises on you."

"Shouldn't we be grateful he *won't* break my bones?" I muttered, flinching as Constance tried touching my jaw again.

"I suppose you have a point, but I've elected to ignore it."

"No, we're *definitely* grateful that he can't. At least, he hasn't chosen to yet," Lyle cut in from his spot leaning against the counter. He looked over to me with a hint of concern. Or maybe it was pity. I couldn't tell.

"He could be holding back for a larger fight, trying to weaken her so that it's easier. You said he noticed that you got stronger, right?"

"Yeah."

"Just means he'll be working harder to get something on you," Minerva piped in. "Not that it took much this time, but you seemed to have handled it better than the last time. No bloody noses and only one sore spot."

"What should we do then? I can't just stand by and do nothing, outside of the occasional search of the garden. I need to get stronger, somehow. Without magic."

"You could continue your training with Minerva."

All of our eyes turned to Ray. Had he been there the whole time?

"Don't look at me like I said 'go to the moon.' It could totally work. You had done it before facing me, and you made it out of that good enough. Not unscathed, but you're still alive and going, so it clearly helped."

I wasn't sure whether or not to tell him that we had, in fact, gone to the moon at this point. I glanced down at where he stood, which was when I noticed he's *standing*. His cast was gone, and he's crutch-free. Other than the slight weight on his other leg, it's almost as though he had never gotten hurt in the first place.

"Ray, your leg!"

"What?" He looked down. "Oh, yeah. Constance took off the cast while you were gone, and I can walk for the most part now. It's crazy how much quicker ghosts heal compared to when we were alive."

What's crazy is that ghosts can get hurt in the first place. I thought that them being dead would mean no injuries, but Minerva had also hurt her ankle a couple weeks ago, so I guess anything is possible.

Minerva's training wasn't a horrible idea. The training had felt like an eternity ago, even if it was only around three months. She *did* have insane skills for someone who's only eighteen, at least when she died. And even if she didn't like to admit it, she's a great teacher. However stubborn she was.

I turned to look at her with a raised eyebrow, pestering the question towards her. In the end, it's her decision about whether or not she'd want to continue training me. By now, she's probably thinking that I was a lost cause who had no hope. Either that, or she actually had a bit of hope in my abilities. Not much, though—this was still Minerva. I waited for an answer.

Eventually, she sighed.

"Alright, fine. We can get started later today. First though, I believe we're expecting a visitor, according to Constance."

Elias. It had to be him. What could he have this time, if anything? I had to wait a week just for him to come back with the mysterious item he had mentioned. But that's assuming he had it at all—he might not have gotten it. I hoped he did, though. Did this mean he's finally ready to help the investigation for the next, and possibly final, ghost?

"What time is he coming?" I couldn't conceal my excitement. Or maybe it's anxiety, I couldn't tell.

Minerva glanced at Constance.

"Well, we are unsure, but it should be soon."

I sighed. "Elias Everard, everyone. King of consistency."

I wheeled myself around to the couch, flopping myself down on it. I swung my feet onto the coffee table, ignoring Minerva's grumbles about how disrespectful it was. My body was too tired to handle her at the moment.

Lyle found a spot next to me and put his feet on the table next to mine, although I guessed it was out of spite for Minerva and not because he cared at all about it. I could hear Minerva's offense from the kitchen.

He ignored it, turning to look at me instead. "Are you really going to the garden again after what just happened?"

I shrugged. "When else would I go? I can't just stop because of Wick, even if I wish I could."

"Well then, what's going to happen if Elias *doesn't* show up?" He twirled his hand lazily in the air. "You said yourself that he wasn't very reliable. Are you going to go anyway, or will you give yourself a break? You don't give yourself those very often."

"It's 'cause I always have things I need to do." I pushed myself up on the couch, suddenly concerned about how close he's sitting to me. Thinking about it made my heart beat faster.

Get yourself together. Jesus.

"I guess I'd just try going to the garden again. I mean, Wick wouldn't try attacking me *again*, right? He *just* did. He has to recharge somehow."

Lyle shook his head with a smile. "Your stubbornness never ceases to impress me, princess."

The nickname sent a hot flash in my cheeks that made me want to slap myself. I was tempted to bring up that calling me princess sounded a *bit* like flirting, but I also didn't want to discourage it, so I kept quiet.

"If you think *I'm* stubborn, just wait 'til you meet my mom. She's where I get it all from."

He smiled even more, leaning his head back. "If she raised a woman like you, she has to be great."

Could he calm down for two seconds? He didn't always need to sound so...*him*. It'd make things much easier if he didn't.

I tried thinking of a response, but before I could say anything, there was a knock at the door. Or, more like four knocks.

Well, at least he's consistent with his knocks, I guess.

My feet carried me to the door before I could process that I was walking over to it. I swung open the door and was greeted by a relieved if not somewhat startled Elias.

"Oh, uh, I didn't think you'd heard me the first time..."

I noticed he was holding something, but I couldn't quite tell what. When I looked back up at him, his eyes kept flitting around. He did *not* look like he wanted to be here. But we needed his help, so no use giving him the chance to back out now. "We've got some stuff to catch up on. I missed a few details last time."

There's only one thing I could distinctly remember forgetting: Wick. Clearly Wick knew who *he* was, so I just had to hope that he had any clue how we could deal with him. I ushered him in, though he still didn't seem very happy to be here.

"You wanted me to come help with the girl in the garden, correct?" He asked as we started the walk back.

"Yep." I glanced down at his hands again. "Is that what took a week to get?"

Elias nodded as he revealed what it was: a very vintage looking teddy bear. One of the button eyes was missing, but other than that it looked put together. If you ignored the uneven bright red stitching on the side that I guessed was from Elias' own attempt at it. "My neighbors showed me a picture of it while they were cleaning their house. I believe they said it's from the seventies. They were originally going to give it away at their garage sale, but I said I'd take it. I was waiting all week for them to find it."

He offered it to me, and I felt around it to make sure there was nothing sharp. It still felt really soft for how old it must've been. "Good find."

Constance came up to us and snatched the bear from my hands. "Goodness, what is that stitching? Elias, by chance did you bring a sewing kit so I can mend this? Possibly a button as well?"

He grumbled something about giving it his best chance and handed over the smallest sewing kit I had ever seen, along with a single button that looked nothing like the one on the teddy bear. Why did he even have that stuff?

"I will be as quick as I can, but this is going to take a bit." She scurried off before we could answer.

Elias blinked slowly, staring at the spot where she had just been. "Well, that was certainly...strange, wasn't it?"

"Definitely. It's like we summoned her with your horrible sewing."

He turned back to me. Thankfully, he didn't seem as nervous as before, but he still didn't look comfortable yet. He crossed his arms over his chest, avoiding my eyes as he spoke. "Now then, what was it that you needed to tell me?"

I brought us over to the couch so we could sit. I mentioned Wick first so that I couldn't forget about him this time. As soon as I said his name, Elias' face went pale. I could practically see the color leave his face real time. "And then he- uh, is something wrong? You look sick."

"Oh, erm, I suppose it's just bizarre to think about having a name now. And that he's trying so hard to get you to stop. You know what I mean, right?"

"Not really."

"It's alright, you don't need to. It's not important."

I knew that Elias was an anxious person in general, but this was pure paranoia. I desperately wanted to believe him, to think that he really didn't have any idea what's happening. But his vague answers, even if they really were because of a lack of knowledge, made it hard to. Sure, I had walked into this whole experience more than a bit skeptical. But now I've lived with them for three months; it would be impossible to argue with Elias that this wasn't real.

But just because I knew all of this was real doesn't mean he wasn't hiding other things from me.

I finished explaining all that Wick had been doing, from the bizarre appearances he'd made to the shadows peeling off of the wall, leading up to the most recent attack from earlier today.

"He doesn't like to get his hands dirty—I think that's why he's been refraining from fighting you himself, at least most of the time. But he must have finally realized that you're fighting back and aren't going to leave. That would explain why he's finally starting to take a more...proactive approach to this. If he can't sway you to leave on your own, he's going to try forcing you out with brute force." He kept on rambling on, getting to the point where I couldn't hear him anymore.

"I think I should go," he said at last, barely a whisper.

"No."

He turned to me. "What?"

"You heard me. You're not leaving, especially not now. You seem to know how to read Wick really well, and if you can understand him like that without even seeing him, then you'll be a ton of help with this ghost. Good thinking on the teddy bear—she's clearly a small child, and those go perfectly together. Even if you can't actually calm her down, you can at least help me find her in that giant garden."

He wrung his hands before sighing. "I suppose you're right. Actually, can we eat something first? I haven't eaten yet."

I stood up with a sense of victory. "Yeah, what do you want? I can't guarantee we have that much, though."

"Do you have any noodles left from my last trip? I've been craving them for a day or two but didn't have time to run to the store."

What else have you been doing? Feeding your cats? "Oh, definitely. I think you forget that there are only five of us here with how many you get."

He let out a breathy laugh. "Thank you, Quincey."

I fled to the kitchen where I saw Ray reaching for something in a higher cabinet, sitting on the counter. "What are you doing?"

He startled, almost falling backwards. I managed to catch him before he fell off the counter. "Uh, nothing."

I looked up and noticed a bag of caramels, tucked behind a pancake mix. A smile tugged on my lips. "So *that's* where you kept getting them. Was Elias sneaking them in for you?"

"Maybe, maybe not. You'll never know."

I rolled my eyes, playfully nudging him. "We're having an early lunch. An all noodle buffet. Do you wanna help or would you rather be kicked out of the kitchen and separated from your sweet, sweet caramels?"

He put his chin in his palm, thinking. "Hmm, now what kind of decision would that be?"

"Hurry up, we have a hungry Elias waiting in the living room. And the faster we make this, the faster we can continue the search of the garden."

"Fine, I *guess* I'll help you make the noodles." Even as he said it, he's still smiling wide. He snatched up one more caramel and popped it into his mouth as we got started.

I was grateful that Elias had picked something quick and easy, even with how much of it we had to make. We got done in a little under an hour and Ray made a quick round of calling everyone into the kitchen.

Elias found a spot before everyone else, with Minerva and Constance coming shortly after. Constance handed over the teddy bear, which looked much nicer now. Elias accepted it with muttered thanks and set it beside him.

Lyle came last, and I could see anger flash across his face as soon as he walked in and saw Elias. Before he could say anything dumb, I hurriedly set down the last dish of noodles and found a spot between them so that they wouldn't be able to look at each other.

After we ate a bit, I finally told them the plan.

"Hopefully we'll be on our way to the garden right after we eat, assuming that we have everything ready." I turned to Elias. "Do you think we'll need anything else?"

He looked down. "I wouldn't know. You're the one in charge here."

"I guess that's good enough for me."

The rest of the meal went by in silence. Elias' nervous energy spread to the rest of the table, and soon I was antsy to just get up and out of there. I quickly finished my plate and collected everyone else's, bringing them to the trash. It was starting to fill up again.

"Ready?" I called over my shoulder as I quickly cleaned them off.

"Oh, uh, I guess as ready as I'll ever be."

He's definitely *not* ready, but I wasn't sure he'd ever be.

As I was putting the plates back, I felt a hand on my shoulder again. I turned and saw Lyle, who quickly pulled me into a hug.

"Stay safe, okay?" He whispered into my ear. "I've lost enough as it is. I can't handle losing you, too, especially not now."

Everything in me felt like it went into overdrive. As he pulled away, I prayed that he hadn't felt the way my heart had pounded in my chest like it was about to explode. He glanced back at me one more time before walking away, not sparing Elias a hurried glare as he passed him.

"Uh, I think we should go," I said quickly, pulling Elias in the direction of the garden.

Chapter Forty-Three

Secret Tunnels Are Cool

"I don't trust this. Not one bit," muttered Elias from beside me. "I've told you repeatedly, I've already tried helping them. I couldn't calm them down then, and I can't do anything to help you now, either."

"Maybe you can't calm her yourself, but the least you can do is try helping me so *I* can."

Elias gave me a sideways glance before deciding that his feet were suddenly the most interesting thing in this mansion. I examined his shoes—they were sleek and black. Dress shoes didn't seem very appropriate when ghosthunting, or whatever you would call my job.

Neither did the rest of his outfit, though. He's always so well dressed to the point where I didn't question if he had that money he had offered when this first started. Even as I thought about the reward, a sense of guilt blossomed in my chest. Maybe it had been about the money at the beginning, but it wasn't anymore. It hadn't been for a long time. Though I couldn't deny that the cash would still be helpful.

"How come you can't calm the ghosts, anyway? And what happened with Constance? She's clearly calm, but it wasn't you," I asked.

He hesitated—at least he wasn't staring at his shoes anymore. "With Constance...well, she did that all for herself. I just stood and watched—I doubt she even remembers what happened. That's when I started teaching her English."

"Well, what about Wick? You've been coming for a while, how come you've never seen him?"

"Oh- uh- it's not that I haven't seen him. I had, towards the beginning. I'd just thought that he had left. Years ago. That's why I hadn't mentioned it, you know, in the beginning."

I couldn't tell if he's lying or not, but it seemed reasonable enough.

"And I'm not really sure *why* I can't calm the ghosts down. I tried desperately, but nothing seemed to work." He looked away from me with what I assumed was guilt, and for a moment my heart panged with empathy. I had felt that way for those three weeks with Ray, and for how long he had been doing it, I wasn't sure I could stand it. It must have felt even worse when he had to start dragging other people into it.

The empathy quickly disappeared, however, because the next words that came out of his mouth were extremely stupid: "You know, I'm somewhat surprised, what with you being…you."

"Excuse me, *what*?" The reply came out before I had time to think about it.

"Well, erm, you're still a teenager. And you're just as anxious as I am. So the fact that you've made it this far is impressive."

I wouldn't say I was *quite* as anxious as he was, but he still—annoyingly—had a point.

"Is that a compliment or an insult?"

"However you wish to take it."

"Okay, so it's *definitely* an insult. No one says that when it's a compliment."

I hadn't even realized we had reached the garden until I walked right into a plant. Elias stifled a laugh, prompting a particular finger from my right hand after I freed myself from the plant. My response only made him laugh harder.

"Oh, shut up. Don't act like you've never walked into a pole by accident."

He shrugged. "You wouldn't know."

Well, that seemed to loosen him up a little, at the expense of my dignity. Not a fair trade by far, but it's better than having him hunched over all the time like a worried rat.

"Now then, which one of us should take the bear?" I had a hunch what he'd say, but it still felt like the polite thing to do by asking.

"You should, as it would mean nothing coming from me." He offered it to me and I held it in the crook of my arm. There wasn't a good way to carry it if I needed to run, but this was the best option I had.

"So, let's say we *do* find the mystery girl, what do we do? Like, if you find her, how will you relay that to me if I'm across the garden?"

"We can't yell, that may scare her off. If we pull out our phones, that may *also* send her into a panic, so let's not text or call. How about we simply plan on meeting back here in fifteen minutes and see where we are?" Elias suggested.

"Good enough."

We finalized the rest of the details, like how I should approach her if I *do* see her, and dispersed. I could hear Elias mumbling something as he walked away, though I couldn't tell what.

It didn't take long for me to lose sight of Elias, despite his tall stature. The plants grew insanely tall considering they probably weren't well cared for. The only thing reminding me that Elias was still in there with me was the sound of his footsteps and his muttering.

As I turned towards a bouquet of flowers, the giggling came back. I wasn't as startled as I had been the first time, but the same couldn't be said about Elias—I heard the sounds of his shrieking from somewhere on my far left. I burst out laughing.

"I'm fine!" He called back, his voice still high.

The laughing still continued, though it had gotten stronger, as though she were laughing at Elias right along with me.

That means she saw it, or at least heard it. Could she be close?

"Uh, kiddo?" I wasn't exactly sure what to call her, so kiddo would have to do, however stupid it sounded. "Wanna come out and play?"

Something shifted in the bushes beside me, and I lunged before she could get away. Except there's no one there; all that I found was a mouthful of daisies. I wiped my mouth as I stood up, dusting the dirt off my clothes. They might end up stained, but that didn't matter. At least Elias hadn't seen it—if he had been there, I would have never heard the end of it.

I continued through the garden, recognizing the chill and the discoloration—I remembered to wear a sweatshirt this time, so it wasn't as bad. The sound of humming filled the air around me, which was when I realized that it's the only sound around me. I quickly stopped, and sure enough, the sound of the girl came back. Except she wasn't giggling anymore; she's actually *talking*.

"Are you going to come find me?"

Was she seriously taunting me? Really?

"I'm trying if you could just *show yourself*!" I threw my hands down beside me, turning in circles. Her voice had the same effect as her laughter, as though it's coming at me from all angles and from nowhere at once. It reminded me of the loud speakers at the high school football field that always overwhelmed me. Maybe that's why I never went. Or maybe it's the fact that I didn't care about football.

"I am certain you will eventually!"

The way she speaks reminds me of how Constance does, very formal, but hearing it through such a young voice felt weird. When was she alive? Maybe she's from around Constance's era.

I needed to stop getting lost in my thoughts, because I always ended up flailing into *something*. In this case, I had tripped on something on the path. I winced as I hit the ground, my palms scraped from trying to catch myself. Thankfully there's no blood, but the stinging wouldn't go away.

I pushed myself up and tried finding what my foot had hit. It's hidden well, but now that I knew to look for something, I saw it easily; a handle, the same color as the stone. I reached out to touch it, and as soon as I felt the cold metal, something unlocked. A trapdoor with a ladder that led down to something underground.

I pulled my phone out from my pocket and shone the flashlight down—I could probably fit into it. It didn't look too deep, either.

Found something. Will let you know how it goes.

I hoped that Elias would see the message, but I didn't keep my hopes very high. We had made it very clear: no phones. Still, telling him eased a bit of the anxiety. I put my phone back in my pocket and stared down at the tunnel before deciding that I needed to go down.

I made sure to grab the bear and tucked it into the crook of my arm again.

"If this is what kills me, I'm going to haunt Elias' ass for all eternity," I muttered as I started my way down the ladder.

I landed on the ground with a thud. I heard the girl's voice again, though it's now unintelligible, right as I got a text back from Elias: *ok.*

"Thank you *so much* for *all* the support," I whispered angrily.

As I got farther from the entrance, it started to feel like the tunnel was suffocating me. It's musty and tight, and I had to crouch down so I wasn't hitting my head against the top. The lightest touch sent dirt and small rocks tumbling from the sides. The heat wasn't helping, either. I prayed that Elias wouldn't walk over top and send a cloud of dirt my way.

With no more light provided from the entrance, I pulled out my phone and turned on the flashlight. As I shone it in front of me, I couldn't see the end yet. I used my free hand to pull my shirt over my nose and mouth, hoping it could help.

I wasn't sure how far this tunnel was or how long I had been in it, but it slowly became easier to breathe and cooled down. The sound of the girl got louder—could she have been waiting at the other side for me? That would make this so much easier.

I turned off my flashlight and saw a patch of light ahead of me.

The door's open.

I silently cheered as I got closer, putting my phone in my pocket and making sure I had a good grip on the bear. I did *not* want to try figuring out the door from this side of it.

The girl's talking stopped for a moment. I heard the sound of a twig snapping and thundering steps above me, sending dust clouds down on me. I hacked as I ran towards the light; I had to catch up to her if I had any chance at finding her this time.

I climbed up the ladder as fast as I could. With one final push, I got myself out of the tunnel, and found myself face to face with the fifth ghost.

I had thought she sounded young, but she looked even younger than she sounded. Her face was round and flush, with freckles scattered all across. Even her eyes were full of life, green and glittering with anticipation.

She wore small black shoes that were stained with dirt, though I didn't know if it's from the garden or from when she was alive. A yellow dress was covered with a white but clearly dirty apron. There's one part of her outfit that stood out most, though—the red-brown stain at her side, surrounding a hole. It had to be blood.

Her hands were clasped in front of her as she looked at me with curious eyes. At least she wasn't trying to fight me, not that a child could put up much of a fight. Then again, Ray had handed my ass to me too many times to count, so I wouldn't put it above her.

As soon as I was on my feet, she took a step back. I couldn't tell if she's trying to be taunting or if she's sincerely scared; her face gave nothing away. I tried taking a step toward her, holding a hand out, but she continued backing up.

"Hey, I won't hurt you. I just want to talk."

I started reaching for the bear when she spoke.

"Can we play a game?" Her voice was soft but carried through the garden easily. We had to be close to the center, because everything's duller than it had been at the tunnel entrance.

"I thought we were just playing hide and seek."

She shrugged innocently, rocking back and forth. Even as she put on the harmless-little-girl facade, something told me she's much more intelligent than she's leading on.

"If you don't want to play hide and seek anymore, what *do* you want to play?"

Instead of telling me, she decided it was best to show me by running in the opposite direction. I cursed under my breath—seriously, tag *again*?—as I started after her.

Chapter Forty-Four
Tangled Up

I always hated playing tag.

Usually I couldn't run to save my life, which made me lose regardless of whether I was the tagger or the tagged. But after less than a week in this damn mansion, I was able to say that I had, indeed, run to save my life. Did that make me any better at tag at that moment?

To answer that question: no, it did not.

It just meant I was stuck in this situation, which would hopefully *not* be life-or-death, and had a significant possibility of ending in me falling on my face.

I lost track of the girl within moments of her bolting. She had gone to the left, and that's all I had to go off of. Determination and regret flowed through me as I chased after her, holding the bear in my grip as tight as I could. I knew the plan was to *give* the bear to her, but maybe chucking it at her back would work the same.

She continued to taunt me from wherever she hid, though the sound of her voice didn't narrow the search down. It always seemed to be coming from opposite directions than where she had just led me. It's as if she's just ahead of me at all times but not quite there. Or maybe I was just starting to lose focus…

I turned the corner and ran right into Elias.

"Damn it!" I yelled, sounding much angrier than I meant to.

"Woah, slow down. Where are you running off to?"

"The ghost! I saw her, and now I'm stuck in this game of tag, and—"

Elias' eyes widened with a mix of fear and curiosity. "What was she like?"

"I don't know! Young, I guess, but we already knew that! She has this weird stain or something on her apron, but I could get a closer look if you *get out of my way* and let me catch up to her before I lose her again!"

He got out of my way, practically pushing me forward. "You need to go!"

"I already knew that!"

I ran forward, hoping I could make up some ground. She had stopped her teasing, which cleared my head, but also made it even harder to find where she could be. Maybe I'd get close enough to hear her footsteps, but I doubted I would be that lucky.

I had no clue what the odds of finding her in this giant garden were, but I had a hunch they weren't in my favor. If I was being honest, when was *anything* in my favor nowadays? This wasn't one of those lucid dreams where I could just make everything go my way and everyone would be fine—this was the real world, however insane and dangerous it was.

It didn't take long for her sound to come back. I tried following it as best as I could, but I may as well have been hearing the voice in my head the whole time. I was losing my mind, and the pounding of my head didn't make it better. I had no clue what to do.

There's no use trying to think about where I was going anymore. At this point I was running on pure instinct, hoping my feet and my gut could lead me in the right direction. My eyes glimpsed at the foliage as we passed, hoping that they could find a glimpse of the yellow dress or the flow of her brown hair.

I hadn't even realized how far I had gotten until I almost rolled my ankle in front of the lake.

This could have been easy for both of us, but *no*, we had to play the absolute worst game from my childhood.

I groaned as I pushed myself up again. I told myself I wasn't going to give up repeatedly, but it's getting *really* hard to keep up that mentality when everything around me seems to be pushing me to the limits.

I dealt with being chased by Minerva, the difficult training from her, constant fighting with Ray, the mental strain of trying to beat Lyle in poker, and this was going to *be what pushed me over the edge? God, I need to get my life together and stop being so pathetic. I'm better than this.*

However harsh the internal critique had been, it worked. My ankle could handle a bit more—if I could walk, I could run.

Just as I was about to continue to the back of the garden, I heard a yelp.

I hurriedly spun around to find where the sound had come from when I locked eyes with the girl.

It's her, and she's completely entangled in vines.

The shadow.

The memory of Ray stuck in the grasp of the shadow Wick had sent after us flooded my mind, sending my heart into a panic. I knew they couldn't die again, but the fear still struck me like an arrow to the chest.

Now, I stared at her in terror as she cried, the vines wrapping around her mouth. She struggled against the hold with everything in her, but she was small and thin—she didn't have much strength going for her in the first place.

The voice in my head kept screaming at me to *do something*.

I ran over to her, my heart beating faster and faster in my chest. I tried figuring out what to do, but everything's happening all at once, it's too much. If this was how freaked out *I* was, I couldn't imagine how terrified she must be.

"I- I'll get you out, I promise!"

Her eyes widened as I tugged at the vines, and she shook her head with what little movement she had. Either she wanted to do this herself, which was doubtful, or she knew something I didn't and I was doing something wrong.

"What do I need to do?" That's stupid—she couldn't answer if she tried. I had to try solving this myself.

I frantically looked around for a tool, anything I could use to fight the vines off, when I saw a stick. Grabbing it off the ground, I tried stabbing the vines, praying that I wouldn't hit the girl as well. They flinched back at the contact, almost as if they were alive, sending goosebumps up my arms. As I tried to hook them and pull them apart, they just squeezed her tighter. Even though her scream was muffled, it still hurt my ears.

Useless, I thought as I threw the stick back on the ground.

There had to be something else around here. The ground was rough beneath my hands and I ignored the stinging of the dirt from where I was scraped. I finally found something: a jagged rock.

Maybe I can cut through the vines?

It's the best shot I had at the moment, and I didn't have much time, so I grabbed the rock in one hand and a vine in the other. I squeezed the vine as tight as I could despite its struggling underneath my hold.

I sawed at the vine, and it quickly went limp in my hand.

Gotcha.

I tossed the dead vine to the side and moved on to the next one, going even quicker than before. The rock was starting to draw blood from how tightly I was holding it, but I wasn't focused on that; she needed help.

The pile of vines at my feet had grown so large I couldn't see my shoes.

When I got the last one, the one that bound her mouth shut, she finally looked me in my eyes.

"You—" she took a breath. "You win."

"Finally."

I was relieved that this hopefully meant no more running, at least for the time being. That meant I had time to both catch my breath and give her the bear, which was still the original plan.

There's no guarantee it'd even do anything, but I had to hope.

"Now then," I said as I reached for the bear, "what's your name?"

She hesitated before speaking. Or maybe she's still trying to calm down. "My name is Mary."

"Well, Mary, it's nice to finally meet you."

Mary still looked uncomfortable, which definitely wasn't good. If I had any chance at calming her down, she needed to be comfortable around me. If she wasn't, this whole plan could backfire right in my face.

I held up the bear in front of me and cautiously offered it to her; I couldn't risk scaring her off. I didn't know if the phrase 'stranger danger' existed back whenever she's from, but someone dressed weird trying to offer you something would be sketchy no matter what year you were born.

"Can I...give this to you? I didn't name it yet, in case you wanted to."

Mary's eyes were set alight, and she reached out for it at first. But then she must have remembered that she had no clue who I was and that it could *definitely* be something dangerous, because she quickly recoiled her hand. I grumbled under my breath—it's good that she knew not to trust strange people, but it's making this way harder.

"You can trust me," I tried again. This time I set the bear on the ground and took a few steps back. I held my hands in the air to show there's nothing else. "See? You don't have to come close to me. You can just get the bear and run, if you want."

If that happened, it definitely *would not* help, but I had to at least pretend to be on her side. Well, it's not that I *wasn't* on her side; I *was*, in the long run, just not at that moment. I just wasn't sure how to make her see that.

I started to turn around, putting my hands on the back of my head, and counted to three in my head. I made a mental decision that if the bear's gone with Mary, I would leave with Elias and come back later on my own. If the bear was still there, then I would probably do the same thing, because that meant I'd need to think of a new plan.

I slowly turned back around, and the bear's still there, but Mary's gone.

Just my luck.

How did she leave so quietly? I hadn't heard anything, but she clearly wasn't there anymore. For all I knew, she could be on the other side of the garden by now.

I remembered how quiet the rest of the garden was, especially if I was closer to the center, and realized maybe that's just it. It wasn't her, necessarily, but the garden itself. She probably had some kind of connection with the garden that let her stay hidden this long.

"You know what? I give up!" I yelled out, hoping that Mary could hear me from wherever she was hiding. "You win! I'm going to leave, but I promise I'll come back!"

Now to find Elias.

Since I was no longer chasing Mary down, it felt fine to enjoy the view of the garden on the way back. If you were ignoring how insanely large and creepy it was, the garden really was impressive. I wondered who kept it up to date when the owners lived here. If it's not them, maybe it's the magic of the mansion itself that made sure it stayed constantly and eerily beautiful.

That brought up a different question, though: who *were* the owners? Nothing about this place made sense, if you put it all together—the size from the inside compared to how it looked on the outside, the way the exterior was modern but the interior was vintage, the fact that ghosts from all over the world and vastly different time periods had found themselves here, all of it. Had the mansion been magical the whole time?

If anyone could answer these questions, it'd be Elias, even if he claimed he didn't know much. On his last visit he seemed to be hiding something, but I thought I was overthinking it. But after today, I wasn't so sure it's all in my head.

"Elias! Are you still here?"

Silence.

I tried again, but nothing came in response. Not even an echo.

Right, I thought. *We said no yelling*.

"Damn it," I muttered under my breath as I kept looking. At this point, he's either ignoring me or left without telling me.

I pulled out my phone and messaged him: *where are you??*

I stared at the screen for a couple minutes as I kept walking, willing him to respond with a 'hey, I'm at the front, I definitely didn't ditch you.' But things weren't in my favor at all today, because he didn't even read it. I *really* didn't like him at the moment.

I tried remembering which way led to the door, but trying to track down Mary had thrown off any sense of direction I had before. Maybe I could try finding the tunnel, but then what? Hopefully I could find my way back from there, but I wasn't going to bet on it.

So, in simpler times, I was screwed.

After what felt like days of wandering, I reached the door. I could have cried from joy the moment I saw the hallway, without any stupid living plants or little children who loved to play tag for some reason. Even if Elias wasn't there.

As I tried crossing the border that led to the rest of the mansion, I was bumped back.

"What?" I mumbled.

I tried again—still nothing.

The feeling of joy from earlier quickly changed to frustration. I kept trying, harder and harder, but still couldn't get out. All I wanted to do was get back, recollect myself, and maybe throw some choice words at Elias.

It's useless. Clearly *something* was keeping me in this garden, and I was determined to figure out what.

"Okay then," I started to talk to myself, evaluating what happened. "I'm stuck in this giant garden, most likely alone if I don't count Mary, and I have to find a way to calm her down when she is constantly running from me. Plus, she probably knows this garden like the back of her hand and can find places to hide easily."

I paused.

"Honestly, this is probably the easiest thing to happen to me since coming to this stupid mansion. Not like that's saying much."

I took a deep breath and turned around to face the garden. I looked it over, all the vibrant colors that came from the entrance and the overwhelming smell, knowing that Mary had to be hiding in there somewhere.

I was about to start wandering around aimlessly when I heard it: the sound of rustling leaves. Grinning from ear to ear if only to keep my confidence up, I prepared myself for what was about to happen.

Time to find a ghost. Again.

"I've got this," I whispered as I ran into the garden.

Chapter Forty-Five
Okay, Who Gave Her a Rock?

"Why won't this damn mansion ever give me a *break*?"

That thought had been running through my mind since the moment I had my first run-in with Minerva, but it's especially true now. I had bounded through the garden and probably went through the whole thing three times, but I still had yet to find Mary. I felt as though I should have found her by now, but the garden might as well have been ten times bigger than the space it occupied. At every twist and turn, it felt like I had passed it several times before. Maybe I was just going in one giant circle over and over again hoping to find something new, and it's driving me insane. Someone said that's the definition of insanity, right?

I was honestly proud of myself for not breaking down yet. Sure, I wasn't *physically* fighting anyone, but this was a different kind of torment, the kind that left you so mentally exhausted that all you wanted to do was give up but knowing you couldn't.

I stared up at the ceiling and saw the sky from between the panes. The sun started to set, and I could see all the gorgeous colors of the clouds. Wow, had I really been here so long that the sun's setting? Or did the time here work similar to the casino, just not as drastic? Either way, I needed to get out of here, and soon.

If I couldn't figure out a way to calm Mary down, what would happen then? Would I just be trapped here forever? Or could some sort of magic teleport me out of here before I died from dehydration?

I slapped the side of my head, as though it would shake out all the random questions. None of them were helpful and they didn't need my attention. What I *should* have been focusing on was the bigger, much more important question of the moment: how in the world am I supposed to calm down Mary?

I had nothing to go off of, no plan, and no real chance of finding her.

Great. Just *great*.

I brainstormed ideas, typing them out on my notes app, but a majority of them ranged from idiotic on my part to idiotic on all parts. There were only three, maybe four, that made any sense.

One: I could beat Mary in her game of tag. It'd have to be for real, like full-on tapping, and maybe she'd calm down. It made sense, but when's anything ever that simple?

Two: I could figure out how she died and give her some kind of closure. I remembered seeing the bloodstain on her dress, so if I had to guess, she died after getting attacked by a wild animal or something and bled to death. Imagining her just being left to die made knots in my stomach. Besides, I had no idea how I'd even give her any sense of closure. It wasn't like I was there when she died.

Three: maybe all I needed to do was hear her out. I knew it's a bit of a stretch, but there had to be *something* she could talk about. Maybe she didn't have a family that she could bond with, and that's why she died all alone.

Jesus, that's sad to think about.

The last idea wasn't much of an idea at all—I'd just hope that I could do it by accident. There's probably something I wasn't thinking about that's the obvious solution, but until I came across that obvious solution, I'd have to go with the other three. If they didn't work, well, that would be a problem for Future Me.

I didn't even realize I was still staring at the ceiling until I felt the ache in my neck. Rubbing the back of my neck, I looked around.

Wait...

I went back and forth between the ceiling and the layout around me. I was in a relatively open part of the garden, and I could see pretty far in either direction—it had to be close to the center.

Maybe I was going insane, but did the ceiling match the layout of the garden?

If I lined up where I hopefully was with the ceiling, then I'd only be a couple turns from the center. I tried walking as straight as I could while still keeping my eyes glued to the ceiling, and as I made the final turn, I saw the clear pond staring back at me.

"I don't know who the hell made this mansion, but props to them." From the hidden area in the ballroom to the *whole underground casino*, whoever designed this really had thought of everything. Even if it's just the magic that added some of these things, it's still wicked impressive. And, in this case, it made my job just a bit easier.

There's still one problem, though; I couldn't keep my neck craned up to the ceiling the whole time. Both because it would have hurt my neck like hell and I needed to pay attention to my surroundings for any hint towards where Mary could be. I had enough problems with distractions as it was.

I quickly pulled out my phone and took a picture of the ceiling. The lighting wasn't the best, but it's enough to show the pattern.

There we go. Now I have the map with no neck pain.

I creeped my way farther into the center, trying to breathe as quietly as I could so that I could hear Mary. As I thought about it, I realized that she had many advantages I didn't—she's smaller, probably faster, and if *she* fell on her face, at least she wasn't that far from the ground.

I wished I could go back to the others. Constance would tell me to keep going. Minerva would probably annoy me but generally she's well intentioned. Ray would make me laugh. Lyle would remind me that everything's okay and that I could make it through. Even if they all became draining every now and then because I didn't have any real alone time, at least their presence gave me some stability. Right now it felt like I knew nothing anymore, that everything I had ever known was falling apart and slipping through my fingers like falling sand. Having anxiety surely wasn't helping—anxiety for the win, am I right?

I could practically feel the disappointment of every person with anxiety frowning down on me because of that thought.

The chill of the center was starting to catch up to me. I shivered as I felt a cold breeze tickle the back of my neck, and immediately froze. My heart started beating faster as I looked around frantically. *Where's Wick? He has to be here somewhere.*

It wasn't like him to show up but not reveal himself. But as I made one more sweep of the center, I realized he wasn't there at all. Was I just imagining it? Even if it's all in my head, the antsy feeling didn't go away.

No matter how many times I walked through the center, I would never get used to the complete lack of the color. I knew that in nature the poisonous animals would have bright colors to ward off predators, but this had the same effect in the opposite way. Every time I found my way here, all I could think was *I'm in danger.*

I found a spot by the water and sat on the sand, slipping off my shoes and dipping my feet in. Despite how cold the rest of the area was, the water's surprisingly warm. As I leaned my head back, I heard the sound of rustling leaves.

I quickly put my shoes back on and turned around. There's Mary, standing at the edge of the center on top of a bench. She's by one of the pathways off to the right that I guessed led to more parts of the garden.

I walked over to her, which was when I noticed she's hiding something behind her back.

"Mary? What are you hiding?"

She hesitated before bringing it to the front—a decent sized rock, which I was kind of surprised she could carry. For a second I wondered what she could have been doing with it, but I wasn't left wondering for long as she started to raise it over her head. She's taller than me on the bench; she could easily swing that onto my head.

My eyes widened as I held my hands out. "You don't need to hurt me, I promise I'm safe."

It was at that moment I saw the vivid blue ring around her eyes.

Wick. He has some sort of control over her.

"He told me to," Mary whispered before hitting it over my head.

The force knocked me down to the ground. I could feel blood from where I had gotten hit, but it's a miracle I hadn't gone unconscious immediately. My head pounded as I saw Mary quickly scurry away, dropping the rock beside me. Was she...scared?

I tried to figure out where Wick had been hiding, but I couldn't before I blacked out.

Chapter Forty-Six
Ouch! Part Three

When I woke up, I wasn't on the hard ground anymore. I groaned as I pushed myself up on the couch, rubbing my eyes. Bandages were wrapped around my head, and I fought the urge to take them off so I could scratch the itchy skin underneath.

People were talking next to me. I looked over and saw Constance and Lyle in a hushed conversation, Lyle pacing back and forth while Constance was clearly trying to calm him down. I shrugged the blanket off as I watched them for a bit, my eyelids still heavy as I tried to wake up.

"Uh, what?"

They both stopped and turned to me. I could see relief on both of their faces as they came over to me, though Lyle was still kind of hectic. "How- how are you feeling? What happened? If Wick did this to you, I *swear*—"

Constance shushed Lyle. "Give her some time to wake up. That was a pretty hard blow to the head. It is a miracle she only has minimal injury. It seems that the only real damage was to the exterior." She looked at me again. "Whatever happened, it appears to have been lighter than we expected it to be."

I tried sitting straight up, but got hit by a rush of dizziness and quickly laid back down.

"I would advise you not to sit up yet," she clarified.

"Wow, I never would have thought," I muttered under my breath as I pushed myself against the arm rest. If I couldn't actually sit, I could at least have my head up.

"Well, it didn't knock the sarcasm out of her, so that's a good sign. I don't know what I'd do with myself if our princess wasn't sarcastic anymore."

I motioned to myself, emphasizing on the bandage around my head. "If you still think I'm some sort of princess while looking like this, you must be delusional."

He rolled his eyes and smiled, sending my heart in loops. Even when I just got hit over the head with a rock and been knocked out for who knows how long, my feelings *still* somehow managed to focus on Lyle's stupidly attractive self. Jesus, I needed to get my priorities set.

I especially needed to distract myself. "So, has anyone seen Elias? I lost him at some point and thought he might've come back."

Constance glanced at Lyle nervously. "None of us have seen him—"

"Good riddance," Lyle grumbled under his breath.

"Cut it out!" She swatted at him. "I know that you do not like him, but we have more important things to worry about."

"Okay, quick question. How did I even *get* here?" I asked. "The barrier had kept me trapped in the garden earlier, which was really weird. It's the only reason why I didn't come back sooner."

She frowned. "That *is* bizarre. But what may be even more bizarre was the fact that you just...appeared outside of the garden. We had assumed that Elias had been the one to get you out, because when we went to check on you, you were lying on the floor unconscious. That was certainly off putting, to say the least. But you said you had lost him?"

"Yeah. We had gotten there and split up. And when I found a secret tunnel, I texted him, and that was the last I heard from him. I thought he had just ditched me. And if he *was* the one who had taken me out of the garden, why wouldn't he have just brought me straight to you guys?"

Constance sighed. "That is a fair point."

"Now that we have *that* settled," Lyle cut in, "can you explain *what the hell happened?*"

I did my best to explain everything that happened since lunch, from meeting Mary to discovering the map in the ceiling to getting hit in the head with the rock. As I was describing the end, I barely remembered the last thing Mary had said before I got knocked out.

"She said 'he told me to' before she hit me. And she had a blue ring around her eyes—it was super weird. It was like she was under some sort of mind control. And, sadly, there's only one person here who could be capable of that."

Lyle groaned. "Wick."

"Ding-ding-ding, you got it right."

Of *course* he's the one making this harder for me. It's almost as if he made it his *job*. I wished that he could just go away, but he's probably stuck here with the rest of the ghosts. Why else would he spend all this time just messing with me? He probably had Mary under his wing already! That's why she would let the mind control happen, if you even had a choice. If only Wick could stop being a little brat and leave, that'd be *great*.

I didn't realize I'd been thinking out loud until I heard Lyle's contagious laugh. "You're totally right, that *would* be great. Or, even better, I could punch his annoyingly stupid face. That would be amazing, too."

I raised my fist for a fist bump, which served as a brutal reminder that none of the ghosts knew what it was. Lyle stared at me with his head tilted like a confused dog, but I was pretty sure it'd confuse him more if I just put it away without any more explanation, so I did my best.

I grabbed his hand with one of mine, ignoring the brief excitement I felt as I did so, and curled it into a fist before tapping it against my own. "Okay, so this is a fist bump. It's a modern thing that shows, like, recognition. It can also be used as a greeting, or a congratulatory thing. It's kinda similar to a high five, which is the same thing except your palm is open, like this." I unfurled his hand again. It's *really* weird trying to explain this stuff.

"Wait, I gotta try this now." He looked like he was going for a high five, but instead of clapping our hands together, he latched onto my hand and interlocked our fingers. He smiled with satisfaction as I hoped he couldn't tell how red my face probably was. "Did I do it right?"

"Uh- close enough."

"You two shouldn't be allowed in the same room anymore," Ray said with a smile. I hadn't even realized he came in. I guess he had a talent for slipping in places undetected.

Lyle let go to turn and face Ray. "Hey, are you alright? You've barely left your room since she came back from the garden."

"Oh, I'm fine. I just had something saved up for Quincey."

I raised my eyebrow as he dumped a large pile of caramels onto my lap. "For you to enjoy! A sweet feast!"

I chuckled as I rubbed my hand over the stash. "Thanks, but I don't think I'll be able to go through all of this. I need to get back to the garden as soon as I can. Which reminds me...how long was I out for?"

"Well," Constance announced, "you came last night around sunset, and it is currently noon."

My eyebrows shot up. "Really? It's already noon?"

"Yes, already. And you better not be eating all of those now."

I put my hand over my heart. "I, Quincey Drew Oaks, promise to not eat all of these caramels right at this instance."

She bit back a smile. "It truly is good to see you better." She leaned in for a hug, and whispered in my ear as she did so. "Lyle has refused to leave your side since you came back."

She pulled back with a proud smile as my gaze instinctively flitted to Lyle, who's still keeping an eye on me. Just imagining him staying with me was enough to make my heart race, however small and stupid it was. Everything he did gave me butterflies—he's just so freaking awesome.

Of course I finally met an amazing guy and he had to be *dead*.

"Okay," Lyle started, "I'm no medical expert, so I really don't know what we should do for Quincey's head, but I'm willing to help any way I can. Do we need to let her rest? Ice? Pain medication?"

Ugh, stop being so nice. "I don't know either, but I really don't need to be coddled. I'll be fine—" I tried pushing myself off of the couch, but it just led to another dizzy rush. Lyle quickly grabbed my arm and gently guided me back down to the couch.

"No, no, I'll be *fine*. It's just a bit of vertigo. I need to get back to the garden and try finding Mary. Maybe I could try something else, but without Elias, I—"

"Quincey, you are *not* going back. Not yet."

There was a sternness in his voice that I hadn't heard before. He's still holding onto my arm, but his grasp was still as gentle as it had been earlier, his thumb tracing over my skin. In the end, I knew he just wanted what was best for me, even if it made me frustrated.

I glanced at Constance, who was watching me with a smug look, something I never thought she could do. "He is right. It would be extremely…irresponsible for you to go back now, especially like this."

"Are you gonna make me stay in bed rest? I'd hope you know by now that it wouldn't work very well."

"I suppose not. Just stay in this part of the mansion, please. No dangerous exploring."

Well, that made me feel a bit better. "Okay, fine. I can wait. Can I try going back tomorrow?"

"We will see how you are feeling when we get there."

It may not have been my original plan, but one day wasn't so bad. I could make it that far, even if it's annoying. "*Fine*."

Lyle smiled at me. "Thank you."

Just seeing him smile made me smile back. "You're welcome. It makes sense, anyway. Don't want to be getting hit over the head two days in a row."

And it'll give me time to figure out a plan for tomorrow. Unless I pass out again, I'm going tomorrow, whether they like it or not.

Chapter Forty-Seven
Mary's Story

The headaches didn't last much longer once I started getting up and doing stuff. I still had a bit of pain throughout most of the day, but now it's much easier to handle. Without the random dizzy spells, I succeeded in going through the day without passing out once.

With a clearer head, I was also giving myself time to figure out what I would actually do once I went back. I looked back on my ideas from the notes app and cut out the second one—unless she'd been killed in her sleep, she probably knew how she died. While Lyle and Constance's deaths may have been left a mystery, they also didn't have an obvious bloodstain on their clothes.

So, other than the 'relying on chance' idea, I was left with two options: beating her in tag and listening to her life story. I was still planning on starting with the tag method and thought through the labyrinth of the garden. I had consulted the picture of the map on my phone repeatedly, even if the blue light made the headaches worse. My drawing skills weren't the best, and neither was my memory, but I tried my best to mark down the important parts of the garden: the center, the shed that led to nowhere, and hopefully the area where the secret tunnel had been. I didn't expect to calm her down the next time I went, but hopefully I could make some progress.

The rest of the day went by easily, and despite how late I had woken up, I managed to fall back to sleep easily. And when I woke up the next day, I was energized and ready to go back to the garden, even with a bit of a headache.

"Quincey, are you certain you can go back? I am aware that you say you are feeling better, but I would rather not risk it and have you come back to us unconscious again," Constance asked me again. It was her third time asking me since we sat down for lunch and I told them my plan.

"I am completely sure. If it helps, I can try bringing Elias back here to help me look, but I'm not sure how much we can rely on him—"

"Not at all," Lyle cut in. I still couldn't tell why he hated Elias so much, but I had to agree that the inconsistency was *extremely* annoying.

"Well," Minerva said, "I guess you better get going. Go, get that small child!"

The enthusiasm in her voice was clearly forced, but it still made me snort.

"You better not get a rock to the head again!" Ray called out, bringing our dishes to the trash.

"I'll try my best, but no promises."

As I said goodbye, Lyle stood up abruptly. I was going to wait to figure out what was wrong, but he sat back down again after a moment. *Weird.*

Ignoring the small bit of disappointment I felt in my chest, I started my way to the garden yet again. On the way, I pulled out my phone and searched for Elias' contact.

Checking out the garden again. The bear didn't work. Come if you want.

I had no clue what he would do or if he'd come at all, but at least I was giving him a chance. Something churned in my stomach as I looked into the garden again.

"Third time's the charm," I reassured myself as I stepped inside.

Instantly I was hit by the cool air. I took a deep breath, enjoying the freshness of it. The weather in the garden was much nicer than it's bound to be outside. We were nearing the colder season, though it didn't really get cold in Scottsdale.

I instinctively pulled out my phone to check the date.

"Tomorrow's Thanksgiving. I won't be with my mom for Thanksgiving."

I wasn't sure why I said it out loud; it wasn't like anyone else could hear me. But even just saying it out loud made my heart ache. Maybe she'd have Rachel and her family over, if she wasn't invited to my *abuela*'s. I knew she'd have Dad and Mimiko. God, I hadn't seen or talked to them since my birthday.

I missed them so much.

I told myself that I'd call them when I got back and put the phone away, knowing I couldn't handle thinking about it much longer. Even if I wanted to call them right then, I had a more pressing task ahead of me.

I had completely forgotten that I needed my phone for the map and hurried to pull it up. My first idea was to check the center again. That's where she found me last time, so she might be there again. Hopefully she wouldn't be under Wick's influence.

When I got there, I was greeted by Mary. Except she wasn't running from me this time; she wasn't even standing. She's sitting on a bench, the very one she had been standing on yesterday when she clocked me over the head. She must have been waiting for me. At least I assumed she had been—she had been watching the spot I entered from, so that seemed like a pretty big indicator for me.

Mary patted the spot beside her on the bench, setting down the flower she had just been twirling. "Hello again. Please, come sit."

Everything in me screamed *this is a trap*. It's way too easy.

From the corner of my eye, I noticed the bear, right where I had left it. I had completely forgotten about it after she ditched it, but it wasn't going to serve much at that point anyway. Still, I found myself instinctively going over to grab it. Now armed with a stuffed bear that would do nothing if she decided to attack me again, I made my way over to Mary and sat beside her.

I noticed her eyes—pure green, no blue to be found—flickering over to the side, probably debating whether or not she should run *now* or try hearing me out before eventually running *later*.

"Please don't run again."

I didn't bother to try hiding the exasperation in my voice. I was tired of constantly playing, and I was ready to just *talk*. I wasn't sure what we were going to talk about yet, but I knew I would think of something.

"Alright."

Relief flooded through me. I was still on edge but managed to relax a bit in my spot as I set the bear down beside me.

"*You* were the one who wanted to talk, correct?"

I would have thought that was obvious—how many other living people tried chasing her down in the garden? Other than Elias, I guess, but he had already ditched me. "Yes?"

"Then speak."

"You know," I said, "you seem pretty mature for a ten year old."

"Nine."

That sent a weird feeling through me, a mix of curiosity and sadness. Thinking about a *nine* year old dying wasn't something that crossed my mind every day. "Okay then, for a *nine* year old, you are pretty mature."

"Thank you. Now then, what was it you would to speak to me about?" Well, at least I didn't need to worry about her being silly. There's no more fun and games with her.

Okay, plan one doesn't really work if we aren't playing tag, so I guess we're trying plan two.

"Tell me about your story. If you're comfortable with that, of course," I quickly added. "Like, what was your life like before? How...how did you die?"

She looked caught off guard, and for a fleeting moment I thought I saw *something* strong in her eyes. It's probably the most emotion I had seen from her yet. "I-I suppose that I can tell you."

Did she really just say yes that quickly? I thought it was going to take more than just asking. Not that I had much of a plan if she refused to.

She took a deep breath, preparing herself. I expected it—I had learned from Ray that for the ghosts who *did* remember how they died, it wasn't an easy topic to talk about. It's easy to imagine why. I couldn't begin to think about what it would be like to remember how you died. Maybe ignorance *was* bliss, like the saying went.

"When I was younger," she began, "I loved stories of adventure. I grew up on a ship with my family and friends, and I was told of all the treasures they had found on their journeys across the seas. Whenever they went on one, I would be hiding below deck, reading my books. A large amount of the books were handwritten by my family, talking of sirens and mermaids and other sea monsters. They all loved to put their adventures to pen and paper. While most of the stories were exaggerated to make it more intriguing for my youthful mind, they never shied away from the bigger parts."

I wondered what type of stories she's talking about. If I had met her before all of this, in a completely normal way, I would have thought it was just her childish mind that believed the unbelievable. That part of my mind's the same one that had read those stories when I was her age, delving myself knee deep into the adventure. But if I had learned anything from living here in the mansion was to never disregard anything. *La Surnaturelle* had mentioned sirens, right?

"One day, our ship crashed while we were returning to our home town in England. The memory of the crash itself is both unclear and the clearest thing in my mind. I remember the small details—the boots of my father, the pearls from the necklace my mother wore. The whole crew was lost. The whole crew except for me."

Something about the way Mary told the story made me feel like a little kid again, curling up in the corner when I was supposed to be asleep and reading fantasy novels until the sun came up.

"I was impaled by a piece of wood in the wreck, right around here." She pointed to the stain on her apron, which suddenly looked more off putting than it had before. "I could never get it treated. No one was willing to treat the daughter of a criminal, especially as we had gone through that town before. I still have the scar that it left behind."

She gently pinched her fingers through the holes and revealed an ugly scar. The scar itself wasn't horrible, a rough circle half the size of a dime, but the red around it made it look even worse. Like it had decorated itself.

"What- what happened next?" I asked.

"I was outcasted by the town and was forced to live in the nearby forest. Specifically in a garden. Not quite as beautiful as this one, but still stunning."

She grabbed the flower that was on the other side of her and began twirling it again. "A few of the older women had been kind enough to give me food and water, and I am still thankful for them now. I believe one was named Elinor." She smiled ever so slightly as she said the name. It was only there for a moment before it faded away.

"After that, I was all alone. My memory is hazy, but I do know that I would occasionally go to the market and steal food. There was a river nearby that I could get water from. I must have died shortly after, because one night I had gone to sleep and woken up in this garden. I was angry, though now I have not the faintest idea why."

That's...a lot.

"I'm...glad I know that now. I—"

I got cut off by the sound of a loud crash.

Something big happened, just outside of the garden. My heart raced in my chest as I thought about what it could be.

I turned to face Mary, and she's standing before I could even ask.

"I heard it as well. We must hurry, in case someone is in danger."

With that, we ran straight towards the chaos.

Chapter Forty-Eight
I Challenge Thee to a Duel

Before we could reach whatever caused the crash, though, we needed to find a way out of the garden.

Sadly—or maybe thankfully—the crash did not come from the way I had entered from. As annoying as it would be to try finding my way around if Mary ditched me, it brought a sense of comfort to know that the ghosts were most likely safe. All of my faith rested in Mary and her hopefully not leaving me in the dust.

I followed her blindly through the twists and turns of the garden, which she navigated with ease. She pulled back the leaves from one of the tall standing plants and revealed another ladder leading down to a secret passage.

"There's no way I could have beat you in tag, man."

She smiled as she offered for me to go down first.

I cautiously lowered myself underground and reached out to help Mary as she climbed down. She swatted at my hand and hopped down after a couple rungs. My eyebrows shot up, but now wasn't the time to ask her about the workings of the garden. We had to find where that crash came from.

We ran through the tunnel with Mary leading the way. When we popped up on the other end, we were within view of a door. Where the door could lead anyway, considering the fact that the map said the garden was the only thing back here, I had no idea.

Mary gestured towards the door. "Would you like to open it?"

Not really, I thought to myself as I reached out nonetheless.

As I twisted the knob, I prayed that there wasn't another shadow creature as I swung the door open. All that stood before us was a hallway.

"Maybe we were tricked?" I suggested.

"Doubtful. Let us go down the corridor."

Without any further thought, Mary started briskly down the hallway. I scurried to follow her, knowing that I couldn't leave her alone, especially not after what just happened. I tried thinking back to where in the mansion we could be—there wasn't anything *behind* the garden, but I think there might have actually been some rooms on the right of where we usually were. Taking a couple steps back but keeping Mary within my line of sight, I quickly pulled out the map of the mansion.

How had I never paid attention to the whole second half of the mansion? All of the mansion that I explored up to that point was all on the left side.

As weird as the inside of the mansion looked, it didn't seem to line up with what it looked like from the outside that first day.

"This mansion is just weird," I grumbled.

"Hmm?"

I hadn't realized I'd started to fall behind. I hurriedly caught myself up to Mary again, who's practically jogging at this point. It's getting harder to see her—this side's less lit and even colder. Even though I knew we were still in the same building as before, it felt like I had stepped into a different plane of reality.

The darkness must have been intended, because it helped conceal Wick.

I skidded to a halt, Mary slowing down as well.

"Damn it..." I muttered.

I heard the sound of banging from beside him and looked around to see Constance, Lyle and Ray all trapped in some kind of bubble. It *looked* like glass, but it had to be some kind of magic, so anything's possible.

They were yelling, but it all came out warbled, like they were underwater. I had never seen them look more terrified; what had Wick done to them? But something else had caught my attention that raised a different and slightly more terrifying question—*where the hell was Minerva?*

I whipped my head back to Wick. "Where is Minerva, and why are *they* here?!"

He shrugged. "Do either of those things really matter?"

I looked at him like he was stupid. "*Yes.*"

He flicked his hand as though he could dismiss the thought as a tangible object. Then, he turned to Mary with a warm smile.

"Mary, why don't you come and help me? We can get revenge on those who wronged us. We can finally be free! They will all *listen*. Why trust *this* adult when all others have proven to be corrupt? Selfish? *Untrustworthy*?" He walked over and squatted down, holding a hand out to her. "You know you can trust *me*, right?"

I looked at Mary, praying she wouldn't go. How would she be able to trust *him*? He's only ever been angry and violent.

But then I remembered what she had said. *He told me to.*

They must have been talking already. With my luck, they probably already become best friends, however sick a way someone like Wick could bond with someone.

Then Mary ran to Wick, wrapping her arms tightly around him. Feeling deflated, my fears came true—I had no chance in the first place, because he had gotten to her first. Even from the hug, I could see Wick's sick smirk.

I had no idea what I was going to do now. In all the rest of these fights, I always felt like I had *someone* by my side.

Now I had no one.

Wick let go of Mary, directing her to his side. She stood restlessly, avoiding my gaze. If I could do anything to wipe the smug look on Wick's face as he turned to face me, I would.

Well, I could certainly try.

With a surprising amount of courage that I didn't know I had, I rolled up my sleeve before I ran up to Wick and socked him in his dumb and annoying face. As I had mentioned before, extremely punchable.

Despite the pain in my hand, the punch felt *amazing*. When I glanced over at the others, Lyle and Ray were cheering from inside the bubble.

Without warning, Wick began laughing drily. It wasn't loud and psychotic like Minerva's had been that first day, but it was terrifying on a whole different level. Angry people laughing out of nowhere was *never* a good thing.

"Let's take this somewhere else, shall we?"

With a twirl of his wrist, the three of us were transported to the ballroom, except everything that had filled up the room had been shoved to the outskirts. Not only that, but somehow the ground that had just been hardwood changed to grass beneath my feet. I stumbled backwards, looking up in fearful awe. What kind of spirit *was* Wick, and how could he have done all of this?

Wick threw open his hands and spun slowly, giddy with glee. "Violence is the only religion known to every man." He opened his hand and it engulfed in fire, sending me a few steps back. "And the battlefield is the church."

I ignored the panic that was growing in my chest. "How long have you been waiting to say that line?"

"Very long, thank you very much."

He smiled as his other hand caught ablaze. "Now then, what do you say, Quincey? How about we settle this once and for all?"

Wick's taunting me; I *knew* that. He's hoping that I'd go down without a fight, without any struggle. It'd be easier for him if I just took the defeat and left.

But that wasn't going to happen. I had risked too much for everything to go down in flames without even a bit of a fight from me.

"I've waited so long to beat your ass," I said with a grin.

"How about we make this a little more interesting?" Wick announced. With another twirl of his wrist, the bubble and all of the ghosts inside were cast to the side. It's almost as if they were in a spectator box. "We'll have your little friends watch as I torture you slowly, hearing all of your agonizing screams until death sounds better than continuing the fight. How does that sound?"

"Leave them out of this," I said through gritted teeth.

"I *am*. I'm just making them watch as their souls' savior is tortured and killed," Wick answered nonchalantly.

I looked over at them. I could practically hear them telling me to be safe, find a way to get out of this unscathed. They knew that compared to Wick and all of his magic, I was a mouse in the cat's paw.

The problem was, no one ever made a change when they went down quietly.

"If you think I'm going to go down that easily, think again."

He raised an eyebrow before lifting his fists. "Oh, I'm going to enjoy this."

I tried finding something around the room that I could use to my advantage, but I wasn't given the luxury of looking before Wick cast the first spell.

Chapter Forty-Nine
Epic Battle Sequence: Activated

I could barely dodge in time before he blasted the wall with his spell right where I was standing, leaving a scorch mark in its wake.

"What, are you so afraid to use your fists that you have to hide behind your magic?" I taunted him. I had no idea if it's smart to anger your opponent, especially when they had a significant upper hand. But hey, I always saw trash-talking in movies, so might as well.

"It's not wise to tease during a losing battle, now is it?" Wick said as he cast out another spell.

"No idea!" I almost got hit again, but I somehow managed to dance my way out of the spell's range.

I accidentally rammed myself into the bubble that the three ghosts had been trapped in. When I turned around, I saw Lyle and Ray aggressively pointing to something at their right. I didn't have enough time to figure out what it was, however, because I had to dive away from another fireball.

The heat of the flames brushed against my skin as the fireball flew over my back, just barely touching it. Not enough to burn it.

I put myself up hastily—I didn't have time to stay on the ground and become an easy target. Didn't people say that if you were getting shot at, you should run in zig-zags so it's harder for your opponents to hit? I would guess that the logic applied here, too.

Then again, I was in a completely open room, and despite the large size of it overall, there wasn't much I could actually run *towards*.

Wick started circling me, probably thinking about which way he should cast his fireball at me next so I couldn't dodge it. I tried matching him so he couldn't surprise me from behind, but I was dealing with a ghost who had *magic*—anything's possible, and that was scary as hell.

My gaze flicked over to what Lyle and Ray had been gesturing to before: a variety of glasses, silverware, and plates. Where were these hiding?

What the hell was I supposed to do with those? Throw them?

That actually isn't a bad idea. But maybe I just loved the idea of throwing things at annoying people.

I stared down Wick, trying to figure out in the back of my mind when I could get back and grab the plates. This time, I actually saw him forming a fireball. Maybe that's the only spell he knew, or maybe he's just bad at everything else. Both made sense to me.

I waited until he was about to throw it, then I bolted.

"What?" It clearly caught him by surprise. "What are you *doing*?"

"Why would I tell you?" I shouted back.

I made it to the dishes when something shiny caught the corner of my eye—the reflections of a few empty wine bottles. I imagined smashing them over Wick's head and knocking him unconscious, but I doubted I had enough strength to do that. And there was no way I'd be able to get close enough. So, throwing them at him for mild inconvenience would have to be enough.

I started with the silverware. They were small enough to cause a distraction, but none of them did any damage. They bounced off of him harmlessly until he regained his wits and ignored them. Groaning, I rolled over to miss another fireball. If I kept this up, I was either going to leave this fight with third degree burns or an extremely annoyed wizard, neither of which would end up well for me.

Wick's just getting angrier and angrier the more I chucked silverware at him. Soon, I was just throwing in a wild panic.

As I was running low, I heard a yell.

At first I was worried that it had come from one of the ghosts, but they were still safe inside the bubble. Instead, it had come from Wick—somehow, in some way, he had managed to hit *himself* with his fireball. It didn't burn him, but it still caught his sleeve on fire. On the ground next to him, there's a bigger spoon that looked like it was steaming. Had the fireball somehow hit off the spoon? Either way, it's a win for me.

Lyle and Ray were cheering, but they quickly quieted down as Ray's eyes widened in terror. He motioned for me to turn around, but by then it was too late; a fireball had hit my shoulder.

I screamed in pain, kneeling to the ground. Tears spilled over onto my cheeks, and my hands were shaking. I felt like I could barely breathe.

No. You can't give up now. No matter what happens, you need to keep fighting, or else Wick wins. That prick doesn't deserve it.

I grunted as I pushed myself up. My shoulder still hurt like hell, but I still had the clothes on my back and I wasn't going to die, so that was good enough for me. I gently reached over my shoulder and felt the edges of my sweater and shirt where the fireball had broken through—at least they hadn't caught on fire.

I slowly turned around, feeling the anger rising in my chest.

Wick watched me with a raised eyebrow, keeping his fists up by his chin. "Wow, Quincey. I was certain that would keep you down. You've never been one to underestimate, though."

"Says the guy who underestimated me on *several* occasions."

He stomped the ground, and soon I was surrounded by pillars of dirt.

Well, that explains why he wanted the grass.

I felt my way around my cage, which was when I realized the dirt wasn't very stable. In a matter of seconds, I was able to kick down every pillar.

I was about to taunt Wick about how easy that'd been to knock down before I froze in my tracks. My smile dropped as I saw him doing a much, *much* bigger spell.

It didn't take long to figure out the pillars were a distraction, but it took me longer than it should have to realize that another ball of bright white fire was being hurled my way. I covered my head and squeezed my eyes shut as I felt small chunks of rock hitting my skin.

When I opened my eyes again, all I could see were large dark spots clouding almost my entire vision. All I could see were small slivers in the gaps, like water running between stones.

"Damn it!"

I could practically hear Minerva telling me off about how I had done something similar during our first encounter, but it wasn't the time to focus on that.

I heard the smirk in Wick's voice as he spoke. "Oh, are you having a hard time *seeing* your victory?"

"Seriously? A pun?" One hand shielded my eyes as the other middle finger graced the presence of the direction I heard his voice from.

The black blobs were still taking over my vision, but they slowly started to go away as I blinked more. It's a painfully slow process, though.

I ducked down to miss another fireball.

I heard the door opening and instinctively turned to see who it was even though I couldn't see anything. I hoped for it to be Minerva, but my luck was never that good.

"Elias?!" Wick exclaimed. I couldn't tell if he was angry or confused, or maybe even afraid.

"Hello again, Wick." Elias' voice, usually reserved, had a degree of confidence behind it.

Even though Elias had said he thought Wick left, something about the way he said that told me otherwise. Could Elias have known Wick's been here the whole time? And if so, what kind of history did the two have to make Wick so angry at him?

"Where'd you come from?! You totally ditched me in the garden!"

"What? I've been lost wandering the garden for the past couple days. My phone died so I couldn't find you, and *you* said no yelling. I only found you because of the sound from the crash!"

"How do you even get lost for two days?! You know what, nevermind! Now isn't the time to be arguing about this!"

"Have you come to watch the show? I was just getting around to beating your pawn." Well, the surprise didn't last long. Again. And what did he mean by *pawn*? This was too confusing.

My flash blindness finally went away, and I could see Elias standing at the entrance to the ballroom, staring out onto the field. His eyes lingered on the bubble that the ghosts were in—would he realize that Minerva's gone, too?

"You won't win. You never did, and you never will."

Wick started to laugh. "Oh, but you see, I already have! All I need to do is throw one final spell at your little...*minion* here, and she's *dead*. Everything will go back to the way it was, and I'll still be here to haunt your dreams. These poor souls and I will serve to remind you that you were *so close* to making everything right, but you *didn't*."

Elias' eyes widened as he took a step back.

"Sadly, I can't have you ruining my plans. I'm going to have to deal with you."

Mary was still by Wick's side the whole time, watching the fight with wide eyes. She was taking this in like a sponge; it's probably reminding her of the battles on her ship. She had grown up with pirates—of course she saw violence like this often.

I was so focused on Mary, I didn't even realize that Wick had fired at Elias until he was already on the ground.

"No!" I needed all the help I could get, even if it was from Elias.

"Oh, boo-hoo. Do you actually *like* the old man?"

"He's only, like, twenty-eight."

Wick opened his mouth to say something, but Elias cut him off. He had pushed himself to his feet, albeit weakly. "I'll help you, Quincey. I'm—" he inhaled sharply— "I'm done waiting for other people to fix my mistakes."

I still wasn't sure what kind of mistakes they were talking about, but I was grateful for the help. "Are you sure you can fight? You aren't looking too hot at the moment."

Before Elias could answer, Wick cast another spell. A ring of fire grew around us, blocking the two of us out from Elias and the ghosts.

"Let's end this now, Quincey. No more playing nice."

When was he ever playing nice? "You're on."

Chapter Fifty
This is Clearly Not Fair

Wick continued to cast his spells, and I continued to dodge them. But his spells were starting to become slower and smaller, and his breathing was labored. I wasn't sure how much longer I could keep up with the fighting myself.

It's a miracle that I hadn't lost yet, but clearly Elias' presence had unnerved Wick for some reason. What had he done that left Wick so freaked out just by him being in the same room? I kept catching Wick stealing fervent glances in Elias' direction, who I could barely see over the flames. I already knew that they've met before, but how? Elias only knew about the mansion because of the ghosts, but Wick had already been mad at Elias. What could have happened? He's been stuck here in the mansion…

…or was he a ghost at all?

I swerved from another spell as the thought danced across my mind. None of the other ghosts had magic, but he could have just been a very powerful wizard when he died. I tried wracking my brain for everything *La Surnaturelle* had mentioned about wizards and other magical people, but fighting for my life didn't help me think very much.

Wick threw another attack, but it missed by a few yards without me even needing to move. Maybe I could keep up my luck, but I didn't want to press my chances with fate.

Wick raised his arms high above his head before slamming them back down. I could barely process the burning chains that were hurling at me until they were only a few feet away. I slid off to the side, but I didn't completely dodge the attack—they had still grazed my better arm.

If I hadn't been afraid before, the fear definitely kicked into overdrive now. What could I do to fight back? I had ditched the dishes earlier, but I wasn't sure what else I could do with plates and bowls. Even if I could find a way to push through the fire, what would I do with the dishes and a few wine bottles?

Beneath my foot, I felt something hard. As I looked down on it, I grinned.

May not be the perfect weapon, but I could work with this.

If only I could find a way to reach him.

My chest felt like it was about to explode, but I didn't have enough time to pause and take a breather. The heat from the fire reached my neck. I scurried forward. I had almost forgotten about the ring, but was it just me, or was it getting smaller?

I stared up at Wick, who was heaving now.

Now or never.

I tightened my grip on the steak knife as I bolted toward him and plunged it into his side.

He gasped as I slid past him. His hands slowly reached to where the knife was embedded. I gave him a nice kick behind the knees, sending him down to the floor.

In between shaky breaths, Wick asked a simple question. "Tell me, Quincey, would you like to know about Minerva *now* or *later*?"

"Now!"

Suddenly, Wick stilled. Slowly, he stood back up, grabbing the bloody knife and dropping it by his side. Blood soaked his cream shirt, and his forehead glistened with sweat. "Suit yourself."

Through the fire emerged Minerva, but it wasn't quite her. Her stance was more rigid, and her face was completely blank. She usually had a good poker face, but the way she looked right now was more robotic than anything that could be natural.

"Minnie, it's time to help."

Oh no.

As Wick limped away, probably to tend his wound, Minerva's dark brown eyes gained a bonus ring of vibrant blue, just like Mary had.

Minerva could easily beat me. She's the one who had trained me to fight at all, and I had already forgotten a majority of what she taught me.

This was *not* going to end well, for me specifically.

From my left, I saw Mary running towards me. She fell side by side with Minerva, having a matching ring around her own eyes. I glared at Wick, who's standing in the direction Mary had just come from.

"*Now* the fight is equal!"

"*How the hell is this equal?!*" What does he think I can do?

"Just wait—I know Elias. He's going to join in the fight and *play the hero*, isn't he?" Wick turned to face Elias with a raised eyebrow, beckoning him to try running through the flames to join in. What *Elias* could do, I had no idea. But if it freaked Wick out this much, I'd take it gladly.

I could see Elias' fearful eyes above the flames. *He's not going to come. Not yet.*

"Oh, that's pathetic." Wick's exaggerated frown quickly flipped over to a wide smile. "Well, more fun for me then."

"Get him, Q!"

I whipped my head around to see the rest of the ghosts were out of the bubble. While I was glad they weren't trapped, now they were right in the line of danger. If the fire spread outward, they were on the opposite side of the entrance—there's no way they'd get over in time. I didn't know what magical fire would do to people who were already dead, but it couldn't be good.

Ray was cheering loudly, which surprisingly gave me a confidence boost. Lyle and Constance both looked panicked, though the former could have also been debating how fast he'd have to run to get through the fire and strangle Wick.

Lyle's eyes widened as he pointed to something behind me. "Watch out!"

I dropped to the ground, just low enough for the fireball to go flying over my head.

"Are fireballs the only offense you have?" I called out to Wick, whirling around.

"Has anyone told you that you talk too much?" Wick turned to Minerva and gave a small nod. I didn't know what kind of telepathic communication they were using, if any at all, but Minerva began marching her way over to me.

"Surprisingly enough, nope."

One of the perks of Minerva being in this mind-control-trance-thing was that she couldn't run very fast. I just had to power walk out of her grasp and I'd be good to go.

I knew I jinxed myself the moment I noticed, because Minerva went right into a deadsprint. What, could she hear my thoughts now?

Fleeting memories of the first day came back to me, getting chased by Minerva through the mansion. Except now I only had the small ring of fire to keep enough distance between the two of us to leave unscathed.

Wick yelled to me as I ran. "This is a losing battle, Quincey! Give up now. Go home. Forget everything that happened in the mansion and go back to a regular life. Let Elias face the consequences of his actions, let him know that lives can't be easily thrown to the side!"

"What did he even *do*?"

"I'll let him tell you that himself, once you surrender and go down easily."

I was toward the edge of the ring, running up to Ray, who's aggressively pointing at something in front of him. On the ground was the collection of dishes—he must have thrown them across the fire.

Thank God for Ray's quick thinking.

I slid across the grass, coming to a halt in front of the stash.

"If there's anything you should know about me by now," I called out to Wick, grabbing a large silver platter, "it's that I never go down easily."

With that, I stood up and whacked Minerva over the head with as much force as I could muster.

She fell to the ground, but I knew that the hit wouldn't keep her down for long, so I bolted as soon as she hit the ground. I apologized to her in my head, knowing that she'd yell at me about it later if I made it out. Hopefully it could buy me at least a couple minutes.

As I passed Wick, I gave him a nice hit with the platter, which I was still holding.

"You really are annoying, Quincey."

"I could say the same about you, candle boy."

Even with all the other noise, I could hear Elias' attempt at stifling his laughter, though he's failing miserably.

"Shut up!" Wick snarled at Elias.

Suddenly, I felt sharp hits on my back and arms. Sharpened rocks shredded my clothes and were scattered on the floor around me. I bit back a scream as some hit my burnt shoulder.

I turned around to see Wick grinning as he threw out more. A quick dodge couldn't get me out of this, and there's no safe way to turn to minimize the impact. Everywhere was vital.

It's painfully obvious—I was losing.

I shook my head to try and clear my thoughts like one of those digital sketch pads. I needed to focus if I wanted to have any chance of winning this.

I only had one thought in my mind as I faced Wick.

Let's do this.

Chapter Fifty-One
Elias Seriously Lacks Communication Skills

"You know, if you had magic this whole time, why didn't you use it in any of our fights before this?"

"Because fists are much more satisfying, wouldn't you agree?"

"Quincey! Less talking, more winning!" Elias shouted from the sidelines.

"You know, two against one isn't that easy, *Elias*!" I snarled back at him. He had said he was going to help, and Wick's clearly scared of him, so why wasn't he doing anything? He needed to hurry his ass up.

"Well then, let's make this a bit more balanced, shall we?" He must have heard my prayers, because before I knew it, he was by my side with his fists up. He had ditched his long coat, revealing his absolutely *ripped* arms. Definitely not what I was expecting from the anxious nerd.

Wait, did he just walk through fire?

Wick's eyes widened with fear, bringing up the question once again: what's Elias capable of that had him so terrified?

"You focus on those two," Elias muttered to me. "I'll get Wick."

Before I could say anything, Elias charged, leaving me with Minerva and Mary.

I had almost forgotten about Mary until she was right next to me and holding my hands behind my back. I tried breaking free, but maybe it was Wick's magic giving her newfound strength because I couldn't. She's literally *nine*, how else could she have that much strength *other* than through magic?

Minerva, who had since gotten off the ground and rejoined the fight, raised her fist. I ducked out of the way just in time as she threw a punch. Her face was still slack, but boy did she have strength in her fists. I looked over my shoulder and saw that Mary's face was also robotic, completely neutral and staring at nothing.

I glanced over at the battle between Wick and Elias.

"Elias, you have *magic*? And you didn't think to tell me before?!"

"Oh, yes, sorry about that!"

Sweat was glistening off Wick's forehead. Elias' fists had been set alight in fire—the only reason I even realized he had magic. I didn't know the specifics about magic, but it seemed like they both liked fire. A lot.

I got a hard hit to the gut from Minerva, right where my bruise had been. I swore under my breath and doubled over, though being bound behind the back made my movements somewhat limited.

Suddenly, Mary let go.

I looked back up at Minerva, who's breathing heavily and rubbing her head. Her eyes were wide, and they were back to normal. No more blue rings around them. When I saw Mary wrap around the corner, her eyes were the same green they had been before. Wick's losing his grip on them.

The fire around us was still burning, but it wasn't quite as tall as it had been before. Maybe I'd be able to burst through the fire if I needed to.

Minerva and Mary stayed by the edge of the ring as I ran up to join Elias, ready to continue fighting.

That's when I heard the yelling, stopping me in my tracks.

"Why are you doing this?!"

"Because," Wick started as he threw another fireball, "you *left* me. Do you know how hard it was to lose our mother and father? And then my own *brother* left me to pursue magic, completely forgetting I existed! I was *thirteen*!"

Hold up, they were *brothers*?

The sense of familiarity I had felt when I had first seen Wick was starting to make sense. But Wick had been at the mansion for who knew how long, and Elias was from the present. What was happening?

"I still wanted to be like you at first," Wick continued through grunts. "That's why I followed your path into magic, even becoming immortal like you!"

Well, that explained a bit about Wick. But Elias? The most paranoid man I've ever met is an immortal?

"Even as I went with you on your journeys for *years*, you never even noticed me! Oh, how dumb I had been. But you were even dumber. I had seen what you did to these poor souls, and I saw how much you regretted it, and that's when I knew. I finally figured out how to put you through all the pain you put *me* through! And it's working! You've never forgiven yourself, have you? You ruined their lives, just like you ruined mine!"

I took a few steps back; this was clearly a fight for them to handle alone. If Elias needed me, I could hop in. While I watched the battle unfold, I tried to process everything I had heard.

Wick and Elias were brothers, and their parents died.

Elias left him to pursue magic, and Wick secretly followed him.

Apparently Elias did something to the ghosts that only the two of them knew, but instead of doing the smart thing and trying to help the ghosts, Wick uses them to get back at his brother for...leaving him?

Wow. Angsty teenager much?

They fell into silence as they hurled spell after spell at each other, primarily made of fireballs. They *really* needed to spice up their repertoire.

Wick rammed into Elias, sending them both my way. I hurried backwards as they fell where I had just been standing. My back found the wall, and I took deep breaths.

Wait, the wall?

As I looked around, the ring of fire was gone. Relief crashed down onto me, and I almost fell to the ground right there.

"Quincey!" It was Lyle.

Before I knew it, Lyle had his arms wrapped around me as he squeezed me tightly, lifting my feet off the ground. It felt like he was crushing my ribs, but I didn't care. Having the comfort of someone next to me overruled any of the pain I felt.

As he set me down, his eyes frantic. He was speaking at a thousand miles an hour, and his accent didn't help. "Are you alright?! You were such a badass out there, but those hits looked awful. Just say the word and I will beat Wick's ass to a pulp right now. That fireball was awful, and- I'm just glad you're safe now." He hugged me again, and I yelped as his arms brushed against the burn on my shoulder.

He swore. "Did I touch something wrong?"

"It- it's fine, I can handle it later." I glanced over at the fight. "Right now, we really need to get off the battlefield before we get trampled."

"You are right as always, princess."

Before we could move, there was an explosion.

Chapter Fifty-Two
Meaningful Conversations Behind a Table

The explosion was mere feet away from us. If we had been only a few feet to the right, we would've been dead. Or, in Lyle's case, dead *again*.

My heart jumped into my throat, and by the look of panic on Lyle's face, he must have been having a similar experience. We stood in fear until I came to my senses.

"Run that way!" I pointed to the left, and Lyle went over and overturned a table for us to hide behind like the others, who were on the other side of the ballroom. When I glanced over at the fight, Elias seemed to be holding his own. He wasn't even sweating as Wick pounded out more and more spells, his timidity nowhere to be found. Feeling confident, I ran over and joined Lyle.

"So, I take it that calming Mary didn't go very well for you?"

"Wow, you really *are* a genius."

"What can I say? It's just the way I am," Lyle answered with a smug grin. If we weren't literally in the middle of a battle, I would have shoved him.

I peeked my head over the table, trying to see if they had reined it back in. The table that the others were hiding behind was scorched. I held my breath, watching the scene play out and hoping Elias would win. It's just like I was watching a movie, except the stakes and my anxiety were both way higher.

"Quincey?" Lyle asked.

"Yes?" I didn't take my eyes off of the fight.

"Your shoulder."

I sighed as I sat back down. My shoulder and arm had hurt like hell since I got the burn, but I didn't exactly have time to think about it. It's a bit more bearable if I ignored it, but the adrenaline rush must have helped the pain a bit. Now that I wasn't on the battlefield, the pain was worse.

"How can I help?"

I turned and looked at Lyle. When I was with him, it's so easy to forget about everything else. All the pain, the fear, the fighting. It's like the world I was drowning in was put on pause, and I finally had a moment to breathe. As he watched me with his searching eyes, I had no idea how to answer the question.

Eventually, I reached out for his hand. I traced my thumb over his knuckles, and his hold was gentle. "Just stay with me. Please."

He slowly moved so he was next to me, never letting go of my hand. "I can do that."

Him being so close to me made my cheeks and neck feel warm, but I didn't even care if he noticed. Everything in me just wanted to be close to him and get as far away from this place as possible. I just wanted to go home.

"I can't believe I'm not dead yet."

"What?" Confusion crossed his face. "What makes you think that?"

"What would make me think otherwise? Like, I've gone through so many near death experiences. Honestly, it's crazy that nothing has kept me down yet. I keep wondering how I ended up being the one to actually do anything. Elias said he had been searching for people for, what, five years? And then this random teenager comes across and suddenly I'm more capable than all the adults who had come before me. It just feels too…I don't know. Too unrealistic. Not that magic or anything else about this damn place was realistic *before* I went through all of this, but…"

"But?" He prompted me to continue.

"I don't feel like I should have been the one to make it. There are so many incredible people out there, and somehow *I* was the one who ended up here. I don't have much going for me; I'm just this anxious mess that can't do anything right. I- I overthink everything, and it keeps me from actually getting anything done. Even after all the training I've gone through with Minerva, I couldn't handle Wick. It's like I put myself into this position and life just said 'hey, how much harder can we make this?' And to think that the biggest worry I had before this was how I would pay for college." I laughed despite the pain I was feeling. "That seems pretty damn stupid now, don't you think?"

I took a deep breath, trying to calm myself down. There's so much on my mind that I hadn't even known I was struggling with, and I definitely didn't mean to spill it all out on Lyle. Again.

"You know," he said slowly, "there was this saying that my father always said. Not an Italian one. 'Heart of gold and mind of steel.' That's what made the best people, at least in his head. I may not have always agreed with him, but I could agree with that. It was kind of ironic, coming from him. He wasn't much of the friendly type."

Then he turned to look at me, studying my face. "You don't come across those people very often. But when you do, you want to keep them close."

He had an arm wrapped around my shoulder—avoiding where the burn was—and rocked me back and forth with a smile. "And I'd say I'm doing a pretty good job at that."

My brain short-circuited like a robot. Maybe I was overthinking it, but part of me thought that he might have gotten the same rush that I had.

"There's actually something I feel like I should tell you—"

Before he could explain, something—or someone—slammed into the table.

We were both thrown forward, my body hitting the ground with a hard thud. Lyle rolled over to the side, and the only thing that kept me from getting pinned under the table was the wall. I heard grumbling from above me.

"Elias?"

"Quincey? What are you doing under the table?" He sounded bewildered.

"I wasn't under it until you *slammed* into it, now get off so I don't get crushed!"

He quickly pushed himself off, bringing the table back up with him. There's a crack down the center of it that's barely being held together. If he had been just a bit heavier, I would have gone splat.

I pushed myself back up and stared down at Elias. Though he still seemed to be holding up better than Wick, his entire body was trembling. Neither of them could keep this going for much longer.

"I can't do this," he said breathlessly. "I really thought I could. I'm so sorry I let you down—"

"Elias!" I snapped to get his attention. "I know it's draining, but you need to keep going. None of us can get to Wick—you're the only one who can do that. Now get your ass up and go get some sense knocked into him."

That must have done the trick, because he just nodded and got up. His legs were weak, but he still ran forward to get to Wick again.

I stared at the table, which was about to break in half. "Well, there goes our table."

"Should we try finding another one?"

Before we could start the search for another hiding place, Ray's voice carried across the ballroom. "Get over here!"

Lyle squeezed my hand. "Are you ready?"

"Ready as I'll ever be."

With that, we started the race towards the others.

Chapter Fifty-Three
The Power of Friendship and Apologies

We kept towards the sides, putting a safe distance between ourselves and the fight that's still going on in the center. It was honestly impressive that they were still going at it; they were both much stronger than I gave them credit for.

There were several scorch marks on the ground and on the wall from the fight. A large ring of dead grass surrounded the center, almost reminding me of markings on a basketball court. A loose fireball almost hit Lyle, but he ducked down in time.

We reached the other side, but we couldn't tell which table the ghosts were behind.

Well, not immediately. Minerva's grumbling certainly helped.

"Get down here before I strangle you both!"

I found the table where it was coming from and grabbed Lyle's wrist, pulling him behind me as I hid behind the neighboring one.

"What took you guys so long over there? And why didn't you just come over here the first time?" Minerva hissed.

"We didn't exactly *choose* to almost get obliterated, thank you very much."

Minerva looked me up and down, and for a moment I thought I saw her eyes glisten with tears. But it only lasted a moment, because she quickly coughed. "I- uh- I'm just glad you're not dead yet. I couldn't handle spending the rest of my afterlife stuck with your sarcasm."

Even as she said it, I knew that she was glad I was alright. I lightly nudged her with a smile. "Aw, you know you'd miss me, don't even deny it."

She rolled her eyes, but she still smiled back. Her genuine smile was actually really cute—if only she wasn't so cocky all the time.

Constance peeked over Minerva's shoulder. "Are you feeling alright?"

I gestured towards myself, all my stained and tattered mess. "I mean, all things considered, at least I'm not dead yet- no offense to you guys."

"No, no, we agree. Being dead is boring," Ray piped in. "Though we really don't seem dead, do we?"

"Definitely not."

We talked so easily, it's almost like things were back to normal. It's weird to think of this place as having any kind of *normal*, but it's true. When I was with them, it didn't feel like I was with ghosts...it felt like I was with family. Every one of them—Lyle, Ray, Constance, even Minerva. As I thought about it, I noticed a smaller figure standing only a few feet away, watching us with her curious eyes.

Mary.

I looked over to her, wondering what's going on inside her mind. Something about her told me that even though she's younger than all of us, she knew a lot of things that we didn't.

I wanted to include her in the group, to make her feel welcomed, but I had no idea if she would even look at me. To be fair, I had just been fighting the person who she had been siding with the whole time, so that couldn't have helped.

When Mary noticed that I was watching her, she looked right back at me, showing no fear. There wasn't much she showed on her face, anyway. The only thing that showed any glimpse of her thoughts were her eyes, always searching for something. Right now, it looked like she was searching for a way out.

"You can come over here, if you'd like."

The others turned to face where I was looking at, all noticing Mary as well. They were all meeting her for the first time, and Constance seemed a bit perturbed at how young she was.

Mary bit her cheek, turning the offer in her head, before scurrying over. She found a spot by Minerva and crouched down, keeping her eyes on the fight before us. I was honestly surprised that Minerva had been deemed the safest, but she didn't even seem annoyed.

As we watched the fight, something inside me urged me to join the battle again.

It doesn't matter if you get hurt. You need to keep fighting until you can't anymore, because it doesn't matter what happens to you as long as it's for the better.

I pushed the unsettling thought from my mind, remembering what I had said to Elias earlier. *He* was the only one who could calm down Wick, not anyone else, even me. Clearly whatever he had done was the reason Wick's trying to stop me from calming the ghosts in the first place, which still didn't make a lot of sense. But, in theory, if we could get Wick to listen to him for long enough that he could apologize, would that be enough to calm Wick down?

Wick looked to his side and his eyes widened when he saw that Mary had left.

"Damn it! Why does this keep happening?!"

He threw a punch at Elias, no magic involved, and Elias managed to catch it—barely.

"Wick!" Elias finally screamed, making me jump. "Please, just listen, for once!"

Wick was stunned into silence. Hearing the usually jittery man yell was one thing, but hearing him scream is a whole different level of terrifying. By the look of it, Wick hadn't heard it before, either.

Elias' voice broke as he spoke.

"I'm sorry! I wanted to be with you, but I wasn't there! I thought I wasn't going to be enough for you, and that's why I left! I didn't think I could raise you to be who I knew you could have been! I didn't leave because I hated you—I left because I hated *myself!*"

We all held our breaths. Elias' cheeks were stained with tears, and Wick looked ready to cry himself.

"I absolutely *despised* myself, because I knew I'd never be someone who could take care of you. You're right! You were only *thirteen* when we lost them. I was twenty-three! I should have been there for you, but I wasn't! I—" his voice hitched. "I was too scared. I was a coward. And I am *so* sorry that I left you."

Now both of them had tears streaming down their faces.

"I know I don't deserve your forgiveness," he whispered. "But—"

Before he could say anything else, Wick ran up and wrapped his arms around him. I saw Elias freeze for a moment before squeezing his brother as tight as he could. All of the anger melted from him. Wick's chains, which had previously been wrapped around his arms and feet, lay still on the ground.

"I think it's safe," I whispered, not wanting to disrupt the moment.

I slowly stood up, Minerva looking ready to drag me back down. Elias and Wick weren't hugging anymore, but both still had tears trailing their cheeks and staining their shirts.

"I need to do something," I whispered to the ghosts. "I'll be right back."

I slowly made my way over to the door as quietly as I could, hoping I wasn't ruining whatever peace we had, and left the ballroom on a search. There's something I had left behind.

When I got to the garden, I pulled out my phone to check the ceiling map. I kept it as my backup as I made my way towards the center of the garden that had been haunting me since Ray discovered it.

As I found the center, I immediately saw what I had come here for: the small stuffed bear that Elias had brought as a peace offering. It may not have worked before, but maybe it could work now.

Grabbing the bear, I began to retrace my steps back to the entrance, then to the others. For the first time since the battle began, I had really paid attention to all of the destruction that had fallen upon the ballroom.

There were various dents and scorch marks on the walls, and the ground was littered with burns and other discarded materials. A few pieces of silverware glinted, including the one stained dark with blood. Some of the tables had been smashed to pieces, others lit with fire. Other smaller fires burned around the room, staying comfortably in their spots.

I walked over to one of the smallest fires and stamped it out before joining the ghosts. They had left the safety from behind the table and also began fixing the chaos. Even after everything we'd been through, this was our home. At least it was theirs.

All eyes turned to me as I made my way over to Mary, holding out the bear, silently pleading that it would work. After all of the mess we had just gone through, I had to hope that it hadn't been in vain.

I stared down at Mary, who's looking up at me with expectant eyes.

She's ready.

We gave each other a small smile, and I heard her whisper 'goodbye' as she took the bear.

Chapter Fifty-Four

Mary's Perspective

I had been playing by myself for so long, I couldn't begin to express my excitement when someone new came along.

I didn't know for certain how long it had been since I first woke up in the garden. The passage of time had become irrelevant fairly quickly.

The days had begun to blur together near the fifth week.

I had stopped counting near the eighth.

Over the time I had been in the garden, I began to memorize where everything was. I knew the secret tunnels, the doors that seemingly led to nowhere, even some of the flowers that surrounded the walls. When I looked up at the ceiling, the stars glimmered through the glass in beautiful patterns. The moon always shone over the lake at night—I knew this because I would always watch it.

I knew there was a way outside of the garden, but I was unable to cross it. Despite my efforts, the barrier had always kept me in the garden, as though to protect me from whatever lay on the other side. I never thought I would see anyone else or get to experience anything outside of the garden.

One day, however, someone came *inside*.

My ecstasy was hard to contain. After so long, I had more to talk to other than the voice of the boy. I could see someone's face again, make contact with skin.

I heard her footsteps before I saw her face. I couldn't help myself; I began to laugh softly in pure elation. I was on my own for such a long time without so much as someone whom I could see, and now I finally had someone whom I could play with.

Though I was excited, I wasn't willing to give myself away so easily. She looked like a friend, but it couldn't be her. Possibly an older changeling, like the one that had invaded the crew a couple years before the crash.

Instead, I hid in the foliage as I watched her. She couldn't see me, but I always saw her as I crouched low to the ground.

Abigail had been my favorite member of the crew, as well as my best friend, with the exception of my parents. That had been until the shipwreck that took her life, along with so many others. Even after the shipwreck, while I was hiding in the forest, she had never once left my mind. Imagining her brought an odd sense of comfort. I missed her more than I could describe, so I hadn't questioned it when she had made her first appearance.

That feeling of joy hadn't lasted long. The further along in the game we went, the more I remembered. I remembered seeing the tangle of her hair in the water. Her limp arms by her side as she floated. The way she was so deathly still; it could have been Death's arms themselves wrapped around her, refusing to let go.

I knew for certain it wasn't her by the time she found me.

But I couldn't simply pause the game now. We hadn't even begun my favorite part: the chase. So I spoke to her for only a matter of moments before sending myself through the brush of the garden once more.

If it hadn't been for those nasty vines, I would have won. Despite her aid, I wasn't willing to admit defeat quite that easily. If the voice of the boy had taught me anything, it was that I shouldn't give up after one try.

We continued playing this game, and I found delight in seeing her try and find me. Eventually, however, I realized I wanted someone to talk to more than I wanted the game.

When I had told this to the boy, he was not happy. He told me the safest option was to protect myself. So I grabbed a rock. As I had hit her, something in me turned.

I made a decision with myself that when she came next, I would simply wait. I knew that she would find me—she seemed to be a clever one.

When she found me, I had not expected her to be so calm with me. The voice of the boy had always been more aggressive, but I knew that he had cared for me. Why else would he talk to me every day, but to not make me feel as lonely?

She spoke to me gently, asking questions. I knew my story, but I hadn't known that I needed to talk to someone in person until I was granted the opportunity to do so.

I cautiously explained my story as simply as I could. I told her about how I had lived on a ship with my family and friends, as well as the shipwreck that had taken them away from me. My stomach hurt as I described the wreck.

Then we heard the crash.

The woman disguised as Abigail startled, but I guided her through the garden to the source of the crash. When we got there, we saw a man with startling blue eyes.

I may not have seen his face before, but I knew his voice.

I glanced hesitantly at the woman before running into the man's arms. From the edge of my vision, I saw her shoulders sag. Guilt took its course through my veins, but I trusted him more than I trusted her. Why would I trust someone who wouldn't show me their real face?

To the side, there was a bubble containing more people. Their looks varied—a woman in a long red gown, a young boy in dirty clothes, an older one in formal attire...I didn't know them, but they appeared to be friends of the woman I was with.

The man with the blue eyes cast me aside, and the two began to fight.

The fight was all a blur to me. All I remembered was blacking out and then being somewhere else, away from the group. A woman in trousers and a jacket had been next to me, blood trickling from her head. She began speaking to me in a soft voice, just like the other woman. Everyone was behaving so gently with me.

Another man came into the room. He looked very similar to the man who had been speaking with me—perhaps they were in some familial relation to each other? He waited on the side as the two continued fighting.

Before I realized it, the battle was over.

The two men were trapped in a warm embrace, tears streaming down their faces. The woman disguised as Abigail had disappeared, and everyone who was with us behind the table had begun to mingle.

"Kid."

I turned around and saw the dark woman crouching down.

"You're Mary, right?"

I shifted around, avoiding her gaze. Eventually, I nodded.

"It's a pleasure to meet you, Mary. I'm Minerva."

I stood there, looking at her in silence. She *seemed* safe enough.

"Quiet type, are you?"

I nodded again.

"Well, that'll be a nice change around here." Minerva smiled. I returned one.

The woman who looked like Abigail returned from the entrance of the room, holding something that resembled a bear. I remembered that she had carried it around with her whenever I had seen her—perhaps it was a good luck charm.

She looked down and handed it to me.

"Goodbye, Abigail." I whispered. I gingerly took it, still unsure of what it was. It was soft to the touch. I slowly brought it to my chest and squeezed it, feeling comfort while holding it. Could it have possibly been similar to a doll?

When I lifted my gaze up towards her, I saw not Abigail, but someone else entirely.

She had the same messy hair, but it was a dark brown. Her eyes were no longer a lively green, but instead the color of storm clouds with exhaustion imminent. She was taller and thinner, and she didn't carry as much grace as Abigail had. Her face was dirty and bloody, her breathing shallow, yet she still smiled at me.

"Uh, hi?" she said.

"Hello there. What is your name?"

She sighed, relieved. "Quincey. I'm glad to meet you."

I debated on what I should do next. Hesitantly, I wrapped my arms around her. She bent down and returned the embrace, though I could tell it caused her pain. It had been so long since I was truly held; I didn't want to let go.

After a few seconds, she was the one to release.

Suddenly, a wave of cold air blew through the room. Considering we were inside, it was a bizarre occurrence. Four other people shuddered—Minerva as well as the people who had been encased in the bubble earlier. How come Quincey and the two others didn't feel it?

The cold air got colder. It wasn't long until I was shivering. The others who had felt it had their arms wrapped around themselves.

Then it disappeared as abruptly as it came, leaving no trace of its existence. I looked down and saw that my stomach had healed. The injuries that Minerva and the young boy had sustained disappeared as well.

How bizarre.

Chapter Fifty-Five
Uh Oh, Do You Have Insurance?

"Now that I see you as you are, I can say that you are quite beautiful."

I stared down at Mary, who's looking up at me with her curious eyes.

I still couldn't believe that I had finally calmed her down. Maybe the fight with Wick had played a part, but I couldn't be sure. All I knew was that I was ready for a break. If she wasn't the last one, hopefully I'd have a bit of time before continuing. But even then, something about this time felt different. I couldn't put my finger on it.

"Who did you see me as?"

"A wonderful woman named Abigail. She was one of the crewmates on the ship, as well as my best friend. She loved to play chase with me on the ship."

I smiled, glad that it hadn't been like Ray's. "I would much rather be a friend than an enemy."

"Not an enemy at all. But I knew you could not have been her."

"How did you know?" Minerva asked calmly. She's acting surprisingly nice to the child, considering I had previously thought she hated kids. She just seemed like someone who wouldn't like them, but maybe I was wrong.

"Abigail was already dead."

"Oh, uh, I'm sorry." Minerva tried patting Mary's back, but the child pulled away from the touch.

"You need not shed tears for me. All that would do is turn Abigail's memory bittersweet. Let me enjoy her memory so I may let go."

How did that sentence just come out of a little kid's mouth?

I looked over the ballroom again. Elias and Wick were talking, though the former was still frustrated with his younger counterpart. The rest of the ghosts joined us, Constance wrapping her arms around Minerva.

Ray was grinning, bouncing around excitedly. "Quincey, you did it. You actually did it. And you're *alive.*"

I hadn't taken the time to think about it, but he was right. Maybe not unharmed, but I was still breathing and moving nonetheless. Euphoria flooded my chest, and soon I was smiling right back at him.

"I knew you would make it, princess."

I turned to Lyle, who's also beaming. His gaze kept flitting towards my arm, though I pretended not to notice. All I wanted to do was wrap my arms around him and feel the comfort of his embrace again, but I wasn't sure how much more hugging my arm could handle.

"I really did it."

Everything in me was sore, my throat was desperate for water, and my chest was burning, but I did it.

"Oh, uh, what were you trying to tell me earlier?"

I could have sworn I saw Lyle's smile falter, but if it had, he's good at hiding it. "It- it was nothing, it's fine. Just glad to have you here."

I wondered what it could have been, but my thoughts had been interrupted by the sound of rumbling. I looked up to the ceiling and watched as the rubble began to fall. Chunks of the ceiling were raining down on us like hail.

Elias and Wick looked at each other before the former turned to me. "You need to get everyone out! The ghosts, too!"

I threw my hands over my head to protect myself from the debris as I yelled for everyone to get out. If the room was going to collapse, none of us would be there to see it. Elias and Wick left first, then the ghosts. I followed shortly after.

The ground shook beneath our feet. The paintings on the wall trembled in their spots, and some even fell down. The lights flickered. The rumbling kept getting louder and louder until it was almost deafening.

It didn't take long to realize what's happening; the mansion was going to fall. The horrifying realization of what that meant crept in on me quickly.

This could be my last time seeing the ghosts.

I tried to push the idea away but couldn't. I didn't want to say goodbye, now or ever. Tears started to fall down my cheeks as we ran through the hallways.

The walls and my mind were caving in on me.

It was loud. It was so loud, like a tornado.

What would happen to the ghosts if the mansion was gone? Would they just disappear, never to be seen again? That seemed to be the only explanation, as much as I hated to think about it.

I remembered that all of my things were still in the bedroom and quickly ran to get everything. The shaking hadn't been so bad at the front—I thought I had time. But soon the room was trembling, too. Scurrying to zip up my bag, I left.

I pulled the suitcase behind me as I saw Lyle holding the door open for Elias and Wick. He narrowed his eyes at them as they went by, and I was just thankful he didn't try locking them in here. I had no idea what would happen if he did.

I thought again about how it would be the last time seeing the ghosts, and tears pricked the back of my eyes again. I watched them go, likely for the last time.

Lyle glanced back at me before running to get me.

"We need to get out of here!" I could barely hear his voice—the roaring was getting louder.

I looked into his eyes and wrapped my arms around him as tight as I could, ignoring the pain in my arm. He didn't hesitate to hug me back.

"If this is the last time—"

"Quincey, I mean this in the nicest possible way, but you better shut the hell up. No use thinking about that now...but if this *is* the last time, I need you to know that no one else has ever made me happier than you have. Now go!"

He let go and sprinted ahead of me. I grabbed my suitcase and followed suit. I left the mansion and all of the memories inside it behind as I ran out the door.

I only made it six steps before the mansion collapsed.

I ran as far as I could, but I couldn't beat the debris. Dust clouds suffocated us, making me cough. The rubble, the remains of the mansion and everything that came with it, pooled around my feet and up to my calf. As soon as the dust cleared, I opened my eyes to see that everyone was standing in front of me.

And it was quiet.

I turned around.

The mansion. It's *gone*.

Wick stood the closest to me, looking at me with intention. He walked closer to me, and I took a step back, almost falling backwards. I didn't want him to get close to me. I could see Lyle beginning to protest from where he was, and I wondered how the ghosts were still here. They couldn't leave the mansion before, right?

Wick crossed his arms as he reached me.

"What do you want?"

"Well, I *guess* I have to say that…I'm…*sorry*."

Everyone was taken by surprise. Everyone except Elias, who motioned for his brother to continue. More likely than not, the apology in itself was his idea.

Wick crossed his arms, his eyes averting my gaze. Now that he wasn't angry, he really *was* a lot like Elias. "I realize that my actions were, well, not so good—"

"You almost killed me repeatedly!"

"Like I said, not so good. Still, I wanted to say that I'm sorry, and I understand if you don't want to forgive me. I was a pretty bad person, wasn't I?"

"Yes, you were."

He rolled his eyes, but there was still some guilt in his face.

"But I guess I can *try* forgiving you."

Lyle and Minerva stared at me incredulously. Lyle opened his mouth to intervene, but I cut him off with a 'talk to the hand' motion.

"That does *not* mean that a single thing you did to me or my friends was okay. All that means is that you need to prove you're not that person, and only then will I even *think* about it. You did some absolutely horrible things, but I also understand that anger makes you do things you don't usually do. So not only do you need to apologize to *me*, but you also need to apologize to the ghosts as well. And you've got some explaining to do about that whole 'I'm not the one who wants to kill you' thing."

Wick turned around and muttered an apology.

"Like you mean it."

He sighed. "I'm sorry for doing that to all of you. You didn't deserve it."

They all looked between each other—I think they were all still getting over the shock of still being there. Wait, how long had Minerva's head wound been gone?

"Okay, that's step one. Now, do you want to explain *who wants me dead*?"

"I'm going to be completely honest, I don't even remember. I feel like there *was* someone, but maybe it was all in my head. Anger can make you do crazy things, I suppose."

Maybe he was trying to hide it from me. Maybe he really didn't remember. I had a feeling that it's going to be a while until I get a real answer, to this and more.

I whirled around to Elias and climbed out of the rubble, storming over to him with a finger jabbed at his chest.

"And don't you *dare* think you can get out of an explanation that easily. You owe us one. Actually, there's a lot of things you need to explain."

"I- I'll explain everything in detail, uhm...later. Later sounds good."

"Then give us the basics now. I think we *all* deserve to know what the hell is happening. For example, in theory, *shouldn't they be gone*?" I gestured wildly toward the ghosts, knowing they were all thinking the same question.

Elias sighed. "How badly do you want to know?"

I turned back to them, getting a read of their faces, before crossing my arms. "Pretty badly."

"Uhm, alright then."

Elias stopped there. I could feel everyone's eyes on us, looking for an explanation.

"Are- are you *sure* you want to know? Right now? Because maybe it would be better explained at- at dinner, or something. Or would coffee be better—?"

"Elias, we want to know *right now*."

He finally got the hint that we wouldn't be leaving without knowing what the hell happened, so he got started.

"Well, you had mentioned seeing other ghosts in the casino, correct? The figures that were nothing more than gray silhouettes?"

I nodded.

"Those were *real* ghosts. Most if not all of them were spirits from the people who had come before you, I would imagine."

Gears were turning in my head, trying to figure out what he meant. If those were *real* ghosts by Elias' terms, then that meant...

"So what you're saying," I started, "is that they aren't *really* ghosts?"

Elias nodded. "At least, not in the way *you* see them."

The silence let that sink in for all of us. But if they weren't really ghosts, then how did they get there? The answer just led to a million more questions.

There was one that was easy to ask. "So what are they?"

Instead of Elias answering, it was Wick. "Their psyches were trapped inside the mansion, yes, but the big difference is that they were sent *before* they died." Wick eyed Elias, and it became clear that even though Elias apologized, there was still a lot to work on.

Something clicked. "I think I read something about that, in the book we found. It was like something about the difference between spirits and souls? Ghosts was more of an umbrella term, I think. I don't remember much about it, though."

Elias looked over at me, impressed. Wick took over the rest of the explanation. "You're right. While spirits are people whose psyche moved to that plane of reality after death, the psyche of people who were alive that got forced into it are known as souls. They're held in contraptions—in this case, it looks like it had been the mansion. Now that they've been calmed down and the contraption has been destroyed..."

"They will continue to age regularly, having been brought back," Elias finished.

"Really?" Ray said breathlessly.

"Wait, follow up question," I interrupted. "Why did the mansion collapse in the first place?"

As Elias spoke, he sounded a bit more confident, or at least more comfortable. "Some magicfolk have the strength to perform a spell that helps create a physical manifestation of negative emotions—a Fearspring. It can be any emotion that they want—anger, depression, anxiety. In my case," he glanced back at Wick, "it was shame. But, once the root of those emotions is handled, the manifestation crumbles." The answer sounded like it came straight from a textbook; how many times had he explained it to people? It still didn't really explain how the ghosts were involved, but I still have my theory that Wick is the real reason why they're there. Maybe Elias felt guilty because he created the thing they were trapped in? A Fearspring or whatever.

"So, what you're saying is that we are free from that monstrosity of a house because you and your brother are finally on good terms?" Lyle said.

"Yes, something like that."

Just when I finally thought I had gotten used to all the madness of the mansion, I got thrown into this. I couldn't imagine what the ghosts—or should I say not-ghosts?—were thinking right now. This whole time they thought they were dead, but they weren't. It had to have been a harder pill for them to swallow.

"Okay, wait."

Everyone turned to Minerva.

"Now that we're...alive, what's going to happen? We don't have any paperwork, like, oh I don't know, a birth certificate! Or a social security number! People still use those, right?"

It's crazy to think that they weren't dead. They were alive, just as much as I was. They could continue on with their normal lives, at least as normal as possible after what we've been through.

I don't have to say goodbye.

Just thinking about it almost made me cry again, but I blinked the tears away.

"*That* I can help with."

Elias snapped his fingers, a stack of papers forming in his hand. They were all in manilla folders—five folders, to be exact. One for each ghost. As well as five bags with lots of fabric inside. Regular clothes? "I have been saving these for when the day would eventually come, though Lyle and Mary's paperwork were a tad rushed. I'm so glad to give these to you."

He walked over and handed a folder to Minerva first. "Minerva Mitchell."

He continued down the line as he handed everyone their things. I didn't even think about the fact that I hadn't heard most of their last names until now. "Constance Almary."

"Ray Farwell."

"Lyle Merrick."

"Mary Delly."

Constance and Mary were both a bit confused; were birth certificates around where they were from? Or *when* they were from?

They all peaked inside their bags with various responses to the contents inside. I stifled a laugh as I saw Minerva pull out a light pink shirt with ruffle sleeves. "Absolutely not. This is a disgrace to the entire clothing industry. Constance, you can have this."

Once Elias was done, he looped over back to me. "Quincey, I need you to make me a promise."

"What is it? Because the last time I made a deal with you, all of *this* happened."

"Keep you and your friends safe. You've been exposed to the magical world. Once magic enters your life, even if you aren't practicing it, life always gets more dangerous. And you *must* keep it a secret. You can only tell people on a need-to-know basis, so your parents or possibly someone you told about the mansion *beforehand*."

I nodded. "*That* I can do. And I only told my mom and my friend Rachel."

He sighed, relieved. "That's perfect. I'll keep all of you safe to the best of my abilities, but there's only so much that I can do without arousing suspicion. I don't know who may try to come for you, but Wick was right about one thing—there *is* something special about you, even if you don't know it yet."

"If you mean that she's a *total badass*, I think we all know that!" Ray grinned.

Elias smiled. "I suppose you could put it that way. You have a fighting spirit that a lot of us from older generations don't. Maybe that's why I always admired your generation. I know that you'll do great things, Quincey." He cleared his throat, going serious once more. "I'll try to keep all evil away since you are all more susceptible to it now. Your lives are about to change—do you think you're ready for it?"

I looked around at all my friends and only saw determination.

"I think we are."

Elias nodded before his eyes widened. "Oh, I almost forgot."

Huh? I watched as he dug through his bag, which I hadn't noticed before. After a bit of searching, he pulled out an envelope.

"I know this was more than you bargained for, but I hope the cash can still help."

The others looked at me in confusion.

"You were getting *paid*?" Ray asked.

"Uh, yeah..." Waves of guilt went through me. "It's like...okay, when I first took the job, I thought it was fake. I had seen the ad in the news, and was like, 'hey, I need cash,' so I took it. Then I got stuck here...but Wick actually offered a way out, a little after Ray was calmed."

Elias' eyebrows shot up, and everyone else seemed just as stunned. Wick averted his eyes—I hadn't even considered it, but now I wondered if the offer was a hoax.

"But at that point, I didn't even care about the money, you know? I had met you guys, and you...became like a family to me. I wasn't going to just leave you guys like that."

It felt so cheesy as I said the words, but I didn't even care; they were completely true. Now that I had gone through everything with them, I couldn't imagine trying to live a life without them.

Especially since now I didn't have to.

"That was so corny," Minerva grumbled, though she was wiping her eyes with her sleeve.

When I turned to ask Elias about what to do next, he was gone, and Wick had gone with him.

"So, I'm guessing Elias didn't plan somewhere for us to live?" Lyle asked.

I swore. "Sorry, I completely forgot about that. I'm sure we can think of something, though."

"As long as it's not a mansion, I think we'll be alright," Minerva grumbled. "I think it's safe to say we've all had enough mansions for one lifetime, let alone two."

I laughed, turning around to stare at the rubble again. I rubbed the dirt from my face onto my sleeve—I was a mess.

Lyle came up next to me, grabbing my hand and squeezing it. "I think it's safe to say we're all glad to be back. As much as you didn't want to say goodbye to us, we didn't want to say goodbye to you, either."

I smiled and leaned against him slightly. "No more goodbyes."

I heard the sound of footsteps as Ray came on my other side. "Is it weird that I might actually miss it?" he asked as he looked at the debris.

"No, I don't think it is."

I faced the ghosts again. "So, are you guys ready to live again?"

I looked at each of them, and they were all grinning. Even Mary, who was usually reserved, had a small smile.

Minerva was the one who spoke for the collective. "Yes, I think we are."

Chapter Fifty-Six

What Happens Now?

I stared at the front door, illuminated by the porch light, debating what to do.

"Why didn't you just tell your mom you were coming?" Minerva asked from over my shoulder. "It'd be a welcome surprise. And she could unlock the door so we aren't looking like stalkers outside of your own house."

As much as I missed Mom, I couldn't figure out what to text her. How was I going to explain all that happened in the past three months? She had to have been planning for tomorrow's dinner with Dad and Mimiko, and she's probably already stressed enough. Having her child randomly appear from out of the blue wouldn't help. Besides, it's the middle of the night—if she wasn't cooking, there's a good chance she's already asleep. For all I knew, she was already on her way to Mexico for Thanksgiving.

"Oh, for Christ's sake," Minerva pushed past me and moved to push the doorbell.

"The doorbell's broken," I quickly added.

She sighed and knocked before retreating back behind me. "See? Easy."

I inhaled slowly, my excitement kicking in. After three months of sporadic texting and vague answers, I was finally going to see Mom. And I could explain everything to her.

But my anxiety also kicked in. *What if something happened to her? What if she got in a car crash? What if she had another heat stroke and I wasn't there to help her?*

My spiraling *what-if*s got cut off by the sound of the door opening.

She looked frazzled, but she was definitely still Mom. Her blue eyes were shining despite the dark circles. Her messy hair was all over the place, and her sweatshirt was covered in flour—she must have been baking for a while.

"*¡Dios mío!* Quincey? Is that really you?"

I ran up to her and hugged her as tight as I could, not caring about the flour that was definitely on my shirt. "I missed you so much," I said into her hair.

She pulled away, her eyes flitting across everyone behind me. "Who are all these people?"

"Well," Ray started, "I'm Ray, and this is Constance, Lyle, Minerva, and Mary! We're the ghosts! Or, not-ghosts?"

I saw her jaw drop. "It's...a long story. I'll try explaining it as best as I can, but right now we need to figure some things out. Can we come inside?"

"Quincey, you're my daughter, and these are your friends. Of *course* you can come inside. Pardon the mess. It's just- wow, I wasn't expecting you to come back *now*."

I motioned for everyone else to follow, and immediately we all began to tell the crazy adventure of what had been happening since I arrived at the mansion.

Reasonably, Mom had a lot of questions. For a moment I was worried that she wouldn't believe us, but she caught on fairly quickly. It's kind of hard to argue when you were talking to the former souls themselves.

I became breathless as I explained what I was feeling, practically reliving every experience. As the others described what I did, they made me sound way more heroic than I had been.

When we finally reached everything that happened today and made for a close, she watched us for a few seconds, her eyes locking with every one of us.

Her gaze landed on me last before she sighed. "Well, you better come help in the kitchen, because now we have five more mouths to feed and less than 24 hours to prepare. If any of you know how to cook, we're gonna need as much help as we can get."

Constance stepped forward. "I would say I can work my way around a kitchen."

"That's an understatement," Ray piped in.

Over the next several hours, we all pitched in to help make Thanksgiving dinner. Mom kept asking the others questions about themselves, and they never shied away from anything. It was a relief to see they were all getting along—Minerva even managed to keep her bluntness down to a minimum, something I didn't think she could do.

When we were done, Mom came to the same question we had earlier. "So, where are you guys going to live?"

"We…haven't been able to give that much thought," I muttered. "Elias could get them all the essential paperwork but he couldn't find them somewhere to sleep."

"Oh, well we can help, can't we? I mean, we have the spare bedrooms, the couch, Marcus and Zander were renting out one of their rooms as well…why don't you all crash with us until you get your own places to live?"

I had to admit, even though living with all of them could get exhausting at times, it would be hard to get back to living with just Mom. And we weren't stuck—we could actually *leave*, which would be a great relief.

Lyle spoke for the collective. "We would love to, Miss Oaks."

"Oh, please, call me Annie."

Before we knew it, it was already dinner the next day. We even invited Elias and Wick, much to Lyle and Minerva's annoyance. Dad and Mimiko brought Marmalade to play with Ollie. Thankfully, none of Mom's family had reached out this year—something about a bout of stomach flu. The ghosts wouldn't be able to handle all that Spanish.

I hadn't explained what I had been doing to Dad, so we had thought of a cover story; I had met them all over the past few months, and they didn't have any family in town, so they're enjoying Thanksgiving with us. It wasn't foolproof, but it worked.

The meal was great—I hadn't had Mom's *arepas* or *paella* in so long, I'd almost forgotten what it tasted like. All the accents clashed over dinner—with Lyle's

New York accent, Constance's French accent, Dad's Arabic accent, the British accents of Mary and the Everard brothers, and occasionally Mom's Spanish accent, the conversations sounded comical. Even with that, everything felt *normal*.

Well, as normal as it could be when a majority of your friends had been sort-of ghosts that were given a second chance at life.

As we ate and laughed, all that was going through my mind was *let's keep it like this forever.*

Five months had passed since the mansion, and a lot had happened.

Only a month after we got back, Minerva had turned 19. It's bizarre to have her my age now, even though I was still technically older according to her new birth certificate. I made sure to tease her relentlessly about it. At the beginning of March, Constance also turned 24, which was another weird adjustment. I always thought she was older, and I would always see her like that.

Overall, they've all adapted to their new lives relatively easily. It took over a month for me to teach them all the new technology, slang, and as many pop culture references as I could remember. I'd even tried making a slideshow but eventually realized there's no way I could fit everything. They can all blend in, if you ignored the accents. Even Constance figured out how to speak in English fluently, including the weird rules. I still haven't decided whether or not I regret teaching the slang to Ray, who now intentionally messes with me by mixing up slang or saying it slightly wrong.

A couple of weeks ago, Constance, Minerva and Mary left the house and moved into a small apartment together. Between selling Constance's jewelry, getting some financial help, and both of them working when they can, it was enough for them to make it work. It surprised me that Minerva chose to work at the craft shop of all places, but I guess she knew a lot about fabrics. Mom made a considerable contribution as well, which they have been thanking her profusely for since.

Outside of smaller jobs and errands, they didn't leave the house very often. I knew Minerva's still worried about law enforcement because of her skin, but she's seen that things have definitely improved since her time, even if they aren't quite perfect yet. I couldn't hold the fear against her, but it was something she was slowly unlearning. I also knew they were still worried people would find out about their…unique circumstances. But no one had questioned them yet, so I think Elias' spell did a bit more than just give them paperwork.

After being taught some basics, Ray decided he wanted to try high school despite my warnings. Not surprisingly, a lot of the kids liked him. He even became good friends with this girl named Kasey. I'd met her a couple times, and she's practically his twin. Ray's still living with us, and Mom's been showering him with love. I didn't realize I wanted a little brother until he came along.

Lyle moved in with Marcus and Zander, though they didn't make him pay because of something Mom wouldn't tell me. I'd been teaching him more about literature and a few other subjects, but he caught on quick enough. Thankfully I didn't really need to work on math with him—he was a whiz when it came to that. It's a miracle for that, because I was never good at math myself. His goal was to try coming to NAU with me this fall, though I told him it might take more time than that to learn everything, despite the fact that he technically had a high school graduation certificate.

"You never know, maybe I'm secretly a genius," he'd said.

"Come on, if you were a genius, you wouldn't bother keeping it a secret," I'd responded.

Spending all that time with him was great—it's one of my favorite parts of the week. My heart always felt like it was going to burst when I was with him, despite my best efforts to calm it. Now that we weren't stuck in the mansion with the constant threat of a goodbye hanging over us, it felt like I could enjoy being with him more. I tried ignoring what my heart kept whispering to me every time I saw him, though there was still a bit of hope with every conversation. My anxiety still got in the way of me mentioning my feelings, despite however many months it'd been.

He even got a job working at Uncle Driver's as one of the waiters. He became a customer's favorite easily, which didn't surprise me; it's so easy to get drawn in by his magnetic self, and it took everything in me to not go see him every day.

Mom had taken a liking to everyone quickly, and decided to claim them as her children as well. She spoiled them every chance she got, and she even got everyone phones for Christmas. They weren't anything too fancy, but they made communication so much easier.

I kept up contact with Elias and Wick—now that they were living together, they seemed to be getting along a bit better. They actually started to act like siblings, with Wick constantly trying to find trouble and Elias needing to reel him in. I've had to intervene many times, and it's always hilarious to see their shenanigans when I come by.

I had asked Elias if he had any idea how the ghosts got into his Fearspring in the first place, but he always looked away in embarrassment and didn't give me much of an answer. After a couple tries, I decided not to pry—I was pretty sure he still felt guilty for all of it. I assumed that his Fearspring was why he couldn't help the ghosts, similar to what *La Surnaturelle* had said.

Maybe we would never know how they had gotten there, but they seemed more than happy to leave that part of their past behind. I couldn't blame them.

My scar from the fireball never went away. Elias had explained it to me once—since it was magical fire and I hadn't been treated by a Healer, the scar's likely permanent, though it didn't hurt anymore. He also said that my body seemed to handle the burn much better than most Regs—that's what he called those without magic—did, so that's a good thing. I tried avoiding it, but sometimes I would still catch myself staring at it in the mirror. Thinking about it made my stomach knot. It was easier to just put on a jacket and ignore it.

Today, we were all meeting at Rachel's coffee shop; I hadn't even realized until then that I had never taken them there. If she was working, they might even get to meet Rachel. She'd heard all about them from me, and I knew they had heard me talk about her a lot during the mansion.

I grabbed the paper Elias had given me from my desk, looking over its contents one more time. He had given it to me a few days before, and I finally decided what I was going to do.

I folded it up and tucked it in my pocket.

Ray was already waiting for me in the car, blasting the rock music so loud I could hear it loud and clear as soon as I stepped out of the front door. I slid into the driver's seat and turned the volume down.

"I'd rather you *not* blast my ears out, thank you very much."

He groaned and turned it back up, though it wasn't as loud as before. Soon we were screaming the lyrics to one of our favorite songs. I was glad to have someone I could share my love of rock music with.

As we pulled in, Ray was out of the car as soon as I stopped it. He blitzed into the cafe, and I laughed as I followed behind him.

I scanned the cafe and found him excitedly talking to Lyle, who already looked drained. For someone who had worked in a casino and was used to chatting people up, he had a pretty small social battery when it came to Ray's endless conversations.

Lyle's gaze found me and his face lit up, making my heart flutter.

He hurriedly motioned for me to come over, and I smiled as I sat next to him. His hand rested on top of mine as I got settled, and I interlocked our fingers, resisting the urge to look. *Don't be dumb.*

Not long after I sat down, I heard the chime of the door opening, and Constance, Minerva and Mary stepped into the cafe. The couple was hand in hand, while Mary followed shortly behind them.

When they joined us, I asked for everyone's orders—making sure that Ray got a drink without caffeine—and went up to the back of the line. Caffeine may have a different effect on people with ADHD, but until I knew for sure he had it and wasn't just energetic, I didn't want to take my chances.

Sadly, we had come at rush hour, but they always made sure to get your drinks to you quicker than anyone else around did. That was probably why it's always so busy.

I noticed Rachel skirting around with drinks and food on a platter. I was tempted to say hello, but she looked stressed, so I waited. As I made it to the front, I saw one of my favorite cashiers.

"Hey there," Krista said, her black lipstick complimenting her tan complexion. "How's it been?"

"Well, I've got some new friends with me." I motioned towards the ghosts—even after all these months, I still caught myself calling them that—and she waved.

I listed off everyone's drinks, surprised that Minerva liked hers on the sweeter side, and finished with my own. Krista gave me another smile as I finished and began clicking away with her black nails before she waved me off so she could get the next customer.

It only took fifteen minutes for the order to come. Lyle joined me to help pick up all the drinks and passed them out to everyone.

"I know it's been a bit since we've all seen each other, so how's everyone doing?"

Everyone answered with some variation of 'good,' except for Minerva, who answered with a sarcastic 'absolutely horrible, actually' while drinking her hot coffee, the steam fogging up her new blue light glasses.

"Well, that's good enough for me, because there's actually a reason I brought you all here. And it's pretty important, if you ask me."

They all looked at me with expectant eyes. Excitedly, I pulled out the folded up paper from my back pocket.

Even though I knew what it said, I leaned over with everyone else to read the paper:

Siren Infestation at Oceanside House in Florida.

"Elias has given us a new job," I announced proudly.

I could hear Lyle groan beside me at the mention of Elias. While I couldn't blame him after everything that happened, I still couldn't contain my excitement at the new task. Even if the mansion was dangerous, I was excited at the idea of getting back into the magical world.

"So, who's up for round two?"

Epilogue

Elias was only in his twenties when he left his brother and friends behind in pursuit of magic. After losing his parents some months before, he had soon turned his focus and attention to something else. He was new to the concept of magic, and even dabbled into the idea of immortality. Not knowing how to cope with his parents' death, he stopped taking care of himself, as well as his brother. When he was about to turn twenty-four, he left for good.

He was known in his town to have a hot head and a short temper. Even then, he didn't know how to handle his emotions. As soon as he learned how to, he manifested them into a Fearspring in the form of a house. While it wasn't foolproof, it did help release some of his frustration and guilt.

His reputation with the town followed him when a French man slandered and hit him in an argument. Elias hadn't learned much about the consequences of magic and lashed out. To punish the man, he didn't harm *him*—instead, he took his wife, a woman by the name of Constance. She became the first resident of the ever-changing mansion. It was petty, Elias knew, but he was young and naive. He didn't know any better. At least that was what he would say to himself.

Knowing he had an eternity to live didn't help with his anger issues. It just stewed up all that anger until he had someone else to take it out on with no concept of remorse. Because what was the point of remorse if they were only a small part of his life? He would meet new people, anyway.

But he knew he had crossed the line when he was visiting Britain, nearly a century later. He came across a small town by the shore and was exploring when he came across a curious young girl. She was frightened and tried kicking him out of the beautiful garden she had been living in. In a fit of delirious rage, he sent the girl to his Fearspring. That was how Mary became the second resident.

After that experience, he realized what he had done. Not only had he taken a young wife away from her husband prior, but he just took a *child*. He promised himself that he would never put that fate upon someone again.

A quarter of a millennia had gone by. Since that day in the garden, Elias had become less angry. He hadn't sent anyone to the mansion in many years, and he thought he had left it all behind. No one had wondered about either of the residents; all evidence of them had turned to an unfortunate end. Meanwhile, the warlock was visiting the great country of America in the late thirties. In Kansas, he came across a young boy, merely a teen. His shoes had broken soles, like he had been running for a long time. Loaves of bread and piles of fruit were scattered around him. Blood soaked his hands as he felt the boy's ribs. In an attempt to save the unconscious boy, he did something he had sworn he would never again do—he sent him to the mansion.

Ray became the third resident.

Once again, anger filled him. But this time, it was for a completely different reason than before. How could someone simply attempt to kill an innocent boy with no remorse? He was painfully reminded of when he sent Mary to the mansion, and his heart ached. How could he have done that in his youth? He didn't know.

In an attempt to calm himself down, he brings himself away from the place where he had found the boy. For the next few years, he was unsure of what to do with himself. He stayed hidden from the prying eyes of society, and he became paranoid about the residents. Would they come back to haunt him? He quickly became a nervous man.

One day he was making his way through New York during a blizzard, shortly after World War II. He searched for the nearest entertainment and came across On The Rocks Casino. It surprised him to find a casino at all—gambling had been outlawed, but he supposed that people found ways. A prohibition didn't mean the demand wasn't there.

He went up to one of the workers, a chatty young man with a certain knack for card games. His eyes, an unsettling blue, reminded Elias of his brother. His heart twisted with ache every time he thought of him—perhaps, one day, he could go back. His brother would be long gone by now, but he could visit the grave. If he had one.

The two began to chat, but Elias couldn't hear him, for he was focused on the angry policemen storming in.

The cold chill of the wind outside rushed in. People began to scream as shots were fired. Elias teleported away in an attempt to flee, not realizing that the man behind the counter had been making contact. There was no way he could get back to the casino safely. Before the worker could come to wits, he sent the young man to the mansion. The fourth resident.

That was where the story started to end. Elias would think about the souls in the mansion often, how they were trapped there because of him, whether his intervention was good or bad. He wished he could go back and do better. But he was an old man now, at least he felt like it in his heart. He had one more stop to make, though. This one was by request. He was face to face with a young colored businesswoman, dark braids flowing down to her hips. The fifties was a dangerous time to be that, even in Washington.

Main Street was bustling with tourists from all walks of life, but the woman kept her eyes on him. She intrigued him—he had been sure to keep as low a profile as he could, in case something were to happen. He hadn't the faintest idea what she would want with him, or if she knew of his magic at all. Maybe she'd just heard of the strange man found across the country and wanted to see for herself.

She smiled at him, though it seemed a bit forced, and thanked him for coming, her eyes glancing to the side. As she went to shake his hand, he saw a man with a brick behind her. Without thinking, he disappeared, bringing her with him. She became the fifth and final resident.

Even now, Elias still didn't know if Minerva had planned it all. She wouldn't know, either—most memories surrounding the time of their 'deaths' would become hazy, he'd learned.

It had been many decades since she joined the mansion. Everyone alive believed the residents were dead, as well as themselves. They were neither dead nor alive, though. He knew now that he had made a mistake, but he wouldn't be able to fix it without the help of somebody else.

He had been following the moving mansion for five years, and hope was starting to seem like a distant thing. The mansion always seemed to know where the best person would be, and all he had to do was find them and get them there. But even sixteen tries later, no one had managed to get past Minerva before being met by a gruesome fate. He had a small graveyard, hidden by magic, where he kept memorials of those who lost their lives for his mistakes.

In a desperate attempt to find the latest person, he created a news ad. It was a risky move—if the spell didn't work and the ad didn't get directed to the one person who needed it, there could be a lot more on his hands.

When the voice who called him belonged to that of a younger woman, something in him stirred. *This had to be it.*

As he saw the car pull up the mansion, he looked at a girl with curly brown hair. "Hi, my name is Quincey. I'm here for your ad?"

A sneak peek at the exciting sequel…

Siren Song

It was the middle of the night when the Captain arrived.

There were tales of her appearing more and more, but the Deirdre siren tribe didn't believe they had anything to worry about. While they knew the Captain still roamed the waters with her ghostly ship, she was rarely seen except by a few frightened sailors. What would the captain want to do with their tribe? There wasn't anything that made them special, and they were close enough to the shore that the Captain shouldn't come.

Something must have caught the Captain's eye, however, because her ship sailed above them as the moon was at its peak. The anchor forced its way down, the force waking up the sleeping sirens. The soldiers huddled around the Elder—the Elder's survival came before anyone else.

The pirate ship started its descent downward. They heard of the Captain's raids; she wasn't afraid to leave destruction in her wake. The spell cast on her ship allowed for her to peacefully walk across the deck as it slowly became submerged.

Her crew, filled with ghosts, started pouring out into the Deirdres' territory. They held enchanted weapons that broke the barrier between the living and the dead as they held the sirens at knifepoint. Children cried as their mothers desperately tried to quiet them.

With only a motion of the inconvenienced Captain's hand, the throat of a crying child was slit. His mother watched in shock, cradling the small child in her hands. The other children cried harder, but their mouths were muffled by the webbed fingers of their guardians. They didn't want any more lives lost tonight, so being complacent was their only choice.

The Deirdre tribe was large, but the ghost crew was stronger.

All they could do was watch as the Captain ran through their territory.

She didn't want their treasure. She didn't want their women or their children. She didn't want their artifacts. So what did she want?

She passed by all of their homes before settling in front of one: the Elder's.

The soldiers stood by the Elder, keeping him away from the intruders, but she didn't walk up to him. Everyone watched as the Captain walked right past the Elder and instead crouched down into a locked chest.

She demanded for it to be unlocked.

When a young soldier protested, he got a knife to the chest.

The Elder, stricken with grief, relented. He asked another soldier to unlock the chest—the safety of his tribe mattered more than the treasure inside.

When the Captain left, she was holding something large wrapped in cloth. With a nod, her crew followed behind her onto their ship before it rose again. In only moments, the only evidence that the ship was there at all were the bodies of the deceased.

The General spoke quietly with the Elder. The regular sirenfolk didn't know what had been taken from them, but she knew. She also knew how important it was to get it back.

The General gathered together as many soldiers as she could. They would mourn their fallen the next night, but they didn't have time to wait. They needed to start creating their plan.

They were going to find the Captain.

They were going to take back what was rightfully theirs.

And they were going to make her pay.

Acknowledgements

Y'all, it has been a crazy two years since I first started this project. I'd started many other books before this, but this was the first one that I actually plotted, and look how far it's come. Now it's getting published—my words will be out there. As a teen writer, this is one of the craziest things I've ever imagined.

I'd like to start by thanking the younger version of me. She was always telling stories, whether it was on the playground or writing them down. If I hadn't sucked at one point, I wouldn't have become the author I am today.

Secondly, I would like to thank each and every reader who picked up this book and somehow made it to the end. These characters—and this story overall—mean so much to me, and I'm very happy to get to share that with the rest of the world. I hope that you enjoyed reading the book as much as I loved writing it (saving the several hours of screaming that has gotten me to the end).

Next, I'm going to thank all of my friends who put up with my rants when this book was still in its earlier stages. If you know me in real life, you know that once I start talking about my book, it's hard to get me to stop. Thankfully, I had friends who seemed at least somewhat okay with my long tangents.

So much thanks goes to two of the biggest people who helped in the production of my book, Michelle Reese (my editor) and Alexis "Hatter" Lynch (my beta reader). I know that my book would not be the same as it is now without the feedback from these wonderful people.

I'd also like to thank my parents, who were two of my biggest supporters throughout the whole process! They were the ones who encouraged me to finally finish.

There are so many more people I could probably thank, but since most people don't read these anyways, I'll keep it short. Thank you to everyone who helped bring me (and my book) to where I am today, and I hope the books keep on coming!

About the Author

I.R. Miller has been telling stories all of her life, from running around on the playground to writing assignments for Language Arts class. After several failed attempts to write these stories down on paper, she finally got enough inspiration and willpower to finish her debut novel, "Soul Savior."

She has moved around several times in her life, but finally found a place to settle with her family in the Midwest. Growing up with autism and ADHD, she didn't always understand what went on around her. Stories became a means of escape. Starting in third grade, people would often find her with her nose in a book at any opportunity she got. It was in fourth grade when she realized she could create her own. Several years later, her first novel is finally out in the public.

When she isn't writing, you will often find her singing or playing with her pets. She works hard to keep up A's in school and can be seen doing many activities throughout the school year (other than sports). After struggling for several years with anxiety and getting diagnosed with Tourette's, she turned to writing even more and has become a stronger person than she ever was before. One of her goals with her writing is to discourage the stigma that is often seen around neurodiversity and mental health through her characters.

After two years of writing, drafting and editing, she's elated to finally have her first book published, and is hoping to have many more.

kdp.amazon.com

Copyright © 2023 I.R. Miller

All rights reserved.

9798853678576

Printed in Great Britain
by Amazon